SPECTERS OF DARKNESS

They dwell in the halfway places between life and death, bound to the world and the living by things left unfulfilled—vengeance, sorrow, love, honor, lust, memory—and all the many emotions and needs of those they've left behind. Now these haunts, hidden from most, are revealed to you in twenty-eight tales that will leave you afraid to go to sleep at night, such heart-pounding chillers as:

"The Hound Lover"—What was there left for a writer who couldn't write? Perhaps all she needed was "true" inspiration. . . .

"Specters in the Moonlight"—It was a cry for help that woke him, a plea that he could not deny—even if the one who begged for his aid seemed beyond any mortal's help. . . .

"Cages"—He met her at a party and she had the most incredible pickup line he'd ever heard, "I'm dead. . . ."

PHA
OF T

D1495705

PHANTOMS
OF THE
NIGHT

EDITED BY

Richard Gilliam

&

Martin H. Greenberg

DAW BOOKS, INC.

DONALD A. WOLLHEIM, FOUNDER

375 Hudson Street, New York, NY 10014

ELIZABETH R. WOLLHEIM

SHEILA E. GILBERT

PUBLISHERS

First Printing, June 1996
1 2 3 4 5 6 7 8 9

DAW TRADEMARK REGISTERED
U.S. PAT. OFF. AND FOREIGN COUNTRIES
—MARCA REGISTRADA
HECHO EN U.S.A.

PRINTED IN THE U.S.A.

ACKNOWLEDGMENTS

CONTENTS

A FEW WORDS
ABOUT GHOSTS
by Richard Gilliam

I suppose I really should say a few words about ghosts and whether or not I believe in them.

The question is an interesting one which reaches much farther than can be sufficiently answered by a simple yes or no. Unlike many of the other classic supernatural creatures of popular fiction, ghosts have unavoidable connections to the questions of the existence of God, and to the spiritual structure of the universe. Consider that a werewolf might be explained as a hormonal reaction to strong moonlight, or that a vampire could be the result of plague and mutated viruses, and so on. Ghosts, though, rarely have scientific explanations. A reanimated dead person who returns with body intact is probably a zombie, but one which returns without physical form is said to be a ghost.

For the record, I do not believe in vampires, zombies, or werewolves. I do believe in God. The word *believe* is important. As enlightened people, we should remain open-minded and consider the possibility that we may be wrong, or that we may see only a part of the truth, and in particular that we do not seek to impose our truth on others.

Who is the keeper of the truth? Thomas Aquinas held that all truth is God's truth, while George Bernard Shaw liked to claim that all great truths began as blasphemies. Maybe they're both right, though I think Shaw's clever comment a bit too doctrinaire to be universally true. Where Shaw was more interested in challenging the establishment view via iconoclasm, Thomas Aquinas attempted to develop a structure where reason and faith could comfortably coexist. Guess which one ended up challenging the establishment more, the cynic or the philosopher?

Reason and faith do not yet comfortably coexist, and while people aren't burned at the stake nearly as often as they once were, you can still get a good argument against Thomas Aquinas from your local neighborhood inquisitor.

Science, which can be considered a branch of reason, is validated through observation and analysis, and with time the opinions of science can change. Light and sound, for example, were once thought to be unquantifiable and without physical characteristics. Light could be observed though, so the existence of light was agreed to well before the properties of light began to be understood. Even after quantification, much of science believed that the speed of sound could not be exceeded, a theory that was not disproved until the middle part of the 20th century. Today, much of science believes that the speed of light can not be exceeded, even if science fiction writers frequently exceed the speed of light with alacrity.

Much as light can be observed to exist, thought can be observed to exist also, yet the prevailing view today is that thought can not be quantified, just as earlier peoples doubted the quantifiability of light. Many leading scientific thinkers of our time have sought to discover the one great equation that will unify all the observations of science. Thus far they have failed, and I have a theory as to why. The great thinkers of science have for the most part ignored the existence of thought, the effects of spirituality and thought on the universe, and the basic energies that are exchanged in the interaction of living beings. Can thought and spirituality be quantified? Thus far we have not yet come to grips with the concept that these *should* be quantified. All truth is God's truth, but there are many who believe that there are some things that we were not meant to know, or, more accurately, that there are some things that we are yet afraid to discover.

In his novel *The Grapes of Wrath*, John Steinbeck writes about how one day the preacher Casy went out in the wilderness to find his own soul, only to find that "he didn't have no soul that was his, but rather just a little piece of a great big soul. A soul ain't no good in a wilderness," continues Steinbeck, saying that each little piece of soul needs to be with the rest to be whole. This was the passage brilliantly spoofed by Bill Murray during the 1995 N.B.A. playoffs ("A fellow doesn't have a game of his own, just a little piece of a bigger game.") I wonder how many of the viewers knew the source origin?

Using Steinbeck's theory, there is, I think, a significant

logic for the possible existence of ghosts. Two types come to mind quickly—the sort of ghost that is lost in the wilderness and doesn't know how to reach the greater whole, and its counterpart, the sort of ghost who knows the way to the whole, but returns to help us find our way out of the wilderness. For an example of the latter, I recommend W. P. Kinsella's outstanding novel *Shoeless Joe*, or the very fine motion picture *Field of Dreams* which was adapted from it.

There is at least a third type of ghost—the ghost as a plot device creature. This ghost, I think, exists more on paper than in the real world. One of my all-time favorite storytelling surprises was when I got to the end of Peter Straub's excellent novel *Ghost Story* and realized it wasn't a ghost story at all, though it had expertly manipulated many of the conventions associated with traditional stories of ghosts.

Good stories need internal logic, and ghost stories are no exception. Hopefully, you will find stories you like in this book. We've tried to allow a wide range of ghosts into these pages, from retributive to redemptive, and from whimsical to sardonic.

Can I prove to you that ghosts exist? No, I think not yet, at least not in the empirical ways that the existence of light and sound can be proved. Do I believe that ghosts exist? Yes, I think it possible that they do. If souls exist within bodies, then so should there be conditions where souls are able to exist without them. A few perhaps will join the whole more slowly than others—some lost in the wilderness, but others choosing to stay and help travelers find their way.

Someday we will tackle the task of quantifying the energies that are exchanged when living beings interact, and then the great thinkers of the world can unite and produce the one great theorem of all things. Until that day, reason and faith will occasionally continue to seemingly be in conflict, neither discipline fully understanding why each so strongly needs the other.

I thank you for joining me for these few words about ghosts. May the road rise with you as you travel.

Green Bay, Wisconsin
July 1995

HI, BOB

by Howard Kaylan

Howard Kaylan is a vocalist for the venerable rock group, *The Turtles*, and can be heard prominently on such classics as "Happy Together," "It Ain't Me Babe," and "You Know She'd Rather Be With Me." An avid reader and longtime fan, this is his first short story.

> "He left his chair—it's empty now,
> so vacant and so still;
> he's laid aside his earthly care,
> a place no one can fill."
> —memorial epitath,
> Brookings-Harbor Pilot, 1952

"Quite a place you guys got here," Powers observed. "Where's the euphemism?"—Tim's way of asking directions to the can. Serena, after the giving of the customary hugs, settled down on the sofa and faced the blue Pacific with a cigarette in one hand and a glass of wine in the other.

"Not at all what I expected, Susan." She carelessly tossed ash in my wife's direction. "I mean, I'm looking at rocks and seals here, for crying out loud. Don't get me wrong: it's a postcard, but you guys were always so 'rock and roll.' "

"Yeah, Kaylan; what gives? I mean, you cut yourself off from your showbiz lifestyle to move up to this little story-book fishing village? Too many drugs in the sixties . . ."

"Oh, yeah," I wittily replied. "Like I should move back to Los Angeles and worry about whether my kid's going to be a Crip or a Blood by the time she hits kindergarten? Or be able to breathe the air in her own backyard? And how about the . . ."

"Yeah, yeah . . . the earthquakes, the freeway killings, and the fires and the mud slides."

Okay, so they were all riffing on me. I guess I laid the rap down a few too many times, but I believed it. Still do.

"And you don't miss it?" Serena had that sneaky half-smile on her face. "Not even a little? Come on! You were runnin' in the fast lane for the last, what, thirty years? It's not like you and your buddy George Wendt can just pick up and jam off to a Soul Asylum concert when the wives are in bed ..."

Now Tim was into it. "Right, Kaylan ... what do you guys do around here for excitement? You've gotta admit, this place *is* a bit on the remote side. Pretty, but remote. Back in L. A.—hell, everything happens there."

So, I told him. We go bike riding. We help out down at Noah's Ark Preschool. We hang out with our neighbors, the Dragos ... and there's Azalea State Park and the Azalea Lanes Bowling Alley—Brookings *is* the home of Winter Flowers, you know. There's Amy and Dennis, Marc and Patty, the Chetco Pelican Players, the Friends of Music. . . . Oh, and of course, every night, there's "Hi, Bob!"

" 'Hi, Bob'? Like we used to play in college?"

"Exactly, Powers. The very same."

"Hold it, you guys," Serena piped in. "You lost me. What the hell is 'Hi, Bob'?"

Susan was the first to answer. "You remember the old *Bob Newhart Show?* The one where he plays the psychologist from Chicago ... ? Well, there's this famous, like, frat party thing where every time some one on the show mentions the name 'Bob' everybody has to take a drink."

Powers finished the thought. ". . . and when somebody in the cast says, 'Hi, Bob,' everyone in the house has to chug their drink down."

Mrs. Powers was not impressed. "That's the big whoops in Brookings? Play dormitory drinking games till you pass out in a puddle of spew? Blaach! Get me back to Santa Ana and my trusty ol' gun ... drinking games ..." her voice trailed off.

"Yeah, but it's not just a game here in Brookings, it's more like a ceremony. We're talkin' *The Bob Newhart Show* now, and folks around here take their Newhart very seriously."

After the babysitter arrived, the four of us piled into my

'82 Grand Wagoneer, avoiding the gopher holes and backing down the long, dark driveway onto Dawson Road.

"Damn gophers! I get these Vector Control traps for the stupid rodents, but they're useless. Like it or not, you just got to shoot the bastards."

"Aww, but they're so cute and cuddly," Serena sympathized. "Besides, isn't that illegal?"

"Serena, my dear," I explained, "Sometimes a man has got to take the law into his own hands."

Now it was less than half a mile to Highway 101 and the sign with the pelican or the seagull or whatever it is welcoming travelers to Lovely Brookings—Home of Winter Flowers. I told you.

In two miles 101 widens out, becoming the town's main drag, Chetco Avenue. The last of the full-blooded Chetco Indians, one Lucy Dick, had gone Happy Hunting here in 1840, and though many of her relatives were herded onto reservations like prisoners, many still hang out here where the Chetco River meets the Pacific at the southernmost spot of the rugged Oregon coast.

"Check out that restaurant up on the right," I advised my traveling companions. "The Cliff House By the Sea."

"Looks deserted."

"Is deserted. Once upon a time, it was going to be a casino . . . back in the '40s when Oregon was all set to legalize gambling. Well, they never did make it legal, but the owners decided to open her up anyway. They were raided, of course."

"Of course. And it's been closed since the forties?"

"Naw . . . it's been a nightclub, a meeting hall . . . you name it, but according to the townfolk, that's Indian burial land and only a medicine man can exorcise the demons."

"Oooo, good story, Kaylan." Serena was using her best imitation of a child trying to mimic Lugosi. "Goats . . ." she wailed. "Moan-stairs . . ." She meant ghosts and monsters.

"We're not going up there tonight anyway." Sue told them. "That's another story. No, tonight we're going to watch a little TV with some loggers, some fishermen . . . oh, and, of course, Bob."

We pulled into the parking lot of the old cedar tavern at about 8:45. It being August, colors from purple to orange reflected the lingering sun on the waters of the calm harbor. *The Pine Cone Tavern* read the carved wooden sign, and the only other sounds in town emanated from Ken's, Brookings' only other drinking spot located curiously next door.

"Man, it sure wasn't this crowded when we drove up here."

Powers was right. Ken's and the Pine Cone did just fine during the day, all right; what with sports channel 30 on at the Cone for all of Curry County's unemployed finest, and Ken's flooded with a younger, wilder crowd ... working mommies who made it a custom to drop by on their way back to pick up the rugrats from daycare: A quick game of pool, a little flirting and a seventy-five-cent brewski. Yet, here at night ... every night ... parking was a major bitch.

An old Dodge pickup with the bumper sticker, "My Idea of Gun Control—Use Both Hands" pulled out of a space with my name on it, and I escorted our guests into my favorite new watering hole.

"Pretty damned colorful, Kaylan," Tim observed.

He was right, you know. Certainly by Los Angeles standards, this was a place right out of Twin Peaks or at least Northern Exposure: You name the animal, and its head was likely as not mounted somewhere on the walls of the Cone. Fishing trophies and handguns were proudly on display and—oh, yes—then there were the locals.

It just isn't cool to walk down Hollywood Boulevard in bib-front overalls. These guys had invented the grunge look, but they sure weren't getting any royalties for Nirvana or Pearl Jam. They were just trying to hold onto their previous livelihoods in a world that seemed to be spinning just a little too fast. But not here at the Cone.

Powers scrambled in first, and even though he's sworn off the sauce these days, old habits die hard and he proceeded directly to the bar.

"I wouldn't sit there if I was you, son." said a grizzled woodcutter in red flannel and khakis. "Not on *that* stool!"

The high-backed chair looked ordinary enough; positioned centrally along the bar rail, although upon a second glance, yes it did appear to be occupado. There was a pack of Marlboros next to a pristine ash tray. To the left of the ash-tray was a freshly poured draft beer and what seemed to be a shot of whiskey—neat—on the side. Powers, ever the gentleman, was apologetic.

"Sorry, sir ... I didn't realize anyone was sitting here."

"Ain't nobody sitting here now, ya' darn fool!"

Well, that broke the ice in the place. At least half the clientele was laughing.

Louise, a fortyish waitress with a pioneer look and a heart of gold, sauntered by with a couple of cold ones for some tourists at table six.

"Don't you pay them no mind, honey. How was you supposed to know?" She craned a weathered neck, taking inventory of her customers before she picked me out of the pack. "Hey, Turtle-Boy! This one a friend of yours?"

I nodded. I guess I felt a bit responsible for Tim's embarrassment.

"Sorry, Louise. Louise, these are my friends, Tim and Serena, and of course, you know Susan."

"How are ya', honey? All right, you come in here on a Monday night at nine o'clock and expect that I'm gonna tell the tale, don't ya'?"

"Well, I was sorta hoping . . ."

"Yeah, yeah . . . okay, city kids, have yourselves a seat over there by the poker machines and I'll be right over to take your orders."

We did and she did. I had my usual Bud. The ladies opted for white wine and Powers reluctantly settled for a diet coke. Then, when Louise returned with our drinks, she spoke in the hushed tones of Legend.

"That there stool . . . that's for Bob."

It was as if all the air had been sucked out of the room with the mere mention of his name. Louise waited for Tim to get uneasy at the receiving end of her piercing blue stare before she continued.

"Bob Hartley his name was; just like that psychologist fellow on the TV . . . you know, *The Bob Newhart Show?*"

A toothless trucker in a stained work shirt piped up with an unlikely addendum.

"Had a few shows, actually—that one in Vermont where he played the innkeeper, and then he tried a comeback as a comic book writer or was it a greetings card writer . . . ?"

"It was *both,* Rocky, and that damn show ain't on the air anymore, no how. Anyway, it don't pertain to this particular story, now does it? We're talking about Bob Hartley here."

"Which one? The TV character or the real guy?" Powers was hooked already.

"Both. See, Bob Hartley . . . *our* Bob Hartley, had come

from Chicago, too; just like the television Bob. And, even wierder, he was also a shrink. Had himself a big-time job down on the California side of Pelican Bay Prison. Now, that's no Leona Helmsley hotel down there you know . . . we're talkin' lifers . . . killers and worse . . . maximum security . . . and the Doc was in charge of the hardcore wackos.

"Now, this Bob was a regular customer 'round here; said he needed the spirits to calm his soul after a day with the inmates. Came in here every night regular as clockwork—9:13 p.m. . . . ordered the same: Chivas straight with a draft back. And no matter what game was on the tube or whatever song was on the box, when Bob walked through those doors, time stopped.

"Made everybody say hello to him, too . . . 'Hi, Bob' . . . 'Hi, Bob' . . . just like on the show."

Serena was not going for it.

"Oh, please!"

"Just let her finish, Reenie." Powers, the voice of reason.

"Like I was sayin', this here Bob Hartley was a bit of a loon. Not enough he got his rocks off hearin' 'Hi, Bob' every night here at the Pine Cone; he'd have all the prisoners doin' it, too. Saved up his money and when his vacation time rolls around, he drags his wife and kids off to Chicago to see the buildings Newhart used to walk past in the opening credits. He went absolutely mental, I swear . . . learned all the words to every episode; had us knowing which ones Peter Bonerz directed. . . ."

"He was the guy who played Jerry Robinson, the dentist." Powers educated his wife.

"Orthodontist, but you're close. And now every time someone on the show says his name or *especially* 'Hi, Bob,' *our* Doctor Hartley feels like we're all drinkin' a toast to *him,* like he's real important and shit. Only that there prison job of his was just eatin' his insides away."

"Serena, do you want to go to the little girls' room?" Susan whispered, but Serena was too inside the story now to let little things like bodily functions ruin a good bar tale, so Sue went alone.

Louise looked up like a teacher catching two cheating students and took a dramatic extra second to regain her composure.

"So now two things happen that sorta coincide: first, this low-life local dude named Hawthorne—real sicko . . . folks 'round here always hated this guy . . . all the way back to his school days—used to wave his Bobbit around at all the girls . . . he gets himself sentenced to life down there at Pelican Bay for raping this little gal from Pistol River . . . couldn't have been more than twelve years old."

Susan returned from the bathroom just then, noticing the absence of color on Serena's face.

"Did I miss anything?" she queried.

"Oh, God!" Serena took a gulp of her wine and shivered noticeably. She wasn't the only one in the place that was creeped out.

Louise savored the moment before she went on.

"So, Hawthorne, he gets himself a good Jewish lawyer and, sure as shit, gets acquitted on a blatant technicality. Then, he just up and disappears."

"You mean he got away with it?" Powers was livid and evidently having a rough time accepting small town truth.

But Louise has a knack of saying one thing and yet hinting at something entirely different and vaguely ominous.

"Sure looked that way . . . that is, till a few months ago. That's when folks started seein' Hawthorne hangin' around town again. He was real bold about it, too. Next thing you know, Nadine Sturgess—that was the little girl, only she's about sixteen by now—she comes home from school one fine afternoon and finds all her underwear on the floor and her bed all violated, too."

"Eyooo!" Serena put it best.

"Worst of all, the bastard used her toothbrush."

"Let me have another one, Louise." I took this well-rehearsed pause to order, knowing that Louise could talk, pour, and smoke simultaneously. My Bud in hand and her cigarette dangling, she went on. The setup was tres-Hollywood.

"Now, can you guess who Nadine's uncle is?"

Of course, only the Powers were allowed to guess.

"Bob, right?"

"Right as rain, kiddo. So he comes in here like usual one night a few months back, and we leave the doors wide open for him—just like tonight, rain or shine—and we can see he's bubblin' inside, seein' as how Hawthorne's been seen in the area and all. He's just beside himself with rage."

A rowdy cowboy in the back interrupted. "Hurry up, Louise, it's almost time!"

"Hang on to your britches, Ray. I'm just gettin' to the good part. So, we all say, 'Hi, Bob,' and proceed to turn off the Blazers' game and switch over to Nickelodeon, you know, that kiddie network . . . show used to be on TBS, but now Nick at Nite's got 'em . . . only *this* night is the beginning of one of them marathons."

"What the hell is a marathon?" Powers asked.

"Eight solid nights of *The Bob Newhart Show,* that's what! So now, OUR Doctor Hartley would leave work about eight, all distraught on account of his job and his niece and this here lunatic stalkin' around. The shows would start comin' on, one after another, and Bob'd start just chuggin' 'em down. Good ol' Bill Crowley'd have to take him home in the taxi the first couple of nights.

"He'd show up at work—at least at first—and then he'd come straight here. Nadine was too petrified to leave her own house, so Bob had private security dudes around her family's place twenty-four hours a day. So . . .

"On Monday night, Bob thinks he sees this Hawthorne guy comin' out of the Sportshaven bar in Harbor, but before he can do anything about it, he has a few too many and passed out just when Howard Borden, Newhart's next-door neighbor proposes to Bob's TV sister, Ellen."

"Hey, four beers back here, Okay? Honey?"

"Comin' up! Tuesday, he sees some guy in a pickup with California plates, follows him around for a couple of hours, and then comes in here and pukes on my bar, right over there, during the show where Jerry goes off to Tahiti.

"Then, on Wednesday, our friend Ray back there tells Bob he's seen the guy at the Brookings Bruins game. Well, Doc Hartley just wandered off by hisself that night and never made it into work the next morning. Seems he spent the night in his Cubs jacket snugglin' up to the old dumpster out back. Oh, but he was back in here on Thursday, all right.

"Thursday night, among other things, Bob and Emily get locked up in a basement storage locker and then one of Emily's students gets a crush on her and then Bob's old buddy, the Peeper, comes to visit . . ."

"Tom Poston!" several customers shout in unison.

"Right. So there's this concert by the Friends of Music down at the Redwood Theater, and Karl Johnson swears up

and down that Hawthorne was there in the third row; leerin'
and makin' obscene gestures up to where Nadine's on stage,
pretty as a picture, singin' 'Surrey With the Fringe on Top.'
Nadine never saw him, I guess. Anyways, that one just about
put the good doctor over the top. He takes the day off work
and picks up Hawthorne's trail down at Hanscam's General
Store. Then, Bob coldcocks the bastard, ties him to the back
bumper of his truck, and drags him up the North bank of the
Chetco River to some campsite near Loeb Park."

It was 9:05 according to the old Hamm's Beer clock, and
the Pine Cone was filling up quickly. Customers were rou-
tinely leaving their drinks or their girlfriends over at Ken's
to take part in the nightly ritual.

"See ya' later, honey . . ."

". . . back at ten o'clock!"

No one came near the place at the bar reserved for Doctor
Hartley.

"Don't stop now, Louise. You're killin' me here." Tim
was sucking up a second diet soda and wiggling on his seat
like a schoolboy.

"So, ol' Bob pulls the truck into an empty campsite and,
calmly as you please, gets out, lights a cigarette, and just
puffs away whilst Hawthorne lies there a'bleedin' all over
the ground. They found about a dozen Marlboro butts at the
spot, so they figure Bob must have talked to Hawthorne for
about an hour as the man bled to death and pleaded for a
ride back to the hospital. And all the while, so I heard, Doc
Hartley, he's whistlin' the Newhart theme: ba ba ba ba ba
ba . . . Jerry and Myrna Music wrote that song . . . oh, wait,
that was after they changed their names to Lorenzo and Hen-
rietta Music. Anyways, Hawthorne's life goes squirtin' all
over the dirt, and after he's stone cold dead, the Doc goes
and cuts off his willy with a hunting knife."

"His what?"

"His Johnson!" a voice in the room impatiently added.

"Oh." Serena took another drink. We all did. "His
Bobbit!"

Louise motioned to an unlabeled jar between the hard-
boiled eggs and the pig's knuckles.

"And thar' she blows!"

"That's it? That's his . . . Bobbit?"

"Uh, yep. Brought it in that very night. Came in here just

like usual, actually a lot happier than usual, and just hands me the jar. Everyone says their 'Hi, Bob's' and we all watch the marathon together till . . . what was it . . . ? About midnight, Bob asks to use the phone over there, calls Wayne up at the police station, and turns himself in. Ol' Wayne strolls right through those doors and carts Bob off to the pokey."

Serena gave Tim a "let's-get-out-of-here" look, but Susan poured some of her wine into Serena's glass and said, "Hold on. Story's not over yet."

Back to Louise.

"Well, the really sad part is that Doc Hartley wound up getting the death penalty on account of the jury said he premeditatedly tortured a technically innocent man to death and disregarded his requests for medical help. Damn shame, too. Hartley was a fine American—a real hero, ya' know? I mean, he did the right thing. Just goes to show ya'. They gave him the electric chair anyway."

"Almost time, Louise."

"I hear ya! So, they give the Doc his one last request before they fry him up and what do you suppose that was?"

For the first time since I've known him, Powers was at a loss for words.

"Ain't you been listening, son? His last request was simple. He just wanted to see one more Newhart show. All them death row guys, they got televisions in their cells, did ya' know that? It's a fact. Cable, too! Shit . . . more'n I got.

"So, that night, the Doc's favorite episode was on: the one where Emily goes off to see her relatives and Bob's left to celebrate Thanksgiving with his single male buddies. They get really plastered together, and Newhart winds up on a ledge dressed like Zorro. It's a great one. Now, the *real* Bob, the Brookings Bob, orders a dinner of moo goo guy pan, just like on the show; he watches every second—even the commercials—smokes himself a few Marlboros, and ZAP, at exactly ten p.m. he's as dead as a carp."

A cold breeze whipped through the open doors of the Pine Cone some time before the opening credits of the *Newhart Show* hit the screen. The room was still except for the television above the bar. It was jingling away . . . "Nick at Nite . . . for TV done right."

"It's starting!"

"Hi, Bob!"

"Hi, Bob!"

"Hi, Bob!"

The entire tavern whispered the greeting in reverent tones. It was the episode where, on a drunken binge, Emil Peterson and Elliot Carlin decide to move in together. The name "Bob" is spoken exactly seventeen times and the line, "Hi, Bob!" pops up no fewer than six. Needless to say, we were soon three sheets to the wind except for Powers, our designated driver.

By the time the MTM kitten meowed at the show's end, Tim was completely blown away.

The people of Brookings were as silent and holy as if in a church during that program. They lifted their glasses and bottles to their lips as if receiving the Host itself. At the first "Hi, Bob!" of the show, their glazed expressions changed to trancelike smiles; indeed there was a calm and spiritual radiance inside the Pine Cone that felt very much like an actual visitation had taken place.

And then, at ten o'clock, the show ended and all the lights in the tavern dimmed.

Afterward, folks began to file out of the old bar; back to Ken's or home to get a good five or six hours' sleep before their backbreaking work began again. Needless to say, the glasses at Bob's barstool were empty and at least six Marlboros had been puffed and snuffed in the once virginal ashtray. Seconds after the lights came back on, Travis Tritt was a-singin' on the jukebox and it was business as usual at the Cone. Louise was laughing with the locals again as they played darts or gathered around the pool tables and the state-owned poker machines.

I left two twenties for Louise as we began to head back to the Jeep, but Powers wasn't done with her yet.

"You mean to tell me this goes on here every night?"

"That's a fact, sonny." Louise seemed pleased with her tip money. "Can we expect you kids back here tomorrow?"

"Uh, no, I mean . . . don't you think this is all just a little weird?"

"Nope, this ain't weird. What's weird is that every night Bob picks up the tab for the whole place: puts the cash in that there brandy snifter by the register. Hell, he's kept this damn bar open all by himself for the last four months. Besides, honey, remember: This is Brookings—Home of Winter Flowers—nothing ever happens here.

* * *

The Pine Cone was emptying as Louise bussed the tables and pocketed the change in her flannel workshirt.

"Good night, Louise."

" 'Night, Louise . . . see ya' tomorrow."

"Good night, Carol."

"Good night, Emily."

"Bye, Jerry."

"See you later, Mister Carlin . . ."

All four of us were unusually quiet on the way back to Dawson Road. Finally, Powers broke the silence.

"Kaylan, this is one of the strangest nights I've ever had."

Susan laughed and I must have been smiling myself. Powers was beginning to catch on.

"Tim, my friend, welcome to Brookings."

The Jeep bumped over two unexpected depressions on the way down my driveway.

"Damn gophers!"

UNFORTUNATE OBSESSION
by Matthew Costello

Matthew Costello is one of the rising stars in writing for
interactive media, including the highly successful CD-
Rom project, *The Seventh Guest*. His impressive cre-
dentials for the more traditional storytelling media
include appearances in many leading anthologies and
magazines.

I admit it.

There were warnings, small signs that something was
wrong, that my life was slipping beyond my control.

And though you might assume that it was *all* about sex,
that it was as simple as that, I would disagree. Strongly. But
in the interest of your understanding—and that is what we're
after here, isn't it?—let me be as honest as possible. Let me
be—what's the word?

Unflinching.

Yes, I won't flinch from any important detail.

I noticed my problem first when I was traveling. On the
road. Away from home. I'd be sitting in the airplane and I'd
find myself examining the pretty flight attendants too
closely, smiling at them and letting my gaze travel from
their cherry-red lipstick down to their not-quite sensible
pumps.

Sometimes, a stewardess would spot me looking at her
and offer a not-unfriendly smile back. And a delicious icy
chill would hit me. There was the slight promise that maybe
something could happen here.

It was only a game. A cheap thrill.

Nothing ever happened. No, though when I found myself
in a new city, in a dreary hotel room after two Scotches and
a satellite movie that usually sucked, I'd look out at the unfamiliar city and think of all the sexy women I'd seen that
day.

I never thought of my wife.

Ellen didn't seem relevant anymore.

Then—as I suppose these things must progress—I found my yearnings overwhelming me. My head would turn at the click of a woman's steps, the sound of heels hypnotically catching my attention. I would study the way a woman's long chestnut hair flowed, a dark wave breaking over slim shoulders. Or how a simple sheath dress gently suggested the wonderful curves beneath the material.

I'd marvel at the heat that eyes could generate.

And all the time thinking, *I'm losing it*. This is what they talk about, in articles, on the talk shows. Men reach an age, and—*boing!*—something snaps.

I'd stand in an elevator, and a woman a few feet away would be wearing some perfume—and I'd be transported. The images, the fantasies, the smells would linger long after the woman innocently left the elevator. I'd imagine the texture of her skin, and my fantasy touches captured me completely.

In my work, in my life, I became a robot, a zombie. I only lived in my fantasy world.

And that world was full of the sensual beauty of women.

Reality slipped away . . . and I didn't give a damn.

The day I met Julie didn't seem any different. She was hired as a associate accountant, an entry-level position. Julie was a blonde, very tall and sleek. When Jack, a full partner, introduced her to the accounting staff, I probably wasn't the only one looking at her, savoring her.

She was twenty-three, or twenty-four . . . and her skin was marble white. She wore expensive clothes—and I thought that somewhere there must be a rich daddy. Sure, *everyone* was looking at her.

But then I saw her look back at me. She smiled, a sad little "I'm at sea here" grin, and I smiled back. But it was a gesture, a connection.

Later I went to the washroom.

I thought of *her*.

I stayed there, replaying that little look, the smile, then how sexy she looked, and—God—the way she might look in bed, making love. . . .

I stayed there, thinking of her, lost in my fantasy. . . .

I didn't plan for what would happen.

At least—I don't think I planned for it to happen.

Tax time came, always a real nut-crusher, and the office kicked into hyperdrive. Everyone worked late. Even those guys with a home full of kids stayed to 9, 10 o'clock, even later. Everyone had to ride out the tax wave. And if they were lucky, if they did good work dodging the nasty tax man for their big-ticket clients, they might get picked to be partner.

Working late was no problem for me. All I had at home was Ellen, and Kelly—so busy with her high school friends. Thinking of Ellen brought me no interest, no excitement. And for her part, Ellen gave no indication that she sensed that something was different with me, that I was lost, floating away.

Then one night Julie was working. There were only a few of us that night and it was very late. . . .

She came by my office to drop off some corporate returns that I had been saddled with.

I looked up when she came in.

I remember so well what she was wearing. It was a simple blue dress . . . with buttons. And though the top buttons weren't provocatively open, still I could see her neck and then—when she put the papers down—a bit more, the tiniest flash of her black bra.

I must have frozen.

"You *okay?*" she asked smiling.

I nodded, quickly forcing a smile back onto my face. I looked down at the tax reports. "Fine. Just what I need. More returns . . ." It passed for a joke.

She stood there a minute.

"Are they particularly difficult?"

I shrugged. "No, but these clients have some tricky liabilities and capital gains problems. It's going to be a long night." I looked up at her. It was so quiet in the office. It seemed as if it were only the two of us here, though I knew that there were still a handful of people working into the night.

She kept her eyes on me. And I felt that chill again, her blue eyes locked on mine. She said: "I—I'll be working late, too. . . ."

It sounded like an opening. I kept replaying in my mind the scene of her bending over like that, wondering if she meant to tease. I was nearly twice her age.

I took a breath, trying to say something.

"Well," I said—and I heard how hoarse my voice sounded, how transparent. I cleared my throat and made a hollow laugh. "If we're still here later, how about a drink before we head home? We'll swap tax stories."

I smiled. My invitation meant *nothing,* I tried to project. *I'm a married man. My wife's picture is on my desk, next to one of my teenage daughter, Kelly.*

Julie looked at me, and she cocked her head, The move was fetching, alluring, devastating.

She nodded. "That sounds nice. You can let me pick your brains."

I kept smiling. "Everything I know about capital gains and estate planning is *yours.*" I looked down at my watch. "Let's say . . . one hour."

Julie started out of the office. "Don't leave without me."

God, I thought, she must be crazy to think I'd even dream of doing that.

Nothing happened that night.

Though we ended up having two drinks and she told me about growing up in Grosse Pointe, and all about her father, who owned a successful real estate business. Nothing happened . . . but I saw the way she listened to me. And she must have seen the way I looked at her when she spoke, the way I followed the movement of her lips, watching her speak but really concentrating on the gentle play of flesh as she said words, *any* words, lost to my erotic dreams.

Only when she looked up and said, "Oh, the place is clearing out," did I make myself stop. I got the check, walked her to her parking lot while recommending that she use a different lot a block away, "A place less likely to add dents to your car," I told her.

And then—an extraordinary moment—

She leaned close and gave me the slightest little kiss good night.

It was nothing. Only a friendly kiss.

I thought of it all the way home to Mamaroneck, driving home to Ellen, Ellen who would be asleep, Ellen who would still be asleep when I got up at 6:45 tomorrow morning.

I was happy, blissfully happy with my fantasies, imagining Julie kissing me harder, taking off her clothes for me, looking me right in my eyes, daring me. . . .

But I wasn't sated. I knew that. I knew that—and it scared me.

It happened at one of those tedious two-day planning conferences, this one in Boston. The topic was the new Clinton tax changes. There were long seminars all day in the meeting rooms of the Boston Hilton.

Julie was surprised that she got to go, being such a junior accountant. She didn't know that I had arranged it.

And that night, we lingered in the Hilton's bar. And a few guys I knew from other "Big Five" accounting firms, KPMG, Bache, looked over, and I'm sure saw what I was up to. But we were out of town. Later, some of them would surely hit the tittie bars still flourishing in the combat zone.

Nobody carried stories home.

It was a code.

I nearly jumped when Julie covered my hand with hers.

"You've been really nice to me," she said. I looked at her, wondering if she suspected that I got her to come here. Her hand felt so smooth, the fingers thin, the nails perfect, glossy.

My hand patted hers, thinking I would only cover her hand. But it stayed there. Our eyes met, and we said nothing. I felt her leg brush mine. It could have been an accident . . . her leg touching mine.

Excuse me. I didn't mean to—

I let my leg rest against hers, pressing back.

Her hand squeezed mine. I was frozen, immobile. She would have to be the one to move to the next step.

"Walk me to my room," she said.

I nodded, dug out my wallet, and held up my Gold Card to catch the eye of the skinny waiter.

The lovemaking was overwhelming. I couldn't get enough of her body, tasting her as if I was starving. Her muscles were tight—she played tennis, she worked out. She was tight, sleek. And she acted as if she wanted to fulfill every wanton dream I ever had.

She slid down me, tracing a line on my chest with her perfect nails, planting kisses on the way down.

Then—before she let her lips surround me—she looked up at me.

"What do you want?" she said, teasing me, playing with me.

I looked in her eyes. There was nothing else, only this fabulous young woman, and her total power over me.

"Do you want this?"

She brought her lips down.

But funny—it was as if I was the one drinking ... from a spring that was totally compelling, demanding. She was all that I wanted.

Later, back in New York, I felt scared.

She had so much power, and there was so little I could do to resist.

God, even the very word *resist* didn't exist.

In New York we began a pattern of meeting in hotels, or occasionally at her apartment—though I felt this was risky. I never mentioned my wife, and she never asked.

I arranged for us to attend the same seminars, and we even hit the sleazy motels out on Long Island where we could spend a few hours together.

No guilt came—and that surprised me. I only worried that it was impossible to keep this affair secret from Ellen. Surely she would notice that I had *nothing* for her, no interest, nothing at all.

As for work, I was in a fog, and Julie seemed to enjoy the fact that she had me so befuddled. She'd stop in my office unannounced.

Sometimes she'd say something:

"I thought about you last night. When I was alone ..."

She'd stand there, mocking me, and drift away.

Other times, she'd walk in and—looking around—slip a hand into her blouse, undo a button, and I'd see her bra of the day, black, white, cream, scalloped or underwired. A little game she played.

Her appetite for sex was voracious.

And then, just as I was beginning to feel that there had to be some way to turn off the tap, to slow things down ... when I couldn't function anymore ...

I made a mistake.

As part of our love play, Julie had stripped me, kissing me as she undid my shirt and opened my belt. And somehow, there had been a bright red lipstick stain on a shirt, something I didn't see.

It was stupid. I wondered whether Julie planned it. Though she never asked about Ellen, never begged for me to get a divorce. But then I was already backing away from her . . .

Ellen saw the stain, and now she knew. When I got home she spent the night crying and yelling at me. No matter what room I went to she was *there,* following me.

That's when she made the first threat.

She told me: *I'll kill her.*

I told Ellen that the affair was over. That it was my midlife crisis. I told her that I was all done with Julie. And God, I meant it, I really meant it.

But now Julie wouldn't let me go.

Instead, Julie grew more bold, more demanding.

She'd do crazy things like shutting my office door, walking over to me, kneeling by me . . .

I admit. I was weak. I didn't stop her at first.

The people in the office started to give me funny looks as if they knew all about my affair.

And Ellen knew too that it wasn't ended. She'd still be awake when I came home now, and she could read me like a book. She screamed at me. And I'm sure the neighbors heard. Have you asked the neighbors? They *must* have heard.

Ellen screamed at me.

"I won't let that bitch take you." She cried, and I started to feel some guilt over what I'd done to her.

And I knew that I had to do something . . . before Ellen did something. . . .

I had to end the affair with Julie. That was it, I decided. End it, plain and simple. And at this last meeting there would be no sex, no matter what Julie did. She's unbalanced, I told myself. I was crazy to get involved with her.

I agreed to meet her at her apartment for dinner. A last dinner, but she didn't know that. Then—God—I hoped we could part as "friends," that she wouldn't try to destroy me at the office.

I took the elevator up to her floor. I had a key to the third-story apartment.

But I didn't need it, because the door was open a crack.

I closed the front door behind me. It was odd that it was open. Julie was scared of the city.

She liked to feel safe.

I walked into the kitchen . . . it was the first room you entered, a surprisingly large bright kitchen with modern appliances and a sparkling linoleum floor. And I smelled it. The blood, you know. The coppery smell, just like they describe it in the murder books. Only it was so strong, overpowering.

I looked in the sink and I saw a knife. A big white carving knife, the type you'd use to slice roast beef paper thin.

I picked it up. That was stupid, I know. Really stupid, picking it up like that.

The kitchen light made the linoleum floor sparkle . . . except where there were bloody steps leading into a bedroom. Maybe I stepped on that blood. I probably did. I felt sick, with the smell, and the way the blood looked—like syrup— not realizing what had happened, and what I should do.

I walked into the bedroom.

The light was off.

Julie's bedroom was lavender with a pale rose rug. When I had visited her here, it seemed to be full of her perfume. Then, later, it mixed with the smell of our sweat, our lovemaking.

Now there was just the blood smell, and the pool of blood on the carpet, and—

Wrapped up in the sheet, a shape.

I shouldn't have touched it, I know that. But I walked over and unwrapped the shape, the body.

Julie's head, her face, her lips, were untouched. I kept peeling away the sheet.

Then, there were the great tears, bloody gashes running from her neck and down, and vicious cuts running straight across those tears. And what had been a tightly wrapped package seemed to come all undone.

I was about to call the police.

That was what I was going to do next. Call the police and tell them what had happened.

Of course, I knew who had done it.

I recognized the knife.

Ellen's father had given it to us for our tenth anniversary. "Never needs sharpening," he said. "Best knife in the world."

I recognized the knife.

I knew who had killed Julie. Ellen said she'd stop her . . . and she did.

And now . . . they're telling me crazy things.

They're asking me so many questions, *where I was, what I was doing*—Christ—as if I could possibly kill Julie.

And telling me stuff—I have to laugh—that's so crazy.

Telling me that Ellen is dead, that Ellen and Kelly have been dead for two years.

They say that I live alone.

One of the detectives said to me, "Your wife died in the car crash."

"You were driving," he said. A snowy night and something happened. And yes, now I remember a crash. The Acura, spinning around in the snow . . . no matter how many tens of thousands of dollars it cost.

Yes—I seem to remember that.

But this is *crazy*. They're looking at me and telling me that my wife and daughter died in that crash . . . and that I lived?

It's a trick.

They're playing a *trick* on me. After I've been so honest.

Because, if she's dead—why then, who—

Who killed Julie? Who cut her up so terribly and wrapped her up all nice and neat, like a present?

If my wife is dead—I have to laugh—

Then who killed Julie?

WHEN A CHILD CRIES
by Michelle Sagara

Michelle Sagara has written four novels and many short
stories, and has gained significant critical popularity
within the past couple of years. This is her first horror
piece, because, as she explains, until she had her first
child she never really experienced the sense of queasy
responsibility, of bone-deep fear, that she feels is necessary to do the genre justice.

I must tell somebody this.

I have come here, Father, although I am not a Catholic. I
know you have no reason to listen to what I have to say, but
I ask you to grant me the same favor that you grant to any
sinner with a burden that must be shed.

I ask you to listen in confidentiality, to tell no one but
God, yours or mine, what I say to you here. Please.

Thank you, thank you, Father. I'm—I'm sorry. I don't
mean to cry. I know that you aren't going to save my soul
in one night. My wife was Catholic. She didn't always go to
church, but she was a believer in many of the tenets of the
church. I listened to some of them, and some I tried not to.

Do you mind if we don't use the box? I'm not a Catholic
anyway, and I—I want to see a face, a reaction. I want to
know I'm talking to another person.

Thank you. Thank you, Father. I don't know where to
begin—but I said that already, didn't I? Let me start with the
worst of it.

I killed my wife last week.

No—wait, don't look like that. Let me explain it. I can explain everything. It's just like I chose the wrong place to
start.

I met my wife ten years ago, when we were both in University. She was—she was so special. All full of ire and

righteous wrath. Her eyes had this way of sparking that reminded me of flint and steel, and she tried to take on the universe, to make things more just. We were both young then. We thought we could change the world.

I didn't know how much I loved her until four years ago. I liked her, I respected her, and I knew enough about her love life that I swore I would steer clear of it forever. Almost did. Things started really strangely between us. We'd been friends for so long that we didn't know how to be in love—not the normal way.

We invented our own. It was fun, and we argued a lot while doing it, but we did it. We were married three years ago—we even survived her relatives and my friends when we planned a wedding. I'm happy that we went through with it, tradition and all—but she still says we'd have been better off eloping. I mean, that's what she used to say.

What? Of course I loved her. I loved her more than anything. We made plans. We had the whole future mapped out. Do you know what it's like to finally meet someone you can *plan* a future with? I mean, that you can talk to with certainty about the next ten years, and the ten after that, and never wonder whether or not you're going to break up or be left? Do you know what it's like to trust someone so completely the idea that they could break that faith just makes you laugh?

We were like that. We were young.

We bought a house. Together. We bought a car. We built the beginnings of our careers. And we decided that we weren't going to get any younger. We both wanted children.

It took longer than we thought it would—the doctor says it almost always does—but Amy finally got pregnant almost two years ago. Well, maybe a year and nine months ago. She was sick from the second week until the twenty-sixth. Couldn't walk anywhere without throwing up.

Your sister was like that? Give her our sympathies—no, my sympathies. God, I can't believe she's dead. I can't believe I killed her. But I had to, I had to.

I'm sorry. Let me just sit a minute and then I'll keep talking.

Our son was born a year ago; a year to the day. It was snowing when we tried to drive out to the hospital. I had to dig the car out, and when we took to the roads, the brakes presented a challenge. But it was three in the morning, and there weren't that many people on the road. I drove slowly. Well, I tried to drive slowly. Depends on who you ask—Amy says I drove like a maniac. She—

We got to the hospital in one piece. We found out we were early, but the nurses didn't want to send us home in the blizzard, so we sat it out in the waiting room, getting more nervous and more excited as we waited.

My son was born twenty-eight hours after we arrived. He had quiet, little lungs, but he cried and we heard him. I thought he'd be messy and wrinkled and ugly, because that's what our prenatal course told us to expect. He was beautiful.

The nurse cleaned him up and wrapped him in some sort of swaddling cloth while my back was turned. It didn't take more than five minutes, and he went from being a tiny, flailing creature to a green bundle of cloth with a face. Amy even let me hold him. I'll never forget the way he stared up at me and cried quietly. Each little cry got softer and softer—and I swear he was curious and almost content a few hours later.

We got to take him home after four days of hospital life. Amy nursed him, and that was a big battle—these little kids, they don't know what they're doing. You'd think nature would make it obvious and simple, but no—obstacles and challenges apparently start from birth.

He cried night and day, and he didn't sleep for the first two months. We were so tired all of the time that we barely had the energy to speak to each other—we took shifts with the baby and wondered if our life was ever going to settle down.

But it did, of course. It always does. Those first two months felt like eternity while we were going through them, but after they'd passed, we wanted them back so we could take the time to enjoy our son as the newborn he was never going to be again.

He learned to laugh early. And he got so fat his cheeks took up his entire face, except where the three chins were. His arms and legs looked like little sausages, and his fingers—he had the chubbiest little fingers. It was so strange, that he could be so fat and so tiny at the same time.

There's nothing as wonderful as the first out-and-out laugh. Because a baby has no inhibitions, nothing to dampen his spirits. He just laughs for joy, and his eyes sparkle, and his face lights up. I know it sounds like a cliché—I always thought it did—but there're reasons that descriptions become clichéd, I guess. When I worked at home, I'd often stop because I could hear him shrieking and squealing with joy at some simple game.

Did I tell you he was stubborn? He got so stubborn so quickly. And he learned to roll over before he was six months old, so we couldn't put him down anywhere without keeping a constant watch. We did have a playpen, but he hated it, and we were weak enough that we couldn't just put him down and let him cry.

At night, Amy would nurse him in bed. She'd set him down between us, and let him suckle himself to sleep. I loved to watch them together. I loved to watch the way he could go from tears and unhappiness to quiet contentment while she cradled him. The most powerful I've ever felt in my life was when I could take that baby and comfort him. I could be his whole world for a few minutes, and I could make everything better. Amy felt the same the way.

Everyone said we'd spoil him. That he was going to end up running our lives. Maybe they were right. We told ourselves that it was better to love him and give him all the security that he needed now, because if he felt secure in the world—in us, really—he wouldn't grow up with the insecurities that we'd faced.

But we'll never know.

When he was six months old, he died.

Oh, my little boy.

They don't know why he died. They have a name for what killed him, but it doesn't mean anything except that it happens without warning, and there isn't a damned thing we could do to prevent it.

Amy found him.

She had rocked him to sleep in the afternoon. That's when he took his nap. She'd smoothed down his hair, and caressed his chubby little cheeks, and talked quietly to him while he nursed. I know it because I'd seen it done so often. She put him to bed, in his crib. She kissed his little forehead.

Mommy loves you, and she always will. If you call her, she'll come, she'll always come for you. She said it like a song, cooing it more than speaking it. That was what she did in place of a lullaby. She hated her singing voice—and she was smart in that; she couldn't stay on key if her life depended on it.

But he never woke up.

And when she went to check on him, because he was sleeping for longer than normal, she found out that he never would.

I wasn't there for it. I don't know what she did next. I don't know if she screamed, or pulled out her hair, or broke things. I don't know if she picked him up and tried to shake him—I don't know if she grabbed him and held him and talked to him and tried to wake him up, even though it was obvious that she couldn't.

I don't know because I never asked her, and she never told me. She called me just before the ambulance arrived. I met her at the hospital. She didn't have to tell me that he was gone. I knew it the moment I saw her face.

They let me hold my son. My little boy.

Ah, Father. I'm sorry. But I'd've died before I'd've let anything bad happen to him. And Amy would have, as well. Nothing—not one thing—has ever hurt me as much.

Please just give me another minute. I'll be—I'll be all right in a minute.

The night of the funeral is still a blur to me. People came. Relatives. Friends. Coworkers. We were brave, Amy and I. We didn't cry where anyone could see us. We didn't have an open casket ceremony, though—that would have killed us both. And we didn't kill the person who told us the best thing to do was to go out and have another one as soon as possible. I don't know why people are so insensitive sometimes.

After the funeral was over, we—just we two—attended the burial. We'd always agreed that if either one of us died, we'd cremate the bodies. But we couldn't do that for our boy. We just couldn't. We had to know where he was resting.

We cried. And we probably screamed, quietly. And then we went home. Home.

His diaper pail was still full. We had to get rid of it. And the change table still had a half-jar of zinc cream and Vaseline. Half an open bag of diapers. There were bottles of frozen milk, just in case of an emergency, in the basement freezer. Those were only the little things.

His infant bed was still in our room. He had his own room, but we somehow never got around to moving him out of ours at night. His dirty laundry was in a separate basket in the corner, and his clean laundry was waiting to be put away. His toys were all over the place.

We started to pick them up. It was terrible. Every single one had a memory associated with it, and picking them up was like saying good-bye again and again and again. We shouldn't have done it—but we wanted something of his to touch, we wanted comfort.

And we didn't know how to comfort each other.

So we talked about him. We had to. We talked about everything we loved and everything that we'd had together. But it wasn't enough. We cried and laughed and cried; we were hysterical in our grief. It was only when we were utterly physically exhausted that we managed to fall asleep.

I told you Amy was nursing him, didn't I? Well, at his age—and his size—feedings in the middle of the night were necessary. He'd start to wake up with a little cry and that was enough to wake Amy. She'd get up, walk over to his bed, and pick him up gently.

Sometimes he wasn't hungry—he just wanted to be held and comforted. Baby nightmares, I guess. If that happened, I'd pick him up and walk with him for a couple of minutes. I sang to him; I could hold a key.

If either of us managed to sleep through the first little cries, he'd start, eventually, to wail. There's something about a baby when he's wailing that's so utterly despairing that you couldn't sleep through it, even if you were dead.

Well, that night, Amy woke up because the baby was crying. He was hungry, I think; it was that little aaaa-waaaa sound that he makes first. I mean, *made* first. She walked over to his bed, bent down, and tried to pick him up.

And her arms passed right through him.

That's when she screamed, and I woke up. I would have been awake in minutes anyway, because the baby's cries were getting louder and louder and more insistent. He was hungry, you see, and Amy couldn't pick him up.

Oh, she tried.

And then I tried.

He was lying there as plainly as you're sitting, but our arms passed right through him. We didn't feel any unnatural cold, or warmth, or anything; if we closed our eyes, it was as if he wasn't there. Except for the crying. He kicked his little legs and he screamed and screamed, and there wasn't a damned thing we could do.

An hour later, his cries trailed off into exhausted moans, then into sobs, and then silence. With the silence, he disappeared.

It was a nightmare, of course. It had to be. But we were awake until the sun came up, holding each other and crying.

The next day was a normal day. We put a few more of the baby's toys away, and then left everything, except for the diaper pail. We couldn't part with anything yet; it was all important to us, and if we gave a single thing away, it would have felt like we were saying he didn't matter anymore, that he wasn't part of our lives.

And the day was normal, if that loss can ever be normal. We went to the grave, and we took one of his toys with us, to leave at the headstone. It wasn't his favorite toy, but we couldn't bear to part with that.

"He'll understand," Amy said, but he'd never understood anything that deep while he was alive, so I didn't believe her.

"Was that him? Was he really there?"

"No," I told her. "We're tired. We're hysterical. We drank too much after the funeral."

"Oh."

That's all she said. Just "Oh."

He said the rest. That night. Same as the night before. He woke her up crying, and woke me up crying as well. And then we both got up and tried everything we could think of to pick him up, starting with prayer. We were in tears fifteen minutes into his second visitation, and he stayed for a full hour, until exhaustion overcame him.

We'd always comforted him—did I tell you that? We always picked him up when he cried.

"Where is he?" Amy shouted, after he'd disappeared. "God damn it, where is he? He needs us!"

I felt it, too, but hers was always the more expressive temper. She shouted and railed, and I sat, silent.

On the third day, we tried moving his bed. And that helped, if you can call the distant cry from the next room help. It was terrible, that cry. Even when it wasn't so loud, it was piercing and painful. Reminded us of how we'd failed him in life, and were failing him still.

On the fourth day, we stayed out past the hour that he normally woke up. That didn't work at all. He just came after we'd fallen asleep, late.

On the fifth night, we sat and watched and listened and prayed and cried. We'd barely managed to get enough sleep to function, and Amy always got depressed when she didn't sleep. I got more obdurate, and more stubborn, a little more bullish. But her—she got weepy.

On the sixth night, she called a priest, and after explaining the situation, managed to convince him to come and see us. That's when we discovered that our son could scream at the top of his lungs with a cry that was only meant for our ears. The priest couldn't hear him. He offered us counseling and sound advice on dealing with our guilt, and we tried to follow it—God knows Amy did, at any rate. But it didn't help. Nothing helped.

It was his tears that hurt the most. They caught the dim glow of the night light, and as they fell out of the corners of his eyes, they painted a little trail in the darkness, a steady stream. His cheeks would be red, and his eyes, squinched shut. I sang to him, but he didn't hear me. I sang for a week straight, and then screamed for one solid night.

Amy went back to work two weeks after he died. Maternity leave was supposed to last the year, and returning early was painful for her because some of her business associates didn't know why she was suddenly back, and they asked how the baby was. Me, I was lucky enough to have the continuity of my work, and no one even alluded to the fact that I had had a child for fear of causing some sort of breakdown.

They just didn't know.

I think I hated my little boy by the end of the first month. I hated that he haunted us, and made us feel that even grieving for his loss, we were never going to escape from the helplessness and the horror of it.

I don't know if Amy ever reached that state, because we got very good at lying to each other and hiding from each other. It started with the usual things, the little things that all couples do. You know, I'd ask her how she was, and she'd smile sort of wanly and tell me that she was fine. Leave me no opening, no real way of getting to the stuff underneath her pale smile. I'd do the same to her—it was my way of making sure that she didn't have me to worry about as well.

I think, if I could do it again, I'd tell her every little thing. I'd empty my soul onto the breakfast table, and dissect each turn of mood and thought. And I'd make her do the same. Because, if we had, maybe we'd have been able to balance our days and our mornings with our evenings. As it was, we drifted in isolation, and each one of us grew to think—or at least I did—that the other one was less affected, less drained, by the experience than they were.

We found out that our friends couldn't see or hear him when an old University friend of ours came to stay during the summer. He was worried about us both, I could tell—but like anyone else, he was afraid of intruding upon the privacy of our grief. He talked a bit, here and there, and he let us show him pictures and talk about the life—not the death—of our little boy. It was the first time he'd had the chance to look at the face of our baby.

But at night, he heard nothing when we woke. I talked to him—I had to—and it made him uneasy; he was a scientist of no little worth, and the supernatural wasn't real for him. He was very, very worried when he left, and so was I. Maybe the words that he'd never spoken were true; maybe we were mad.

I sought counseling in August. Amy wouldn't go with me. We've never fought about anything—before or since—the way we fought about that. She was openly scornful. And she was right about it, but her words made it hard to come out and admit it. Another bit of wall cropped up between us, a little bit of fear and shadow made real.

I started to travel a bit, with work, taking jobs that would get me out of the house for a week or two at a time. If there is a God, and he's Amy's God, then I beg him for forgiveness. If there is no God, and there's an afterlife, then I beg Amy for it. I think I cracked then, and I had to get away, but I was too much of a coward to just do it. I had to find reasons, and work was a legitimate, adult reason.

Amy understood, of course, in that silent way of hers. She always did. But we weren't being honest—I told you that—and while she was gracious about it, she was also cool. I'd phone her in the evenings, the first few nights, and I'd stay on the phone during the difficult time. But I stopped doing it after a while; I was exhausted, and I'd sleep like the dead. He didn't come to me when I wasn't home.

I guess that's why I failed to notice the change in Amy at first. I didn't want to see it. She lost weight, she lost interest in the world around her. She began to look as if she were part ghost herself, pale and drifting through the day as if it didn't really belong to her anymore.

She started to make mistakes at work; little ones, at first, that could be overlooked because she was still in mourning. But they got bigger and bigger, until her boss—a woman we both admired—called her in to tell her that, unless her performance improved, she would have to be let go. We understood it, and Amy tearfully promised that she would do better.

She never did, and a month after that, Amy was trapped in the house, with a ghost for company. Oh, yes, he started to come to her in the day, when I was working, and in the evening, when I was working overtime. She told me about it, reluctantly, two weeks after it started. Asked me for help.

This was as honest as she'd been with me for a long time, and I tried to be honest in return. But I was still hiding from him, and I couldn't be home with her as much as she needed me to be there.

Give me just a little more time, I asked her. *Just a little bit more. I can't—I can't keep feeling so helpless.*

She nodded, said sure, and became as much a ghost to me as he was; I just didn't see it until later.

But what I told her was true; I needed time. I don't know when time finally gave me a bit more strength and the distance I needed to come back to them both. Maybe a month ago. Maybe two. It blurs now, because now it doesn't matter.

I remember the first day because I bought her flowers and came home for lunch. They were forget-me-nots, which were probably a poor choice, but they were her favorites. She took them without a word, and burst into tears. She even let me hold her, but the tears didn't stop. I guess that's when I knew I'd failed her, too, but at least with her, I had a hope of redeeming myself.

I think I knew that it was too late when I realized what her daily routine was. She would clean the house, almost top to bottom, while our son wailed in the background. Then she would quietly eat lunch, have her customary cup of tea, and stare at the paper. Reading it made no sense of the life she was leading.

After this strange ritual, she would go to the cemetery and sit by the grave, as if that was the closest she could come to comforting him. Or herself.

I know this because, one day, I snuck out of work a little early and went to the grave myself. I found her sitting there, with her forehead pressed into cold marble, shadowed by the shortening day. I walked quietly, because graveyards always make me quiet, and because I did, I didn't disturb her—or her quiet prayer.

The prayer itself was a shock to me. It was simple.

Please, let us be together. Please let us be together soon.

I touched her shoulder, and she turned without even jumping. *Hello,* she said quietly, as if meeting me there were the most natural thing in the world.

"I've come to take you home," I told her. And I did.

That night, she stood by the baby's bed and hugged herself hard. I could see her fingers biting into her upper arms the way her teeth bit into her lower lip. I put my arms around her and rocked her gently, and she cried and cried and cried.

"I'll be home from now on," I told her. "I'll never leave you again." But that didn't stop her tears. And it didn't stop her quiet prayers.

I can see that you understand it already, Father.

But it took me a lot longer than it took you.

I don't know when I realized that she didn't want to live anymore. I thought it was a depression that I could fight by myself, but I didn't see the implacable desire that lay at the core of it.

Because she never said a thing about it. She couldn't. Suicide is a mortal sin, as you know. She wasn't afraid of dying—she was afraid that, by dying, she would lose any chance of joining our boy, and of finally being allowed to comfort him. Paradise, for her, wasn't some Dante-esque heaven; it was the feel of her child in her arms, and the sound of his voice as she realized that she could hold him again, and that she never intended to let him go. Not, of course, that he would realize that at his age, but still.

Her tears became a quiet counterpoint, and then a harmony, to his. Days passed, weeks, in which she would cry when she thought I wouldn't notice; her eyes took on that swollen, reddish look almost all of the time. She wouldn't talk to me about it; I'd lost the right to demand honesty from her.

But it was more than I could take, to stand by, as helpless for her as I was for him. I told you that the ability to comfort my son made me feel powerful; in some measure, the ability to comfort Amy had also been a pillar upon which I'd built my confidence, my identity. That was crumbling, and I had to do *something*. So I started to do some research of my own.

I found out that most poisons, while neat, are not painless. I found out that most drugs, while neat, are not painless. And those that are painless are next to impossible for someone like me to lay hands on. I tried to think of something that would leave no mark—and nothing that pointed to me—but there wasn't anything obvious. After a couple of weeks, it didn't matter.

I wasn't planning the perfect crime, after all.

The most painless thing, in the end, was the simplest. I got a gun. I learned, with some pain, how to fire it. I brought it home, with proper permits, and hid it beside the bed. Then I spent a week building up my nerve.

Because suicide is a sin, but being murdered isn't, you see.

I prayed, you know. I prayed to Amy's God. I prayed to Amy and to my son. It was like a meditation.

That night, when we went to bed, I asked her if I could hold her. She said yes—she didn't say no to much—and came into my arms quietly. In quiet moods, she was not so much woman as child; she could put her arms around my neck and snuggle into my chest as if for warmth and protection. At least, that's what she did before he died.

I wanted that, briefly, again. I didn't care about the sex, but I wanted that closeness back.

I had a dream last night, I told her. She listened, passively, her ear against my chest. *I saw David.*

She tensed slightly, and then raised her head. *Was he— was he happy?*

I swallowed. *He was happy,* I told her. *He was happy because he was with you.*

Really? With me? I could hear her voice break, and I could feel her heart against my rib cage. Her arms tightened.

With you, love. You were both together, right here, beside me. I could see them, if I closed my eyes. I could see her, holding him between us, talking in whispers because she was afraid to wake me up. I could hear him shriek with joy as she tickled him in the darkness. *You were,* I said, swallowing again, *both happy.*

You dreamed this? Tell me about it. Her voice was thick, but it was somehow alive in a way that it hadn't been for far too long. *Tell me everything. Don't leave anything out.*

I did. And I held her until she slept, and when she was deeply asleep, I put her down gently beside me, on her side of the bed. Then, Father, I shot her once, in the head. It wasn't so hard as all that. I didn't watch. But I did clean up afterward.

After I'd finished, I waited.

He came. His crying was soft to start, as it always was. But this time, it didn't have a chance to get any louder. Because she stood up, from the bed—although she wasn't in it anymore—and walked to him. Bent over, her hair shadowing her face so that I couldn't see her expression.

She picked him up, and put him over her shoulder, and rocked him back and forth, talking in shaking, tearful whispers. He chewed on her shoulder and mumbled and grumbled, and she carried him to our bed, and laid him gently down between us.

And then, facing me, she began to nurse him, and he to suckle, and for a moment, they were both more alive, and more real to me, than *I* was. She was so happy, and he was so content, that I reached out to touch them both.

I—I couldn't, of course. Because they were dead. But I wept for the first time in months, for the sheer joy of seeing them, happy at last, because of something I had finally done.

I know why the Madonna is a mother with a child.

I called Amy, but she couldn't hear me, and I had to be content with watching as both she and he trailed off into sleep and disappeared. I was at peace that night, Father.

And when I think of it, of that last night with them both, I can remember a little of that peace. But with each day, it gets less.

Because after that night, they never came back.

It was okay to begin with, but now—now I'm just so damned lonely. They're *gone,* and there's nothing that can change the fact that I'm here alone. I thought—I don't know what I thought. I thought that she'd haunt me like he had—

that they'd both come back to me, happy, night after night after night.

But never since the first night have I seen them.

And I only know of one way to join them.

Oh, Father, Father—give me strength. Because now I understand her desire almost as well as I understand her fear. Can I go to them? Can I make us, finally, whole?

Will your God—will *her* God—have mercy for me?

BLOOD TIES
by Craig Shaw Gardner

Craig Shaw Gardner is the author of the *Ebenezum* trilogy, and his more recent *Dragon Circle* series, which includes the novels, *Dragon Sleeping*, *Dragon Waking*, and *Dragon Burning*.

It was so hard, once you'd been away.

Stephanie walked through the half empty house. Her heels clacked with a hollow sound against the bare oak floors. Most of their parents' furniture was still here, but their Aunt Betsy had spirited away the Oriental rugs, saying they had been promised to her by her sister. Steve hadn't felt strong enough to object at the time, and Stephanie hadn't been around.

Now their aunt had been calling Steve again, demanding some of their mother's jewelry; the so-called "family heirlooms." Stephanie would put an end to that.

She looked in on the living room. The center of the floor had been swept, but there was dust in the corner, back by the bookcase. And she saw another gray clump, dust mixed with cat hair, most likely, half hidden by a sofa leg. The place needed a good cleaning around the edges. It was the sort of thing Steve wouldn't see; the little details that made a room just right. Just like a man.

She smiled. Now that she was back, she'd take care of everything.

Steve hadn't known what to do.

His parents had died when he was out of town, a car crash, brake failure, his father no doubt stewed to the gills from whatever party they were attending that weekend and insisting on driving anyway. Nobody, not even Steve's mother, could keep him from that.

Not that Steve would ever know for sure. There had been

no reason for an autopsy. The crash had been so bad you couldn't tell where metal left off and the people began. That's what the EMT had said anyway. Bunch of jokers—those EMTs.

But there'd be no hint of impropriety when it came to his parents. His father, the judge, was a man who got special privileges even in death.

So Steve had gotten called back from one of his rare weekends out of town, one of the few times he'd ever been away.

He'd moved out of his parents' house a decade ago, when he'd turned twenty-one. But Mother and Father were only a phone call, or a few minutes' drive, away. "Long apron strings," his girlfriend Cheryl had said. His ex-girlfriend, Steve reminded himself.

Now, back in this house, he realized that he'd never really left. He knew which floorboards squeaked, and where you could sit in the dining room and feel that draft that his father could never stop, no matter what he did.

But this house was more than that. Memories of his parents were everywhere. Steve expected to see them when he turned a corner, walked into the kitchen, looked up from reading on the couch.

His father sat at the head of the dining room table, hid behind his paper on his overstuffed chair, disappeared behind his forbidden office door. But Steve remembered his mother in every room.

There had always been something a little frail about his father. But his mother—

When he first heard the news, it had actually surprised him that anything as small as a car crash could kill a woman like that.

She had always been the strong one in the family. A car wreck was only a couple of tons of twisted steel and plastic. His mother should have shrugged that off easily.

"Steven-James-Conner!" His whole name, strung together like one long curse word, one long accusation. "What have you done now?"

He stared down at the broken vase. It came from someplace old. Little Stevie couldn't remember the name. But it was someplace old that sounded important.

"Why can't you be more like your sister?" his mother had

said, not for the first time. "Aren't twins supposed to be alike?"

Steve blinked. It was almost as if his mother was right there before him. The words, the tone, the anger and condescension, everything just the way it was so many years ago, but right here in this living room.

He remembered his father's answers, too, the explanation of the difference between identical and fraternal twins, the soft suggestion that Steve was only a boy, the even quieter comment that it might be a good idea to put the more fragile things around the house away for a year or two. But those comments were distant, the words not quite so exact.

"What, am I not supposed to have my nice things out because we have a little terror running around the house?" Steve's mother frowned down at him. "No, everyone in this house obeys the rules." Her hand shot toward him. "Steven is going to learn to be civilized if I have to take down his pants every day and give him a good paddling!"

Steve slapped himself sharply across the cheek and nose. The pain brought him back to his senses. It was like he had been falling into some sort of trance.

His mother was gone. He was alone in the living room, staring at the table that had once held a vase.

He had work to do. As executor of his parent's estate, he wanted to catalog their belongings, make sure everything was the way it should be.

He pulled the notebook from his pocket and quickly wrote down the contents of the living room. If he could help it, he didn't want to see his mother here again.

He kept his memories at bay through the dining room and the foyer, and on into his father's study, a room he had only really gotten to know as an adult. He wasn't sure how exact he was supposed to be. Should he list every single volume in his father's library? He'd have to talk to the lawyers again.

He wished, not for the first time, that he could hire someone to do all this for him. But he didn't have that kind of money, had hardly any money at all, really, until the estate came through. If there was any money in the estate after they cleared up his parents' debts. Money was something his parents never discussed with Steven; one of many somethings they never discussed.

And he had to face it, there was another reason he was

doing this. He wanted to see this place one more time, to walk through it with his parents gone, to be done with it.

If he could ever finish this. He was feeling overwhelmed by the sheer volume of things around him. The rows of books blurred before him, the titles fading with the evening light. He had to get out of here for a minute, stretch his legs, maybe walk outside.

He stepped out into the hall, and stopped.

He had heard a noise. Someone else was in the house.

The noise was so faint, he didn't realize for a moment that somebody was crying. It came from the other side of the house, from the kitchen.

"Who's there?" he called as he moved quickly across the hallway and into the dining room. The sound seemed even fainter now, farther away. Maybe it was coming from somewhere else, even the house next door.

He pushed the swinging door to the kitchen open anyway.

A little girl stood before him, too busy bawling to know that he was there.

It was his sister, Stephanie, when she was four.

Something had broken, slipped through Stephanie's delicate fingers to shatter on the floor.

"Oh, don't cry," their mother cooed. "Come to Mama. You're God's perfect little girl."

Stephanie sniffled into her mother's apron. And mother's face lit up in that beatific smile she only got when she could hold her daughter.

Steven remembered how he used to hate his sister for that.

"What are you doing, standing in the door like that?"

With the sudden anger in her tone, Steve realized his mother was talking to him.

"He's a little sneak, isn't he?" their mother murmured to her daughter. "Stephanie isn't a little sneak. Are you, my perfect little girl?"

Steve had had just about enough of this. "Mom—" he began.

"Don't talk back to me, young man." His mother never would let Steve get a word in.

What was he doing, anyway? Talking to a memory?

"This is crazy," he murmured.

"What was that?" his mother demanded. "What have I told you about talking back to me?"

The same thoughts and emotions welled up in him again. He had done something wrong, let his mother down. This was all too real.

It wasn't real. He didn't have to do this anymore. His mother was dead. He could leave this behind.

He slapped himself again.

His mother took a step toward him. "Don't hit yourself like that! I swear, I don't know what gets into you."

She was still here. But she couldn't be here.

He took a deep breath. "No, Mother. You're not real."

"What nonsense. I'll show you who's real, young man."

Steve closed his eyes. He could feel a line of pain, a dull ache that crossed his jaw to the bridge of his nose, where the heel of his hand had met the meat of his face. When he hit himself like that, he was alive. The pain let him know.

"Don't you dare close your eyes! Are you trying to ignore me?"

He listened to the blood pounding in his ears. This was real, not those memories of his mother. He was alive. The blood kept him separate from the ghosts of his past.

"Steven James Conner! You will look at me when I'm talking to you!"

"No!" Steve shouted. His fist lashed out, banging into the woodwork to the side of the door. Pain shot across his knuckles. He cradled his fist in his other hand and looked back into the kitchen.

His mother was gone. The kitchen was quiet.

One of his knuckles had split open. A line of blood ran down the back of his hand. He licked the back of his hand clean, sucked at his damaged knuckle. It tasted salty. It tasted real.

For a moment, he thought it strange that he should see Stephanie here with his mother. But then, Stephanie would have been the one his mother would have wanted to take care of things, the one to make everything right.

But his mother couldn't have Stephanie. No one had Stephanie, except Steven's memory.

After all, Stephanie was dead, too.

But he'd had enough of this house for one night. Maybe, when he came back in the morning, he could leave his memories outside.

* * *

A gentle breeze blew in through the bedroom window. Stephanie remembered what her father used to say about this house. "It always got the air."

The night was turning suddenly cool, the autumn chill replacing the Indian summer day. She really should go back to her room and get a sweater to put over her thin blouse.

But she couldn't bring herself to move. Not quite yet. Not when she could smell the grass and leaves and feel the wind against the starched cloth of her collar. She was alive now, more alive than ever before.

She ran her hand through her sandy brown hair. It was clipped much too short. She'd have to let it grow back the way it was. She'd have everything the way she wanted it.

It was just so good to *feel* for a change.

She stood in the window and looked out at the night. She felt better with every passing minute. This house was hers, the way it was always meant to be.

She never wanted to leave.

The next day was worse.

His Aunt Betsy had woken him out of a sound sleep. Steve groped for the phone, almost knocking it off the nightstand as he grabbed the receiver. He muttered something that might pass for hello.

His aunt had already started talking, that kind of rapid patter, one sentence after another, that told you not to ask any questions.

At first, Steve had thought it was his mother.

Aunt Betsy was already at the house. She had her own set of keys. Steve's mother, her sister, had trusted her with the keys, and wanted her to have the carpets.

Steve tried to sputter out some explanation about the estate. Aunt Betsy wouldn't listen to him any more than his mother would.

By the time Steve got to the house, the carpets were gone.

Steve felt the fury rise up inside him as soon as he stepped into the living room. He hadn't protected the place well enough. He could never protect anything well enough. He wanted to smash his hand right through the picture window.

He could never control anyone in his family. His mother was proof of that.

He wished again that Stephanie could be here, instead of

him. She had always been so much better at this sort of thing. Better at keeping everything together.

Ironic that she had been the first in the family to die. Murdered, by a lover maybe, or a total stranger, when she was home alone. The police had never come up with a suitable suspect.

It was possible that she might even have killed herself. But no, her parents never would have permitted that. A suicide? They certainly wouldn't allow anyone to say it out loud.

He was the one who should have died. Instead, he was the only one left. He should be glad that his parents were gone, that he could finally be free of his mother's disapproval and his father's aloofness. But instead, he felt empty, as if he couldn't be whole until he found—what? Something that had been missing all his life.

He shook his head. It was the house that was doing this to him. He'd take a quick inventory of what his aunt had removed and get this over with. Three Oriental rugs were gone from the living and dining rooms. The rest of the downstairs was untouched.

He'd have to check upstairs, too.

He realized, as he climbed the stairs, that he'd resisted going up here the day before. As many painful memories as waited for him down in the house's common area, the pain upstairs was much more personal.

Steve reached the top of the stairs. He knew what was in each of the rooms without taking another step.

Steve no longer had a room up here. What had been his bedroom at the end of the hall became his mother's sewing room on the day after he moved out.

His sister's room looked the same as it had for years. His mother had kept it that way, a shrine to Stephanie. She had never moved out of the house when she was alive, and her parents would be certain she would never move out after she was dead. All his sister's things, her clothes, her books, her personal items, kept neatly arranged and dusted, waiting for the day Stephanie would return.

He walked into his parents' room. It was dark, the windows masked by heavy, ornate drapes, starched white layers crowded by red plush ruffles. Everything was plush; heavy curtains and heavy bedspread. The air was heavy with his mother's perfume. You could air out this room for years, and her presence would still be there.

He glanced quickly around the room. All of his mother's little keepsakes seemed to be there. He opened the jewel box on the top of her bureau. Her ruby and diamond broach lay in the top compartment. Aunt Betsy would have taken this if she would have taken anything. Unless she coveted his mother's mink.

Steve walked quickly to his mother's closet. It was jammed with so many clothes that he had trouble pushing his hands through the layers of cloth. As he pulled one dress after another aside, he felt resistance in the pile of fabric, as if something was pushing back.

Steve took a step back. Surely, the fur was somewhere in that jumbled mass. He didn't want to look anymore. He needed to get some distance from his mother.

He walked quickly out into the hall, then into his sister's room.

He felt calmer as soon as he stepped inside. He often referred to this room as some sort of shrine, but, compared to his mother, his sister really was some sort of saint. She would take the time to listen, to laugh, to actually reply in a way that showed she cared about what Steve thought. And he felt this room still held a little bit of his sister in it, even after all these years.

His aunt wouldn't have taken any of Stephanie's things. He looked quickly around this room, afraid somehow that some part of his sister might be gone.

"Steven."

The voice was as faint as the breeze, yet he was sure he heard his name.

"Steven." The voice was stronger now, and held a melody he hadn't heard since his sister died.

"Stephanie?" Steven whispered.

The breeze laughed gently.

"You're here?" Steve's voice grew louder.

"I never left." Her voice became louder in reply.

Some noise came from the back of Steven's throat, maybe a laugh, maybe a cry of pain. "Oh, Stephanie, I wish you really were here!"

Hangers rattled in her closet, as if she were hiding behind all those things that once were hers.

"Stephanie?" He pushed his way among her things, looking for her among the dresses, skirts, and blouses.

"But I am here, Steven," said the voice that came from nowhere, and everywhere, "if you want me to be."

He stopped, and waited for her to continue. It felt very reassuring to be here, among all these physical objects that were once a part of her life.

"I know you've wanted my help," her soft voice said to him. "As I've wanted yours. We really need each other."

Steve smiled at that. They had really grown to depend on each other as they'd battled their way through adolescence. None of this was Stephanie's fault.

A wool skirt brushed the back of his neck. His hand rested against one of Stephanie's blouses. The silk felt cool beneath his fingers.

"Take these things. Only you can give me form."

For the first time, he didn't feel like lashing out. There seemed to be two pulses inside his temples. She gave him peace, he gave her his warmth, his blood, his life.

It was the little things that were giving her trouble; the buttons on her blouse, the clasp on her necklace. Her fingers felt too big, too clumsy, at first.

Stephanie was guiding his hands. They'd get better with practice.

She stood and smoothed her skirt. She was getting hungry. Time to venture out and see what was in the kitchen.

Mother stood in her doorway.

"What is the meaning of this, young man?"

Stephanie stared at her. What was she talking about?

"What do you mean, dressing like that?" Mother shouted, her anger in full force. "What kind of sick pervert would—"

"Mother," Stephanie said, her hands calmly clasped before her. "Look at me."

Her mother's frown changed ever so slightly, anger falling from the corners of her mouth. "Stephie? My little girl?"

Stephanie found herself laughing at that. "I'm not so little anymore. This was the only way I could come back."

Her mother's mouth twisted upward into a wistful smile. "You'll always be my little girl."

Stephanie took a step away. There was anger here, inside her. Steven's anger.

"You won't listen to me, will you, Mother?" she said,

wanting to put an end to this. "You never listened, to either of us."

The loathing was back on her mother's face. "Your brother's been talking to you, hasn't he? Filling your head with his lies? Such a willful child. I never could do anything with him."

Now Stephanie found herself getting angry. "My brother never wanted anything—" She paused, sensing Steven deep within. "—except maybe a little love."

Mother went rigid at that. "How dare you suggest that I didn't love him? What kind of freak are you?"

"Freak?" Stephanie answered slowly. "Mother, I'm—"

"You're nothing!" Mother barked. "Nothing but a memory. You weren't strong enough. That's why you're dead!"

"Shut up, Mother! I won't listen to any more of this." She looked down at her hands, her favorite silver bracelet, her graduation ring. She was real.

But her mother pushed at her. "I kept you safe. I kept you near me. Without me, you were nothing!"

Stephanie began to cry. Great, wrenching sobs racked her body. Her knees trembled. She felt very cold.

She was nothing without her mother.

Stephanie had to get away. She panicked. She struggled to get out.

She had never planned for this.

"No!" Steven's deep voice burst through his sister's tears. He couldn't lose her now.

His mother's smile was triumphant. She had won it all.

Steven wouldn't let her get away with this. Not if he had to tear down the whole house. He pushed past his mother.

He almost tripped. He wasn't used to his sister's heels.

"You drove me to this!" he shouted at his mother as he swept the bottles and boxes from her dresser. They crashed to the floor. "Now I hope you're happy."

Stephanie cowered somewhere deep inside him. He'd have to be the strong one now. He ripped down curtains, up-ended drawers.

"Stop it!" his mother shrieked. "You're horrible!"

"You can't beat me, Mother!"

"Freak!" she called.

He'd smash every piece of furniture in the room.

"Not my child—"

When he was done, there'd be nothing left of his mother's room.

"Never my child—"

He toppled the vanity, tripping as the mirror shattered beneath him.

He looked down at his arm, startled enough to ignore his mother's cries. He'd cut himself on the mirror; a jagged gash just below the palm of his hand. It was blood that made him different. Blood would save him. He pulled at the piece of glass still embedded in his skin, slicing it back and forth to make the wound a little larger. He was amazed how quickly it flowed, bubbling from his arm onto the carpet.

"Never—" her voice whispered. His mother was fading. She was nothing but a shadow. She couldn't compete with life. Red poured from the wound.

But Stephanie was screaming. How could he quiet her down?

All he had was blood.

THE HOUND LOVER
by Laura Resnick

Laura Resnick is the winner of the John W. Campbell Best New Writer Award, and the author of numerous popular short stories and novels.

She welcomed him in the night, welcomed his sleek, hard length between her thighs, welcomed the salty velvet of his tongue in a cold-lipped embrace. There was no delicacy in this demon, no tenderness in the incubus that pressed her heavily into the aged mattress, hurting her with his unrepentant passion. No word, no whisper, no sigh escaped his lips. His breathing was feather light despite his exertion, and its soft, reliable rhythm coolly brushed the vulnerable hollows of her throat as her head lolled backward.

She could find no voice, either for pain or pleasure, and her mind, like her tormentor, would not let her separate the two sensations. Her thighs quivered limply against his hard flanks, and her arms lay at her sides, leaden and unresponsive, unable to touch, scratch, grasp, or clasp the unseen sorcerer invading her body with such intensity.

She strained for breath, throwing her head back even farther, hot pleasure mingling with terror as the weight on her chest grew heavier, suffocating her. Her throat tightened against her futile efforts to scream, to sigh, to draw air into her burning lungs.

Her helplessness only served to incite him, and he drove deeper, engulfing her in his chilly fire. Surely she would faint, she thought, as he rode her faster, harder, bearing her down into the abyss. Surely she would die.

Pitiless in his ardor, he led her into the underworld where Pluto had taken his captive bride; and, like Persephone, she followed him blindly into the heart of darkness. And there she found a force stronger than death, a consummation devoutly wished and greedily grasped.

Then, to her sorrow, he withdrew like a shadow at dawn, disappearing even as she strained toward him, even as her skin flushed and her body shook with a new tremor of ecstasy. She was alone when unconsciousness enfolded her in its sheltering arms, more alone than she had ever been before. She could never forget the dark wonder he had shown her; she would never again be the woman she had been before the haunting echo of his cry had roused her to seek his embrace.

She knew he would return. He would come again to suck her soul out of her body, to terrify and enthrall her, to lure her ever deeper into that undiscovered country. Yes, like the night itself, he would come again; and she would be waiting for him.

He came again last night, with the oily stealth of a predator, like a raptor, like a hungry wolf, like a great dark hound come to devour me ...

Grace went utterly still and stared at the words she had just scrawled upon the stained folds of the brown paper bag which lay flattened before her. Spread out on the kitchen table, the bag stank of last night's Chinese food, bought in haste and eaten with disinterest. The bag bore pale splotches of grease and darker stains from the black bean sauce Grace had injudiciously ordered; smearing as it came into contact with these, the sentence she had written was already soaking into the paper and growing cloudy.

"He came again last night," she breathed, her heart pounding with sudden exhilaration.

Cautiously, as if fearful of being snared, she opened a cabinet, pulled out a briefcase, set it on the table, and opened it. Her heart pounded with mingled fear and anticipation as she stared at its contents: a laptop computer and a thick, tattered dictionary.

After a long moment, she lifted the laptop with shaking hands and cradled it briefly in her arms. Her longtime companion, her significant other. She had carried it around like some useless appendage for so long, she now nearly choked with pleasure, with reconquered pride, to realize she might actually use it today. How long had it lurked accusingly in the corners of her life like a guilty secret, a bashful lover, an elusive dream? Today, after such a long and painful drought, she might actually justify the obsession which had made her drag the damned thing through two hospitals, a psychiatric ward, a new apartment, and two prescribed vacations. Christ, she had even started carrying it to her analyst's waiting room, as if she really expected to break through the barrier while waiting for another hour of self-torture.

Eager to get started, to find out if the first line she'd written in over three years was going to lead to a second one, she looked around for an electrical outlet. She had just found one when the telephone rang, making her jump like a scalded cat.

"Shit." She lifted the receiver, already sure of her caller's identity.

"Grace! How's it going up there?"

"Fine," she mumbled.

"Missing the city? The smog? The crime? The subways and pimps and crack addicts?"

"Sure, Jo," she said absently, gaze fixed on her computer. She longed to be left alone with it more ardently than she had ever longed for any man.

There was a brief silence. "Uh, finding everything you need?"

"Yeah. No problems."

"Seen much of the town yet?"

Jo had bought this little house in the woods ten years ago, and ever since then she had been regaling Grace with stories about the town, its inhabitants, and her own summer and weekend adventures in country living.

"No, I haven't really been out much yet." Grace's fingers brushed across the keyboard. She shifted the phone to her other ear and sat down. "It's only been four days."

The silence was a little longer this time. "How are you feeling?"

"Better." For once, that was true. "Really. This was a good idea. Thanks for offering to let me stay here."

"Offering? Offering, she says. Last week you called it nagging, badgering, pushing, manipulating—"

"Well, now I'm glad I came." She smiled. No need to retract words that had indeed been true at the time. They had been friends since their college days, some twenty years ago. "You were right. It's good to get out of the city, breathe fresh air, not worry about traffic, muggings, bumping into people I don't want to see, getting calls from my lawyer."

"Good. I'm glad. You *do* sound better. I'll be up on Saturday."

"See you then."

She rose to hang up the phone, then turned and looked again at the keyboard. The interruption had been untimely. It had broken her concentration, doused the sparks she had felt. She begged for help, addressing her silent prayers impartially to heaven or hell, and approached the mute laptop with all the trepidation of a sinner entering the confessional.

By dusk, she had exhausted anger, tears, and even physical violence. Smashed crockery—which she would have to replace before Jo's arrival—lay upon the floor. The table was covered with crumpled tissues, coffee stains, an overflowing ashtray, and a small burn mark where she had stubbed out a cigarette without looking. She stared at the cursor on the small computer screen, watching it blink hypnotically. It goaded her, mocked her. She hadn't written a word since typing that single sentence hours ago: *He came again last night . . .*

Numb and drained, Grace finally turned off the computer as the sky outside lost its amber glow. Her shoulders slumped as she poured a generous amount of Scotch into her coffee cup. Oppressed by the scent of failure which overpowered the little kitchen, she opened the back door and stepped out onto the porch. The April night was cool against her skin, and it smelled of greenery and promise. A breeze ruffled the trees. They sighed in response and swooned like maidens. Grace sat on an old lounge chair and closed her tired eyes.

This was worse than before. The coma her imagination had fallen into was bad enough. She never thought of it as writer's block. That was far too innocuous a phrase for the thing that had destroyed her life. Anyhow, she had always despised that trite cliché as a convenient excuse for Ivy League idiots, hopeful housewives, and pompous professionals whose Great Novels would never be written simply because they didn't really want to do the blood and guts work of sitting down day after day and writing a goddamn book.

She wanted to do it. It was all she had *ever* wanted. And for years, she'd done it well and successfully. Then—burnout. It had just happened. Then came her first internment in a hospital. "Exhaustion," they said, after she collapsed on West 85th Street in the middle of the day.

She'd demanded to be released against the doctor's advice. She had a book to finish, dammit. She had a deadline to meet. She couldn't get anything done in that hospital, it was too noisy and there was no privacy. *That's* why she hadn't written a single word on the laptop she had insisted on having with her.

But she still didn't write after returning home. Her second visit to the hospital lasted longer. She knew, though she resented being told, that she had brought this illness upon herself. The publisher extended her deadline, urged her to take some time off, get away, relax. Their kindness, of course, was based on the fact that her last two books for them had been national best-sellers.

But their kindness—not to mention patience—was wearing thin by the time she realized that she would never finish this book. She hadn't written a word in over a year, and when she looked at the first few chapters of the book, she had no idea what she had planned to write after that.

Grace absently traced the scars on her wrists. Such a dramatic thing to do. So classical a method. Why hadn't she simply taken pills or used a gun?

She sighed and took a healthy swig of Scotch. An owl hooted, crickets chirped, a truck drove past the house. Country sounds, soothing sounds. But she would not be soothed.

After her release from the psychiatric hospital, she told her editor she would write a different book, a better book. She'd have to, she realized, since the advance money they'd already paid her was trickling through her fingers very rapidly: hospital bills after her insurance was canceled, psychiatric treatment, expensive prescriptions, a couple of vacations to help her relax and gain a new perspective, legal fees, old debts . . .

By now, of course, her editor realized that, some three years after signing the contract, Grace wasn't going to write a book. The publisher wanted the money back. According to the terms of the contract, Grace had to give it back. The problem was, she didn't have it anymore.

Burnout. Hospitalization. Psychiatric treatment. Public humiliation. Professional death. Personal hell.

None of it, though, had prepared her for this, for today. Could anything hurt more than hope? Had anything ever wounded her as much as that first tantalizing sentence, the promise of a paragraph to come, the hint of a story blossoming in the wasteland of her imagination?

"Oh, God." Too deep for tears, too deep.

What the hell did that sentence mean, anyhow. *He came again last night* . . . He, who? Where did he come? Who did he come to? What had sparked that fragment, that notion, that shadow of a thought?

"Shit." It taunted her, flooded her with anger.

"Fine. If thy right eye offends thee . . ." If the sentence wasn't going to go anywhere, wouldn't lead to anything, she'd erase it. Right now. She pushed herself to her feet. *"Fine."*

A cry arose from the woods, a desolate cry that would not be ignored, that echoed through her mind and made her turn to search the darkness with a wide-eyed gaze. Something about that sound was hauntingly familiar. It stirred a response in her belly that was almost sexual in its heat and immediacy.

She stood at the edge of the porch, peering into the night. She thought she saw a dark flank catch a flicker of light from the sickle moon before disappearing into the woods. A dog? An incredibly big one. It howled again, calling to her, and she had to steel herself not to run across the lawn and follow it into the woods.

She reached for her drink, hand shaking slightly. She was breathing fast. She hoped that thing out there wasn't dangerous. How long had it been lurking around the house? When it cried out again, she backed quickly toward the door and entered the house with more speed than grace. She slammed the door shut behind her, locked it, and stood with her back pressed against it, listening.

There was no sound from outside. The howling had ceased. The black dog had gone away. But somehow, she knew he would return. Yes, like the night itself, he would come again; and she would be waiting for him.

Grace was still asleep when Jo arrived on Saturday. She awoke to the sharp sting of her friend's palm against her face.

"Ow!" She opened her eyes in time to see another blow coming. "Stop it! What are you doing?"

White-faced and breathing hard, Jo snapped, "What did you take?"

"What?" Grace touched her tender cheek and winced.

"What did you *take?*" Jo practically shrieked the last word as she shook Grace's shoulders.

"You're hurting me! What is the *matter* with you?" Grace shoved the other woman away. "Jesus, I took nothing. Nothing! Why are—"

"I've been trying to wake you up for five minutes! I thought you were drugged or in a coma or something." Jo glanced suspiciously at the empty glass on the bedside table.

"One glass," Grace said clearly. "That's all I had all night. The dregs of my bottle. It was too late to go out for more."

"Then what's the *matter* with you?"

Grace blinked and sat upright. "Did you say five minutes? Really?" She looked around, disoriented. "I must have been really tired."

"Tired?" Jo repeated incredulously. "You weren't—"

"What time is it?"

"What does . . . Never mind. It's almost noon."

Grace rubbed her cheek again and looked around at the tangled sheets. "I was having this wild dream."

"Uh-huh." Deflated, Jo sank into a chair.

"Really . . . erotic."

"Oh?"

"Kinky."

"Oh?"

"Something about . . ." She squeezed her eyes shut and tried to recall the details. A *frisson* of remembered sensation shivered through her. Dark, elusive images. "Something half-man, half-beast," she murmured.

"Sounds more scary than erotic."

The memory quivered and faded. Grace opened her eyes with a sigh. "Maybe." She studied Jo. "Why don't you take a nap or something?"

Jo looked surprised and shook her head. "Let's go out for lunch."

Grace clenched the cotton sheet between her hands. She was ready to write it down: her daily sentence. That's all she was being granted so far, but it was more than she had hoped for. A special gift from whatever capricious gods had chosen to torment her. Each day she awoke with one perfect, crystal clear sentence in her mind; and each one followed the previous day's sentence as perfectly as ripples on a lake's surface.

She yearned to turn on her laptop, write down the sentence, and study the way it linked with the four previous sentences. My God, a whole paragraph. The steep, square shape, with its irregular edges and strange gaps; the flow and development of one idea, smooth as glass, changeable as a dangerous current. To see nine rough-edged, word-filled lines on the screen. Nothing could equal that feeling—except possibly knowing where the story was going, which she didn't.

Patience, she reminded herself. *Just let it happen.*

"Okay, Jo," she said at last. "Let me just shower and dress, and we'll get out of here."

"You're sure you're all right?"

"I'm fine. Go unpack or something."

The moment Jo left the room, Grace found a pen and a sheet of paper at the desk and wrote down her sentence before it could escape her. She'd add it on to the others later.

"Do you know anything about a black dog?" she asked Jo after lunch as they strolled around the quaint streets of the local town. Antique shops and galleries, handmade chocolates and designer boutiques attracted visitors in droves.

"How do you mean?"

"I keep seeing one around the house."

"Really?"

"He's very shy. Only comes around after dark. I've put some food out for him, but he never touches it."

"*You've* put food out? You don't like dogs."

"I feel sorry for him. He sounds lonely."

"He talks to you?"

Grace gave her a look. "I wonder if he's feral or if he belongs to someone."

"I've never seen him." Jo shrugged, then after a moment said, "Maybe he belonged to that Racinet woman. She used to live about a mile away, at the edge of the woods."

"Used to? She left without her dog?"

"She died. About two years ago."

"Oh."

"Yeah, it was weird. She was only about thirty-five. She was a completely unknown artist when her husband bought a weekend home up here. Not even a very good artist, I gather. But living up here had a profound effect on her work, and she quickly decided to live here full-time. She and her husband separated a few months later, and she got the house in the divorce settlement. She didn't live for very long after that, though."

"What happened?"

"Nobody knows. They found her in the woods one day, naked and dead. It was January."

Grace stopped walking and stared at Jo. "What was she doing naked in the woods in the middle of winter?"

Jo shrugged. "No one knows. Insanity, I suppose. Apparently she just walked out there one night and died of exposure. No signs of physical violence or trauma . . . Just dead."

Grace resumed walking. "What makes you think this dog I've been seeing might be hers?"

"Apparently she had this enormous black hound she was very fond of."

"What do you mean, apparently?"

"I never saw him. No one ever did. He wasn't in her house or yard when her body was found. But everyone knew about him. He was in all of her later paintings."

"She put a *dog* in all of her paintings?"

"Yeah. Painting her dog made her famous." Jo smiled. "You never know what's going to become fashionable, do you? She did about twenty paintings of this dog the year before she died. They were snatched up like *that*." Jo snapped her fingers.

"A dog," Grace repeated, shaking her head.

"Come on, I'll show you. She's a real celebrity around here, especially since her death. Most of the local galleries have prints on display. Signed, limited-edition. Ridiculously expensive."

Someone recognized Jo as soon as they entered the gallery and came over to say hello. Grace glared at her friend when she introduced her to the woman. Jo knew perfectly well that she would have preferred to melt into the depths of the shop and forgo meeting anyone. And, of course, this turned into a worst case scenario.

"Grace Wedeck? Ohmigod! This is such a thrill! I've read every single one of your books. *Destiny's Hand* is my absolute favorite. How on earth do you come up with all those ideas?"

"Damned if I know," Grace mumbled. "Nice shop. Is that an original?"

The ploy didn't work. "Oh, I wish I had one of your

books here for you to autograph. When is your next one due out? It's been so long since your last book. I just can't wait to see the next one. It's going to be terrific, I just know it is."

"Oh, thanks. We just came in to—"

"What's it about?"

Grace blanched. Whereas she had once enjoyed the effusive praise of genuine fans, she now felt like an imposter. The Grace Wedeck they so admired was dead but not buried. As for discussing the future—it was hard enough to admit to herself and her analyst that she was terrified she'd never write again; there was no way she was going to tell total strangers.

"What's it about?" Grace repeated. "Uh, you know, it's . . ."

Christ, this was why she avoided people. After three years, she still hadn't found any easy responses to the casually cruel questions everyone asked a burned-out, washed-up writer.

By now, Jo was having the good grace to look guilty for having instigated this disastrous conversation, and she intervened. "Oh, that's top secret. Grace won't even tell me. You know how writers are."

"Oh? Oh. Of course." The woman smiled, apparently trying to put Grace at ease. "Can I at least know the title?"

"The title?"

"I'm going to tell my bookseller that I want the very first copy that comes in."

"The title. Well, it's . . ."

"It's still untitled, isn't it?" Jo piped up.

"It . . ." From nowhere, a warm wave of calm washed over Grace, and she heard herself say, "It's called *The Hound Lover*."

Both women looked at her with surprise. *"The Hound Lover?"* Jo repeated.

"It's just a working title."

Jo stared. "Do you mean you're actually writing . . ." She glanced at the other woman and stopped awkwardly. "I mean—"

"Yeah," Grace admitted. "It's something I'm, you know, working on."

"But that's *wonderful!* Why didn't you tell me?"

"Has your visit here inspired you, or did you come here because of Louise Racinet?" the gallery owner asked.

Grace frowned. "Because of Louise Racinet?"

"You know. *The Hound Lover*. Her last painting."

"Her what?" Grace snapped in surprise.

"Surely you knew? No? What an extraordinary coincidence. I've got a print on display over here. Personally, I think it's her best, though opinions do differ. This is it. Here."

The woman rattled on for some time about form and influence and substance, but Grace didn't hear her. She heard, saw, knew nothing except the picture before her.

This vision was an echo of the strange words which had started flowing through her fingertips recently. It was a reflection of the darkly erotic dreams which held her in their grip all night long, leaving her disoriented and unable to grasp the elusive fragments of memory and sensation. He was much more than a hound, this thing that Racinet had painted. He was a bestial intelligence, a poetic monster. He summoned spirits, he defied the gods, and he dominated a submissive feminine form whose presence was more suggested than portrayed. He was a demon lover, powerful, merciless, and irresistible, neither real nor imagined, but existing somewhere between fantasy and reality in an eternal purgatory of the imagination.

"This is what he looks like," Grace murmured at last.

"He who?" Jo asked.

He came again last night . . . like a great dark hound come to devour me . . .

"How much does this thing cost?" Grace asked, reaching for her checkbook.

The sentences turned into paragraphs which turned into pages. Each day saw Grace's output increasing until she found herself writing nearly twenty pages a day, every day— more than she had been used to writing even at the peak of her professional productivity.

The impulse had become an idea, which had in turn metamorphosed into a situation and finally developed into a story. She still didn't know the ending, an extraordinary position to be in after having written over a hundred pages. She didn't particularly care. She clawed her way out of a dazed, drugged sleep each day to virtually fling herself at the laptop, filled with exhilaration and passion. She turned off the computer each evening, worn, drained, and terrified that she had finally depleted her reserves in this last, brief burst of glory and would now wander through the empty days and hollow years with an unfinished book clutched in her arms like a dead child.

She kept the Racinet print near the table she worked at, studying it every time she lost her train of thought. Though they were separated by time and death, she and the Racinet woman shared a vision, for this was the thing that haunted her dreams with increasing clarity. This was the creature that filled her nights with a hot twist of erotic rapture and dark horror. And this thing was both hero and villain in the novel she worked on feverishly day after day. *The Hound Lover*. This was his story as surely as if he whispered it to her with his cold lips during the nightly rape of her unconscious mind. She didn't have to know how; she only knew it was happening.

Shaking with fatigue, she poured a large glass of orange juice and took it out onto the back porch as twilight enclosed the yard and filled the woods with the shapes and shadows of another world. She hadn't touched a drop of alcohol since she had started writing again, though her throat was raw from smoking one cigarette after another.

Jo hadn't come up last weekend, but she'd be here again on Saturday. Grace sighed and let her mind turn to mundane matters. She supposed she'd better tidy up the house, get some groceries, and do a couple of loads of laundry. She'd been wearing the same clothes, right down to her underwear, for three days. It wouldn't be smart to let Jo think she was cracking up just when she was finally getting her life back on track.

She had learned to expect the howling to come soon after dusk, so it didn't surprise her tonight. She had never caught more than the faintest glimpse of Racinet's dog—for surely that's what it was—nor did the poor thing ever eat any of the food she put out for it. She had ceased to worry about its lurking in the woods, though. Hadn't the black hound brought Racinet good fortune, turning her from an unknown painter into a famous artist?

Arthur Conan Doyle's *Hound of the Baskervilles* notwithstanding, mysterious black hounds weren't necessarily evil. There were numerous stories of black dogs in folklore, tales of ghostly hounds who protected children, haunted battle-grounds, and guarded sacred sites against the devil. There were legends about shapeshifters, too: werehounds, canine demons, and men who turned themselves into black dogs to woo maidens, wreak mischief on local communities, and avenge wrongs.

Well, if that thing in the woods was a creature from the Other Side, she could only welcome its presence in her life. Haunting and possession were a pleasure after the hell she had been through these past three years.

Jo knew her too well to interfere with her work. Nothing else had ever mattered to Grace—which was why she had few friends, no hobbies, and one ex-husband who was now happily remarried to a normal person. Jo was openly happy about Grace's breakthrough, a little surprised by her refusal to let her friend look at the manuscript, and plainly worried about the way Grace was driving herself.

"Now, I've never tried to tell you how to run your life," Jo began as they sat on the porch one evening.

"Bullshit."

"But I think you'd be well-advised to pace yourself. Isn't this exactly the way this whole burnout thing began? You were working too hard, never exercising, never eating anything but junk food, never relaxing or socializing or taking time off."

"This is different."

"How?"

"This isn't like work. This book just flows, as if someone were telling me the story. I'm just writing it down."

"All the same—"

"And I'm much more relaxed than I used to be. For the first time since I was twelve, I'm not having any trouble with insomnia. I'm asleep almost as soon as my head hits the pillow, and sleeping hard for about ten hours a night."

"And talking and crying out in your sleep," Jo added.

"Really?" Grace frowned.

"And when I come into your room, you're impossible to wake."

"I was probably just having a nightmare."

"It happened last time I was here, too."

"Well, I'm . . ." The howling came.

"You're *what?*" Jo challenged.

"Shhh. That's him."

"What's him?" Jo blinked at her.

It grew louder. "That howling."

"What howling?"

It seemed to reverberate all around them, making Grace tremble. "It grows louder every night."

"*What* does?"

Grace stared at her. "Can't you hear it?"

"Hear *what?*"

"Hear him calling?" She closed her eyes and felt the physical pull. It was both a summons and a promise.

"Grace? *Grace.*" Jo's hands on her shoulders startled her into dropping her glass of juice. "I don't hear anything. What do you hear?"

"That dog." She didn't like the way Jo was looking at her.

"Are you sure you're all right?"

"Oh, for God's sake. You're the one who's half deaf. That's it, I'm going to bed."

"It's barely ten o'clock."

"I'm tired. I've been working all day. Good night, Jo."

Upstairs in her room, she undressed, turned out the light, and started to climb into bed. She heard the hound's cry again, at once sinister and beckoning. She went to the window and looked out at the moon-streaked landscape. The night was filled with magic and mystery, with the scent of ripening summer. One shadow separated itself from the others and came toward the house.

He stood beneath her window, and she saw him, full and strong in the moonlight, for the first time. The silvery light shone on the straight, dark length of his back. His chest was broad and deep, his legs long and gracefully swift. He raised his proud face to hers and met her gaze, deliberately and intently. Held frozen in her position at the window, Grace looked into those strange, intelligent eyes and knew why he never ate the food she put out for him, why he never left footprints in the woods, and why no one else had ever seen Louise Racinet's dog. She felt his glowing amber gaze move over her face, her hair, her body, and she knew. Only she would ever hear his voice in the woods. Only she would ever see him take shape in the shadows and glide through the night to call upon his chosen one. And in her heart, she had known it all long before this moment.

Obediently, she turned to the bed and waited for him.

* * *

The book was finished a month later. Grace delivered it personally to an astonished editor, then returned quickly to Jo's house in the woods. She didn't like to be away at all, and especially not at night. The erotic, inspiring whirlpool of her nights was manna to her now.

The telephone call came only two days later. "Grace! My God! I couldn't put it down. This is *incredible,*" her editor raved.

"Oh, good. Glad you like it."

"Like it? I *love* it. I devoured it, I absorbed it, I . . . I . . . I . . . Oh, wow, this is the most exciting thing I've ever read. It's erotic and spiritual and lyrical and surprising and mysterious and dangerous . . . Grace, this is an extraordinary book! The sky's the limit for this thing."

"Oh, good. Look, I'm trying to work right now. Could you just send me the rest of the advance money, and we'll talk more next week?"

There was a slight pause. "Sure. Of course. Look, are you okay? I mean, I think you should take some time off, Grace. You've earned it. Why don't—"

"Thanks. I'll talk to you later." Grace hung up.

At twilight she heard him. His cry came from deep in the heart of the woods. He hadn't come to her since her return from the city. And he didn't come tonight either.

"I want you to leave," Jo told her.

"I can't." She hadn't written a word in two months. Not since summer's end. Not since finishing *The Hound Lover.*

"I don't think this place is good for you anymore. Quite the opposite," Jo said.

"He'll come back. I know he'll come back."

Jo stared at her. "Who? Grace—were you having an affair?"

Grace drew in a sharp breath and tried to pull herself together. She hadn't mentioned the howling in the woods—or anything remotely connected to it—since the night she had realized the nature of the Hound Lover. Jo would certainly force her to leave—and probably go back into treatment—if she mentioned it now.

"I meant *it,*" Grace said. "*It* will come back."

"The writing? Of course it will," Jo said instantly. "It did once already, didn't it? But it's time for a change of scenery."

"No. I like it here. Am I in your way?"

"You know that's not the problem."

"Then what *is* the problem?"

"Jesus, look at yourself. You're smoking three packs a day. You're drinking again. You never eat. You never see people or go out or do anything but stare at your laptop all day. Then you sit alone on the porch like a zombie at night, just staring off into space." Jo shook her head. "You're acting even stranger than before you wrote that book."

"And I haven't written a word—"

"Can't you just give yourself a break? You just finished writing a book after three years of thinking you'd never write again. You've done it, for God's sake!"

"For God's sake?" Grace tilted her head back and blew out a wreath of smoke. "No, I don't think it was written for His sake at all."

"What? No, never mind. Look, I don't want to fight about this. But will you at least think about moving out of here?"

After Jo left the room, Grace murmured, "Where in hell would I go?"

The torment was unbearable. She could hear him, faintly, so faintly, from very far away, but she never saw him. Each night was an eternity of yearning unfulfilled. Each day was an endless, dismal hell. It was a tremendous effort to endure Jo's visits. Grace knew she was thinner than ever, with dark circles under her eyes, a hacking cough from too many cigarettes, and a faintly unpleasant odor when she forgot to bathe.

Autumn ended with an early frost, and the cold, bleak landscape suited Grace's mood. At Jo's insistence, she started seeing a local psychiatrist. He prescribed something to help her sleep, but her prosaic dreams frustrated her even more than her insomnia and she quit taking the pills. She was afraid that if she told the psychiatrist the truth, he'd have her removed from the house, so her sessions with him were vague and pointless.

I will never write again. It's over.
Grace sat staring at the words she had written.
The cursor blinked, its staccato rhythm urging her to write

more, but she ignored it. She saw the truth before her. She had just written the last words she would ever write. Her life had been about writing. Without that, what was left?

She took a deep breath and looked out the window into the dark night. He answered her for the first time in days. Faint and far away, but unmistakably an answer.

Had Louise Racinet known what that thing out there was before she gave herself to it in the final embrace? Grace still wasn't sure even *she* knew. The dark, secret places of the forest were his domain, and had been for centuries. His story, his image, was both a lure and a warning, for the untamed, bestial power he had sought had eventually engulfed and enslaved him. The paintings were symbolic and disturbing. The book was a dark fantasy. Both were products of tormented hearts. But neither Grace nor the artist were insane. The Hound Lover existed; not alive, not of this world, but unmistakably real.

He had used their gifts for his own ends. Grace turned off the kitchen light and went to the door, staring sightlessly into the dark as the voice in the woods continued to beckon her forth.

He had found a willing vessel in her; talent without inspiration, imagination without direction, genius without hope. In the silence of dark nights and bleak days, he had offered her a bargain she could never have refused, even if she had fully understood its implications. He had paid in full, and so had she. And now that it was over, she was nothing but a drained, empty husk, ready to embrace for all eternity the sweet oblivion of the night.

She pushed open the back door. The night was bitterly cold. It didn't matter. He would take her long before the cold killed her, just as he had taken Louise Racinet. And as with Louise, they would find her empty body and never know why she had gone with him. How could they know? How could they possibly know?

Jo met the new tenant of the old Hamilton house the following summer. "That place on the other side of the woods, right?"

"That's right," the woman answered. She was young, Jo noticed, twenty-five at the most. "I'm renting for the whole summer. I came to get away from all the distractions in the city."

"It's great up here, isn't it? I've got to come up more often." Her visits had been infrequent since Grace's death. The message left on the laptop had said it all: *I'll never write again. It's over.* Rationally, she knew Grace had rejected all help; but guilt was never rational. It had taken a long time to recover from the sight of Grace's body lying in the woods. Jo had berated herself for ever telling her about how Louise Racinet had died; clearly that story had planted the seed in Grace's fertile imagination. Trying not to think about it anymore, Jo asked, "What have you been doing since you arrived?"

"Long walks. Trying to work." The woman sighed a bit and added, "And reading. I've just started the new Grace Wedeck."

Jo blanched. "Oh?" She hadn't yet been able to bring herself to read her friend's final book. Maybe she never would; the memories were too sad.

"It's fabulous. Such a pity she died so young. Suicide, you know. Her second attempt, the newspapers said."

"Yes. She was very unhappy. Unstable." Jo omitted the jargon explanations of Grace's local psychiatrist.

"I just wish I could tell her what an inspiration this book is."

"You're a writer, too?"

"No. Composer." She shrugged self-consciously and added, "Or trying to be. I haven't written anything really—you know—really *exciting* yet. That's why I came here. To concentrate."

"Well, I'm sure it'll happen for you up here. A lot of creative people have found this area very inspiring, you know."

"Yes. I can see why." The woman nodded. Her eyes sparkled with hope as she smiled dreamily. "At night I hear, I don't know—call it music—in the woods."

SPECTERS IN THE MOONLIGHT

by Larry Segriff

Larry Segriff's work has appeared in numerous genres. His first novel, *Spacer Dreams,* was recently published to excellent reviews. Larry's short fiction can be found in such anthologies as *Frankenstein: The Monster Wakes, Wheel of Fortune,* and *The Book of Kings.*

"Please, Daddy. Please don't."

The soft little voice cut across my dreams, jerking me awake. There was that moment of disorientation that always accompanies waking up in a strange room, especially in the middle of the night.

I looked over at the pillow next to mine, knowing damn well there was no one there. But that voice had been so real, that note of quiet desperation so heart wrenching, that I just had to look.

The pillow was empty except for the wan, pale moonlight shining through the frost on the window and the little lace curtains. It lit up my room, and touched my heart with its chill. For a moment it lay there, black and silver on the pillowcase, and then a cloud swept across it and took it away.

A cold night in the middle of nowhere. This little bed and breakfast had been recommended to me—so much so that I stopped a hundred miles short of my destination to stay here, and that with a big presentation in the morning.

I glanced at the clock beside the bed. 2:30. Only three hours before I had to get up, and I needed my sleep. I'd been a sales rep for the same pharmaceutical company for a long time, and it seemed that these days I had to work harder than ever just to keep up. Opportunities like this one were fewer and farther between than they once were. I couldn't afford to blow it.

Rolling over, I plumped the pillow beneath me, pulled the

quilt up over my shoulders again, and settled down once more.

"Please, Daddy, please not again."

"Damn!" I said, flinging the covers back and sitting up in bed before I even knew what I was doing. Automatically, I glanced once at the little sample case I kept on the floor of my bed, but then I looked away. There was nothing in there that would help this.

Not yet, anyway.

Feeling the beginnings of anger stirring within me, I got out of bed and, not even bothering to fumble for my slippers, stalked around to the other side. That voice had sounded like it was right next to my head. There had to be a speaker in the pillow or the headboard or something. Presentation or no, I was going to find it, and then I was going to raise some holy hell.

Grimly, I set about stripping the bed.

I found nothing. The bed was an old four-poster. Oak, I thought, but in the cloudshot moonlight it was hard to tell. I searched it as carefully as I could for about fifteen minutes, and came away completely empty. No hidden compartments in the wood. No lumps in the pillow or the mattress. No hollow sounds in the wall behind the bed.

Nothing. Not a damned thing.

Frowning, my mind racing as it examined options and possibilities, my hands went through the unthinking process of making the bed up again. Not that I was necessarily planning on returning to it—I hadn't decided about that yet—but out of old habit. One of the first lessons I learned was to leave things as I found them. There weren't many bridges in this business; it wasn't safe to burn any of them.

I had just finished replacing the pillows and had stepped back from the bed to survey my handiwork when I heard the voice again. This time it was just a single word, "Please," softer and more drawn out than before, and the pain in it was enough to break my heart and drain away the anger building within me.

But that wasn't what chilled me to my very soul, nor was it the faint sobbing that followed on its heels. No, what froze me in place was the fact that the moon had come out once again, and from this vantage point I could see the pattern it made as it passed through the lace on its way to the pillow.

That pattern was a face.

Oh, not like Rembrandt might have painted—the eyes were too big, and the mouth too wide, and the nose more of a suggestion than an actual representation—but it didn't take much imagination to see it as a face. And the longer I looked, the more lifelike it became.

Had there been moonlight that second time I heard the voice? I couldn't recall. I'd been angry, and not paying attention to such things.

I shook my head. What was I doing? Was I really starting to think—?

Again a cloud passed before the moon and the sobbing cut off.

My God, I thought, sinking slowly down on the edge of the bed. *What's going on?* This was . . . this was madness. Such things simply didn't happen.

I leaned back and felt the solidity of my sample case. *This* was reality. Not specters in the moonlight, but *this*.

But that voice, that pain . . .

I don't know how long I sat there, or what decision I might have reached on my own, because eventually the moon came out again and all choices were taken from me.

This time, the moon lay full upon the bed, and in the patterns of shadows I could see more than just a face. I could see a full person. There were the shoulders, and there the arms, raised in futile defense. There were the legs, spread shamelessly, and the back arched in pain.

"Oh, sweet Jesus," I whispered as her sobs once more filled the room. "How can I stop this? What can I do?"

But there were no answers among the shadows and the sobs. Just the silver moonlight, and the sounds of suffering.

"Daddy . . ." That single word hung on the night air, a loud cry that came as a plea and an accusation, and pierced me with its pain.

I knew then that I was going to do something foolish. The second rule of business is Don't Get Involved. Well, that rule had just shattered along with my heart.

I was involved, whether I wanted to be or not.

Pulled to my feet by the pain in that voice, I stumbled over to my sample case. There was a gun concealed in a side pocket. When I'd first started out in this business, such a thing was unthinkable. Now it was mandatory.

I wanted that gun. With it, I might be able to force some

answers from someone. Besides, I needed to feel its comfortable, deadly weight in my hand.

Pulling it out, I turned back to the shadowy form on my bed.

"I'll be back," I promised her. She didn't react at all, didn't acknowledge me in any way, but I felt certain she'd heard me—heard me and understood the promise I was making.

Then, the sound of her sobbing still echoing in my head, I went out to find the man who'd put them there.

He was in the living room on the floor below, waiting for me. He was sitting in a rocking chair, an afghan across his old, withered knees, his chair turned slightly toward the picture window. His silhouette was black against the moonlight.

Beside him, on the floor, I could see his wooden cane. He'd used it when he'd met me at the door, and when he'd shown me up to my room. It was all a single piece of wood—rosewood, I'd guessed, and its handle had been carved into the shape of a rose. Exquisitely wrought, I'd thought it a wonderful thing to own, its beauty almost worth the pain its use must cost him.

Now it just lay there like a guilty burden he'd tried to cast aside.

I thought he was sleep, but his head lifted as I came down the stairs. As I drew closer, I could see that he held something in his lap. It glinted briefly and for a moment my finger tightened on the trigger, but it wasn't a weapon. It was a picture, an old framed photograph of a young girl, and any doubts I may have had fled at the sight.

"Damned weathermen," he said as I came up beside him. He gestured toward the window with the small photograph in his hand. "Said it was supposed to be cloudy all night. Wouldn't have put you in that room otherwise. Wouldn't have put you there anyway except we're all full up. No choice."

But I didn't want to hear that. I was surprised to note that my hand had grown sweaty on the grip of the pistol I held. That was unlike me, but then this whole situation was unlike me.

"Tell me," I said. "Tell me about her."

He looked once at the gun in my hand. "You can put that away," he said. I didn't, and after a moment he sighed and looked down again at the picture in his hand. "Her name was Rose. She was my daughter. When she was fourteen, she took a whole bottle of sleeping pills—they'd been her mother's; I guess I'd never gotten around to throwing them out after Lydia died. Rose died in her bed. It was late October, and there was a Harvest Moon that night, shining down full and bright. I like to think its light showed her the way home."

My hand had started to cramp around the grip of my pistol and I flexed my fingers once to keep them loose. "Go on," I said.

"Not much more to say," he said. Reaching down, he fumbled around and came up with his cane. Reflexively, I took a step back, and kept my gun leveled at his chest. "I carved this out of the same wood I made her cross from. You can still see it. She's buried in the cemetery at the top of the hill, just down the road a ways."

He sighed again, and sort of slumped deeper into his chair before lapsing back into silence.

I flexed my fingers a second time. Listening to him speak, I'd felt my anger lessen a bit, but now it was back. "That's it? That's all you have to say? No apologies? No excuses?"

"Son," he said, and this time there was a hint of fire in his voice, "I made my apologies years ago. I don't see any call to repeat them to you. Besides, that's not what you're after. You're here to lay that ghost to rest, and you know I'm the only one who can do that, so put that gun away and let's get on with it."

I frowned, and flexed my fingers a third time, but neither seemed to help. The truth was, he was right. "How?" I said, hating the fact that I had to ask.

"Simple. I have to die as she did. It's the only thing that will give her peace. It's got to be in that bed, and it has to be an overdose of drugs—which is why I keep telling you to put that gun away. You don't need it, and you can't help her with it. Oh, and one other thing: it's got to be a night like this, with the full moon shining down."

"How do you know all this?"

"I asked, is how. Son, I've been trying to end her suffering for nigh on thirty years. I've had the priest out. The old coot won't admit she's real, but he says that even if she was, there'd be nothing he could do. Demons, yes, he's got rituals for them, but not for ghosts. So I've had others out, over the

years, people who do this for a living. They all told me that
I was the only one who could help her. I wasn't ready, then;
still had some living to do, but that's all behind me now. I'm
an old man, and I don't want to meet my maker with her
spirit still lost in this world."

If he was trying to play on my sympathies, it wasn't
working. The echoes of her pain were still too loud in my
memory. They drowned out any feelings I might have for
him.

"So why haven't you done it?" I asked. "If it's that simple, why haven't you done it yourself?"

He shook his head in the moonlight. "I couldn't do that.
The Bible says suicide's a sin. I told you, I don't want to
meet my maker with her spirit still lost, and that's the truth,
but even less do I want to stand before St. Peter and tell him
I killed myself. No, sir. Rose is my daughter, and I want her
to find peace, but I don't want to spend eternity in hell for
her."

Listening to his words, I decided that I didn't believe him.
I didn't want to, for one thing. I'd seen too much pain and
suffering up in that room to want to believe he was truly
sorry.

But it was more than that. Mostly, it was that his story
was just too pat, too slick. I was a salesman myself. I recognized a pitch when I heard one.

The trick was going to be separating out the truth in what
he'd just said. From my own experience, I knew that the
best way to hook a customer was through honesty. Tell 'em
enough to give your line that ring of sincerity, and then lead
them astray. I was pretty sure that was what he was trying
on me.

The question was, which parts were true?

I didn't have to think about that for long. The answer became obvious as soon as I turned it around: which part was
false? Clearly, I realized, the part about his wanting to die
was a lie. I didn't believe it. I refused to believe it. Which
meant that the other part, the bit about how his daughter
could be helped, that was probably true.

"All right," I said. "I'll help you." And I would, too. Only
not the way he had it planned. "You lead the way," I added,
stepping back out of reach.

He didn't protest, just struggled up out of his chair and
started up the stairs.

At the top of the stairs, he paused. "Pills are in there," he said, using his cane to point toward the bathroom at the end of the hall, "but you'll have to feed them to me. I don't want to do anything that'll make it look like I'm helping you."

And suddenly I saw it all. Of course. It was the pills. Sure, he'd known this would happen someday, that sooner or later someone would meet poor Rose, and come to him for some answers. He must have made up a whole bottle of fakes—probably just ordinary sugar spooned into regular gel caps. All he'd have to do is swallow a bunch of them, go to sleep, and that would be that. By the time I knew he was still alive, the other guests would be awake. Even more importantly, the moon would be gone from the sky, and it would be too late.

That was his plan. I knew it. It had to be. Only it wasn't going to work quite that way.

"All right," I said. "I'll get them in a moment."

He paused outside my room, and I could see his shoulders stiffen beneath the thin robe he wore. Carefully, I reached around him and turned the knob. "After you," I said, and pushed the door open.

She was still there. She was lying on her side, her tear-tracked face turned toward the window, and silent sobs racked her shadowy form.

"Rose." It was the old man who spoke. He took a single step into the room, his free hand reaching out toward the bed.

"Let's go," I said. I stepped up beside him and in one move took his cane away from him and propelled him onto the bed. At that point, I didn't give a damn about his frail old bones.

"The pills . . ." he said, but I ignored him and made my way back to my sample case.

I didn't spend any time thinking about what I was about to do. I could see her lying there beside him, her soft sobs as regular as a heartbeat, and I felt no remorse at all as I spun the locks. A moment later and my case was open, with all my goodies laid out in their neat little rows.

I glanced up at the old man, to make sure he wasn't watching me. I kept my hands below the level of the lid, to block his sight, but I didn't want to take any chances. After all, even though he was pretty much a helpless old man and couldn't stop me if he tried, still I didn't want him waking up any of the other guests.

I saw right away that I didn't have to worry. He was enrapt by the ghost at his side. He had one hand on her shoulder, and though I imagined he was trying to apologize, it looked for all the world like he was caressing her. I nodded once and started thumbing through my supplies.

Soon I had it, a syringe full of liquid death, shining silver in the moonlight.

I looked at them, once, father and daughter, and then I made my move, stepping forward, bringing up my hand, plunging the needle deep into his backside, and driving the plunger home.

He jerked, but by then it was too late. I withdrew the needle and stepped back, ready for almost anything. Anything, that is, except what happened.

He looked at me, looked at the needle in my hand, and smiled.

"Thank you," he said.

I took another step back, this time in confusion. Had I misunderstood? Was he truly repentant?

I got no farther in my thoughts. The stuff I gave him was fast acting, and I saw him slump forward, his left arm flying out and passing through his daughter.

"Rose," he whispered, "I'm coming, Rose."

And there in the moonlight I saw her turn toward him. I saw her eyes go wide, and her mouth stretch in a scream that was beyond my power to hear. And then I saw him rise up out of his body and wrap her in a vile, loving embrace.

I staggered back in horror, looking at what I had wrought. With my mind's eye, I could see the scene before me stretching out for all of eternity. I could hear her screams in my head, her cries of utter anguish, and I knew that I had caused them.

I looked at the two of them and the scene before me burned its way into my heart. I knew in that moment that I couldn't let this go on. I had to stop it, and I thought I knew how.

My hand brushed my sample case as I tossed the useless gun onto the bed. I glanced down into it, and started rummaging through its contents again.

Moments later, I lay down on the bed next to the old man, the rosewood cane gripped firmly in my left hand. On the other side of him, the two spirits writhed, one in pleasure, one in agony.

I thought once, briefly, about my family, about what this would do to them, about what people would think, and then I put them out of my mind forever. There was simply no choice.

For the last time, I looked over at Rose, trying to blot her father from my vision, and then I said the very words he'd said to her.

"I'm coming, Rose," I said.

The silver moonlight lay full upon us as I emptied the needle into my arm and waited for it to show me the way to her side.

CAGES

by Scott Ciencin

Scott Ciencin is the author of eighteen novels, including several major genre best-sellers. His work ranges from contemporary adult thrillers, to fantasy, to horror, and children's fiction, the latter of which include his popular *Dinotopia* novels, *Windchaser* and *Lost City*. He has worked in film and television, and is currently writing for DC Comics.

"I'm dead," she whispered. "I'm dead and I need you to help me *feel* something. Will you help me?"

Jeff stared at the pretty young woman who had navigated the crowded living room and grasped his arm. Even through his sweater, he felt chilled by her touch.

"What do you want me to do?" he asked, finishing off the vodka and tonic that had been stuffed in his hand a moment before.

"Take me home and make love to me."

He glanced down at her perfect body. Her hourglass figure was boldly displayed in a siren-red sequined dress with a choker collar and bare back. Her long blonde wavy hair was piled elegantly above her stunning, azure eyes, high, model cheekbones, and sensuous, slightly parted lips. She reminded him of Sharon Stone in *Basic Instinct*. He caught several men looking her way, saw the envy and desire in their eyes; it made him want her all the more.

Normally, he preferred more of a chase, but she had been direct, and he didn't want to be insulting by giving her lines or flattery. Besides, his life hadn't been normal in quite some time.

"Sure," Jeff said, setting his glass on a nearby table, "why not?"

Her flesh was already beginning to warm.

On the drive, the woman said her name was Candayce. She didn't volunteer any other details until they were in his bedroom and he had her dress off. His hands were all over her, fondling her breasts, which were slightly larger than he had guessed, but still perfectly formed and proportioned. She kissed him, and by now, her lips were on fire.

"Something you have to know," she said, breathlessly.

"If you tell me you're a man, I'll beat the *shit* out of you," he said softly, playfully. The moment the words left his lips he regretted them. From her raw laugh, he knew she hadn't been offended.

In response to his words, she took his hand and slid it between her soft thighs. She was burning up, wet, ready, and definitely *not* a man.

"I want you," he said, unzipping his pants.

"Wait," she moaned.

Suddenly, it came to him. "Protection. Right. What was I thinking?"

"Listen."

Her tone forced him to pull back slightly and stare into her dazzling eyes. "I'm dead. I'm a corpse."

Jeff tried to restrain his growing smile and failed.

"I'm serious. Feel my heart."

"All right," he said, leaning down and pressing his face to her breast, sliding the marblelike nipple into his mouth.

"No!" she said, pushing him back. "Listen to my heart."

Realizing they were at an impasse, Jeff gave in to her wishes. He placed his ear against her chest and listened.

She had no heartbeat; none that he could detect.

"Christ, that's bizarre," he said, feeling his ardor fade slightly.

"I'm dead. I've been dead for a long time."

"Come on." He had read about things like this, people whose hearts slowed to an imperceptible level. The hero of Poe's "Premature Burial" suffered from a disease that inspired similar effects, or so he recalled from a high school English class, a decade earlier. Still, those people looked dead, had fallen into deep comas. Candayce shouldn't have been up and walking around. "Are you sick? Do you want me to take you home? Where do you live?"

"I don't."

"Candayce—"

"I'm not sick. I'm dead and I'm yours for as long as you want me."

He felt the chill returning to her flesh. It had a numbing effect on his desire.

"Do you want me?"

"I don't want any trouble," he said, seriously wondering if he had made a mistake by bringing her to his apartment. She might get pissed off and talk about him to the wrong kind of people, the kind that were looking for him. No amount of pleasure was worth enduring what *they* had planned for him.

Candayce sat back on the bed, pulling her legs up beneath her. Jeff allowed his hand to slip from her now icy depths. She seemed despondent.

Opposite corners, gentlemen, opposite corners.

"Maybe I should just take you back to the party," he said, attempting to mask his fear.

"You don't understand. I'm not crazy, I'm—"

"Dead."

"Yes."

"For a corpse, you put on a pretty good show of being alive."

"Years of practice." She looked up at him. "I can do things for you. Anything you want, anything you've ever dreamed of, and a hell of a lot more."

"All you want in return is a place to crash. No way."

Anger spidered across her magnificent face. "All I want is for you to need me. So I can get warm. It's so cold, you can't imagine."

They stared at each other for a few moments. Jeff had no idea why he suddenly became aroused once more, but he felt himself throbbing, his heart pounding, his brain burning up with desire. This time, she didn't put off his advances. Her skin was cold at first, but it warmed quickly.

The damage is done, he told himself as her lips closed over his sex and took him down deep. She's here. I might as well give her what she came for, and get something out of this myself.

For a time, they were both on fire.

She was right, the sex had been amazing. They had made love for close to two hours and every time he had been on the brink of orgasm, she had scaled him back, drawn it out, and finally allowed him to explode with the greatest pleasure of his adult life.

"By the way," she said with a throaty laugh, "what's *your* name?"

"Jeff Paymer."

Disappointment flashed briefly in her azure eyes. "You don't trust me, yet. That's all right. When you're ready, you tell me as much or as little as you want. I'll listen. You never have to lie with me."

He froze for a moment, his sex suddenly shriveling. A host of possibilities flashed in his mind. She could be a skip tracer, hired by his father, or the prosecutor's office. Or they might have met a long time ago and he had forgotten her, though it hardly seemed likely. What about Benny? If Benny had opened his stupid mouth and told her the trouble he was in, he would gut the little bastard.

She *may* have just sensed he was lying. Damn, he was going to have to get another place tomorrow. More complications, just what he needed.

"I'll stay with you for a time," she said. "If that's what you want."

Jeff closed his eyes. He wanted it, all right.

"You don't know if you can trust me," she said.

"It's not that," he said unconvincingly.

"What would it take for you to trust me? Would you feel better if you knew more about me?"

A ragged breath escaped him. "I don't even know your last name."

"I don't know yours. All I know is what I see. A handsome man who takes care of his body, Irish descent, reddish-tinged hair, a beard and mustache to hide your baby face, and a hell of a nice cock."

"Thank you."

"I also see a man who doesn't own very much."

He rose to one elbow. "What do you mean?"

"This place is a furnished rental. There's nothing in here that says anything about you. No photographs, no books, nothing. Your closet over there, sitting open, shows enough clothes that can go in a suitcase real fast. Those open boxes of junk food we passed in the living room and the plates with the half-eaten Wendy's chicken sandwich on the floor show you could give a fuck about a healthy diet. No eating out. No credit cards. I bet you do everything with cash."

"Who are you?" he asked, genuinely frightened this time. She was sounding less like a night's amusement and more like a serious danger with every passing moment.

"Someone who needs you. Someone who won't be around forever. When you're done with me, I'll move on to another. A man, a woman, a child. Someone who'll have need of me and who will, in return, fulfill my needs. If you want me to stay, that is. I suppose we need a certain amount of trust for that. You have to trust me, and you have to trust what your gut's telling you."

Jeff watched her carefully, trying to find any hint that she was bullshitting him. His instincts told him that she was being completely straight with him. She made it sound so dry, like a legal contract. He told her as much.

"I'm being up front with you, no surprises. I'll be yours as long as you want me. As long as you need me. There'll come a time when you won't want me anymore. Then I'll go."

He couldn't imagine a time he wouldn't want her.

"I only want one thing of you, Jeff. When the time comes, admit to yourself that it's over and let me go. Don't make it drag on so long that you start to hate me. I couldn't take it if you started to hate me. Do you want me to stay a few days, see how it works out, or do you want me to go?"

"No," he said, touching her. "Don't go."

"My last name is Krstulich." She pronounced it *crystal-itch.* "Look me up sometime. I died here in Boston, six years ago Thursday."

Jeff wanted to ask how, but that would reinforce her delusion. *There was no heartbeat. Not even when she came.*

He had no idea that by morning, he would start to accept her statements at face value.

The nightmare came with renewed intensity. Somehow he knew when he closed his eyes and drifted off to sleep that he would have to face the dream tonight. Whenever he allowed himself to relax and actually believe that he had a chance at getting his life back together, the dream came to punish him for his foolishness.

A little after three in the morning he woke with a strangled cry, rocketing to a sitting position in bed. The inhuman screams and the harsh, frantic beating of wings filled the darkened bedroom for a few seconds, then receded to the confines of his memory. He forgot about Candayce until he saw her curled up in the chair across from the bed. Her long, amazing legs were drawn up before her, their silky expanse catching the soft, bluish-white glow coming in from outside. The long hair she had whipped back and forth a few hours ago as she sat astride him hung before her face, allowing him to see only her sparkling eyes and restrained smile. She had been watching him sleep. Worse, she seemed amused by his nightmare.

"Want to talk about it?" Candayce asked.

"Nightmare. Nothin'. Go back to sleep," he said, feigning grogginess. In truth, he was completely alert.

"You were fifteen years old," she said. "Working for the summer at an amusement park called Seventh Heaven outside of Hollywood. Your old man got you the job. One of his old money pals was chairman of the board for the park. People were always looking to do favors for your father, weren't they?"

Jeff wanted to tell her to get the hell out, but his fear stilled the words. How could she know so much about him? Was she working for someone that was after him? He had to know and so he let her talk.

"You were motivated; your father liked that. You knew exactly what you wanted out of life. The only problem was, you wanted everything handed to you. That summer you wanted to stay in Hollywood with friends of the family. You wanted to be a famous director one day and wanted to see what the business was like. Your dad knew he had been too indulgent with you, and if he was going to let you leave Palm Beach to roam around for two months, you were going to have to earn your keep. So he got you the job in the park. The owners said no problem, anything for Hugh Nolan's boy."

Jeff wanted to make her stop, but he was fascinated to hear his memory, his nightmare, come from the lips of this total stranger.

"So that's your name. Nolan." Candayce took a moment, savoring the discovery. "You worked for a man named Ted Duchovy, taking care of the exotic birds for several of the attractions. It was weird because you actually came to like the job and the people you met. At night and on weekends, you got to cruise the top parties, even visit some film sets. But what really did it for you was getting your hands dirty, making money for yourself. Having cash in your pocket that you didn't have to ask for and could do whatever you wanted with was a real thrill.

"One day Ted called you over. It was a special day. You remember what he said, don't you? I can feel the way it burns in your memory."

"He said, 'You're in for a rare treat today, little bro.' That's what he called me." Christ, why was he going along with this? Why was he telling her anything?

"Sweet. He told you it was time for population control. Too many birds running around, fucking their brains out, making more little birds. The thought made you feel bad. You liked the birds. They took to you from the first day, accepted you the way no one ever had."

"Stop," Jeff said. She was peeling open his secrets, describing events as if she had been the one to experience them. Candayce had no intention of stopping now. "Their colors were so beautiful. There was nothing sweeter to you than listening to their songs, and watching the way they behaved. If you loved anything in your life up until then, it was nothing compared to the way you felt about those birds. If anyone had told you how it was going to be, you would have laughed at them. But here you were, finally caring about something other than yourself. Of course, there was Becca, too, but that was different."

"Don't talk about her."

"I just want you to understand what's going on. I need for you to trust me. Our time will be so much better if you do."

"I trust you," he said, hoping the lie would silence her.

Candayce shook her head. "You thought population control meant taking some of the birds away, selling them to private owners, giving them to nature preserves. Then Ted grabbed one of them, handed you the machete, and told you to cut its head off. Fastest way. No pain."

"Jesus," Jeff cried, shuddering. Suddenly he was bathed in sweat and the room was freezing. "No."

"You wouldn't do it. Ted called you a wus and someone else grabbed your arms. You watched as Ted spent the next couple of hours tearing the birds apart, spraying their blood in your face. When it came time for the last one, they put the knife in your hand and made you kill the bird. The guy holding you put his hand over yours, didn't give you a choice. Said you had to be one of them."

Jeff felt ill. The nightmare had been bad enough. This was almost more than he could take. *"Who are you?"*

" 'Just some fucking birds,' Duchovy said. 'So what if they're endangered? Get over it.'

"That afternoon, you went back to the family that was putting you up. Becca Schwegel was the only one home. She was Bob Schwegel's only daughter, two years older than you, your best friend since you had arrived. You were in hysterics and you tried to tell her, but she was so busy trying to hold you and calm you down, that things just happened. You lost your virginity to her.

"I guess looking back on it now, you probably wonder how you could have gotten it up after seeing all that blood, all the killing. You might even feel kind of sick. Did it turn you on? I don't think so. You just needed to escape from those memories. More than anything in the world you needed to get away, to *disappear* for awhile so you didn't have to face what you had seen.

"What Becca did to you made it all go away. That night, you told Becca's dad. Duchovy and the others were fired. The park was almost shut down in the controversy. Later, your father said that was the only decent thing you ever did in your life."

"When he came to see me in prison," Jeff said, suddenly aware that there was nothing he could hide from this woman.

Candayce rose from the chair and came to him. "I know you've done bad things, but I'm not going to judge you."

Suddenly, the moonlight fell on her face and she tossed her hair back. Her features had changed. So had her body. Her breasts were much smaller, she was skinnier, her features more pointed, and acne scars lightly pitted her attractive face. Her voice hadn't changed, but that was the only part of her that didn't look identical to Becca Schwegel on the first day they made love.

Jeff thought there was a way for him to calmly accept Candayce's transformation. He was wrong. The moment she touched him with her lukewarm hands, he passed out.

He woke again. This time there had been no nightmares. Candayce sat on the bed beside him. She had not shucked off Becca's flesh. Jeff struggled to stay calm.

"I can become anyone, anything you've ever dreamed of," Candayce said. "Fulfill any fantasy."

"Don't touch me," Jeff said.

Candayce threw her hair back. "Is that what you want? Wouldn't it be better if I *did* touch you, looking like this? Tell me, how many times have you slept with a woman and closed your eyes, pretending it was Becca?"

"Don't," he said as she reached down and started caressing his cock. Her hands were warmer and he felt himself responding. "This isn't real."

"It *is* real. As real as you want me to make it. I can even take her voice, if you want. Remember how she sounded when she came? I can make it sound like that."

He was fully erect, wanting desperately to hear those sounds. To make the world vanish for a time, to make all his fears and all the horrors he had faced in the last six months go away for a time.

"I'm the only thing that's real," Candayce said, borrowing not only Becca's voice, but the words she used as she climbed on top of Jeff the first time and placed him inside her moist sex. Candayce mounted him and moaned softly, gently, exactly as Becca had moaned.

This can't be real, Jeff thought. A dream. An illusion.

"Take me," Becca pleaded.

Jeff arced his body up like a bow, driving himself deeply into her as their hands entwined and she screamed.

Jeff forgot about everything except the rhythm of their lovemaking. When it was over, Candayce lay next to him. He watched as she transformed into the voluptuous woman he had met at the party.

"I can make you happy," she said. "I can make the pain go away, make it disappear. Will you let me stay?"

"Yes," Jeff said without reservation. "I will."

Over the next week, Jeff barely thought about the reason for his stopover in Boston. All that mattered was Candayce. They were together constantly. Her touch was a drug. For the first few days, she alternated between her seductive, true appearance, and Becca's. One day they were at the mall, and Jeff's gaze fell on a woman with soft brown skin and dark eyes. It was a momentary lapse; he knew better than to openly gaze at another woman when he had one on his arm, but he couldn't help himself. When he tore his gaze from the woman and looked back at Candayce, she had stolen the woman's identity. They made love in the back of his car, in the dimly lit parking garage. After that, there were no limits. They went to nightclubs and bars, anywhere he could afford, and selected women he wanted to fuck. Candayce cataloged them, and sometimes changed several times during a single act of lovemaking.

She would give him head as a Nordic blonde, then drag him inside herself as a black-haired, innocent looking, college student. He liked to touch her as she changed, to impale her and watch her swaying breasts change color and shape, to hear her moans radically alter as he drove himself deeper into her. It was more than the changing of her form that excited him; her personality transformed, her tastes changed, and each time he felt as if he was with someone new.

There was another gradual progression: Their lovemaking became more unusual, darker, bordering on violent, until one night their bondage and role-playing got out of hand and he very nearly struck her for real. When it was over, Candayce flopped across his chest, a satisfied grin on her face. At the moment, she wore the face of an actress he had fantasized about since he was twelve. It had been so long since she had used her true face that he was beginning to forget what she looked like.

Sensing his concern, Candayce changed back. He scrutinized her until she became uncomfortable.

"What is it?" she asked.

"You had a mole behind your ear. It's gone now."

The small birthmark reappeared.

"Wrong ear."

"Does it matter?"

"I thought this is what you *really* looked like."

"This is what you were in the mood for at the time."

"What about that name you gave me?"

"Do you even remember it?"

Her reply pissed him off. He suddenly felt as if he was once again teetering on the edge of violence. "Was anything you told me true?"

"Don't start sounding like a loser, okay? I thought you were better than that. You didn't whine when you skipped bail on those embezzlement charges. When you beat the crap out of that skip tracer that caught up to you in Memphis. Man, you were right on the edge of caving his head in. But you didn't do it. You had him right there, could have shut him down, but you didn't. What's the matter, did you start hearing Tweety-Bird in your head? Did the sight of his blood freak you out?"

"Waitaminute. I didn't tell you about any of that."

"Haven't you figured it out yet? You don't have to. It takes me a while to get attuned to someone. Until then, I need something strong, like a nightmare or a panic attack to start getting details. Right now, I can tell you every grade you got in high school. The hard-on you used to get every time Mimi Thomas wore that white sweater in Band. I know more about you than *you* do."

"You said I could tell you when I was ready."

"Fuck off. This is getting old. Admit it. You're ready for the next big thrill. Problem is, there isn't any. This is as good as it gets." She climbed off the bed and laughed at him. "I bet that pisses you off, doesn't it?"

"Candayce—"

"You really think that's my name? Okay, I'll let you be *stupid* if you want."

"Stop it," he said, sliding off the bed and closing on her. "What the hell's with you? One second everything's fine, the next, you have this bug up your ass."

"I bet you feel cheated. Poor little Jeff. You didn't worry about all the people who took it up the ass because of your get rich schemes, did you?"

"Get the fuck out of here," he said uncertainly, following her to the living room.

"You wish. I'm under your skin. I'm in your blood. You're nothing but a limp-dicked asshole with big dreams but no balls to make your dreams happen. Your instincts are shit, Jeff. Face it."

"Just get out," he said, his rage threatening to explode.

"First it was that record label deal. Take these unknowns, put them out there, compete with the big boys. Only your 'talent' didn't have any and the company went under. How much did your dad sink into that little venture? Or what about the movie, huh? *The Razor*. Oooooh, booga-booga-booga. Scary stuff, kids. Only you couldn't get a distributor. Two strikes."

"I'm warning you," he said, his hands curling into fists as Candayce backed into the kitchen.

"So you were about a million dollars in the hole, half of

that to your dad, and what did he do? Give you a job. He let you manage what, six hotels at once? Put you in charge of the whole chain. He gave you his trust and you raped him. Ripped off cash from your own father to fund the children's book—cool kids, 3-D, holograms, all this neat stuff, only no publisher was interested, and by then, you had been found out. Oh, shit, it looks like three strikes, our poor little Jeffy is going to get bunged up the ass by the Cleaver Twins in Cell Block H. That's if Daddy actually presses charges, which he won't."

Her back was to the refrigerator. Jeff wanted to shut her mouth. Anything to make her stop.

"But he *did* press charges. And you went running—"

"STOP IT!" he screamed, hauling off and punching her in the mouth. Candayce stumbled and touched her bleeding lip.

"That was nice, can I have another one? Or should I tell the story about what finally went wrong with Becca, why you two didn't stay together, or maybe remind you of the hard-on you got when Ted was ripping the heads off those little prizes of yours—"

He leaped on her, striking her again and again, bloodying her perfect face, slamming her head into the wall until she slumped down and stopped moving. For a moment he thought he had killed her. She lay on her stomach, her hair streaked with blood. He couldn't see her face.

No heartbeat.

I'm dead, how many times do I have to tell you that?

Candayce stirred. Jeff stood over her, trembling. She turned over and let him see her face. It was unmarred. "Now didn't that feel better? Why don't you give me another one? I'm dead. It's not gonna bother *me* any."

"You wanted that," he said, horrified.

"No, you did. All I want is for you to be honest with yourself. Everything we've done up until now, it's been fucking mundane. I liked it, don't get me wrong. You gave me some warmth, made me hot a few times. But we're ready to move on."

He wanted to say he was sorry, but he wasn't. The flapping of wings filled his head and he remembered the salty taste of blood on his lips. Turning from her, he put his hands to his face. "Jesus, this isn't me."

"It *is* you," she said. "And it's all right. You know what

they say, sweetheart. Love means never having to say you're sorry."

"This is sick," he said.

"You can have anything you want from me," she said.

"The truth. Who are you?"

"Candayce Krstulich. I didn't lie about that. Born September 17th, 1965, died—"

"Stop that."

"Whatever you want, sweetheart. Whatever you want."

"The one thing I don't want is *you*," he said.

"You will."

Before they went to sleep, he suddenly felt overcome by urges that he had forced down for more than a decade.

"Become Becca for me," he said. "And make her scared."

Candayce smiled and shut the bedroom door behind them. When it was over, Becca lay in the corner, bleeding, crying, begging for forgiveness.

That night, Jeff slept better than he had in years.

Jeff spent the next day taking care of the business that had drawn him to Boston. Over the last ten years, Jeff had started a savings account. He had skimmed a small percentage from every one of his deals and secreted it away in a dozen different hiding places. A thirty-thousand-dollar chunk had been left where only two people, Jeff and his childhood friend Benny de'Oro, would know to look. Jeff rarely trusted anyone. Benny was a little sleaze, but Jeff knew things about him, things that would get Benny dead in a hurry if they were told. For that reason, he was certain he could trust Benny.

The little son-of-a-bitch had ripped him off.

Jeff caught Benny coming out of his favorite nightspot. The stupid fuck didn't even know to change his habits when someone was after him. He also didn't lock the doors on his black Camaro. Jeff yanked open the passenger door, shoved a young woman who was about to join Benny out of the way, and got in.

"Drive."

Benny shook his head. The girl he had picked up was outside the car, screaming. "That was rude, man. Rude and unnecessary."

Jeff reached over, pulled the cigarette lighter from the

dash, and ground it into Benny's hand. The man jumped, then realized it was still cool.

"I'm not kidding," Jeff said. "Go."

They drove off.

"Man, this is not like you," Benny said. "You've always been the reasonable kind. What the hell's with you? That wiggle you took home turn out to have razor blades in her cunt or something? Shit, I thought you'd be in a better fucking mood than this."

"You know something?" Jeff asked. "I never liked you."

Benny nodded. He was short and dark, with raven hair, a curly beard, and the face and build of an ape. "Same back at you, man. It was always business. So what is this? You want your money? I got it. Some of it, anyway. Charged up my credit cards, cashed in my retirement fund. Came up with twenty-four grand. Best I could do on this kind of notice. We go back to my place, I'll give it to you."

"Fine."

They drove in silence for a time. Benny looked over. "You know, I could have just had you popped. Would have been cleaner and a hell of a lot cheaper."

"You don't have what it takes."

Benny shrugged. "You might be right."

"I know I'm right."

"You go down, you might still rat me out."

"Might."

Benny laughed. "You're a real ball buster, man. I'm just glad I got you in a good mood."

Jeff returned to his apartment with the money. He'd had time to calm down and to ease off the high Candayce had given him with her tricks. She was waiting for him in the bedroom. No disguises this time.

"You made it through okay?" she asked.

He nodded.

"I was worried."

He sat in the chair across from the bed. Candayce was naked as she came to him and straddled the chair. She ground herself against his lap.

"Want me?" she asked as she ran her hands over his chest and tried to make his nipples hard.

"Tell me you did it to get me so torqued up Benny would be afraid to try anything."

"Sure," she said.

God, he wanted to believe it. "Get off."

"I intend to."

"Put some clothes on. I want to go out for a while."

"Okay," she said, climbing off him, slightly frightened by his tone. "Whatever you want."

"Yeah," he said bitterly. "Whatever."

The Midnight Arcade wasn't too crowded. It was a week-night. Jeff found the bloodiest game in the house and started feeding in quarters.

"Used to do this as a kid. Calmed me down. Can't explain it."

He zoomed down corridors and faced Nazis armed with every weapon imaginable. Jeff rose to the threat, massacring anything that moved. By the second game he was earning extra points. Clouds of blood splattered across the screen as he made a kill.

"Besides what happened with Ted at the park, have you ever killed anything, Jeff? Have you ever killed anyone?"

"No."

"But you like it. On the screen. When you blow away your enemies, it excites you. I can feel it."

"This is just a game."

"We've played games."

"Not those kind of games."

"We could."

Jeff lost interest in the video screen. He took Candayce by the hand and led her to the street. She now wore blue jeans, black leather boots, a fishnet blouse, and a black leather jacket. She was able to transform her single set of clothes the same way she could alter her body.

"Killing you would be like killing myself," he said.

"No, it wouldn't. Go on. You'll like it."

Jeff was silent. From somewhere far away he heard the beating of nightmarish wings.

"I'm dead, Jeff. You make me warm from time to time. I'm grateful. But I'm still dead. Nothing that happens to me matters."

"Don't say that."

"What I mean is, you can do what you want with me. We don't have to stop at—"

"No."

"—hurting."

She smiled wantonly. "Just a thought."

During the drive home, Jeff resisted the temptation to talk with Candayce about murder. Talking about it, he knew, was the first step toward making something happen. They were back inside, kissing passionately, when he found he couldn't concentrate on anything except her offer.

"What makes you think I'd be interested?" he asked.

"In killing me?"

"Yes."

"Just to see what it's like. To see if you might enjoy it. Besides, you're getting bored."

"No, I'm not."

"You are."

"All I have to do is think of something and you can make it happen. Believe me, I'm not getting bored. I shouldn't have brought this up. Why don't we talk about before?"

"You mean when I was alive?"

"You *are* alive!"

"I'm not."

"I can see you, I can hear you, I can touch you."

"You can fuck me, you can hurt me, you can kill me." She walked to the bedroom, undressed, and reclined on the bed, her legs spread slightly. Her hand went to her sex, manipulating it ever so slowly.

"There's got to be more," she said in a throaty voice that perfectly mimicked a pitchwoman from a phone sex commercial they had seen one night when Jeff was too sore to keep fucking. "Come on. You *know* you want to."

She was right and that terrified him worse than anything that had happened so far.

In the morning he started packing.

"What are you doing?" she asked.

"I thought you knew everything that was in my head. I'm getting out of here. There's no reason to stay in Boston."

She drew her legs up and bit her lip. "There is for me. I was killed here. I can't leave."

Jeff rubbed at his temples. "I'm on overload. The volume's too loud. Do you understand what I'm saying?"

"You're gonna leave the job half done, just like you have everything else?"

"I don't know what you want from me. You tell me you're not judging me, then you rip me open to get what you need. Why in the fuck did you do this to me?"

"So *I'm* responsible," she said. "I made you look at me as meat to be fucked and slapped around, then thrown out when *you're* finished."

"Don't give me that Madonna-Whore crap. If all I have to do to get rid of you is get in my car and drive out of Boston, great. I'm gone. This isn't me. I don't like what I'm becoming with you around."

"You're not done with me," she promised as he finished packing.

Crying out in rage, Jeff threw the packed suitcase at her. It struck her hard then fell to the floor, springing open and spilling its contents. Candayce ran her hand over her split lip, then reached down to pick up one of his shirts.

"I'm going out," he said.

She nodded. "I'll put these away."

Night had fallen by the time she caught up with him at the Midnight Arcade. He had racked up thirty-five kills when she came up from behind and wrapped her arms around him, gently biting his ear.

"I need you," he said.

"I know." Her voice was vibrant, her skin warm and alive. "I'm here for you."

They went back to his room and made love. Partway through she transformed into the raven-haired Latino they had passed on the street a few minutes earlier.

"You read my mind," he whispered as he took her with even more passion.

She moaned in reply. He didn't plan what happened next. In a way, he felt as if he was in a dream. Outside of himself. As if he had disappeared.

Jeff pulled out of her, piled up the pillows from the bed, and turned her over to take her from behind. In seconds he was pounding inside her and the pillows kept her from having to put all her weight on her knees. He eased her down so that she would not lose the position even if she went limp, then slipped his hands around her throat and started to squeeze. She fought against him, but her gyrations only made him come faster.

He barely noticed when she stopped moving.

In the middle of the night he woke up and found Candayce next to him. She was glowing. There had been no nightmares. The future meant nothing so long as he had her.

Her chest was still. She had forgotten to feign breathing. That should have bothered him, he knew. He woke her and she pulled him into a warm and delectable kiss.

"Doesn't it bother you?" he asked.

"Being dead?"

"Yeah."

"Not much I can do about it. Besides, in ways I'm more alive now than I ever was before. So many of us are walking around like that, dead on the inside with no clue there's anything wrong."

"You're not angry at the man who killed you?"

"Who said it was a man? No, I'm not angry. What happened to me was a blessing. I was put out of my fucking misery. Everything I've felt with you, every pleasure we've taken together, has been so much more intense than anything I ever felt when I was alive. Maybe you'll understand one day."

Jeff nodded. He was beginning to think he already understood. Taking Candayce into his arms, he stole back into the comforting arms of sleep, allowing the swirling mass of his thoughts to vanish as he surrendered to oblivion.

Over the next few weeks, Jeff killed Candayce eleven times. The sex became meaningless, this had taken its place. They experimented with every form of murder. For a time, Candayce would wait for him, welcome him to murder her, but that quickly became boring. It was better when she put up a fight, better still when she transformed into a host of different victims and allowed him to stalk her until finally making his gruesome kill.

He wanted to buy a gun and shoot her, and so they found an abandoned warehouse. After hunting her for close to an hour he cornered her. The first shot took her square in the forehead. She teetered, but did not fall until he had pumped three more bullets into her. An odd smile stole over her beautiful face as she collapsed.

He looked down at her corpse and realized that he was numb. He always went numb when the time came to kill her. Why in the hell she wanted it, he had no idea. All he really knew was that if he wanted to disappear the way he used to when they made love, this is what it took.

Still, it was already getting old. There was no real risk to it. No challenge. Candayce was already dead.

From somewhere deep in the shadows, Jeff heard a scream. He reacted instinctively, turning and firing the weapon until only one bullet was left. The roar of the weapon was accompanied by the fluttering of wings. For a moment he thought he was imagining the sound, that it was the screaming of the birds whose deaths he had witnessed so long ago. Those sounds often came as he tore Candayce apart, particularly when she became Becca for him and allowed him to finish destroying all that was left of what he had once loved.

A sobbing came from the shadows. Jeff's legs felt heavy as he walked about fifty feet and saw the woman on the ground. She had been hit twice by his bullets. One shot had entered her hips, the other her chest. Blood leaked from her mouth and she was sucking air with a desperation that reminded him of the bird he had been forced to kill.

Looking away from her bloody form, he noticed the sketchbook laying beside her. She had been drawing the birds that had come to roost in the abandoned warehouse. Somehow, this sight was worse. His gaze shifted back to the dying woman.

She wasn't looking at him. Her eyes were already glazed over in shock. He knew that he could call an ambulance, but how could he explain what had happened? A part of him wanted Candayce to come back and tell him it was all right. He turned and looked for his lover's body.

Gone.

This time, she wasn't coming back. He realized that in the same strange way she had understood so much about him. Panic flared within him and he finally knew what Candayce had wanted from him all along.

In the distance he thought he heard sirens, but it was too soon for that. The sounds might have been the shrieks of birds sensing what was coming next. It no longer mattered.

Closing his eyes, he placed the gun beneath his jaw and slowly squeezed the trigger. A smile played across his handsome face.

This he was going to feel.

"Do I know you?" the woman asked. "You've been staring at me half the night."

They had both come to the party looking for the same thing, but only one of them was willing to admit it.

The startlingly handsome man reached out and stroked the pretty young woman's face. Though she flinched at his touch, she did not withdraw. Her fingers curled around his invitingly.

"You're cold," she said.

"I'm *dead*," Jeff whispered. "I'm dead and I need you to help me feel something. Will you help me?"

The woman looked at him strangely. Jeff didn't let it bother him.

He already knew her answer.

CASTING CIRCLES
by Edward E. Kramer

Edward E. Kramer's credits include more than a decade
of work as a music critic and photojournalist. A graduate
of Emory University in Atlanta, Ed is a clinical and edu-
cational consultant specializing in addiction counseling.
He has edited numerous anthologies and occasionally
contributes short stories to various projects.

The shrill chime on Jonathan's watch sounded. A hand
reached over his and pressed each of the timepiece's buttons
until the tone ceased. Jonathan opened his eyes.

"C'mon, asswipe, it's midnight. Time to make good."

Ralph's face wasn't the first thing Jonathan *ever* wanted
to wake to. A self-proclaimed "bully-of-the-camp," Ralph
was the first to tease him about going out each night during
"free time" to scout around with Ryan and Jenny, the two
photography counselors. Jonathan was teased about almost
everything else, too.

While the rest of the kids in Cabin 15 focused on softball,
skiing, riflery, and any coed activities that would put their
raging adolescent hormones in close proximity to the
fifteen-year-old girls across the lake, Jonathan kept mostly
to himself. His daily activities included photography, arts
and crafts, ham radio, and drama. Even though he was a year
too young to qualify as counselor-in-training, Ryan and
Jenny took him in as their assistant. Eating with them at the
counselors' table in the dining hall and going with them into
town on film runs distanced Jonathan even farther from his
peers. As far as Jonathan was concerned, the farther the better.

"C'mon pansies, it's time to get up," Ralph whispered in
one camper's ear, as he put his hand squarely over the boy's
mouth to prevent any sound from waking the counselors
sleeping in the back room. Jonathan quietly slid off his top

bunk and laced his sneakers. He was already dressed; tonight would be the best performance of his life. In a few minutes, all eight campers were ready to go.

"Keep it down," warned Troy, the cabin's senior camper.

"We don't want to wake any spirits before their time," Ralph quipped.

"Shhhh!" Troy directed his comments to Ralph. "We still have to get across the campgrounds. Keep it down, asshole."

"What if we get caught?" asked Jake. "Will they kick us out?"

"With what our parents are paying," Troy responded, "it would take an act of God before they got rid of even _one_ of us. Besides, we'd blame it all on Jonathan. Ain't that right?"

Jonathan chose not to respond. He continued leading the group to the photography shack, where Ryan and Jenny said they'd be waiting. They were both Camp Dakota "virgins"; Ryan had just graduated high school in the Bronx and Jenny was a freshman at MIT. _They won't come back,_ he thought to himself. _They never do._ Jonathan had attended the camp every summer since he was seven. He was the one who first showed Jenny where the church once stood.

"There they are!" Jonathan exclaimed. He'd have felt like shit if everyone in the cabin made it up to the shack and no one else showed. He'd never be able to do it alone.

"Quiet, you guys." Ryan waited for the last one to straggle up. "Huddle around."

"I—I feel sick," Jake stammered. "I wanna go back."

Ralph clenched his grip around the boy's neck. "Take one step toward the cabin and I'll kick your ass. Understand?"

Jake nodded. He didn't have the guts to ask if he could be excused to use the bathroom.

"Here's the deal," Ryan began, "no flashlights, no lighters. We take one candle. Jenny will lead. Any questions?"

Troy stared at the puddle forming at Jake's feet. "Anyone got a clean set of diapers? I think Jake wet himself."

It was too dark to capture Jake's expression. Even Ryan laughed to himself a moment. "Okay, guys, ante up."

Jenny collected an odd assortment of lights and lighters, then lit a short, stout black candle. Ryan grabbed his notebook from inside.

"Jonathan, you and Jenny lead the way. I'll take the rear."

It was nearly a quarter mile through the woods before they got to Camp Dakota's original site. All the wooden cabins were gone. The gym remained—or what was left of it. Jonathan calculated to himself: Jenny said the camp burned in 1945, that would make it right at fifty years since they moved to the new grounds. As they approached the clearing, the one structure which still stood undaunted loomed before them.

"Shit, this is eerie," Ralph exclaimed.

"You ain't chickening out, are you?" questioned Troy.

"No, I just said it was eerie. Okay?"

"This way," Jenny led. The group followed through a stone archway and down into a square, roofless enclosure about twenty by forty feet. Jonathan had shown it to Jenny the second day of camp. Infatuated with Indiana Jones since she was twelve, Jenny told Ryan and Jonathan she would make this archaeological dig *her* summer project, and dubbed them her partners. Every chance Jenny had, she would dig and excavate around the building that had once been the Camp Dakota assembly hall and dining room. But Jenny soon found that it was much more than that.

Digging beneath a small two-foot square rock piling revealed brittle fragments of paper and a small wooden cross. The piling was positioned, she said, so that something heavy could be placed at that location atop the wooden floor—when there *was* still a wooden floor.

Jenny placed the candle in the center. "Let's make a circle around the candle, and sit close enough so that we can still hold hands."

Ryan and Jenny sat together. Jonathan sat on the opposite side with four of the boys to his right and left (it was customary to count Ralph as two). Jonathan was happy; for the first time since the start of camp, the kids would hear about St. Vincent's from someone other than him.

It was Ryan who suggested the seance in the first place, and prepared the script for Jenny and Jonathan to follow. After a week's practice, only Ryan had trouble remembering his lines, but he would be mostly reading anyway. Jonathan would show *them* who the bravest camper of Cabin 15 was.

"Before we begin," started Jenny, "I want to share with you what Jonathan, Ryan, and I have found during the past six weeks." She smiled at Jonathan; he tried not to grin, but failed.

"In 1896, twenty-four years before Camp Dakota even existed, there was a small colony of settlers from Germany.

Their wooden houses were in the same place as the cabins once stood. This building, with floor and roof intact, was their church. Its name was St. Vincent."

"Aw, c'mon," Troy said doubtfully. "How could you know all that?"

" 'Cause I'm good—"

"I'll vouch for that," interjected Ryan. Jenny swatted at him half-jokingly as everyone laughed.

"Because I'm a good researcher. I found all this out from the records at the town hall and by looking at early photos and sketches. Ryan, show them the one of the cathedral."

He removed a photocopy from the notebook and held it next to the candle.

"Look at the roof on that building," said Ralph, pointing to the huge steeple.

"We're in *that* building now," Jonathan pointed out.

"Then where are the tombstones?"

"Gone," Jenny pointed out. "Well, all but one."

Ryan reached for the candle in the center of the circle and walked over to the far corner. "Here she is!"

"She was buried in here?" asked Ralph.

"No, stupid," responded Jonathan, a bit bolder. "They dug it up outside, where the drawing shows the cemetery ought to be. We just carried it in here."

"Oh," Jenny inserted. "It's a *him,* not a her. His name was Sebastian Gruel. He died August 10, 1905, according to the gravestone."

"And that's who we're going to *attempt* to reach tonight." Ryan returned to the circle, placing the candle back into the center. "I must warn you, though, once the circle is cast, you must not break it until I say so. Understand?"

Ryan peered around to each of the boys until he received a firm nod of agreement. "Good. Everyone hold hands and we'll begin." He laid out the notebook in front of him and pulled a large silver dagger from his waist. When he held it high overhead, the flame's reflection danced off the blade, projecting strange patterns of light on the sheer stone walls.

Jonathan surveyed the others; he could sense their tension. It felt good that *they* would feel some pressure instead of *him* for a change. His hands joined Aaron's on the right and Manny's on the left. Jonathan could feel their palms sweat.

"First, I will cast a magic circle. This will protect us as

long as the circle remains complete." Ryan opened his back-pack and removed a small glass of water, a salt shaker from the dining hall, some sweet-smelling incense, and a metal ashtray. He lit the incense in the ashtray and stood up in place, reading from his notebook:

"I exorcise thee, O creature of water, that thou cast out from thee all the impurities and uncleanliness of the spirits of the world of phantasm."

"Where did he learn to do that?" Ralph whispered to Troy, his voice quivering.

"He's a warlock," Aaron responded in a voice louder than a whisper.

The term is witch, *stupid,* thought Jonathan. But he knew better than to reply now.

Ryan touched the blade of the dagger to the water, then to the salt. He mixed the two together then rose and walked around the circle of campers sprinkling the mixture. As he paced:

"I conjure thee, O Circle of power, that thou beist a boundary between the worlds of men and the realms of the Mighty Ones. A guardian and a protection that shall pre-serve and contain the power which we shall raise within thee, wherefore do I bless and consecrate thee."

Jonathan knew where the verses came from—a role-playing supplement that the three of them had played through that last time Jenny GM'd. She was the best Game Master he ever had.

Ryan sat back down and joined the circle, placing the dagger on the ground in front of him. "Repeat after me: I sum-mon, stir, and call thee up, Sebastian Gruel, to attend our rites within this circle."

One by one, each of the boys repeated the chant, their voices weak with fear. Jonathan strained his voice to sound like the others; but he was not afraid.

After Jenny recites, then Ryan, it's my turn. I can do it, Jonathan thought confidently, *I know I can.*

Ryan repeated the chant, this time at the level of a scream. "I *demand* thee, Sebastian Gruel, to attend our rites within this circle. I demand thee *now!*"

Jonathan's face contorted, as the deepened voice he had practiced roared. "I am Sebastian Gruel. You have summoned me from depths beyond your spirits' reach. I have returned."

Ryan and Jenny looked at each other, then back at Jonathan. Even Ryan felt a bit tense.

"Why does thou choose to return to us on the ninetieth anniversary of your death? What message—"

"Murder," Jonathan burst out. "You bastards put me to death."

Jenny looked confused. She had traced Gruel's death. It was an accident; he'd fallen from the roof of the church. Jonathan must have forgotten his lines.

Ryan continued, "Which—*er*, bastards, put you to death—and why?"

"You," Jonathan spouted at Ralph, "and you," looking at Troy. "All of you will pay. And my revenge will be sweet."

Jenny broke in front of Ryan, "Wait, you weren't murdered, Sebastian, you fell from the steeple. It was an accident!"

"Stupid, foolish child. They *murdered* me. I was *hanged* from the steeple when our Reverend died. They thought black magic did him in and blamed me because of a birthmark beside my heart. Such lunacy!"

Jonathan looked at the expression on each of the boys' faces and let out a laugh that enhanced their fear. "I'll get each of you, just you wait—"

Jake began to sob loudly.

Ryan recommanded the floor. "Enough. I thank thee for being here, in spirit, with us. This rite has ended."

"I am here with you now," Jonathan screamed, "in body, mind, and spirit. I will not return!"

Jonathan's nails pierced Aaron's and Emmanuel's hands, but his grip was too strong for them to break free.

"You will leave this circle now!" Ryan yelled, as his hands broke away from the human chain.

Jonathan screeched "Nooooo!" as the candle flame soared six feet in height—then extinguished.

Silence. Sixty seconds passed; only Jake's sobs could be heard.

Jenny's heart pounded fiercely as she found the matchbook and relit the center candle. Jonathan was lying on his back; his hands free, too, from the chain. "C—C'mon, let's get out of here—slowly." She did not want them running back to camp.

Ryan tried to wake Jonathan to no avail. He checked the boy's pulse; it was weak, but rhythmic. He lifted the boy and carried him in his arms.

"You get back to bed before you're missed," Jenny cautioned. "And, remember, *nothing happened*. We'll take care of Jonathan."

Not another word was spoken on the trail back to camp. The residents of Cabin 15 didn't even gesture a simple "Good-night" as they parted ways at the photography shack. Ryan and Jenny brought Jonathan inside.

"He'll be okay," Ryan said unconvincingly. "We need to make up something quick."

"We were working late, like we often do, and Jonathan couldn't sleep so he came out to see if we needed help." Jenny paced the floor as she spoke.

"Hey, yeah," Ryan continued, "we asked him to mix some acetic acid, like he usually does, and he inhaled too much and passed out. That'll work—won't it?"

"Let's get him to the infirmary, now." Jenny led the way out. "I'm really scared."

"I guess I inhaled too much 'stop bath' in the darkroom." Jonathan shrugged his shoulders. "I don't really remember much."

"Shit man. You were out for almost two days," reported Troy. "They took you to the hospital and even called your Mom."

"I'm fine, really."

Jonathan walked back to his bed and finished folding the sheets. The rash he'd developed still hadn't gone away yet, but they gave him cream to smear on his chest at night for it. He reached between the two layers of mattress and pushed Ryan's dagger to the center. When he went back to the clearing after being released from the infirmary, he was surprised that Ryan hadn't returned for it.

Jonathan studied his calendar. I've got over a week before the session ends.

He smiled to himself.

My revenge *will* be sweet. I'll make those bastards pay.

THE MOST ANCIENT BATTLE
by Michael Coney

Michael Coney is the author of such novels as *Rax, The Hero of Downways,* and *Brontomek,* the latter of which was honored by the British Science Fiction Association as the best novel of 1976. The fifth book of his popular *Song of Earth* series, *The King of the Scepter'd Isle,* has seen publication in France, Germany, Great Britain, and the United States. All told, his works have appeared in twelve languages and been published on five continents.

While cleaning out my father's effects, I came across some old photographs. According to the packet they'd been developed and printed in a one-hour shop in Bristol in late 1973, twenty years ago.

I took them over to the rain-swept window and flipped through them. Shots of the house where my parents had lived until Mom died and Dad moved to Zennor; shots of my twenty-first birthday with friends I hadn't seen in years; Mom sitting on the beach at Weston-Super-Mare; camping with our friends the Tregothnans; the usual kind of thing.

Until I came to the penultimate photo.

A woman stood alone in a doorway. She stood relaxed, the long blue skirt showing the outline of one bent knee, one hand tucked casually into the waistband, the other resting against the doorjamb. She wore a white blouse with short sleeves; straight black hair hung over one shoulder and almost reached the curve of her breasts. I took all this in at a glance, but it was her face that captured my attention.

I'd never seen such a beautiful face. It was almost unearthly, with high cheekbones, slanting eyes, and an expression not exactly challenging; more of supreme confidence. It was the expression of a woman so secure in her beauty that the rest of the world could go to hell, for all she cared. She'd have been about thirty. Thirty, and she'd seen it all, and it hadn't affected her in the least. Thirty, and she'd just gotten showered and dressed and left some lover lying replete and scared in her bed, knowing he'd lose her soon; knowing, in fact, that he'd never really had her at all. . . .

I was getting fanciful. It was a photo of an unusually attractive woman, that was all, and I'd better stop looking at it for my own peace of mind. I'm a married man and anyway this photo was taken twenty years ago. But who was she?

Was she some secret out of Dad's past? Difficult to imagine. Dad was the finest man I've ever known, and that isn't filial loyalty talking; everyone thinks the same. Women tended to gather around him, but it was always apparent he only had eyes for Mom, so the admirers would drift away disappointed after a while, and others would take their place. Mom used to laugh about it. Dad showed no sign of remarrying after her death four years ago. He seemed to lose heart, and holed up in this godforsaken rainy-gray Cornish village licking his wounds until his death last month at the age of sixty-three. His heart just stopped beating, the doctor said. It sometimes happens.

I laid the photos on the windowsill and held the negative strips up to the light. Yes, the photo of the woman was number 35; last but one. The prints were still in their original order. I turned my attention to the woman again, and now I noticed something else. She was standing in the doorway of an inn. I could make out lettering on the lintel above her: *M.F. Minesse, licensed to sell ales, wines, and spirits for consumption on or off the premises.* And above that a hanging sign: THE MOVING FINGER.

Perhaps she was the wife of M.F. Minesse, or the daughter. Or perhaps she was M.F. Minesse herself, maintaining an orderly house by the sheer strength of her personality. Yes, in some trick of the late afternoon light I caught a glimpse of something almost cruel in the perfection of that face. She was not a woman to be messed about with.

Reluctantly, I slipped her photo to the bottom of the pack, revealing the final item; and this one I did recognize.

A simple shot: James and Tom Tregothnan, father and son, looking over the parapet of an old stone bridge. The photographer, presumably Dad, had been standing on the bank of the river. It was a dull day but the subjects' features were clear. James is dead now—a terrible business—but Shirley and I still see a lot of Tom and Molly. The Lecontes and the Tregothnans have been friends for years; for generations, so I'm told. I can never remember a time when the Tregothnans were not around.

As I was about to replace the photos in the envelope, I noticed writing on the back of the last one. *Jim and Tom Tregothnan, 15 October 1973,* written in Dad's careful hand. One could always trust the old man to be methodical. And now I would discover the identity of the mystery woman.

But the reverse of her photo was disappointingly blank. I flipped through the others. Some bore captions, some didn't. In general, the obvious ones were not described, but nearly all bore dates.

So did that mean the identity of the woman, and the date, were so patently obvious to Dad that he hadn't needed to write a caption? Or didn't he care; was it just a random shot to hurry the end of the roll? That was more likely. That the woman was staggeringly attractive might not have occurred to my pure old Dad.

I felt suddenly lonely in the cold little house. I needed to talk to someone. I glanced at my watch; it was five-thirty. The sea-borne Cornish rain continued to drench the land. Boxes lay all around the room, some full of Dad's personal diaries and writings, some containing records of various charitable organizations of which Dad had been an officer—offices which had devolved upon me as his natural successor. Did I really need all this stuff? Probably not, unless someone, someday, wanted to write a history.

I found I was looking at the photo of the Tregothnans, and on an impulse crossed the room and picked up the phone.

Molly Tregothnan answered. "Jack! How are things down in darkest Cornwall?"

"Okay. There's masses of stuff here. I don't think Dad ever threw anything away."

"You're lucky you caught us. We're taking a break. Wayne's got himself in a spot of trouble again, and Tom thinks a fishing trip will help sort him out. You know, male bonding as they sit together drinking beer on some muddy riverbank in the pouring rain."

Wayne in trouble was nothing new. The young Tregothnan, now twenty, is no wilder than Tom was in his day, but that doesn't make it any easier. "What's he done this time?"

"Nothing worse than usual. It's just the cumulative effect. The police caught him on the Post Office roof, smoking pot. Tom's trying to talk them out of adding breaking and entering to the list. He reasons that although Wayne accidentally put his foot through a skylight, his whole body did not enter. And just as well, because the floor was sixteen feet away."

"Lucky Wayne. Was anyone with him?"

"Well, there's that, too. She's rather young. So bloody young, the papers won't be using her name." I heard her sigh. "My guess is, she's pregnant. It's all I need. Christ, Jack, sometimes I wonder what my life is all about. Tom's been all broody this last few months, and I hear his job's on the line; and Wayne, well, it's just been one thing after another. Why can't they be model bloody citizens like you, eh? And Charlie doing well at Cambridge, and all. God, I envy Shirley. It's going to take more than killing a few fish to sort our mess out, I can tell you."

"I'm sorry to hear about Tom's job."

"I don't want to talk about it. I want to get away from here, from them all. I want to see you. You make me feel good. It's the French blood in you."

It's one of life's permanent duties, fending off the flirty Molly. And the French blood was many generations ago, for what it's worth. "Well, you wouldn't like it in Zennor. Why not enjoy yourself talking to the locals in the nearest pub while Tom and Wayne are bonding on the riverbank? Which particular river will have the honor, anyway?"

"I don't know; it could be the River Jordan for all I care. All Tom said was that he knew just the place. It has some kind of family connections with the Tregothnans; the family's been buried there for yonks. He clammed up when I pressed him for details, and looked kind of haunted. Haunted! What's he got to be haunted about?—that's what I'd like to know. I'm the one who has to carry the can. Huh. You want to talk to Tom?" she said abruptly, her tone suddenly unfriendly. She would be a difficult woman to live with. "Tom!" I heard her yell. "It's Jack!"

There was a pause, then the familiar voice. "Jack. How are things?"

"Fine." I offered a brief description of the old man's squirreling habits, then mentioned the photographs. "There's one of you and your dad among them, taken twenty years ago. Would you like to have it?"

"Twenty years ago?"

"There was a date on the back. Fifteenth of October seventy-three."

And as I said the words, I wanted to snatch them back. I'm no good at dates; I rely on Shirley to remind me of birthdays and anniversaries. But now I remembered, too late, the significance of the fifteenth of October, 1973. And, insensitive clod that I was, I'd reminded Tom of something he'd rather forget.

The fifteenth of October 1973 was the day James Tregothnan was murdered.

He'd taken Tom and Angharad for a short holiday, and met his death one evening not far from the inn at which they were staying. The murderer was never caught. I'd been in France with a couple of my Cambridge pals at the time; it was the year I met Shirley. I'd received a call from Mom; she could hardly speak for crying. James Tregothnan had been found murdered in some remote country lane near Camelford in Cornwall; stabbed, it emerged later, just once. I'd caught the next plane home. Dad had cut short his sales trip and we'd all gathered at the Tregothnans', trying to console Angharad, widow of James. Tom, I recall, had been slumped in an easy chair and I'd sat on the arm, trying clumsily to get him to talk. Why, I don't know. It seemed the right thing to do.

Later that evening we couldn't ignore the fact that we were all hungry despite our sorrow, so we went to the local pub for a meal. It was a mistake. The contrast between our glum group and the rest of the noisy, laughing customers was too much. None of us knew how to behave. We didn't want to talk about the murder, and we didn't want to talk about future plans because that implied we'd already written James off. So we talked about the past until Angharad, full of gin, suddenly burst out, "The police suspect Tom and me!"

We uttered a chorus of disbelief. "James went off alone, didn't he?" said Mom. "He left you both at that inn. Somebody will vouch for that, surely?"

I remember Angharad shooting Dad a secret glance. "That landlady says she will, but I don't trust her. She's weird. And there were no other customers; it's the deadest dump I've ever been in. And the pub is only a couple of miles from where they found James. What we need is a reliable witness the police will believe. Someone like you, Bill. A pillar of bloody society."

And Dad's face had frozen, and he'd stared into his beer for a long time. I thought I understood his problem. He'd desperately wanted to help, but was morally incapable of committing perjury.

Mom said quite sharply to Angharad, "Anyway, you had no motive."

People changed after James Tregothnan's murder. Dad lost some of his bounce, and his volunteer work seemed to become a chore. He and Mom grew apart, just a little. Angharad went to live at Amesbury and joined a charitable women's group. Tom married Molly and changed, too, losing some of his carefree charm. Shirley reckoned it was a newfound sense of responsibility. She was wrong.

And now, the photograph.

"Tom, was my father with you that day?"

"With us?"

"Yes. With you and your dad. It must have been him taking the photo."

"Good grief, Jack, I haven't seen the photo. I don't know anything about it."

"There's you and your dad standing on an old stone bridge, looking downstream." The thing was becoming important to me now, and I could hear the impatient edge in my own voice. "It's on a roll of film taken by my dad. The fifteenth October '73, Tom, for God's sake!"

His voice was flat. "No."

"What do you mean, no?"

"I mean your dad wasn't there." It was like a stranger talking; cold and controlled.

"Then who took the photo?"

"How would I know who took the photo? I've never seen the bloody photo. It could have been taken anywhere; your dad probably got the date wrong. Let it go, Jack. My God, don't I have enough problems without you resurrecting some old photo from way back?"

"Take it easy, Tom. I was naturally curious."

"The whole thing is dead and buried. Your dad wasn't there. If he'd been there, he'd have been able to back up our alibi and we wouldn't have had to go through that nightmare with the police. Jesus Christ, Mom and I came within an inch of being charged with murder! You dad's help would have been very welcome, to say the least."

"Sorry, Tom. Let's forget it. Uh, I'm sorry to hear about Wayne. If I can help in any way—"

Shockingly, he suddenly yelled, "You just keep out of it, Jack! It's none of your bloody business, you understand? Just keep away from my family until we've sorted this thing out!"

And the line went dead.

It wasn't so much the violence in Tom's voice that sent me into what, I suppose, was mild shock; I'd had plenty of experience of his moods when we were kids. It was the fact that I'd been disloyal to Dad. Just for a moment I'd seriously considered that he might have been involved in a murder. Not in the actual deed, of course. But I'd found myself thinking that he must have been in Camelford that day, and concealed the fact for his own reasons. And that would have been a totally unDadlike thing for him to do.

I stood for a while looking out of the cottage window at the gray houses of Zennor, remembering him; the craggy, smiling face; the deep and reassuring voice. God, how I'd loved him. And now, sorting out the evidence of his life, trying to put it in some kind of order, I felt as though he were standing beside me in that tiny living room, asking me what I thought of some course of action. Respecting my opinion like he always did.

Not quite always. He'd never discussed his intention to move to Zennor and cut himself off from everybody. And why Zennor? Why this grim little village surrounded by Iron Age fields with their stone walls, close by the cliffs where the storm waves boom in from the Atlantic? Full of Celtic mystery and legends of Arthur, as though Dad was trying to burrow back into the past. He'd become quite the historian these last few years; one of the boxes was packed with books on the Dark Ages and the Arthurian myths.

Since his move we'd talked on the phone weekly, and Shirley and I had driven down here frequently at weekends. But he'd never visited us. It was almost as though he'd lived a life of pretense in Bristol for Mom's sake, and once she was gone there was no need to pretend anymore. But Dad, living a life of pretense? Almost impossible to imagine, were it not for the odd feeling I've always had about him and Angharad.

I have a curious memory from early in my married life. Sunshine and a swing in the garden, watching little Charlie's grip on the ropes as Shirley pushed him gently in the small of the back. Hearing Dad's voice somewhere behind me, his tone strange, almost strangled.

"I hope to God this is the end of it."

And Shirley replying vaguely, "What's that, Dad? The end of what?"

That's all. I'd swung 'round to see Dad looking at Charlie with a tortured, desperate expression, then Mom came out from the kitchen with a tray of drinks, and the weird moment ended.

Dad was sales manager for Bates Brothers Foods. Although he was nominally desk-bound in Bristol, he still liked to get out on the road as often as possible. He'd been enormously popular with clients and was to a large extent responsible for the position the company holds in today's market. Customers looked on him as a father-confessor. They phoned him at home for advice on their personal problems, and I've never known him to refuse to help. Mom used to laugh about it. She was a good woman.

One of the boxes on the floor contained Dad's old road diaries. I found myself looking at it, irresolute. Finally I told myself it was better to satisfy my curiosity than to spend the rest of my life wondering.

I found the diary for 1973 and opened it up. Pages of Dad's neat writing: lists of calls to be made, reminders of special orders, notes of customers' suggestions, a few personal notes such as "*Camelot* on at Yeovil." In those days Dad had been an ordinary salesman, traveling the West Country.

I found I was breathing fast as I turned to October, and there was a queer sick feeling in my stomach.

The pages opened at October 13. "Taunton. Anderson, push meat pies; Charlesworth, new client; remember see Mrs. Jackson—"

Impatiently I flipped the page over. October 14. "Exeter, call home re Jack's football, Moons, pastie w'salers—"

October 15. "Newton Abbot." Crossed out.

All the details for the day in Newton Abbot had been canceled by a single diagonal line. I stared at it for a long time,

trying not to think what it meant. Also diagonally, just above
the line, was written the one word RESCHEDULE. I turned
the page. October 16. "Torquay." Then the customary list.
Business as usual. Nothing else of interest.

So Dad could have driven to Camelford after his Exeter
rounds. It's not all that far. He'd have taken the A30 over the
north edge of Dartmoor, crossed the River Tamar and the
Devon-Cornwall border, through Launceston, then the A395
to Camelford. He'd have been there in time for a nightcap.
Where? The Moving Finger, where that mysterious woman
had been standing in the doorway? They'd all gathered together for a last drink: the Tregothnans, Dad, and the
woman. Then bed, and the next day spent together fishing.
Dad had taken the photo. And in the evening James died.
And later that night Dad had driven to Newton Abbot to
continue his rounds.

It didn't make sense. If Dad had been with the Tregothnans, he'd have backed up Tom and Angharad's alibis and
cleared them of suspicion. Unless Dad had gone to
Camelford secretly with the express purpose of murdering
James for reasons unknown. After all, Tom had simply said
he wasn't there, which could have meant he hadn't actually
seen him.

But there was the photograph. . . .

With the wrong date on the back? Dad was usually so methodical.

What in God's name had happened, that October day in
Camelford? As I settled down for sleep later that evening,
the problem kept revolving in my mind until it became a cycle of hallucinations. Again and again I saw Dad and James
Tregothnan armed with crude iron swords—not fighting
each other, but side by side against a mutual foe, while the
clashes and screams of an ancient battle sounded all around
them.

Three o'clock on another grim Cornish afternoon. No
wonder the Saxons left this part of the country to the Celts.
I'd finished loading the boxes into the van and decided to
leave the furniture. Maybe we'd rent the place out, furnished, as a holiday cottage.

By now I was sure I'd been misled by a series of coincidences. Tom was right. Dad had put the wrong date on a
photograph taken weeks before it had been developed and

printed. And the day crossed out of the diary? Probably he was sick, confined to his hotel room after a supper of tainted fish or whatever.

I called Shirley to let her know I was on my way, took a last look around, locked the place up, and drove off. It was still raining, gray and vile.

It's a funny thing about fate. I'd always been arrogant enough to suppose I was master of my own destiny. I know differently now. Dad knew, too. Maybe that was why he gave up on life after Mom died: he'd fulfilled his purpose on Earth. We're led by fate as though we have rings in our noses.

My personal destiny tweaked me on course near that oddly-named Cornish village, Indian Queens. I'd been following the A30 east for some time and logic told me I should have continued that way, picking up the A38 from Bodmin to Exeter, and thence on the M5 motorway home.

But logic had nothing to do with it. Near Indian Queens I saw a sign for Wadebridge and Camelford. And on a sudden whim—so I thought at the time—I turned onto the A39. I arrived at Camelford in a misty twilight, and wondered what I was doing there.

I called Shirley from a public box, and the lying began. I've never lied to her before, yet now it seemed perfectly natural.

"I've decided to stay another night at Zennor after all. There's a few loose ends to tie up. I should be home sometime tomorrow afternoon."

"Okay," she said, trusting woman, and we exchanged a few items of news before I hung up.

I had an hour before dark; time to drive around a bit, spy out the land, find a nice quiet inn, and settle in for the night. I'd already seen a couple of likely places in Camelford, but I fancied somewhere off the main road. I opened the map. A minor road headed north just the other side of town; there were a couple of likely-looking villages out there, close by the River Camel. I drove on, and in less than two miles found myself in a village. An inn stood beside the road, apparently closed. They don't often open before six out of the tourist season. I had half an hour to kill. The rain had stopped. I decided to stretch my legs.

A couple of hundred yards along the lane I came to a bridge and leaned against the rounded stone parapet, looking

down at the water. If this was the River Camel, it wasn't
much. Little more than a stream, in fact. It hurried noisily
over its bed of pebbles, fed by the recent rains, and as I
watched it, the ring of destiny twitched my nose again. For
no particular reason, I left the road, made my way down to
the riverbank, and looked back.

The bridge was ancient, surrounded by wet and tangled
vegetation, supported on two pillars. Each pillar consisted of
four massive rectangular stones laid lengthways on top of
each other. These supported three lintels at a height of about
six feet above the water level. Sound boomed oddly through
here. In addition to the rush of the water I heard shouting,
neighing, and clanging noises. I underwent a moment of
strange fancies before I recognized the commonplace sound
of activists trying to disrupt a nearby fox hunt. Last night's
dream had affected my thinking.

Perhaps I should have wondered why people would be
hunting so late in the evening. Instead, another thought hit
me like a punch in the stomach.

This old stone bridge. It looked very much like the bridge
in the photograph.

So now I had to swallow another coincidence. Even if
Dad had written the wrong date on the photo, he had never-
theless been near Camelford at some time during the weeks
before James Tregothnan's death. And so had James and
Tom. Unless it was a different bridge. Many of these old
West Country bridges look alike.

Another look at the photo would clear the whole thing up.
The set of the stones would not have changed over twenty
years. I could bring the photo down to the riverbank and
compare it with the bridge, stone by stone. Probably my sub-
conscious had invented similarities where none existed.

I climbed back to the lane and walked toward the village.
All was quiet now; just the drip of wet leaves and the fading
rush of water. The hunt had moved on; maybe there never
had been a hunt. It seemed my imagination was working
overtime that evening. The village came into view; low-
slung cottages waiting patiently for sunnier days. A single
lamp gleamed yellow above the inn sign and now, for the
first time, I saw it clearly. A peeling representation of an
open book with a quill pen laid across it; underneath, the
words THE MOVING FINGER.

I found myself approaching stealthily, as though scared of disturbing a nest of demons. The outer door, black and heavy, stood open; an inner door was closed. White lettering ran along the top of the outer door frame: *M.F. Minesse, licensed to sell ales, wines, and spirits for consumption on or off the premises.*

Suddenly I felt a longing to be home, in the neat house in Bristol where I belonged, away from this weird place of dark windows and hungry silence. Home was only a couple of hours away. Shirley would be pleased to see me; we'd maybe have dinner at the tandoori restaurant down the road. A glass of Scotch before bed. Yes, time to get back on the road. . . .

Except that I couldn't see my van anywhere around.

I'd left it on the other side of the road, opposite the inn. It was not there now. It was nowhere in sight. Either the police had towed it away, or it had been stolen. Together with all the stuff I'd brought back from Zennor; all the memories of Dad. And, a lesser item but one of practical importance: my overnight things.

I'd stared at the place where the van had been for long enough; this was getting me nowhere. I hurried into the inn. The inner door opened directly into the bar; the counter was on the left, the shelves looked well-stocked, and three customers sat around a cheerful fire in a big old fireplace to the right. The everyday appearance of the room fed my anger. I strode up to the counter and slapped it with a open palm.

"Anybody about?" I called.

"She's slipped out for a moment," said one of the customers. Then he exclaimed incredulously, "Jack!"

It was Tom Tregothnan, with Molly and the errant Wayne. I stared at them. "What the hell are you people doing here?" I asked.

"What the hell are *you?*" retorted Tom.

Molly said at the same time, "I told you we were going fishing."

"Yes, but why here?"

"Why not, for God's sake?" said Tom, clearly not in a forthcoming mood.

"Well, I know you head off into Cornwall occasionally, but. . . . This is a hell of a coincidence, isn't it?"

Tom was wearing that slightly unpleasant look I remembered of old. "So we've come fishing. What's *your* excuse?"

It would have been tactless to tell him I'd come looking for the bridge. If, in fact, that was why I had come. "I'm on my way back from Zennor," I said. "I thought maybe I'd take the north Cornwall route for a change. Now the van's been stolen and it looks like I'm stuck here."

"Stolen?" Molly echoed. "When did this happen?"

"Just now. Is there a phone anywhere around? I'd better call the police. We'll catch up with the news after."

There was a phone at the end of the bar. Surprisingly, I got through to the police immediately, gave them a description of the van and received the impression that they were moderately concerned and would look out for it. The kind of day I was having, I'd expected the phone lines to be down.

I rejoined the Tregothnans, wondering whether to ask a few questions, like: Why had Tom brought Molly and Wayne here of all places, so close to where his father had been murdered? Had he been coming here regularly over the years? Did Molly know the story behind this area?

Best not to ask the questions yet. Tom was not in the right mood. "So. What am I going to do now?"

Molly said, "Miss Minesse has another room. Why not stay here tonight? Maybe tomorrow you can keep me company while the boys go fishing. Until the police find your van."

"On the other hand," said Tom, still with that look of his that came mainly from lowered eyebrows, "I could run you into Camelford. There're a couple of good pubs there."

Wayne did not contribute, staring into the flames, his puffy face morose.

"Here comes Miss Minesse now," said Molly.

A door behind the counter opened and a woman entered. It was the woman in Dad's photo; I'd half-expected that. But at the sight of her, the unreality began again.

Because she hadn't aged.

She looked exactly the same; face unchanged by the passage of twenty years, hair still a lustrous black, same rich figure, same white blouse and blue skirt. It was as though she'd come directly in from posing for Dad's camera in the ancient timbered doorway.

I found I was staring stupidly. To cover my discomfort I crossed the room to the bar. "Good evening," I said. My throat was dry; the words sounded to me like a croak.

She didn't look up from a glass she was polishing. "Mr.

John Leconte?" she said in a low, flat voice. "Welcome to the Moving Finger. I have your room ready."

Molly and Wayne went to bed about ten. We'd eaten an excellent supper of game pie and roast potatoes followed by rhubarb crumble and coffee. I'd kept my mounting store of questions to myself, not wishing to embarrass Tom, who seemed to be playing some deep game. Now, however, we were alone in the bar except for the enigmatic Miss Minesse and an elderly man sitting under the dartboard contemplating his empty glass. The fire had burned low.

"All right, Tom. Why did you book me into this place?"

He looked surprised. "Book you in? Why would I do that?"

"So why did that woman have a room for me?"

"I've no idea." His mood had mellowed over supper; he took a sip of Gold Label and flicked an appreciative tongue over his lips. "We'd been here an hour by the time you arrived. Maybe she heard us talking and misunderstood something we said about you traveling through Cornwall."

It sounded highly unlikely, but it was the best explanation so far. "All right, maybe. But why did you bring Molly and Wayne *here*, of all places? Good grief, your dad was killed somewhere around these parts! Do they know that?"

"Water under the bridge, Jack. Water under the bridge. The fishing is good here. I've been coming here for years. The Tregothnans have some kind of connections here way back, so Dad told me once. Should I stay away for the rest of my life because of something that happened twenty years ago?"

Put like that, the whole thing began to seem more reasonable, although it was quite a change from his attitude to his father's death when I'd spoken to him earlier that day. I'd mellowed, too; my room had looked comfortable, the bar was pleasant, oak-beamed with plenty of old pictures and brassware; the kind of place I like. There was even a stuffed grouse in a glass case over the fireplace. And it was good to see Tom and Molly again, although I could have done without Wayne.

I returned to another oddity. "This Minesse woman," I said quietly. "There's something funny about her. I found a photo of her among Dad's stuff and she looked exactly the same as she does now. But the photo was taken twenty years ago."

"Probably her mother."

"*Exactly* like her, Tom? And the writing over the front door saying M.F. Minesse? *Exactly* the same name?"

"The mother probably still holds the license. Maybe she's in the background somewhere. Maybe she handles the food side of things now." He seemed determined to make light of everything.

"So you've been here since your dad's death?"

"Oh, once or twice, perhaps. A few times."

"You'd have noticed a transition from mother to daughter, for God's sake!"

"Good grief, I've hardly looked at the woman! She's a cold fish. I notice she hasn't responded to the old Leconte charm either, and personally I've learned to keep things neutral with her. Anyway, you know me; I'm not really that great with the women."

This was true. Tom's a handsome devil like his father, red-bearded and reminiscent of an Elizabethan seafarer, but somehow he gets tongue-tied in the presence of the ladies.

"It's the same woman," I said stubbornly. I glanced past Tom to the bar. Miss Minesse was looking our way, gray eyes opaque. Suddenly I shivered.

Tom said, "All right. Let's see the photo."

"It was in the van."

He regarded me quizzically. "So I only have your word for it there is a photo. And I only have your word you didn't know I was coming here tonight. You're stretching my credulity, Jack."

It was the wrong time to bring up the topic of the bridge photo, also unavailable. And Tom seemed genuine enough. I introduced a note of manly banter. "She's a good-looking filly, anyway."

He glanced at her. "Too sinister for my taste. You'd be living very dangerously, Jack."

I knew what he meant. She was the antithesis of Molly, who was blonde and bland and slender and had—according to Shirley—a face like a bladder of lard.

Shortly afterward Tom went to bed and I was trapped into conversation with the bar's only other customer. He insisted on playing the role of the local yokel, relating the lurid history of the village and in particular the bridge up the road.

" 'Twere just such a night as this," he said in classic style, "when a gennleman tourist—a gennleman just like you— was done to death right upriver of the bridge. He bled his life's blood into the water and next morning the river ran red under the bridge. Bright red, I tell you. Fair turned my stomach, it did." His eyes assumed a faraway expression. "All of twenty years ago, that were."

I told him I knew all about it, and stood to go.

Beerily frustrated by my response, he redoubled his efforts. "Aye, 'twere not the first time there's been devilry at the bridge. There's been murdering there ever since 'twere builded, and long afore that. That's why it's called Slaughter Bridge."

After a disturbed night I awakened late, showered in the shared bathroom, dressed, and went downstairs. In the bar I found a table set for two, and sat down. Like all empty bars, the room felt as though ghosts were drinking at the tables, laughing and chattering in deathly silence.

"Full breakfast, Mr. Leconte? Bacon, eggs, sausage and so on?" It was Miss Minesse. She wore the same white blouse and blue skirt; or an identical outfit freshly laundered. Yet this time she looked sexy. Her hair rested more softly on her shoulders; her lips looked more full, almost swollen; her gray eyes held an invitation that had been missing last night, and even her voice sounded warmer. She stood with one hand resting on the back of the chair opposite, lending a slight twist to her body that pushed her breasts against the fabric of the blouse. The nipples were erect.

"Yes. . . . Thanks," I managed to say. She smiled as though acknowledging my interest, and turned away.

"Are the Tregothnans up yet?" I asked, possibly to keep her there.

"Mr. Tregothnan and his son left for the river an hour ago," she said, smiling again. "Mrs. Tregothnan is still in bed." It was an odd choice of words. I'd have expected her to say "Mrs. Tregothnan is still in her room." Instead, she'd conjured up an image of warm flesh.

She served an excellent breakfast, possibly prepared by her theoretical mother, smiled a lot but said little, responding to my curiosity about the neighborhood with straight, simple answers. As I ate, the fanciful notion occurred to me of three cloned Miss Minesses: tough no-nonsense Miss Minesse to run the evening bar, a warm and sexual Miss Minesse to tempt lodgers to extend their stay, and a workaday Miss Minesse with dishpan hands and straggly hair but great culinary expertise, beavering away in the kitchen.

As she was clearing the table, I said, "By the way, I found an old photograph of the inn yesterday. Taken at least twenty years ago. It looked like you outside the front entrance."

"That's not why we have the pleasure of your company, is it?" she said, smiling right into my eyes, and I left it at that.

As I strolled up the road toward the bridge with some vague idea of seeing what Tom and Wayne were up to, I pondered on this brief exchange. Why hadn't I asked her outright if she was the woman in the photo? Because I couldn't have produced it to show her? And what did her reply mean? Was it a statement or a question?

I must have walked for over an hour mulling over recent events, before I turned in at the wrought-iron gate of a tiny churchyard. A chill breeze ruffled the long grass and everything looked drenched; the rain had continued most of the night. A huddle of crows watched me from the eaves of a squat, square church, cawing angrily at the intrusion on their territory. Simple gravestones stood all around, and one more recent than most caught my eye.

JAMES EDWARD TREGOTHNAN
Born 28th October 1939
Died 15th October 1973
AT LAST PEACE

I searched around but found no sign of Angharad's grave; she'd died ten years ago and was probably buried in Amesbury. What I did find, was a goodly number of Tregothnan graves. THOMAS CHARLES TREGOTHNAN had been buried here in 1952; JAMES WILLIAM TREGOTHNAN in 1930. There were others. And the strange thing was, every epitaph implied that the Tregothnan underneath was better off dead. A HAVEN WELCOMED. TROUBLED NO MORE. That kind of thing.

I wandered on, seeking out Tregothnans until I reached ancient ground where the inscriptions were too eroded to decipher. I returned to the gate. Molly had been right when she'd said the Tregothnans had family connections here; although, curiously enough, I could find no gravestones for the wives.

I wondered about our families. As I've said, the Tregothnans and the Lecontes have been connected for generations although we have never intermarried. And here was the fount of the Tregothnans, the hub of the family in this remote part of Cornwall. But the Lecontes? We're scattered all over the place. It's said that we originated near Nantes, in Western France. I went there once, only to find that the name Leconte is not exactly a rarity in France, and I quickly abandoned any attempt to trace my roots. In a way, I envied Tom his foothold here.

By noon I was getting tired of walking, so I lunched at a wayside pub, still pondering the connection between the families. Dad had once told me James Tregothnan had shown him a medieval document, some kind of partnership in a water mill. The partners' names had been Tregothnan and Leconte.

And yet, years later when I'd questioned Dad about this in Zennor, he'd denied all knowledge of such a document. Strange.

Then something about the male Tregothnans hit me; something Tom had never mentioned.

According to those gravestones, they had all died comparatively young. Usually in their forties. I could think of two reasons why that might be—both unbelievable. But suddenly I had a presentiment, and I feared for Tom.

As I walked back the way I'd come, working out ways of easing Tom and his family away from this place of ill-omen to somewhere safe and normal like Bournemouth, a more prosaic thought occurred. I must call Shirley.

And I'd have to tell her where I was, because she'd be sure to find out later about the coincidence of meeting the Tregothnans. For some reason I felt guilty about it. Recent events seemed so peculiar, so unbelievable.

It took longer than I'd expected to get back to the inn. By the time I arrived the door was open for evening business, but the bar was still empty. Miss Minesse smiled at me; she hadn't assumed her sinister guise yet. I called Shirley.

"You mean you ran into the Tregothnans just like *that?*" she said incredulously, as I'd expected.

"Small world."

"I thought you said you were staying at Zennor another night."

"I decided not to."

"But Camelford, that's on the A39. Why would you take the A39? You always take the A38."

"Not this time. It was just a whim."

"Funny kind of a whim." Women have a knack of making the innocent feel guilty. "Is Molly Tregothnan there?"

"I've told you already, all three of them are here." I was getting annoyed now. I'd never strayed from the straight and narrow, all our married life together. Yet Shirley had a thing about Molly. She didn't calm down until she'd extracted a promise from me to be home by evening, and I hung up feeling frustrated, angry, and trapped.

"That's marriage for you," said Miss Minesse who'd been standing in the shadows.

"You've never married?" I said, to make conversation.

"I don't need to." Now what did she mean by that? She stood as she'd been standing at the breakfast table, half-smiling. The pink tip of her tongue passed over full lips. I was suddenly breathless. "It's all hypocrisy," she continued. "Everybody knows that. You know it."

"There's no hypocrisy," I said, feeling a pulse beating in my throat. "I love my wife."

"Of course you do." She took a deep breath. Her nipples were swollen. "But right at this moment you want *me,* don't you? Because I'm here and she isn't. And because I'm me and she's she. It's the way human males are. It's good for the species. And it would be good for you and me."

She moved a step closer and one hand dropped below her waist, moving between her thighs as she watched me, eyes suddenly sleepy. I stood motionless, shocked at the crudity of her gesture, appalled at the immediacy of my arousal. I couldn't speak.

"You'd better come with me," she said.

She turned and made for the stairs and I followed, while one tiny sane corner of my mind marveled at the strength of that fateful ring through my nose, because this was only the latest in the string of events over which I had no control.

It was dark at the top of the stairs, and it was dark in the room into which she led me; just a faint rectangle indicated the position of the curtained window. I heard clothes rustling and, in a fever of haste I began to drag off my own. Possessed with a blinding vision of her body, I could think of nothing else.

"Come to bed, Jack." It was a whisper, a promise.

Warm arms reached for me, a warm body opened up to me and soon I knew an ecstasy that came close to killing me. Time slipped by while I lay suspended and mindless.

"Oh God, Jack, we should have done that long ago." This time it was no whisper.

And I froze. The world froze.

A moment later the light clicked on. Wayne stood in the doorway. "Mom, are you okay? I heard . . ." His voice trailed away as he stared at us. His young, unformed face twisted in a grimace of shock.

And I looked from him to Molly's face on the pillow.

We heard Wayne pounding down the stairs. We looked at each other. "Oh, my God," said Molly.

I couldn't speak. My thoughts had scattered and I couldn't gather them into rational shape.

"He's going to tell Tom!" Molly cried. "Jack, what are we going to do?"

I managed to grasp the fact that this was no sorcery; I'd simply been tricked. Miss Minesse had lured me to Molly's bedside, then slipped out. Molly had not objected to what happened next; hell, she'd made advances enough in the past. I stared down at her vapid face, now contorted in fear, and wondered at the peak of joy to which she'd taken me, only minutes ago.

Down in the bar, Miss Minesse had shown me that love is a myth, that she could make me betray Shirley simply by walking upstairs. And now she'd shown me that lust is a myth, too; that any warm body will do the necessary job for a man.

I wanted to roar with despair, like an animal might roar, because Miss Minesse had proved that's all I was, an animal.

Instead I dragged myself back to the problem at hand, and said to Molly, "I have no idea what we can do."

Shocked at the coldness I couldn't keep out of my voice, she cried, "I'm going to kill myself!"

"Pull yourself together, Molly. Let's think. We have to come up with some excuse for this. Some kind of mitigating circumstance." A dull rage began to grow in me. How could Miss Minesse have put me in this position? She knew per-

fectly well I could never explain to Molly the real reason for
my presence in her bed. It was not in me to humiliate her so.

But Molly's expression had turned crafty. "All I was
doing, was taking a rest before supper. I was waiting for
Tom and Wayne to come back from the river. I must have
dozed off. The next thing I know, you're in my bed raping
me."

So much for loyalty. "If that's the way you want it, you'd
better fabricate a few signs of violence," I said sarcastically.

Her composure swiftly recovered, she rolled out of bed
and stood. "That's the way it's got to be, Jack. I'm very
sorry, and all that."

"I've known Tom all my life. He'll never believe I'd rape
you."

"There's no point in us both going under. Anyway, Tom
would never believe I'd been unfaithful to him, either. He
worships me, didn't you know?"

Molly was right. Even after twenty-odd years of marriage,
Tom was still under the impression that his wife was little
short of a goddess. On the other hand, I'd built up a pretty
good reputation with him myself over the years. But I could
only use that to challenge Molly's story. I couldn't deny
what Wayne had seen.

"I'm going to talk to Miss Minesse," I said, pulling on my
clothes. Molly's duplicity had made me angrier than I cared
to show. Was there a conspiracy to shatter every single illusion I had?

"You think Morgan Minesse will give you an alibi?" she
said, smiling at me slyly. "You're wasting your time. Face it,
Jack, you'll take the rap in the end. It's the kind of person
you are. You're a real-life Sir bloody Lancelot, full of stupid
ideas of chivalry, defending the honor of a lady." Then suddenly her face changed. Her shoulders sagged. "Oh, God,
I'm sorry, Jack. I don't know what made me say all that. I
say idiotic things when I get scared.

The sudden switch surprised me and defused my anger. I
considered what she'd said more rationally, and had to admit
there might be some sense in it. Perhaps I should agree to
take the blame. Always provided no charges were laid, and
that Shirley was never told the Molly version. Perhaps it was
the only way, after all. It would cost me Tom's friendship,
but it would save the Tregothnans' marriage.

Molly stood there naked in the harsh light of the room's

central light, head down, blonde hair hanging past her face, small-breasted and hips little wider than a boy's. I could feel no lust for her; only pity. She was vulnerable, and she'd been used. As had I.

By Miss Minesse.

Why? Pure mischief? Hardly; there was nothing mischievous about Miss Minesse. She had to have a plan. And the plan must involve the series of strange events and seeming coincidences leading up to the moment Wayne opened the bedroom door.

And at last I began to get a glimmering of the truth.

I was right—and I was wrong. Unsmiling, Miss Minesse watched me approach the bar counter. She pushed an open book toward me. The page was blank except where she'd written today's date in the left-hand margin.

"You forgot to sign the register," she said.

The pages were thick, ruled with faint blue lines, the book ancient and leather-bound. I turned back to the previous page. Guests were few and far between. The previous visitor had stayed here on 26 April 1990.

Tom Tregothnan.

And again on 14 December 1987. And so on, back through the years. Tom Tregothnan, the only guest. I raised my eyes to Miss Minesse's icy gray ones.

"You reel him in from time to time, and he doesn't even know it's happening. You play him like a fish."

"It's no game," she said.

I turned back another page, knowing what I would find. And there they were, the familiar signatures:

15 October 1973   J.E. Tregothnan
                         Tom Tregothnan
                         Angharad Tregothnan
                         W.D. Leconte.

I flipped the few pages back to the beginning. Mostly solitary Tregothnans, punctuated at regular intervals by small groups each including a Leconte. The first guest in the book was Albert T. Tregothnan in 1846.

But now I knew there had been other books before that, and scrolls before the books. And before that, tablets. There

was an endpaper in ornate, swirling colors with a panel
holding copperplate script.

> *The Moving Finger Inn. Your hostess,*
> *Morgan Faye Minesse.*

"One of my more whimsical moments," she said. "Malory
had recently made the name famous and I rather cared for it.
His facts were grossly inaccurate, though. That's what happens with legends."

I held her gaze for a moment, and it seemed I'd always
known her. "I do crossword puzzles, too," I said. "So now
we're all assembled for your charade. Does anyone ever forget their lines . . . or improvise, perhaps?"

"Never."

I felt curiously calm. Dad must have felt calm, too, as he
faced this same woman twenty years ago, fresh from
Angharad Tregothnan's bed and knowing he could do nothing to alter destiny. But he would have tried, and I was going to try.

"But you will try," she added.

Then I snapped back into the present and the urgency took
hold of me. Wayne was on his way to see Tom at the riverbank, and murder would be committed. I must try to stop it.
What idiots human beings are! I ran from the bar out into
the misty twilight.

A light drizzle was falling as it always had done, that evening. I caught sight, dimly, of people hurrying about the village in some urgency, calling to each other with faint and
echoing cries. The road ahead was indistinct, mist-shrouded.
I ran, like Dad had run before me, hoping to break the endless cycle of events.

The cries of the villagers faded behind. I heard only my
running feet and rasping breath. Then, gradually, I became
aware of the sounds of battle. The yells of the warriors, the
screams of the injured, the whinnying of frightened horses
and the ringing clash of metal on metal. I reached the bridge,
gasping for breath, pushed through the undergrowth to the
grassy bank of the river Camel and hurried upstream. The
battle raged all around me.

I saw little of it; just faint figures in the mist, swinging
swords with desperate energy, horses thrashing on the
ground in their death throes, all the ghosts that have haunted

this reach of the Camel for centuries, possibly millennia. For Arthur was not the first father to be killed by his son at this place. Lancelot and Guinevere were not the only adulterers. They were just convenient legends, like Morgan le Fay. There were more ancient evils at work here. More primal battles.

I found Tom Tregothnan lying on his side, curled up in pain at the edge of the water. His eyes flickered open as I knelt beside him. The bone handle of a knife protruded from the left side of his stomach.

"Ridiculous thing," he whispered. "Wayne came running up with some stupid yarn, trying to make trouble, I suppose. It was just once too often, and I hit him. Then things . . . got out of hand."

"It happens." I watched the blood seeping from around the knife hilt. "Nobody's fault."

"I know." He clutched my hand. A horse loomed up through the mist, dragging a screaming warrior with his foot twisted in the stirrup. Tom gave no sign of having seen or heard the apparition. And I knew, then, that the ghosts were for me alone; another charade directed by Morgan le Fay. It was necessary for me to know everything, just as it was necessary for Tom to know nothing. "I have to get something off my chest, Jack," Tom was saying. "I . . . killed my dad, did you know? I caught your dad in bed with my mom. I was young. I went squealing to Dad, and he wouldn't believe it. We . . . fought. That's why I reacted like I did when Wayne came along with his pack of lies. A story like that can cause trouble. You're the only person I've ever told." He tried to grin but succeeded only in grimacing. "Same place, too. Hell of a coincidence, eh?"

The sons had killed the fathers down through time, but the fathers had never told the sons. How could they? You can't admit to your son: I killed your grandfather. You have to cover it up, but you can never get it out of your system. It changes you, just like Tom changed after that evening in 1973. Just like Wayne would change after tonight.

And I would change, too, like Dad did. And like Dad, I would keep quiet, because if people knew what Molly and I had done, it would destroy the respect I'd earned from Shirley and Charlie and our nice little community. As Molly had said with more truth than she knew, I was a real-life Sir bloody Lancelot. And Molly would go to Amesbury and do charity work.

In the end it would get too much for me, and I'd crawl off somewhere and hide like Dad did, knowing that Charlie would have to go through all this one day after I was dead. Maybe I'd leave some little clue like a photo, to try to warn him. But I couldn't tell him. And it wouldn't make any difference if I did; Morgan le Fay would simply make minor adjustments to her scenario.

"Jack, do something for me, will you?" Tom said. His voice was very weak. "Get rid of this knife. It's our fishing knife and the police will link it to Wayne. No point in that."

I looked at the handle. "I'm scared to pull it out. I'd better go and call an ambulance." It's funny how we get comfort from talking like rational human beings.

Again he tried to grin. "Bit late for an ambulance. Just pull the bloody thing out and leave me here. Find Wayne and drive him around for a while. Maybe take him to a pub somewhere and get him calmed down. Explain there's no need for him to take the rap. Then go back to the Finger; Miss Minesse will help with an alibi. She did as much for me, twenty years ago. . . ."

"You've got it all worked out."

"A knife in the gut sharpens the brain. And try to act normally in front of Molly until it's reasonable to send out a search party. She need never know the truth. . . ." His hand tightened over mine. "Wayne was lying, eh? You and Molly never . . . Did you?"

"Of course not."

"I never thought you did, not for a moment. Hell, Jack, you're the finest man I know. So go on now. Pull out this knife."

The sounds of war had faded by the time I found Wayne. The mist had cleared and the stars were out. Arthur's last battle at Camlann had been refought, and the river was once more the old Camel. I wondered if it would be running red, come daylight. Wayne lay on the bank, staring at the sky. I stood over him, looking down.

"I stuck a knife in Dad," he said. He was crying. "I don't know how it happened." He saw the knife in my hand and his eyes widened. "You pulled it out. Is he okay?"

"I'm sorry. He's dead, Wayne."

He covered his face. "What . . . what are we going to do?"

I led him by the hand to the bridge, and sat him down below the parapet, out of sight of any passing cars. Then I walked back to the village slowly, like a man out for a stroll. My van was back where I'd left it, opposite the pub. All the boxes of Dad's stuff had gone. So it's happened, through the generations. My family has never been able to build up any kind of history. Somehow the documents always get lost; theft, fire, shipwreck, whatever. Maybe I should tell Charlie to deposit my records with the British Museum. But he'd want to know why, and so would the British Museum.

I drove Wayne around like Tom had asked, and after a couple of hours and a few drinks he stopped shaking. We talked about fathers and sons, and the most ancient battle between them, and the way we've been able to civilize ourselves out of it for the most part. And the way that animals haven't been so able, and the way there's a bit of animal in us all. We never mentioned Arthur and Mordred, or all the others. We were just trying to rationalize one single dispute that got out of hand, that evening.

At one point—I think it was after his third pint—he gave me a nasty look that reminded me very much of the young Tom and said, "You were screwing my mother. I can't forgive that. Just one bleat out of you and I'll make sure the whole of bloody Bristol knows." The mists of Camlann were just a couple hours past, yet we were back on solid ground.

"I understand," I said.

"Charlie's worth a dozen of you." He was starting to sound like the churlish Wayne of old. Then he fell silent for a while, and by the time he spoke again he'd been doing some deep thinking. "It's about time I got my act together. I'm going to have to look after Mom quite a lot, for a while. This is going to hit her hard." He glanced at his watch, a huge waterproof thing. "I must get back to the Finger."

"If you're ready for it."

He stared at me, and for the first time he looked like an adult. "I can handle Mom. And the police. We don't need you, it would only complicate things. Much better if you'd never been at Slaughter Bridge, if you know what I mean. I'll square Mom. You'd better drive straight home after you've dropped me off."

Yes, he'd square Molly. And I'd have to square Shirley, and get her to lie about my phone call, if the police asked her if I was at Slaughter Bridge on the evening of Tom's death. Which would mean our marriage would never be quite the same again. It was a big price to pay, but I had no option.

Wayne and I performed one last ceremony before I returned him to the Moving Finger. We drove to Dozmary Pool on Bodmin Moor and I threw the knife as far as I could, out into the moonlit water. There was a splash and widening silver ripples, that was all. No arm clad in white samite rose to catch the knife. As Morgan le Fay said, Malory's facts were inaccurate. He'd probably invented the arm for dramatic effect.

BLOOD GHOST
by John Helfers

John Helfers is a recent graduate of the University of Wisconsin-Green Bay and works as a free-lance editorial consultant. This is his first published short story.

"Stop kid!" The man's voice behind me caused me to brake without thinking. The old car stopped in front of the intersection just before a tractor trailer went roaring through.

Sitting back from where I had been thrown against the steering wheel, my body concentrated very hard on just breathing for a while. Then the realization of where that voice had come from hit me. I slowly looked at my rearview mirror. The reflection showed the cavernous back seat of the Cadillac, empty. Then the voice spoke again.

"Turn around, kid."

I had just bought this car and driven it away from the very pretty female owner not more than five minutes ago.

Alone.

Slowly, I turned around. Resting very comfortably on my back seat was a lean man in a dark gray tailored suit. His hair was styled, and his neatly folded hands were manicured, fairly recently, too. His gaze fell upon me as I examined him and I looked up. He could have passed for anybody's favorite uncle except for his eyes, empty black voids that made my stomach lurch and my gaze drop. He saw me look away and smiled.

"Oh, sorry." He took a pair of designer sunglasses out of his inside jacket pocket and put them on, "Haven't gotten used to that yet."

"Get out of my car." I said. It was amazing how calm my voice sounded, especially after the two shocks I had suffered.

The man smiled again, a normal looking smile that chilled my spine, "I'd like to, kid, but I can't. Watch."

He leaned over and reached for the door handle. A puff of blue-gray mist rolled off his arm as his hand pushed right through the car door. He pulled his hand back and looked at me again, shrugging his shoulders.

I snorted and reached over, careful not to come anywhere near him, "Please, let me help you." The rear driver's side door swung open, letting a shaft of sunlight enter the car.

He smiled again, "All right, here goes, but it won't help." He moved over to the open door and tried to move past it, my eyes on him all the while. As soon as his hand got past the boundaries of the car, it started to fade into that white mist again. This time, however, he jerked it back with a grunt, "Shit, that hurts."

I would have stared at him for the rest of my life if the car behind mine hadn't blared its horn. Turning around and checking the intersection, I started driving again, not saying a word.

"In case you haven't figured it out by now, kid, I'm a ghost."

At that moment, it was the only thing that made sense, "And you're stuck in my car?"

"Well, apparently it's still *my* car just as much as it is yours, isn't it?"

I looked in the rearview mirror again. He still wasn't there. That was really annoying. Then I remembered the woman who sold me the car saying something about how her father always drove Cadillacs. I took a guess, "Wait a minute. You mean you're Mr. Capestan?"

"Yes, I am. Or at least I was. Do you think Jan would have driven a car like this? No, she goes for those foreign jobs, the ones with a back shelf instead of a seat and a hundred miles to the gallon. This beauty and I go way back."

I smiled as I thought of my internal wince at seeing the Nissan parked next to the Caddy. "So, how long are you going to be here?"

"I don't know," he said, wafting through the back of the seat and sitting next to me. The car swerved violently as I fought not to lose control at seeing this. Mr. Capestan shook his head, "Jesus, what are you trying to do, kill me twice? If I wasn't already dead, you would have given me a heart attack that time."

"Wait, wait, wait, just hold on here." I pulled the car off the street into a grocery store parking lot, driving around to the side of the building. Killing the engine, I turned to face him, "All right, I'm a rational guy. And what I see is, for lack of a better term, an entity in my front seat who won't or can't leave, for whatever reason. Let's just say, for whatever other reason, you do exist, and I am talking to a ghost, or apparition, or whatever the hell you are, and not hallucinating from too much time on the Net. Does this mean you'll be here forever?"

He chuckled, a sound I thought should have been a little more humorous and less ominous, "Of course not, kid, I—"

"And stop calling me kid. I'm twenty-five." Now that he hadn't disappeared into mist or revealed himself to be one of my dopey college friends playing a trick on me, I wanted to regain some control of the conversation.

"Sorry. Well, as I was saying, I chose you. My daughter, Jan, whom you've met, held the car until I could signal her as to whom to sell it to. That person is you."

I dreaded the next question, "Why me?"

"Because you can see and hear me," he said with what sounded suspiciously like a sigh of annoyance.

"How did you know I was the one?" I asked, although the answer was becoming painfully obvious.

"Because when I touched you, you noticed," he said.

I thought back to the test drive before buying the car. Jan had insisted on coming with, not that it bothered me. About halfway through the trip, I had felt an unbelievable chill settle on my shoulder and neck, causing me to start suddenly. Then, as quickly as it had come, the sensation was gone. Jan had noticed and asked if anything was wrong. I had shaken my head and passed it off, saying something about the air-conditioning. She watched me with a strange expression on her face the rest of the way back to her house.

"So you were the 'feeling' I got in the car," I said. He nodded.

I held up a finger, "So what? Whatever you need me for, you can just tell Jan to do. After all, you told her who to sell the car to, right?"

He smiled again, "I knew I found a sharp one. Good idea, ki—it's a good idea, but it doesn't work that way. The way I figure it, the only reason I could tell Jan what to do with the car was because of the strong ties both her and I had to it, with her growing up with it, and me owning it. Kind of a triangle-relationship, understand?"

I nodded, then interrupted as anther question struck me, "Sure, but if that's true, where do I fit in?"

"I don't know, I'm just as new to this as you are. Maybe it was your love for the car. Maybe you're just different. Maybe you're crazy, I don't know. But you're the one."

"Insanity would be a welcome break right now," I said.

"Anyway, what I need you for, I can't tell her. All I was able to do was give her a feeling about you, that you were the one to sell my baby to." His hand caressed the leather of the front seat, or would have, if his fingers hadn't melted through the top of it. "Christ, that's enough to piss a man off. Twenty-nine years I drove this car, kept it in perfect condition, cherry, you understand? Now I can't even touch it."

I looked at him, "But how are you able to sit there?"

His shoulders rolled in what I assumed was a shrug, "I don't know. I saw an old movie where the hero, who was a ghost, was held up here by a locket he gave his wife before he died. Maybe that's what the car is, a, what-do-you-call it . . . ?"

"A focus?" I supplied.

He nodded, "Sounds good. Anyway, I have to take care of something for Jan, but, as you saw, I'm stuck in here."

"And you need me for that, right?"

He smiled again, "You got it."

"And I suppose you're going to sit here forever until I do, right?" I asked.

"What choice do I have? I'm not going anywhere," he said.

"What if I sell the car?" I said.

"I'll find another . . . associate. Of course, if you want to pass up the chance to make a little money . . ." his voice trailed off meaningfully.

"How much?" I asked.

"A good piece of half a million," he said.

I gulped. Was he kidding? Another look at his face dispelled that thought. Even though my job made life comfortable, there was always room for improvement. I thought of what could be done with the kind of money he was talking about. Finish paying off my college loans—and my parents, for that matter. Take a very well-earned vacation. Quit my job and look for something with a future, more than factory work at least. Get the hell out of this city, even. But something in the way he said it made me wonder. . . .

"What do you want?" I asked.

He said nothing for a long time, but just leaned back into the seat (which was odd because the seat didn't move, even though he did). When he spoke, his voice was quiet, almost wistful.

"First off, you gotta understand . . ." He looked at me hard, and then laughed quietly, long and low, "Jesus, where are my manners? Jack Capestan. You'll forgive me if I don't shake hands.

I smiled again. "Alec Ryerson."

"Anyway, Alec, you gotta understand that I wasn't a very nice man in my life. I was a Family man, you understand that?"

I had seen enough movies to know exactly what he meant. I nodded.

"Well, I did well enough, but I was careful to keep Jan out of it. Back then, there was honor in the Family, not like today, but that's beside the point. What matters is, I was pulling a job when I got double-crossed and whacked by my partner. He hid the money—of course I know where, the bastard used my own car to drop it off—then got himself busted for a speeding ticket that turned into 25-to-life up at Rikers Island. Charlie always was an asshole. Anyway, I want to provide for my daughter, and that's where you come in."

"So, all I have to do is get the money, give it to her, and your soul is at eternal peace, huh?"

"Something like that."

"What's my cut?" I asked.

"You watch too many movies. Your *share* is ten percent."

I shook my head, "Not good enough. Twenty-five."

His jaw dropped. "I don't think I quite heard you. This money is dropping into your lap and you have the nerve to ask for more?"

I nodded, "Look, call it negotiation, call it compensation for scaring the hell out of me a few minutes ago, call it whatever you want. The fact is, I've got you. If I keep the car, you're screwed, and Jan never sees the money. Of course, I got to put up with you for however long I own it, but I think that's manageable. Now, I'm sure we can come to an amicable agreement, aren't you?"

He stared at me so long and silently that I started to wonder if I had pushed him too far. Then I realized, what could he do to me? As far as he was concerned, I was holding all the cards, so to speak.

"Fifteen."

"Twenty."

"Done."

"All right. Now, where do you want to go?"

He shook his head and smiled. "Maybe you should have worked for us. You want to go to the Square Street Gym."

I drove the car out of the parking lot and plotted the fastest way there, then suddenly had a thought, "What if he's had the money moved?"

That sibilant laugh came from his mouth again, "No way. I know Charlie too well. He doesn't trust anybody. Until a few months ago, I thought I was different. Shit happens. Anyway, there's no way he'd move the money. Poor bastard thinks he's going to make parole one of these years."

I shivered at his implication.

Square Street was in a part of town that was slowly going to seed, although it wore it well. The gym was a three-story brick building that smelled like sweat from across the street. I turned to him, "Now what?"

"Now, you go inside and talk to the manager. Tell him you're getting a package for the Breezer that's in the locker room. He'll give you shit, but don't take it, tell him only you can get that package. New runners come and go all the time, it won't matter. The locker is number 653, the combination is 52-6-42. Got that?"

"Package for Breezer, 653, 52-6-42." I repeated.

"Attaboy, you'll do fine. Now get going."

I left the car and walked over to the cracked double doors. A dark staircase led upward, along with the strong smell of seat and leather. Climbing to the top, I entered the gym.

Everybody, whether they were sparring in the boxing ring, working out, or just shooting the shit, turned and looked at me, then went back to their business.

There was a fat man sitting behind a window set in the wall. I walked over to him. After several seconds, he looked at me again. "Yeah?"

"I need to get a package for the Breezer," I said.

"What locker, I'll get it for ya," he said, starting to walk toward another door. He hadn't been sitting.

"No." He stopped, then turned around. "Breezer said only I could get it."

He snickered. "Look, kid, quit fuckin' with me, I ain't in the mood. Everybody knows that no one goes to the locker room but members, that's the rules."

I smiled and said, "Well, you'll just have to change the rules."

His face grew hard faster than I thought possible. "Get the fuck outta here, kid, before I have a couple of the boys throw you out the window."

"Wait a minute, I'm not looking for trouble." My brow furrowed in thought. "How much is a membership?"

He thought for a minute, taking considerably longer than me. "Fifty bucks a month." I checked my wallet and found what was left of my last paycheck there, sixty dollars. I sighed and forked the money over.

The fat man smiled. "Right this way, son."

A few minutes later, I was looking at the kind of money you usually only see in the movies. Picking up one of the top bundles of bills, I noticed brown stains dotting it. I put it back and carefully closed the lid. Then something Capestan said came back to me. Double-crossed and whacked by his partner . . . what if he was going to try the same thing? I sat down and thought it over, then dismissed the idea. Why? What could he possibly accomplish by killing me? And how would he get the money to Jan if the courier, me, was dead? I shook my head at my suspicions.

Then another idea came to me. What if I pulled the same scam on him? This money could set me up for years, and what could he do? Jack shit, that's what. But I shook my head again, realizing exactly what I was thinking. Even though Capestan was a dead mobster, he was still a mobster. If I could see him, then maybe someone else could. Maybe one of his Mob buddies. That would be bad, very bad. Besides, Jan was waiting for this back at her house. Maybe she would be grateful. *Very* grateful . . .

Seconds later, the heavy suitcase was in my hand and I was trotting down the stairs and out the door. I crossed the street and threw the suitcase in the trunk and myself in the front seat. He was still there.

"How'd it go?"

"Fine."

"That's good. Now we can go to Jan's and then your part of this will be almost over."

"Fine," I said, beginning to realize that I didn't have the stomach for Mob life.

The long drive to Jan's house passed in silence. Finally I pulled the car back into the driveway where I had purchased it, seemingly only an hour ago. That was before I believed in ghosts.

I got out and walked to the front door, the suitcase a reassuring weight under my hand. Ringing the doorbell, I was greeted by the pretty young woman who had taken my check that morning.

"Can I help you? Is something wrong with the car?"

"Not in the way you think," I replied. "May I come in?"

"You look very pale. Would you like something to drink?" she asked, backing up and motioning me inside.

A cup of coffee later, I was sitting at her kitchen table, telling her the story, which ended with the suitcase beside me. Hefting it up on the table, I watched her open it and riffle through the bills inside. Curiously, she was examining the same stack I had grabbed earlier, the one with the brown stains on it.

"I can't believe he did it. Finally, his soul will be at peace."

"Great, well, I'll just take my share and leave." I started to get up, but was overcome with a wave of weariness, causing me to collapse into the chair.

"I'm afraid your part in this is not over yet, Alec. When I said his soul would be at peace, I meant in your body. The money was never important, it was this," she said, pointing to the brown stains on the portrait of Benjamin Franklin. "His blood."

A creeping numbness was spreading from the pit of my stomach into my limbs.

"Poisoned . . ."

"Oh, no, my dear Alec, that would kill you. I need you alive for the transfer."

My last memory was of her looking up at the doorway. With effort, I raised my head before it locked in position. A shadowy form stood there.

"Hello, Father."

* * *

So now here I am, stuck. Once the "transfer" was complete, I learned a lot of interesting things about the Capestan family. I had all the time in the world to watch them. I also learned some of the tricks Jack pulled on me to fool me into taking that job. The turning into mist bit, among others. I look forward to using them on him, soon.

Well, I was right about one thing. Jan was grateful, all right. At least, that's what she kept telling me during the ceremony. Funny, all the feeling was gone in my body, but not pain. . . .

What really irritates me is seeing my body being used like this, while I'm trapped outside, in the void. But someday, somehow, I'll get it back. That's just one more interesting thing about ghosts. One doesn't always need a focus to come back to the world of the living.

Revenge works just as well.

BLACK WATER
by Diana L. Paxson

Diana L. Paxson's novels include her *Chronicles of Westria* series, and her more recent *Woden's Children* series. Her short fiction can be found in the anthologies *Ancient Enchantresses*, *Grails: Quests of the Dawn*, and *The Book of Kings*.

Light and shadow play on the water . . . surface and depths shifting in swift alternation as the willow leaves stir in the wind. . . . I know that this is the fishpond at Gra'mere's house in Metairie, but I don't remember it being so big. I see myself staring into it, the red-haired, freckled child I was then, with a doll clutched in one grubby hand, watched by the grown-up Brigit, who wears linen suits and understands the stock market.

Shapes swirl upward from the deeps and I lean forward to see. Drowned shadows change places with surface reflections. Skeletal limbs waver with the current; a skull-face splits in a malevolent grin. I recoil and see my own childish features. The water boils and they become those of a woman old with experience, a black silk shawl drifts over creamed-coffee skin and garments of purple shot with shadow.

The doll slips from my hands. I grab, but she is sinking already, shattering the image. The shadow surges upward. Something cold and slippery grips my ankle; screaming, I cling to the willow tree.

"Let go—" Even the words are liquid. "There is peace in the depths . . . come to me. . . ."

But the terror of that clammy grip convulses me, and struggling, I try to break free. . . .

I fought for breath, clutching at the hand that was choking me while consciousness flailed up through the black pool.

My eyes were open, but it was still dark. Nearby, someone was whimpering.

"Hank—" I pried his hand from my throat and struggled to my knees. In the dim light I could see him twitching. "Hank, wake up!" I shook his shoulder.

"Wha—?" He stilled, shuddering.

"You had a nightmare," I sat back, feeling my own pulse slow. Despite the air-conditioning I was sweating.

"Hurts . . ." he muttered thickly, and then. "Dammit, leave me alone!"

I bit back the first words that came to mind—I'd been too long learning to hold my temper. Hank had never yet had the privilege of hearing me in a real Irish rage. This time control might have been a mistake, though, because it left room for fear. Last Sunday I had found him lying on the sofa in front of the TV, twitching with open eyes, but he was not watching the ball game. He stirred when I called him, and said the game had half-bored him to death and he was fine, but he went off again twice more into that waking doze before we went to bed. Was this part of the same thing?

Shivering, I padded into the black-and-white-tiled kitchen. The clock showed dawn near. I made coffee and sat down, cradling the warmth of it between my hands as I waited for the day.

Hank and I had shared the apartment in the Marigny quarter of New Orleans for almost a year, and I still found it hard to believe he was mine. Maybe it was because his family had always had money, but he took the world as he found it. Even his job in the import agency didn't seem to weight him down. When my Irish blood set me to weeping, Hank could always make me laugh.

By the time the clock radio in the bedroom blared, I had almost convinced myself it was my own nightmares troubling me. I heard Hank groan, but he had never been a morning person, any more than me. Ashamed of my night thoughts, I made coffee and carried the cup into the room.

The pitiless illumination of early morning showed me his face, still closed against the world. But not in sleep. He lay too tense, lines graven around his mouth, hands clutching the sheet beneath his chin. And I could see, too, how his brown hair lay lank across the pillow, and the scabs where he had cut himself shaving dark against the pallor of his skin.

"Hank, here's coffee—"

He curled deeper into the comforter, but the smell of fresh French Market coffee would wake the dead. After a moment his eyes opened, dull as river mud, and he pushed himself upright.

"*Bien*—put it there—" He gestured with languid grace toward the chair.

I blinked. He was a Vickery, but it had been a long time since people larded their conversation with French phrases to prove their breeding. It was my mother, just one generation away from being poor white trash, who had pushed me to learn French and sent me to Sacred Heart. So far as I knew, Hank hadn't even studied the language at school. I watched him take his first sip.

"Last night you had a nightmare, nearly throttled me," I said. "Do you remember?"

Hank shrugged and drank more coffee. Sunlight glanced from the window, sketching the image of a skeleton in a top hat across the floor.

"Hon, you don't look good. You sure you're okay?"

"Of course I'm okay!" It was his own voice this time, rough with irritation. He was rubbing the back of his neck as if it pained him.

"Well, you don't look it," I repeated. "Maybe you should see a doctor."

"Had a checkup last month, don't you remember?" he snarled. "Will you get off my back?"

I frowned. Something about that phrase—abruptly I remembered old Marie, who had mostly raised me, talking to our cook about Baron Samedi who ruled the graveyard, and "hants" that rode the back of a person's neck. It was ridiculous, of course, said the part of me that had studied Business Administration at LSU. But colored folks and Irish have a lot in common when it comes to superstitions. If Hank wasn't sick—and he'd shown no signs of being crazy before—there was something in me that believed the old tales of ghosts that fed on the living might be true.

"Well, you don't sound like yourself, and that's for sure!" I said slowly. He looked up at me and I recoiled, seeing another man gazing out of his eyes.

I glared back at him. *Get out of there, whoever you are! Hank Vickery belongs to me!* I was certain of that much, but I knew I couldn't beat whatever was after him alone.

* * *

Madame Angeline's front steps were faintly pink in the glaring sunshine. When I looked closely, I saw grains of coarse red grit between the boards. I had heard that red brick dust preserved the wood. Perhaps some folks, scrubbing down their front steps with a brick because their neighbors did it, even believed that. But old Marie had told me that red dust was a hoodoo protection, and I thought maybe I'd come to the right place.

If so, it was purely by chance. Going to work I had to detour around some road construction on Frenchmen Street and I saw the sign above a door. "Mme. Angeline DeLaure, Psychic, Readings." What Marie would have called a "two headed woman," or at least I hoped so. I had stopped at the next convenience store and phoned, then called in sick to work.

I lifted my hand to knock.

"Ms. Halley? Come in—" The door swung inward.

The front room was filled with potted plants, whose leaves fluttered gently in the breeze from a mahogany and brass ceiling fan. I sat at a varnished table covered with a lace cloth, and Madame Angeline brought tea. An old carpet lay across linoleum that was almost as worn, but scrupulously clean. Nestled among the hanging ferns was a bracket with a picture of Mary Star of the Sea and candles and a cut glass bowl of clear water that glimmered in the morning light. I don't know what I had expected—but it was not this middle-aged, tan-skinned woman in a blue housedress with a white lace scarf covering her hair, in this shabby-genteel room.

I felt myself flushing. I had rarely met anyone so completely at peace with herself, a daughter of those free women of color who had become a caste of their own. Madame Angeline probably had more ancestors among the founding families of New Orleans than I did.

Madame set down her cup. "You're not here for a reading, you said?"

"I'm here—because I think my boyfriend has—" I swallowed, "—a 'hant'!"

She looked at me and laughed. "A black woman raised you, *vrai*. And you only know her words. You sure your man's not just crazy? You tell me what's happened and maybe I can give you a word for it a white girl won't be ashamed to use."

I was doubly embarrassed now. Psychic or not, she could certainly see through me. As well as I could, I described what had happened, and felt the sick feeling come back as Madame began to frown.

"Where'd you say you're living?" she asked when I was done.

"On Dauphine Street, in the Marigny. The property has belonged to Hank's family for years. It used to be warehouses, but they pulled them down and put up apartments. Do you think there's something wrong with the building? It was only remodeled a few years ago."

"Maybe," she sighed. "But we try the simple things first. Take salt—sprinkle it all over, but especially where he sleeps. Put some on your own head and neck and cover it with a white scarf. And when your man gets home, you want to sprinkle that salt on his head and neck too and spin him around wrong ways—counterclockwise—three times. Do it while you're kissing, make him think you're glad to see him."

"My kisses aren't *that* hot! He'll catch on," I said ruefully. "What do I tell him?"

"If he feels the difference—" she said slowly, "he will feel better, and forgive you for being silly. If not—it depends what's riding him. But you be careful. If he gets nasty, you get out of there. Think ahead, make sure there's someplace you can go. And call me. Either way, I want to know."

That night would have been funny, if I weren't so scared. I spent the rest of my day off cleaning the house. It was a lovely place, with everything modern, but high ceilings and tall, shuttered windows that gave it a hint of traditional Creole grace. Madame had given me some black salt to use in the cleansing that looked like spilled pepper on the blond wood floor. I cooked seafood gumbo with shrimp and crab, chicken, hot sausage, tomato, and spices the way Hank liked it best and set the table with a white cloth and candles. I told myself that all the fixings might distract Hank from the hoodoo, but the truth is, when I'm nervous I cook.

It seemed to work, anyway. When I put the salt on him, Hank thought I'd gone out of my mind, but I could see he did feel better, and after he calmed down he laughed, and he ate up the gumbo with more appetite than he'd shown in weeks. By the time we went to bed, I had almost convinced myself there had never been anything wrong with him at all.

This is night. The moon is rising, and I find myself walking along the River, the way it looked a century ago. Warehouses crowd together below the levee, but in the gaps between them there are houses, shacks mostly, with shingles half off and tangles of garden around the back and sides. But the house beside the willow tree is well kept, and though the back seems wild, the front path has been neatly swept. There is a light in the window.

It looks so welcoming in that darkness, I find myself moving toward it. The door opens to my touch and then I'm inside.

"Bien, Mam'zelle, you have come—"

I blink, trying to make sense of the riot of shape and color around me—draped cloths and carved screens, chests and tables and shelves all crammed with images, candles, bottles, bones . . . The man who stands in the midst of them is dressed in black, so old his black skin has dulled to a dark gray. A real gris-gris man . . . Panic flickers in my belly and I turn to go, but I can't find the door.

"What do you want?" My unease grows at his answering smile.

"I want what's mine. Don't interfere!"

"I don't understand."

"I had a home in the Big Island—what you call Hayti. I was a man of power. An' any man with power makes enemies. They could not kill—not me—but they capture me, send me here as a slave. Moi! *Isambard Didon, the greatest* bokor *in Hayti! But my master do not own my power, and soon enough I'm free. They do not let me buy land, but the Blanc never asked for rent. He do not dare—I know his secrets, and so this place is mine."*

"Then keep it!" I exclaim. "What does that have to do with me!"

"You tryin' to keep me out, cher. *I don't like that. You stop—you let me take what's mine!" He moved closer, and I smelled raw earth and something ranker, like old bones.*

"Let me go—" I whisper. "I never did you harm!"

"Remember—" His laughter scrapes my nerves. In the flickering lamplight a top-hatted shadow stretches tall be-

hind him, reaching with skeletal hands. I edge away, and suddenly a door is before me. Frantic, I thrust through it. The river is at my feet; I fall, and the foul waters close over me.

I woke, soaked in sweat and gasping. It took me a few moments to realize I wasn't drowning. On the other side of the bed Hank lay still, his breathing quiet and slow. Had my nightmare been silent or was he too deeply asleep to hear? Shaking, I went to take a shower. When I came back to the bedroom, moonlight was slanting through the window. Looking at it, I realized why the house in my dream had seemed so familiar. The moon was rising at just the same angle above the old willow tree as it did here.

Shivering despite the heat of the night, I crawled in beside Hank. In the two weeks since the salt episode, our relationship had been better than ever. He gave a sleepy grunt and reached for me, and I clung to him until dawn, drawing comfort from his solid warmth and trying to forget my dream.

Thank goodness it was Saturday. As soon as it was light, I pulled on some old jeans and went into the little back garden. Working with plants is even better than cooking for settling the nerves. Hank and I managed the building, and it was our job to keep up the garden. Hank hadn't worked out there for a week or two, when he dug out the nicotiana bush, and neither had I. The weeds that seemed to manifest the minute a spot was left untended were already high. I dug and yanked until I had most of the jungle cleared, including the space where the old nicotiana had died. The empty spot looked lonely, and I thought I'd plant the poinsettia I'd been keeping going in a pot since last Christmas.

The ground was still soft from yesterday's rain, and it was no trouble to drive the spade deep into the soil. Suddenly the metal struck something hard. Not a stone, I thought, wiggling the handle—nothing but river mud here so close to the canal. A brick, maybe, from some building now gone. Whatever it was, it didn't belong in my flower bed. More carefully, I probed, and lifted earth away from the object until I could get the trowel under it.

It was a round unglazed earthenware pot, about the size of a skull, discolored around the neck as if something had once been tied there and stoppered with some unidentifiable substance grown rock-hard with time. And it was heavy—too heavy for its size—which was odd, since I could hear something dry and light rattling around inside.

I'd thought to toss it in the trash, but now I wondered. If the pot was as old as it looked, some museum might want it. I carried it to the back porch and looked around for something to wipe it with. My palms were tingling; I set the pot down and rubbed them against my jeans, wondering which of the weeds I'd pulled was causing the reaction.

I could feel a headache coming on. Leaving the pot, I climbed the stairs to our flat. Hank was still in his maroon bathrobe, scrambling eggs to go with the sausages that were already spitting in the pan. They smelled odd. He turned as I came in, solid and familiar. But he, too, seemed strange.

"Brigit—you all right, sweetheart? You look like you've seen a ghost."

"What do you mean?" I glared at him. "While you slept, I have been working!"

"Well, then, you must be hungry. Eggs'll be ready in just a shake—" He poured them into the frying pan. I shuddered at the scent and turned away.

"I do not want them!" The tingling from my hands was spreading and the denim jeans felt unpleasant against my skin. I went into the bedroom and stripped them off, looking around for something else to wear. I pulled a black turtleneck from the drawer and a pair of slacks from the laundry hamper. They were stained, but they were dark, and soft. I felt sick to my stomach, and I was shivering.

When I came back into the kitchen, Hank looked at my long sleeves and raised one eyebrow.

"Aren't you hot, coming' in from that sun?" He frowned as I shook my head. "Have some breakfast! Maybe some coffee?"

That, at least, sounded good to me. I spooned in extra sugar and waved away the cream. Sunlight was coming through the kitchen window as it always did in the morning, gleaming on tile and chrome. It sent pain stabbing through my throbbing head and I looked away.

"There's a new group playing down at Snug Harbor—" Hank said agreeably. "Want to go?"

I shook my head once more. I didn't want to listen to jazz. I wanted—what? I tried to think, and knew only that I had to stay here.

Diana L. Paxson

Hank rested his hand on my shoulder and I struck it away. "All right." He was still trying to keep it light. "You tell me what's goin' on or I'll salt you down like you did me!"

In the past two weeks that had become a joke between us. I still didn't know if Hank believed he had been haunted. I had been glad to laugh with him, not sure myself what I believed. But now I could feel the color draining from my face.

"*Cochon!* You would not dare—" I eased out of the chair. Panic raised goose-bumps on my skin. I had to get downstairs.

But Hank was between me and the door. As I tried to ease by, he grabbed me. I fought with a strength that surprised me. I think it surprised Hank, as well, but he had been a quarterback at LSU. In another moment he had one arm clamped around me and was reaching for the salt shaker, laughing.

I heard myself swearing in French and some other language I did not recognize. A rage darker than Irish temper uncoiled within me. He would see, this *blanc* who had stolen—

And at that moment the top of the salt shaker came off and fine grains poured down over my head and neck and rattled across the floor.

I screamed, feeling awareness divide. I was myself, Brigit, and I was someone else who was struggling for possession of my body and soul. Once, barefoot, I had stepped on a snail. Again I felt that revulsion, but this time the spreading horror was within.

"Oh, God, Hank, help me!" I clung to him and saw the laughter leave his eyes.

"I'll call Emergency—"

"No!" That Other who was within me tried to close my throat, but I forced out the words. "Madame Angeline . . . card . . . in my purse! Call her!"

An alien energy surged through me as Hank let me go. I got halfway across the room before he knocked me down. Before I could get up, he'd pulled the cord from his robe and was tying my wrists to the newel post.

"Brigit baby, if I'm wrong you can hate me later—" he eyed me uneasily. "And if this woman sounds like a flake, I'm calling an ambulance after all."

"But of course!" I spat, tugging at the cord. "Let him look

at me, the *medecin blanc*. He will find me in health, I assure
you, and then where will you be?"

"Where will *you* be? That's not Brigit talking!" Hank began to dial.

The effort to be Brigit again shot pain through my head
and I moaned. I could hear Hank talking. Then he set down
the phone with a look on his face I'd never seen before.

"Are you crazy, or am I?" he muttered. He was already
pulling on shorts and a polo shirt and finding his shoes.
Then he took his trenchcoat from the closet and began to
button it around me, over my bound hands. "Good thing we
don't have any neighbors next door."

Hank laid me on the back seat of his Toyota, where I
swore and fought, sometimes against him, and sometimes
against the being who was trying to steal my body, all the
way across town.

"Get those clothes off her—"

I whimpered as Hank carried me into Madame Angeline's
bathroom. My struggles had exhausted me, or perhaps the
thing that had attacked me could not follow so far. But the
headache had become an agony that filled the world. I hurt
too much to protest as Hank stripped and lowered me into
the bathtub, but the water was warm, and gradually it began
to soothe my pain.

A long time later I realized that I was myself again. For
a moment, feeling the water, I thought I was back in my
dream. But this water smelled fragrant. I recognized the
gritty texture of undissolved salt beneath me and bits of herb
floating to either side. Gradually I became aware of the hiss
of a rattle. It had been going on for some time.

Madame Angeline stood at the foot of the tub, shaking a
gourd covered with a net of blue and white beads. Her hair
was still done up in a white kerchief, but she was dressed all
in white now, and around her neck she was wearing ropes of
colored beads. She looked down at me through narrowed
eyes, her gaze as dispassionate as a surgeon's. I thought
vaguely, *Doctors wear white, too. . . .*

"Brigit, Brigit, do you hear me?"

I made some kind of sound, and her expression softened.

"That's good, child. You've got yourself in a lot of trouble. Let's get you out of that water and maybe you can tell
me. . . ."

* * *

"You're sure that's all?" Madame frowned as Hank finished summarizing our morning.

They had wrapped me in a white sheet and set me down in the middle of a circle drawn with cornmeal in the plant-filled front room. My head still hurt, but it was a residual soreness, not that hammering agony. The agony now was of another kind. What had happened to me had been not a rape but a seduction, so insidious that I hadn't even known the moment when that alien mind had overwhelmed my own. The bath had washed his foulness away, but the sense of violation remained.

"What about before she came in?" The priestess turned to me. "What were you doing in the garden, *petite,* to get you this way?"

"Just weeding—" I said slowly, thinking back to moist earth and sunlight, the mockingbird singing in the willow tree. I heard in memory the spade ring against earthenware. "Until I found the pot. It looked old, maybe valuable, so I brought it in."

Madame Angeline's gaze grew intent as I described my find. "A *pot-de-tete,*" she said softly. "Yes, it might be, in that part of town."

Hank pushed the hair back from his brow. "What do you mean?"

"In the old days, the people of power—the root doctors and voodoo queens—they had to be careful." She smiled a little grimly, as if things were not all that different today. "Some, like Marie LaVeau, had fine houses in the center of town and made their ceremonies outside the city at Bayou St. John. But others lived on the outskirts, by the wharves, wherever there was a little unclaimed land. Everyone knew they were there, but so long as the authorities didn't have their noses rubbed in it, you understand, they let them be."

An image of a house by a willow tree flickered suddenly into memory, and then a face, its features distorted in malevolent glee.

"Isambard . . ." I whispered. "I dreamed of him— Isambard Didon."

"Not so great a *bokor* as he thought," said Madame Angeline when I had finished telling her about my dream. "His name has not been remembered. But he was good enough so the part of his spirit he put into that pot, what in Haiti they call the *gros-bon-ange,* survived."

"Is that usual?" asked Hank uneasily.

The priestess answered with an ambiguous smile. "Not so much here, where the traditions we follow are part voodoo, partly from the *Santeria* of Cuba, and partly pure New Orleans Creole, but in Haiti, yes. When a devotee dies, the pot is broken and the soul goes to rest beneath the waters of Guinée, which is Africa of the spirit, you understand—the origin, the first home. The soul of a Mother or Father of the Spirits is treated with especial care. And a *bokor,* a sorcerer—" she shook her head. "He is the hardest to dismiss. Such souls are right to fear no one will call them back to become *loa,* so they don't want to go."

"That's what was making me feel so sick? And what got Brigit?" Hank asked. A little muscle was still jumping in his jaw like it does when he's upset, but, really, he was handling all of this very well. Better, in some ways, than me. I'd been so smug, so sure I could handle anything in this world or the next. Had my success in dislodging the "hant" from Hank somehow made it easier for the thing to get at me?

"Then I guess we don't want to give the pot to a museum, do we?" he said dryly. Madame responded with a tight smile.

"It must be broken, as it should have been a hundred years ago. M'sieu Isambard must pass beneath the waters to Guinée."

I twitched, remembering how the waters had tried to drown me in my dream. Was death calling me, too, or was it just the *bokor* who was trying to drag me down?

"Can you do it?" Hank asked directly.

"I know what to do, yes. But with you two there is already a connection. I think it was your ancestor, Mr. Vickery, that gave the *bokor* that land. I think you should be there as well."

Hank looked at me and I shuddered, wanting nothing so much as to forget this had ever happened. But I was still bruised in my soul.

"Yes," I whispered. "We'll help. I won't be able to sleep until I see—until I feel that bastard go!"

As Madame went down the hall to find me something dry to drive home in, a door swung open and I saw a room, bright with colors, statues, and candles, and glittering sequined banners on the walls. *Altars* . . . I thought in confusion, *like the ones* he *had in my dream.* But I was sure Madame Angeline meant only good to me. She was a voodoo priestess; of course she would work with such things. So what was the difference, if not in the images and names?

Drawn to them despite my fear, I looked in. The largest of the altars had been set up on what looked like an old sideboard, draped in blue satin and silver lace. In the place of honor was a three-foot statue of the same Star of the Sea whose picture was in the front room, a lovely lady with long dark hair and white gown, rising from the waves of the sea. A blue candle in a tall votive glass burned before her. Pearls were wreathed around her pedestal, and from her neck hung crystal beads.

That was not so different from a church altar, and I remembered suddenly the comfort I had found in gazing at the image of the Virgin Mary as a child. But the decorations surrounding this Lady were more colorful. Seashells, a plate with shell-shaped chocolates, a sequined bottle with the word "Yemaya." There was a large porcelain tureen, a vase of blue glass in the shape of a fish, filled with white flowers. On the top shelf was another image, of a mermaid with a divided tail.

As I looked at the altar, I felt my apprehension ease. Here were only grace and beauty; in the Sea-Mother's waters there was nothing I need fear. I heard a step behind me and jumped back, suddenly afraid I had intruded. But Madame Angeline smiled.

"Yemaya is my mother. But—" she looked at me critically, "I don't think she is yours. Still, she loves all children. You call on her and she'll take care of you."

"And what about the *bokor?* Who did *he* serve?"

"At a guess, Baron Samedi, who lives in the cemetery, though there are others of the Petro line to whom he might turn."

"A death-god?" I shuddered, thinking of the skull-shape of the pot I had found.

"You might say so," she answered, "but you must not think that death is always an evil. Papa Ghede is the life that comes from death—he is sex, he is a glutton, and he is a clown. And then there is his female side, Maman Brigitte, who is a great lady, and watches over the graves. The evil this *bokor* has done is not to serve death, but to cling to life when he should go on."

I nodded, and turned to take the loose shift she had found for me to wear. But as the priestess closed the door to her altar room behind me, I wondered which of the powers who were honored within might be interested in claiming a red-headed Irish girl.

When we got back to the flat, Madame refused to let me go in until she and Hank had gone in with a new broom and some salt and other things and cleaned out the place once more. She had brought along another box, and more salt inside which to bury the *pot-de-tete,* but she made me go into the house before she brought it out again.

"I can protect myself," she told me, "but I don't want you anywhere near that thing, *petite,* until we're ready to get rid of it."

I thought that Hank might hang back from that final ceremony. But when it came time to go, I was the one who was looking for excuses, and only the lingering soreness at the back of my neck kept me from pretending it was all some bad dream.

Clouds had begun moving in at sunset, and by eleven thirty, when we were to meet Madame Angeline at the cemetery, the sky was covered, the air like a black velvet coverlet that smothered with its warmth. The white clothes she had told us to wear glimmered ghostlike in the gloom. That made me feel a little safer; if I had worn anything dark, the night would have swallowed me, and the way I felt, it wouldn't take much to sweep me away.

The cemetery was an old one across the lake in the next parish. Ancient cypresses watched over it—gaunt, moss-draped arms spread against the sky. By the iron gate a white shape glowed. For a moment that made my skin prickle, then I realized I was seeing by the light of a candle set into the ground with an opened bottle of rum beside it. It was not Madame Angeline, but another woman, younger and darker. Without speaking, she waved to us to follow her.

The pallid beam of Hank's flashlight picked out lichen-speckled tombs built above ground to protect them from flooding, and cracked headstones set up later, after they had built the levees; weather-stained angels leaned at drunken angles, pyramids and cupolas loomed suddenly to either

side. We wound our way across the graveyard until the murmur of the river grew louder than the sighing of the wind in
the trees.

Black waters . . . I thought, *waiting to take me . . .* But my
feet carried me forward. I had dug up that damned pot—I
could not run from my responsibility.

At the far end of the cemetery the priestess was waiting
beside a weeping willow tree. The stones of the wall had
tumbled down and I could see the dark gleam of the river
beyond them. More candles, black ones, flickered above a
newly-cleared patch of earth where a design of a cross on a
pedestal had been drawn in brick dust mixed with herbs,
within a circle of the same. Beside her was a covered basket
and a bulky package, still swathed in white cloth.

"Good, you are on time." Madame Angeline's face had
the same focused serenity as when she was shaking her rattle
over me. "Tie these cords around your arms." She handed
two lengths of braided red silk to Hank. "The pressure will
keep you in your bodies. Sit on these mats, not on the
ground."

We settled ourselves, and I tied my white headscarf more
securely. The priestess bowed her head and began to murmur
prayers in a Latin which even Catholics no longer used.
Then, abruptly, she switched to English.

"Legba, Ellegua, open the way for us, open the roads we
travel who are still living, and the road where we send this
soul. Papa Ghede, you give life, you give death, you have
the power of magic, so let this work have your blessing—"
She lifted a bottle of gin to her lips, took a mouthful, and
then sprayed it out in a fine mist over the design on the
ground. "This is all for you, Papa," she set the bottle down
and lifted the napkin that covered a wicker picnic plate full
of some chicken dish so spicy it made my eyes water from
three feet away.

"And you, too, Maman," she added, opening a bottle of
chocolate liqueur and placing it beside the gin, then adding
a dark chocolate petit-four on a lace doily. Ghede's consort
was clearly a lady of refined tastes. "We'll all be sleeping at
your feet someday, Maman. Make a welcome for the one
we're sending now, eh?"

Madame Angeline sat back on her heels and took a deep
breath. She was already perspiring.

"Mr. Vickery, the one called Isambard Didon lived on

your ancestor's land, now yours. In a sense you are his heir. So I ask you to unwrap this box and set what it contains upon the *vevers*." She indicated the design on the ground.

Hank had gone rather grim around the mouth, but he obeyed. I guessed she had warned him about this earlier in the day. I loved the man, but I wouldn't have thought he had it in him. But that no longer surprised me, I had been wrong about a lot of other things today.

And then the *pot-de-tete* was sitting on the *vevers,* and I was too busy resisting the waves of need that radiated off of it to think of anything else at all.

"Hold on to her," said the priestess softly as I gasped. "It is because he had her before that she feels it."

"Isambard Didon!" she said in a commanding tone, taking a round stone from the basket. "Listen to me. You are dead—*mort*—you must leave this world behind and go beneath the sea. It's peaceful down there with the ancestors, you'll find rest and healing. Go down to Guinée, Isambard, go into the water and leave the living in peace. Ghede, he's yours, you take him now!" She reeled off a rush of syllables I did not understand and struck down.

The smash as the pot shattered was lost in a wail of outrage and anguish. I cried out and covered my ears, but it made no difference, and I knew I was hearing with the senses within. Even Madame Angeline flinched, and the younger priestess supported her, but Hank only looked confused.

Then the wail became words. *"I will not go! They betrayed me, the blancs! I served them—I made the gris-gris, the secret charms they required. And when the Yellow Sickness came, they grew frightened and burned me in my home. But my soul was safe underground, and so I have waited, I have waited too long for my revenge!"*

The priestess snatched up her rattle and began to shake it furiously, calling Ghede's name.

"I will take this man," came the reply. *"I had him before, and I know his soul. Did you bring him here because you are a fool, or to prevent me from taking you? He knows nothing, but that does not matter. His body is strong, and his family has power. I will use him to destroy them, and there is nothing you can do. I have read much in his memory. They will not believe a black woman or this white trash girl!"*

The hatred that pulsed from the circle seared my wounded

soul, but it was the threat to Hank that cramped my gut with
fear. I lurched to my knees, trying to get between him and
the *bokor.*

"Ghede, take him! Maman, take him!" Madame Angeline
was on her feet, shaking the rattle furiously. The rhythm
hissed in my ears, and then I was twitching in time to it.
Dizzied, I fell against Hank, but almost instantly pulled myself upright. Some inner convulsion jerked my head to one
side and my body twisted. The priestess was rattling, and
Hank was shouting my name.

"Brigit, Brigit—" but what I heard was *Brigitte!* Every
muscle spasmed as a shudder rolled from head to heels. My
scarf and the red cord on my arm went flying, and in that
moment, between the lightning flash and the thunder, I understood that it was not the *mort* who had me in his grip, but
something else entirely.

A power too immense for my comprehension was trying
to squeeze into my finite soul. Words battered at my awareness. *"Let me in, daughter, and do not be afraid. We will
deal with this pig, but you must let me in!"*

What defenses I still had clenched in revulsion. The *bokor*
had taken me like a trickle of water oozing through a gap in
a wall. This was a dark wave that would sweep the whole
structure away.

*"Do not be afraid. In order to possess, you must be
possessed—do you understand?"*

"What's happening—is the ghost trying to get her again?"
Hank's voice seemed to come from far away.

"Not him, no—it's the *loa* knocking on her head. But
she's not initiated!"

Then the two priestesses were beside me, splashing me
with water, blowing in my ear. For a moment the shock
brought me back to myself, and I stared at them.

"Come on, now, Maman," cried Madame, shaking me.
"You get out of there. This girl's not your head, you leave
her alone!"

Hank cried out and clapped his hands to his head. Fear for
him clenched in my belly and once more the power of the
loa rolled through me. *"You let me in, or that* bokor's *going
to take your man!"* came the voice in my head, and with a
sudden sense of release like the moment when your body
takes over in the act of love, I gave in.

And then there were no more words. My head jerked vi-

olently, a force not my own lifted me to my feet and a cry
scraped my throat, harsh as a raven's call. I knew everything
I was doing, knew at the same time that it was not me, not
Brigit Halley, who was sweeping the two priestesses aside.
I felt my face changing, flesh tight over ancient bones. I re-
membered . . .

*. . . the cool embrace of earth, the weight of stone, the
sweet silence of sepulchers—all those who lie in this graveyard, I know. Memory ranges farther, to the airless heat at
the heart of a pyramid, and a secret chamber beneath the
Temple of Isis where a dark-veiled image reigned in that
time when Ghede was called Khensu. The white man calls a
name and memory ripples; I see a green land studded with
mounds that cover chambered tombs, with triple spirals
graven into their stones. I have received all the generations
of humankind.*

*I remember all the subtle stages of disintegration, until
nothing is left but the holy and eternal bones. . . .*

*Through this body whose actions Brigit Halley is now
only observing, Memory rises like the River in flood time,
and I laugh.*

The priestess is still babbling, trying to make me go away.

"You stop that! You have need of me!" I say. "I take this
girl for a little while, or you have that *malin* taking bodies
all the time! I'm here now, *cherie*—let me help you!"

"Aché, Maman—" *the priestess whispers, bowing her
head in defeat.*

*The other woman pulls a black silk shawl from the basket
and offers it to me. I drape it around me, savoring the unfamiliar luxury of silk against skin, then turn to the circle.*

*Above the shards of the broken pot the shape of a man is
hovering, his form brightening and fading with the fluctua-
tions of his will. A tendril of substance reaches toward the
barrier; I flick the corner of my shawl in its direction and it
recoils. This one was handsome once, but the form that
floats before me now is emaciated and gray.*

"Isambard Didon, your time is finished," *I tell the one
who snarls in the midst of the circle.* "Still yourself! I am
beyond your cursing. You desire to take flesh once more—I
understand, but this thing, it cannot be. Until you
have passed through the waters of Guinée, never will you return
to the living world. In this place those waters run close be-

neath the surface. Sink down, Isambard. Sink down and be at peace."

I extend my arms and the ghost recoils. As I bring them down, his form folds in upon itself until it is a swirl of mist that even the man Hank can see. The bokor's *curses fade until they are no more than the whimper of a whipped dog. But I compel him into the earth and below it, beyond it, until the waters of the Abyss rise up to sweep him away.*

It is very still. I take a deep breath of the moist air, weighted with all the rich scents of the living world.

"He is gone. Aché, Maman," *whispers the priestess.* "Thank you."

"Make his grave here. Bury the shards of his pot and what it contained, and make a pile of stones over it. He will not return."

"Maman, this horse is not used to carrying so great a rider—" *the priestess says carefully then, and I laugh. I have heard this before.*

"She is weak, but she will grow stronger. Tell her so. Tell her she must make a feast for me, and I will go."

The priestesses come toward me. The younger is carrying a jug of water. Indeed it is time to go. As I release my hold on the body, it sways.

"Go now, Maman. Au'voir. It is time for you to go home," *the woman whispers, shaking her rattle over my head, and my eyelids close and I sink down into the depths once more.*

I gasped as cold water poured over my head. "Hank!" I sputtered, "what in hell—"

Then I got my eyes open and realized that I was not in our bedroom. Hank was holding me all right, but the guttering candles on the ground only intensified the darkness around us. I saw Madame Angeline, her face strained and tired, but smiling, and began to remember . . . the *bokor,* and the *loa,* and power. . . .

There had been so much—images flickered, dimming, as the great tide that had filled me drained away. Suddenly I was weeping against his shoulder.

"Brigit, honey," Hank patted my hair with clumsy tenderness. "It's over. Nothing will hurt you now." He turned to Madame Angeline in appeal.

"Don't fear," came her voice behind me. "This is normal,

the emptied vessel mourning what it has lost. But she is too open. She must come to me, get the proper initiations."

"We'll talk about that later." Hank focused on me again. "Brigit, it's okay. I've got you safe, and I love you."

"Yes. I know." I hugged him tight, filled once more by my own humanity, and the waters of Guinée ebbed away.

STAR QUALITY
by Marc Bilgrey

Marc Bilgrey's writing credits include a situation comedy pilot for CBS TV, MAD magazine, Marvel Comics, and material for comedians. He's just completed a novel.

Todd Wilson felt his palms get moist, as he stood in front of Herbert J. Samuels, the most successful movie producer in the history of the medium. Samuels and his young female assistant were seated at a long table in an otherwise empty rehearsal hall. Todd held a page of the script he'd been asked to read. Cold. He was only slightly less nervous than he'd been when a wild raccoon had crawled into his sleeping bag on a camping trip when he was nine years old.

"I like him," said Samuels, in a loud voice, as he turned to his assistant, who was seated to his immediate left.

"He likes you," she said to Todd, who wondered why Samuels needed an interpreter.

"I want him back here in two days and then I'll make my final decision," said Samuels.

"He wants you back in forty-eight hours," said the assistant, "it's between you and one other actor for the part."

"What's the other actor's name?" asked Todd.

The assistant consulted her list, then replied, "Jack Graham. Okay, we'll see you in two days."

Todd thanked them and left the room. He did not mention that Jack Graham was his roommate. As Todd started walking back to his West 56th Street apartment, he wondered what the odds were, that, of all the thousands of actors in New York, he'd be up for the same part, (which, if he got it, would be the most important role of his life), against his roommate. Probably greater than winning the lottery *and* hitting the jackpot in Atlantic City all in the same day.

* * *

"We've got to talk this thing over," said Todd. It was an hour later. He was sitting in the living room of his fifteenth floor apartment, looking at Jack Graham. It was Jack's day off from waiting tables at Swan's, a midtown deli. Todd was between temp jobs.

"What is there to talk over?" said Jack, sipping a glass of grape juice. "We both go in on Friday, try to do the best reading we can, and whoever they pick gets the job."

"You don't seem to understand, Jack," said Todd, "I *have* to get that part, it'd be the biggest break of my career."

"Mine, too."

Todd didn't like the way the conversation was going. True, he thought, they had both grown up in the same small town in Ohio, and had both come to New York ten years earlier to become actors, and yes, they had both worked hard at a succession of dead-end jobs waiting for this very moment. But still, decided Todd, *I* deserve it more.

"Perhaps some cash would make you see things differently," said Todd, taking out his wallet.

"You're kidding," said Jack, as he got up and looked out the window.

"Okay," said Todd, as he pocketed his wallet and stood up, "how about women? You've always had a thing for Kathleen. You stay home on Friday and she's yours."

"I can't believe this," said Jack, turning around, "you're offering me your girlfriend in exchange for this part?"

"I'll even throw in some naked pictures I took of her."

The smile vanished from Jack's face. "You're serious, Todd, aren't you?"

"Damn right, I am," said Todd.

"Look, this whole conversation is ridiculous. First of all, Kathleen is not some object that you can give away as if you own her, she's a human being."

"Don't be so technical."

"And second, I'm going to be there on Friday and that's the end of it. Now, if you'll excuse me, I'm going to start on dinner."

Todd watched Jack walk to the kitchen and decided that the time for talk had passed. He had to kill his roommate. The only remaining question was how.

"I'm going out for a walk," said Todd, as he headed to the door.

"Maybe when you get back, you'll have a little more sense," said Jack.

"Maybe," said Todd, as he stepped out into the hallway and walked to the elevator.

When Todd reached Broadway (a block away), he wondered if he should shoot Jack. The only thing stopping him was the fact that he did not own a gun. He was one of those few New Yorkers that didn't. A dwindling, yet nervous minority. By the time he'd walked to Fifth Avenue he'd decided on a knife. He had plenty of those. The only problem was, he didn't like the sight of blood. By the time he got to Lexington Avenue, he'd decided that poison was the way to go. After all, he reasoned, it was painless, and quick. The tricky part would be trying to figure out how to get Jack's body out of the house. What would the neighbors think? Todd considered the fact that it would be difficult to have a believable alibi when fifty thousand people saw you carrying your roommate's corpse down the street and dropping it in the corner garbage can.

On First Avenue, Todd discarded the idea of doing the dirty deed in his apartment, but had not come up with a viable alternative. Then he reached Sutton Place Park. It was there, while staring down into the murky waters of the East River, that the idea came to him. It was neat, he thought, and simple, and had very few moving parts.

Two hours later, Todd sat on a bench in the deserted park, a newly purchased baseball cap pulled low over his face. He glanced at his watch, then saw Jack Graham walking toward him.

"What's going on?" said Jack. "I got here as quickly as I could. Is it really true what you said on the phone about Steve Kane?"

"Would I lie to you?" said Todd, with the most innocent expression his nine and a half years of acting lessons could conjure up. "In about an hour, Steve Kane, the hottest director in the business is due to start setting up right here in this park to shoot a scene for his latest film, *The Killer Cop*."

Jack looked around at the empty park. "Now tell me again how you know all this. You were a little vague on the phone."

"I was not vague," said Todd, as he walked to the railing

that overlooked the river, "I know a guy who knows a guy who knows the second A.D. on the picture."

"I wouldn't want to intrude," said Jack, as he went to the railing and looked down at the water, a few stories beneath him. "I mean, a lot of directors don't like to have visitors on their set."

"Trust me," said Todd, "we're not intruding. The assistant director is tight with the guy I know."

"You mean the guy who knows the guy that you know."

"Right," said Todd, as he pulled a lead pipe out of his sleeve, and said, "what's that over there?"

"Where?" said Jack, looking off into the wilds of Queens.

Todd smacked the pipe across the back of Jack's head and watched him crumple to the ground. Todd looked around the empty park, to make sure he wasn't being observed, and then lifted Jack's limp body and dropped it over the railing. He watched it bounce off the jagged rocks of the seawall and fall into the water far below. It looked like a rag doll, moving in slow motion, thought Todd. He stood transfixed for a few seconds, then began running.

Instead of going straight back to his apartment, he zig-zagged down strange streets, walking half a block, then running, then walking again. All the while checking behind him, to make sure that he was not being followed. Two hours later, he finally went home.

The next day passed quickly, and then, it was Friday. The day he'd waited a lifetime for. Todd put on a new pair of pants, a fresh shirt and left for the rehearsal studio. When he got there, he was ushered into the same room he'd been in two days earlier. Herbert J. Samuels was seated behind the same table, talking with the same assistant he'd seen before. The only thing that had changed was the odds.

"Ah," said Samuels, "Mr. Wilson, please step forward."

Todd couldn't help noticing that this time he was being addressed directly and not through the assistant. "Yes, sir," said Todd.

"I've been informed that the other actor we are considering for the role has the same address as you, a Mr. Jack Graham."

Todd felt a chill shoot up his back. Had he been found out, he wondered. Were the cops waiting outside? Up to now, he'd managed to take his mind off the murder and focus only on the audition.

"Yes," said Todd, thinking quickly, "Jack had to leave town yesterday, said it was some kind of family emergency."

"Too bad," said Samuels, "I'd like to have gotten another look at him. Well, then, Todd, I guess you've got the part. Congratulations."

Todd shook Samuels' hand, and was then taken aside by the producer's assistant, who gave him a copy of the script and told him that the movie would start shooting in two months and that they would contact his agent the following week to work out the particulars. Then she congratulated him and walked him to the door.

On his way home, Todd picked up some takeout Japanese food, which he loved, but seldom got a chance to eat because of his limited budget. As he entered the lobby of his building, Todd decided that from now on, he wouldn't have to worry about money anymore. This film would make him a working actor, instead of a waiter, or a cab driver, or an office temp, or a thousand other nothing jobs he'd had. As for Jack, well, what was done was done.

It was exactly midnight when something woke Todd up. He sat up in bed and listened to the sound of a door opening in the other room. Was it Kathleen, he wondered? Then remembered that she'd gone to visit her mother in Connecticut for a few days. Todd got out of bed, and, dressed in only a T-shirt and a pair of boxer shorts, ventured into the living room. There, smiling, sitting on the couch was Jack Graham.

"Hi, Todd," said Jack, "what's new?"

"But, but," said Todd, as he felt his heart pounding, "you, you . . ."

"I'm dead, I believe, are the words you're looking for," said Jack calmly.

Cautiously, Todd inched over to Jack, trying to figure out if he was hallucinating, or seeing some kind of imposter.

"Stop tiptoeing like that," said Jack, "you look ridiculous. Yeah, I'm a ghost, what'd you think I was, my own twin brother? Don't forget, I was an only child."

Todd remembered, then decided that he didn't like the idea of talking ectoplasm one bit. "What do you want?" said Todd hesitantly.

"I want to say good-bye," said Jack.

"Oh," said Todd, slipping into a chair. "How is it that I can't see through you?"

"Beats me. I'm new at this. So," said Jack, as he stood up and walked to the window, "why'd you kill me?"

"I wanted the part."

"No kidding," said Jack, rubbing the back of his head. "You didn't have to be so rough."

"Sorry."

"Kind of hot in here, isn't it?" said Jack, as he opened the window as far as it would go. "Ah, that's better." He turned back to Todd. "You know, frankly, I was surprised. I mean, we grew up together and then you murder me just for a role in a movie."

"What can I tell you," said Todd, forcing a nervous smile, "I guess I'm just a little overambitious, that's all."

"Well," said Jack, "I'm not one to hold a grudge."

"That's nice to hear," said Todd.

"Yup, I'm just a kind-hearted ghost. I stopped by to let you know that I have no hard feelings." Jack held out his hand to Todd.

Todd, despite some misgivings, went over and shook it. As soon as he did, he regretted it. Jack's hand felt icy and his grip was strong and he would not release it.

"Hey," said Todd, "what's the idea?"

"The idea," said Jack, "is this." With that, he flung Todd out the open window. Todd sailed through the air and dropped like a rock onto the ground of the alley, fifteen floors below.

Todd saw his body lying in the shadows as he tried to figure out how he could be in two places at the same time. He pinched himself. He didn't feel any different and yet there was no arguing with what he saw in front of him.

"Hi, Todd," said a voice.

He turned and saw that it was Jack. "What happened?" asked Todd.

"You're dead, what do you think happened?" said Jack.

"You killed me!" said Todd.

"Well, you didn't think I'd let you get away with killing me, did you?"

"You know," said Todd, "I'm seeing a whole new side of you."

"What can I tell you? A guy's got to do what a guy's got to do."

"So what happens now?" asked Todd.

"Well," said Jack, as they walked out of the alley, onto the deserted sidewalk, "now comes the next thing."

"And what's that?"

"We move on."

"Heaven?" asked Todd, tentatively.

"You must be kidding. You think they let murderers like us into heaven?"

"I never really thought about it."

"Well, think about it. You killed me and then I killed you. That makes us both murderers."

That was when it dawned on Todd. He glanced at Jack and saw him nod.

"Yup," said Jack, "we're both going to hell."

"That's pretty lousy," said Todd.

"Yeah, but look at the bright side. We've lived in New York for ten years, it's got to be better than this."

"Good point," said Todd, as they crossed the street to Broadway.

"You know," said Jack, "I actually went to heaven for a few minutes, but when I told them about my plans to kill you, they sent me straight to hell."

"No kidding."

"Yeah," said Jack, "in fact, I was in hell a little while ago, just before I came to see you. They're going to be putting on a play down there."

"They have theater?" said Todd. "That's great."

"Yeah, they're doing *Hamlet* this week and I went out for the lead."

"Did you get it?"

"I don't know yet, I'm still waiting to hear."

"Are the auditions still open?"

"Well, yeah, but—"

"I'd make a great Hamlet," said Todd.

"You know," said Jack, as they continued down the street, "you're *really* starting to get on my nerves."

PREACHERMAN GETS THE BLUES
by Tina L. Jens

Tina L. Jens' short stories have appeared in *South from Midnight*, *The Secret Prophecies of Nostradamus*, and *Shock Rock 2*. She lives in Chicago, where she is active in many community events, including organizing weekly author readings at local restaurants.

*"I got the lonesome Blues, but I'm just too mean to cry.
Got the lonesome Blues, baby, but I'm just too mean to cry.
'Cause my man has gone, and I feel like I could die."*

—traditional

"Axman, I know it's a lousy guitar, but the contract says you play the first number on the house guitar—that's the way it's gotta be."

The musician looked fine in a silver silk shirt, black creased pants, and cowboy boots polished to a high shine. Sarah felt plain in her faded blue jeans and white T-shirt, but it was more suited to her work.

"Woman, you don't scare me with your spook stories. You're lucky to get us in here. Me an' the boys got a new album out and a deal goin' with Fender. We're not gonna drive off our audience opening on that piece of shit."

Axman turned his back on the club owner and wandered across the stage, blowing through a series of fancy riffs.

It was show-off stuff. Frustrated, Sarah ran a hand through her tangled blonde hair.

"You want to sacrifice a warm-up number, or a whole set?" Sarah asked his back. That turned the young musician around.

"You threatening me, girl?"

Sarah met his dark gaze. "I'm not the one you have to be afraid of," she said. She turned and walked away.

It was twenty minutes before opening time, but Sarah unlocked the door anyway. She didn't like to see anybody standing out in the rain—with good reason. She struggled to shove the massive oak slab into the corner. Warped by age and rain, she didn't need to prop it open. The regulars at the Lonesome Blues Pub started filing in, soggy and sloshing in their shoes.

Sarah turned up Muddy Waters on the stereo, to give Axman and the band a little privacy. Then she set the early patrons up with their first round of the night.

She stocked a full bar, but there wasn't much call for it. A north-side Chicago Blues club had two kinds of patrons. The young white professionals, in fancy suits and loud ties, chugged Miller Lite straight from the bottle. And the old black men, in black felt hats, each with a single gold tooth that flashed when they smiled, ordered snifters of Wild Turkey.

"Mom, it's raining again, really hard!"

Her daughter came bounding over to the waitress station and climbed up on a bar stool.

"Hey, Little Mustang!" The grizzled patron winked at her over his snifter.

"Hey, yourself, Old George!"

Old George let out a laugh that was equal parts wheeze and chuckle.

Sarah shook her head. "Sweetheart, put out the ashtrays will you?"

"'Kay, Mom."

Sarah smiled as her daughter grabbed the stacks of ashtrays and started distributing them to each table, stopping to greet the regulars.

At ten years old, Mustang's nose barely reached the rail of the bar when she stood up. Sarah had bought the club while she was pregnant. Unable to afford a sitter, she took the child to work with her. Mustang had grown up on the knees of the Blues greats: Buddy Guy, Koko Taylor, Son Seals, Junior Wells.

They'd played checkers with her between sets, sung her lullabies, even changed her diapers in an emergency. When the musicians weren't playing with Mustang, Jayhawk was. And if the baby started fussing in the middle of a set, all the band had to do was break into a rendition of Mustang Sally. It calmed her down and put her to sleep every time.

Sarah had named her daughter Suzy, but she doubted if even Suzy remembered that.

Sarah tried to ignore the booming thunder outside as she continued her prep work, quartering limes and dumping cherries and olives into the condiment box. She picked up a dingy bar rag and gave a halfhearted swipe at the wooden counter, taking comfort from the familiar bumps and grooves. She knew it was clean. She'd washed it thoroughly the night before.

She wandered over to Carl, who was collecting cover at the door. Carl was a senior at De Paul with the linebacker build that set the physical standards among bouncers. This was the second night he'd filled in for Joe, the regular guy.

"It's a wicked night, Miss Sarah."

"That it is, Carl." Nervously she scanned the black, billowing clouds.

"Doesn't seem to be affecting business, though," Carl said, handing her a stack of bills. Mustang joined them at the door.

As Sarah left to deposit the cash in the register, Mustang whispered to Carl, "Mom doesn't like storms, on account of Daddy."

Carl just said "Oh," not knowing what the little girl meant.

Sarah didn't talk about her dead boyfriend much. To her mind, Mustang was still too young to know the whole story.

Jerry had been a computer programmer for IBM, with a fondness, but little talent, for the Blues. Drunk on champagne after proposing, he'd dragged his electric guitar out in the rain to serenade her. Jerry was electrocuted when water seeped into the amplifier and blew several fuses. He'd been playing *Stormy Monday* when he died.

Sarah gave the drummer a nod, picked up the PA mike, and switched on the sound. "Welcome one and all, Blues fans, to the Lonesome Blues Pub. We're very lucky to have with us tonight a band all the way from Mississippi, with a new album, 'Backwater Blues Gonna Get You,' from Chess Two Studios. Give a big welcome to Sonny 'Axman' Williams and The Delta Backwater Blues Band. Come on! Give it up!" she urged the crowd.

The drummer tapped the countoff with his sticks, and the

bass, harmonica, and rhythm guitar jumped into the opening strains of *Long-Handled Shovel.*

A chill went down Sarah's spine. She had a bad feeling about the opening number. But felt hats were bobbing up and down in approval.

"That boy can blow a harp!" she overheard Old George tell his neighbor.

With a whiskey-and-menthol-aged voice, the drummer growled into the mike.

"It takes a long handled shovel to dig a six-foot hole.
Yeah. It takes a long handled shovel to dig a six-foot hole.
But it takes a long-legged woman to make me lose my soul."

Axman slithered through the crowd and climbed the seven steps at the front of the stage.

"And now, a man *so bad* he's scared of hisself. Give it up one time for The Axman!" the drummer encouraged the audience.

The guitarist nodded a cool acknowledgment to the applause. Sarah stepped to the end of the bar and stared at him. Axman winked at her. Feigning left, Axman reached right and picked up his Fender. Crisply plucking an augmented melody, The Axman closed his eyes, dropped his chin to his chest and soared off on a plaintive solo.

"Alright, Axman. You've dug your own grave," Sarah whispered.

The regulars got a firm grip on their glasses and started to mutter.

"The spook's not gonna be happy."

"Jayhawk'll teach 'im."

Sarah moved to fill drink orders.

Carl met her at the counter, handing her more cash. It was standing room only now. She acknowledged the money with a thin-lipped grimace. "Just hope you don't have to pass it all back out," she told the bouncer.

Carl walked back to the door with Mustang. "What'd she mean by that?"

"Mom's afraid Jayhawk's gonna get mad. Axman knew the house rules, *plus,* he was rude to Mom. Jayhawk don't like that."

Suddenly the lights flickered.

"What was that?" Carl looked around. The power

switches were all in a cabinet behind the bar to prevent mischief or accidents.

"That's just Jayhawk warming up," the girl said.

Carl wasn't as dumb as he looked, but he wasn't following the conversation. "Who's Jayhawk?"

Mustang gave him a look that said, *You're an imbecile.* "Jayhawk is the ghost in the guitar."

"There's a ghost in the guitar?" Carl knew he sounded stupid, but he had to ask.

"You've heard of Billy Jay Hawkins?" she asked in a voice that clearly indicated the answer should be Yes.

Carl shook his head No.

With a sigh that spoke volumes, she put her hands on her hips and explained. "Billy Jay Hawkins, *otherwise* known as Jayhawk, was only *the* best Blues guitar player in Chicago in the '70s. He was my dad's hero. And he played right here in this club—before Mom owned it.

"Anyway, everybody says his last night here was awesome! During the last set, the fire broke out. Everybody was rushin' to get out. He tripped over his mike cord and fell off the stage. Impaled himself on his guitar's whammy bar. Died right there at the foot of the steps."

She leaned between patrons to point out the exact spot.

Some of the suits standing near the door snickered.

Carl checked over his shoulder. "Where'd you hear that?"

"Old George and Ratman told me," Mustang said.

"Does your mom know you're going around telling stories like that?"

Mustang gave an indignant shake of her head. "Don't have to 'go round tellin' it,' everybody *else* knows the story."

"Seems like a gruesome souvenir. Why doesn't Miss Sarah just get rid of it?"

"Can't. When Mom bought the club, the guitar was sitting up on the stage. You can move it, but by the next night, it's always back at the same place."

On stage, Axman could tell the crowd was restless, but he knew his playing wasn't at fault.

"That felt so good, think I'll do another," he said, making sure the band caught the cue. He'd nail down the audience with the second half of the solo.

A shriek of feedback shot out of the bass player's amp.

Axman threw him a look that sent the musician scrambling to adjust the speaker controls.

Mustang crossed her arms and leaned against the door-post. "That boy sure is slow," she said.

Carl looked around nervously, to see if any of the patrons had heard. "Mustang, I don't think you ought to be calling the musicians 'boys'."

"Well, if he acts like an idiot . . ."

"And," he said more forcefully, "I don't think your mom would appreciate you walking around telling ghost stories—it could be bad for business."

"Stupid musicians are bad for business."

"Mustang! You better watch your mouth—" He felt a hand on his shoulder.

It was Ratman, reaching up to calm him down.

It was hard to tell how tall Ratman had been before arthritis crippled him up, but he didn't stand taller than five feet now, from the crown of his broken felt hat to the tip of his scuffed and worn snakeskin boots.

"Li'l Mustang," he rasped at the girl, "you been practicin'?"

"Yup!" she nodded proudly. "Got the 'G' down real good!"

"That's my girl. Run along now and help your ma, while I talk some sense inta this boy."

"Ratman, you're the best," Mustang said, giving him a quick kiss on the cheek. He returned the affection with a tobacco-stained grin.

He paused deliberately, until the young girl was well out of earshot. He stared at Carl, considering him mightily. Then he patted through his old coat's pockets. Ratman's eyes lit up. He pulled his harmonica halfway out of a pocket, shook his head, put it back, and continued searching. Finally, he found the ever present pack of Kools.

Carl sighed quietly.

The felt hats had a way of taking their time, moving extra slow, that was designed to drive a person half crazy. But it also made a guy relax. You had to, 'cause there was no rushing them.

When the Ratman was good and ready, he spoke.

"Got a match there, kid?"

Carl sighed again and checked his pockets. He pulled out a pack of matches and lit the old man's smoke.

* * *

Axman knew he had them now, there was no more rustling in the crowd, no one weaving through the audience on the way to the john. He smiled slickly, stepped back to widen his stance, fretted up an octave, and prepared to blow the audience away with the sweet, singing high notes that were his trademark.

Then his strings broke; B, G, and E, in quick succession.

Axman snarled an obscenity into the mike, and the band shut the song down. He stalked off the stage to a round of applause liberally laced with hooting and laughter.

The drummer leaned into the mike. "Don't go away, folks, there's lots mo' Blues ta come."

Sarah quickly fired up the stereo system, slapping in the closest tape at hand.

> *"I've got to keep movin', I've got to keep movin'.*
> *Blues fallin' down like hail. Got to keep movin'.*
> *'Cause there's a Hellhound on my trail."*

She shivered. Too many dark implications in the lyrics tonight. But she wouldn't turn off Robert Johnson, King of the Delta Blues. Some folks said the musician had gained his musical talents by making a pact with the Devil. If there were evil spirits out tonight, it made no sense to offend them by turning off his music.

Carl was too young and inexperienced to be superstitious.

"Speaker feedback, broken strings, flickering lights— those things happen at all clubs," Carl insisted. "You don't have to blame it on a ghost." He was having a hard time believing the stories Ratman was telling him.

"Course they do, son," Old George assured him. "Things like that happen all the time." He chuckled in a way that made Carl squirm.

"But it's the pattern of 'festations, that's what ya gotta watch for," Ratman told the boy.

All three men turned to look at the empty stage. At that moment, the bass player's mike stand toppled sideways into Axman's mike, which fell, dominolike, into the harp player's mike stand. The tangle of metal poles and wires finally fell off the stage onto the nearest table, sending customers scrambling.

"That happens all the time, too, son. I seen it myself, hundreds of times," Old George said.

Shit! Sarah thought. It had to be a table of suits and chicks. She hurried over to help right the table and bar stools, and massage shaky nerves.

"Mustang!" she yelled toward the bar, "get six Miller Lites and three glasses!" Chicks always wanted glasses. "And a bar rag!"

"This round's on the house, folks," she told them, as Mustang came up with the tray.

"Bet Mom'll even set ya up with a round of shots if you say pretty please," Mustang said in a stage whisper.

The hint brought a slurred rendition of "Pretty Please!" from the group. Sarah laughed, relieved. They were drunk and having a good time. The accident would be forgotten after another round of drinks. She took their order and headed for the bar.

Sarah set up the shots and gave Mustang the high sign to pick up the tray. She let Mustang handle the delivery. The girl was good with the customers.

And if it was illegal to let a minor serve alcohol—well, Chicago cops would look the other way, in return for a free beer once in a while. The cops knew it was tough for a woman and child to make their way in the world.

Only after the crisis was over did Sarah stop to chew out Jayhawk. She didn't go anywhere special to do it. He could hear her wherever she was in the bar. And the regulars were used to seeing her talk to the air.

"Jayhawk, I know you're pissed, but what say you don't kill the customers. If the club shuts down, that guitar of yours won't ever get played, now will it?"

It was time to see if she could negotiate with the other side in this conflict. Carrying a tray of drinks, she stopped at the band's table.

"You boys have a good sound. You *could* have a really good night here," she said meaningfully.

Axman was still surly. That was no surprise. He was young, talented, and cocky. It'd be years before he'd unplug his ears to a bit of advice.

"Get that spook of yours under control, woman!"

"He's not a pet," Sarah tried to explain. "Do one number on his guitar and he'll leave you alone. Some of the oldtimers even think it's lucky. When Lefty Dizz played here, he'd do a whole set on it. Said all his gigs after that were twice as good. Came back whenever he thought his luck was changing."

The guitar player slurped his drink loudly over Sarah's words.

"Suit yourself, Axman. But don't think three strings and a couple of mike stands are his limit."

"So, Jayhawk's pretty P.O.d tonight, huh?" Carl asked. A look of uncertainty had crept into his eyes.

"Hell, no, son!" Old George said, giving him a good-natured slap on the back. "Jayhawk's just teasin' now. Givin' the guy *time* to mend his ways. If the kid picks up the guitar next set, everything'll be all right."

"And if he doesn't?" A tremor had crept into Carl's voice.

"Well, then, we'll see what we does see," Old George said, nodding to himself.

"Why, I heard one time, Old Snake Eyes Thompson—they called him Snake Eyes cause he had a bad wanderin' eye, ya see. So's when ya looked at him, it 'peared he was lookin' in two different directions 'twonce," Ratman said, rubbing his gnarled hands together. "Anyways, he and his band was in here. They'd just made their second record, they was ac-tin' like big shots, wouldn't let anyone sit in with them, wouldn't play Jayhawk's guitar, hittin' on all the women—"

"Includin' Miss Sarah," Old George added.

"Jayhawk, he specially don't like that," Ratman ex-plained. "They 'as just making a general nuisance of 'emselves."

"That's 'bout right," Old George said.

The young bouncer was perfectly caught in the old men's double-barreled storytelling.

"Well, what happened?" Carl demanded.

"They 'as killed," Old George said, matter-of-fact.

"Oh, Jayhawk toyed with them first," Ratman said. "Mike stands fallin', speakers cuttin' in 'n out, every string on stage broke: bass, lead, rhythm guitars."

"And fiddle," Old George said.

"That's right," Ratman nodded, recalling. "The strings broke, even the spares in the cases."

"Yessir!" Old George agreed. "They went to put the

spares on and they was no good, comin' straight outta the packet."

"Jayhawk was flashin' lights, flippin' mikes off and on, even locked one of the fellas in the john. Then," Ratman dropped his voice to a whisper.

Carl and George leaned closer to hear the rest of the story. "Durin' the last set, old Jayhawk, he just up and quit. Din do nothin'. By that time, the musicians were so rattled, they couldn't hardly play a lick. They jus' kept waitin' for somethin' to go wrong."

"Never did," Old George said.

"No, sir," Ratman declared. "Not till they was on their way home."

"Then what happened?" Carl squeaked.

Ratman pulled out a cigarette and searched for a pack of matches. Impatient, Carl offered the man a light. His hand shook ever so slightly as he held the match.

"Why, they was killed," Ratman said finally. "Van hit a slippery patch, spun outta control, and ran into a ditch."

"That's it?" Carl asked. "They died in a car accident?"

"That wasn't what killed 'em," Old George said, shaking his head.

"No?"

"Nah," Ratman said. "Their 'quipment did it. The amps and speakers stacked in the rear of the van slid forward. Police found 'em with their skulls crushed. Old Snake Eyes' eyeballs had popped out. They was sittin' up there on the dash, pretty as you please, lookin' round."

Old George snorted.

"Jayhawk got those boys in the end," Ratman assured Carl.

" 'Course, them things do happen," Old George added.

Carl was feeling equal parts scared and foolish. But he didn't have time to give it much thought. The old men had already launched into their next story.

The bassist laid down a standard walking line. The drummer softly filled with his brushes on cymbal and snare. The harp blew a lonesome riff.

The band in sync, the drummer called Axman to the stage. "And now, ladies and gentlemen, won'tcha welcome back a man who learned to play guitar sittin' atop a tombstone in a

Louisiana graveyard at midnight—Mr. Sonny 'Axman' Williams."

"Thank you!" Axman said to the crowd, trying to hide just how thankful he was the audience hadn't cleared out after the first set.

"If ya'll been outside tonight, and we know ya have, than ya know what we're talking about when we say . . . we got 'The Wet Weather Blues.' "

Sarah gave her nerves up as a lost cause and poured herself a double shot of Southern Comfort, slugged it back and poured herself another.

Old George and Ratman hadn't had this much fun since they'd hid Sugar Blue's remote mike in the tank of the women's john.

"Sing it one time!" Axman called to the band.

"Well, it rained all morning, and then it rained all night.
Said, it rained all morning, then it rained all night.
When the wind started howlin', I like to blew away.
Oh, it scared me so awful, I kneeled down to pray."

In the corner of his eye, Carl saw a tall, stern-looking man stride through the door. The massive oak door slammed shut behind him.

Carl looked uncertainly between the door and the new patron. He moved to get the money from the man since he was already inside.

Ratman and Old George grabbed onto his elbows. Carl could have carried them across the whole bar, frail as they were, but he'd gotten in the habit of listening to what they said.

"Boy, don't you know *nothin'?*" Old George asked him.

"Ya don pass the collection plate to the Preacherman," Ratman said.

There was fear in the old men's eyes and voices. Carl decided anything they were scared of, scared him, too.

Ratman felt a tug at his sleeve. It was the little one. "Little Mustang, git behind your ma now, you hear?"

She nodded solemnly and slipped into the crowd.

The band played on.

Preacherman stood, framed by the oak door, a life-sized replica of the old-time, backwoods parson. Round-brimmed, black felt hat, black frock coat buttoned up the front with long black tails flapping behind.

Legs too long and eyes cold as hellfire, Preacherman didn't look all human. But he did look mean.

Preacherman stood, waiting for his presence to seep out in front of him, quietly tapping on a body's shoulder, table by table, whispering in your ear, saying, "Preacherman is here."

The crowd parted for the newcomer. Sarah got a good look at him through the corridor of bodies. The man was completely dry, despite the storm outside.

The stranger thumbed the brim of his hat at her. Sarah nodded stiffly. She didn't care much for the red glint in his eye. She moved to help Carl reopen the door.

Axman felt the change in the room. He cursed the ghost and kept on playing. He'd be damned if he was gonna let a spook steal his crowd.

He didn't know the danger that came in with that thought.

Sarah watched as Carl kicked a wedge under the door. No gust of wind had blown that old door shut.

She turned to find the black-clad stranger standing behind her. His face was deathly pale. Sarah took two steps back before nodding at the man.

His head bobbed and swayed reptilianlike. When he spoke, his voice sounded like the belly of a snake slithering over loose gravel. "I hear this club harbors a spirit."

His eyes flashed with accusation.

Axman's amp, a top of the line, Fender Twin Reverb, cut out for the third time as he led into the intro of "Hoochie Coochie Man." He considered slamming his book through the woofer, but that might scuff the polish. Instead, he slammed his guitar into its stand and jumped from the stage to the barroom floor.

With a silent apology to Muddy Waters, the drummer closed down the song.

Axman tried to brush past the stranger standing at the foot of the steps.

"Ahhhh, ssssson," Preacherman said, "perhaps it would be a convenient time for a guest to play a song or two?"

"Yeah, you can sit in with the band, if you want—if the damned spook will let you do anything," Axman growled, heading for the bar.

"I do not think he will bother me."

The crowd was quiet as the stranger climbed the steps. The drummer covered his mike and quizzed the guest.

"They call me the Preacherman," was all the man said.

"Mom, that man's gonna play Jayhawk," Mustang said, peeking over the bar.

Sarah decided she'd been too quick to judge the stranger. "Maybe things will quiet down a little."

Mustang slipped around the corner of the bar to nab an empty bar stool. "I don't think so," she said.

The Preacherman plucked a couple of chords, testing the action of the old guitar.

Preacherman rambled through a series of arpeggios. The house lights flickered and dimmed. Finally, the wandering intro led into a gritty rendition of Lightnin' Sam Hopkins' "Long Way From Home." As the Preacherman filled out the first verse, the silver tips of his boots began to glow a faint red.

Playing with one hand, the drummer mopped the sweat from his neck. The house lights had never kicked out so much heat. Preacherman's fingers flashed over the strings.

By the end of the number, white chicks were dancing in the aisle. The speakers hadn't cut out once. And the house guitar had never sounded so good.

Axman was happy. Somebody else had played the spook's guitar. Now he could go finish the set. Axman climbed the steps and motioned for the Preacherman to sit in for another number, guest's choice.

"How 'bout a little Robert Johnson ditty?" Preacherman hissed.

"Early this mornin' when you knocked upon my door."

Preacherman fancied up the riff and threw it to Axman. It was a standard variation. Axman had no problem echoing it. Adding a twist at the end he tossed it back. The second line was the same as the first. When the vocals had finished, Preacherman took another turn, then let the harp step in. The Preacherman's fingertips were glowing red.

Mustang was studying the indicator lights on the amplifier behind the bar. When she was an infant, Jayhawk had kept her amused for hours, making intricate patterns with the red lights. Tonight, despite the volume and tuner settings, only four of the eight rows of lights were lit.

Sarah had three taps running as she lined up a row of shot

glasses on a tray. She used her forearm to pop all three taps off just as the glasses were starting to overflow.

"Mom, Jayhawk doesn't—"

"Mustang, can't you see I'm busy?"

Little Mustang's eyes filled with tears as the fifth row of lights slowly faded out. She took a last look at her mom, then slid down from her bar stool and went looking for Old George and Ratman.

On stage a cymbal flared. And the band said, *"Hello, Satan, I believe it's time to go."*

The Preacherman had been showing off mightily. Axman decided it was time to show folks who was in charge of this show. The dueling guitars began. Strings flashed and speakers whined. The drummer muttered a little prayer to himself, but kept playing as he watched his spare sticks float past his head.

Ratman and Old George were in the back corner, deep in their snifters of whiskey, mumbling between themselves.

"Shoulda known the Preacherman would be out in a storm like this," Ratman worried. "Ain't seen him around these parts since Blindboy Richards died."

Now there 'as a man din wanna go," Old George said with a laugh.

"Watch what you say!" Ratman told him. "Lessun you feeling particularly lucky to be insultin' spirits tonight."

"That's not Jayhawk playin'," Mustang said suddenly, her nose peeking over the top of their table.

The old men jumped.

"Child, you just scared a year of life offen me. And I haven' got it to spare," Ratman said.

He looked at her and saw the fear leaking out of her eyes. "Climb up here where we can see you."

Mustang scrambled onto the bar stool beside him.

"You may bury my body down by the highway side."

The old oak door slammed shut. Again. Miss Sarah was busy at the bar. Carl fought to open it by himself this time. Despite his 250 pounds of muscles, he was having no luck.

Sarah tried for the third time to pour a shot of Jack for a customer. The shot glass kept floating away.

"Jayhawk, I've had 'bout enough of this shit," Sarah told the ghost.

The suit was getting more desperate for his drink. Sarah knew he needed it for courage. But courage to stay or courage to go, she didn't know. She took another look at his face and decided her resolve could use some stiffening too. She set two more shot glasses on the bar.

"Hold on to those," she told the suit.

The man clutched the glasses firmly.

She poured them both a double.

"That's on the house, friend."

"Baby, I don't care where you bury my body when I'm dead and gone."

"He's killing Jayhawk," Mustang told the old men.

Ratman and Old George nodded in agreement.

"Reckon so," Old George said.

"What are we gonna do?" Mustang prodded the conversation along.

Ratman took a long, slow look around the club.

"Ta start with," he said finally, "tell that fool ta come over here, 'for he hurts hisself." Ratman waved toward Carl, who was still fighting to open the door.

Mustang brought the bouncer back to the table.

Axman and the harmonica player teamed up against Preacherman. But they were still losing the duel, badly.

When the Preacherman grabbed the riff, Axman stepped back to talk to his drummer.

"It's not right, embarrassin' a man on stage—front of people!"

"Some men is like that," the drummer told him. "It's nothin' you won't live through."

"Gonna send the man back to the woods till he learns some club etiquette!"

"Steady, Axman."

The drummer shook his head, throwing sweat in both directions. "Can't cool a temper in heat like this," he growled to himself.

Axman stepped in front of the Preacherman. In an un-Blues-like manner, he borrowed a move from Pete Townsend and swung his arm wildly, windmill fashion, jamming out a trio of power chords.

Preacherman gave an evil grin, stepped around the young guitar player, and made a roundhouse swing of his own.

Suddenly, claws scratched across strings. And fire erupted

from the Preacherman's amp. The blast blew Axman clean off the stage.

"Believe it's time we did something 'bout that man," Ratman said to his conspirators.

"I could turn off the power," Carl offered. "The switches are behind the bar."

"Well, *do* it, son," Old George told him. Wheezing, the old man eased himself to the floor.

"Where do ya think you're going?" Ratman asked him.

"Thought I'd pull the plug at the wall," Old George said.

Ratman nodded. "Jus don't go gettin' yerself hurt."

Mustang turned to her friend. "What can I do?"

"You stay here with me, lil'un. We'll be the reinforcements," he said softly.

"You can bury my body down by the highway side."

The drummer gave a sickly smile to Old George, who'd sneaked around back of the stage. The musician couldn't do much more. Demon faces had appeared on the heads of his drums. They were talking to him.

". . . then we'll take your guts, dry them across rusty steam pipes, and string the Preacherman's guitar with them. After that, we'll . . ."

"I hear ya! I hear ya!" he bawled.

The drummer was playing for his life.

Sarah had no chance to see what was happening on stage. She struggled to anchor down the glasses. She'd given up on the liquor bottles. They floated in a perfect circle above her head, following her as she moved up and down the bar.

The bar business was heavy. Sarah wondered if Jayhawk was controlling the crowd somehow. Then decided, nah, they stayed for the same reason people chased ambulances or went to horror movies—for the thrill of it.

Squeezing behind Miss Sarah, Carl pulled open the power box. The indicator lights on the amp were already out. But he didn't have time to worry about that.

He flipped off all the switches. No response. He flicked them all on and off again. The power stayed on.

Behind the stage, Old George had eased himself over to the power outlet. He had his hand on the surge protector when the Preacherman spotted him.

Preacherman let out a roar. *"So my old evil spirit can get a Greyhound bus an' ride!"*

A bolt of lightning flashed through the club and hit the stage. Old George was knocked out the alley door. Carl was thrown over the bar.

A great ring of fire shot up to circle the stage. A gleaming, flame-licked guitar began to rise up out of the floor.

"Got the 'Me and the *Devil* Blues,' " Preacherman crowed, flinging the old guitar into the fire, to claim the demon gift.

Ratman turned to his best friend in all the world. "Lil Mustang, you 'fraid of hellfire?"

Mustang shook her head no.

"Well, then," Ratman said, "I ain't either. Reckon it's time we showed that Old Devil how ta play the Blues."

Mustang took the old man's hand. They walked down the aisle, as fast as Ratman's arthritis would allow.

Sarah saw her daughter walk into the ring of hellfire. She screamed and tried to climb over the bar.

Carl hugged Miss Sarah tight as they watched the little girl find the discarded guitar and pick it up. Then she and Ratman climbed the steps to the stage.

Preacherman was caught up in an unholy rapture, flames crawled up the tails of his coat, and his guitar screamed. A hellish band—all tails, pointed ears and claws—could be seen in the flickering flames, backing him up.

Unnoticed, Little Mustang plugged her guitar into the amp. Ratman pulled his rusty old harp from his coat pocket.

"Why don' we show this man where *we're* from?" Ratman whispered to the little girl.

With a deliberateness born of too-little fingers and not enough practice, Mustang strummed out the opening chords of "Sweet Home Chicago."

Through the wailing screams of the demon band, the terrified patrons at the front tables could just make out the words being sung by the unlikely duet.

"Baby don't you wanna go . . . to my sweet home, Chicago."

The front tables cheered the hometown anthem and picked up the beat.

Little Mustang gained her confidence as they moved into the verse. She'd been over this part hundreds of times. This was how Ratman and Buddy and Koko had taught her addition, subtraction and the multiplication tables—the easy ones, anyway.

Still pounding with one hand, the drummer shoved his mike in front of her.

And Mustang sang,

> *"One an One is Two*
> *Two and Two is Four*
> *One thing is for certain*
> *Don't want that Devil playin' here no more."*

Ratman let out a cackle.

Preacherman played on. But he'd lost some of his fire.

Mustang had a handle on the chord progression now. She winked at the old man. Ratman took a turn at the lyrics.

> *"Said, Four and Four is Eight*
> *An Eight and Two is Ten*
> *Old Evil Preacherman*
> *Ain't gonna know where he's been.*
>
>   *. . . Whatcha say, Mustang?"*

And Mustang said,

> *"Two and Two is Four*
> *And Three and Two is Five*
> *Ratman, Me, and Jayhawk,*
> *We're gettin' out of here alive."*

The crowd was with them, now clapping in time and cheering them on. The old oak door creaked open an inch, as the hellfires started to burn down.

The demons were starting to lose their grip on the drum heads. The drummer just laughed and beat the hell out of 'em.

Then the crowd joined in on the chorus.

"Baby, don't you wanna go . . . back to my sweet home, Chicago."

A roaring chasm appeared on the floor of the stage. The demon-band and all the hellfire was sucked down into it.

Then the Preacherman began his slow descent into hell, still clutching the gleaming guitar. The chasm closed. The stage was scorched but solid.

Mustang was still playing Jayhawk's guitar for all she was worth. She could feel the ghost stirring, gaining strength.

"One more time," Mustang called to Ratman.

Ratman took a long look at the cheering crowd, then turned back to Mustang.

"I'll do it—for you," Ratman told her. With a growl from the back of his throat, he sang,

> *"Eight and Eight is Sixteen*
> *And twice that is Thirty-two*
> *Shore 'nough there, folks*
> *We done give the Devil the Blues."*

Sarah had to kick the crowd out an hour later, after a final set. Ratman played his harp, Mustang sang backup, and Axman played Jayhawk's guitar.

Sarah sat with Carl and watched the last set. They had to duck their heads every so often, as Jayhawk floated the stray glasses back to the bar.

Ratman and Old George were at the tail end of the line as the crowd filed out. They stopped at the bar to say good night.

Old George grinned. "Miss Sarah, you sure do know how ta put on a show."

"See ya all tomorrow night," Ratman said, with a wink.

As the group wandered into the night, Jayhawk made the lights wink back.

HELL JUST OVER THE HILL
by George Zebrowski

George Zebrowksi's novel, *Stranger Suns,* was a *New York Times* Notable Book of the Year. His numerous, much praised, award-nominated stories have appeared in nearly all the major magazines and anthologies of the past two decades, along with his novels, which have been translated into half a dozen languages. His new novel, *The Killing Star,* written with Charles Pellegrino, has received excellent reviews. He lives and works in the Binghamton, New York area, Rod Serling's hometown, which inspired the following story.

Rick got on the bus as if entering a confessional, overnight round trip to anywhere, found an empty double toward the middle, and began to drift into self-examination as the half-filled bus left the station. Unlike most who mull while traveling, he usually arrived at his destination and at some definite conclusions at the same time. He had sometimes felt a bit guilty about this, wondering if he was avoiding some terrible truths, and was only too willing to accept simple-minded lies about himself.

But today it was different. After a few idle thoughts about leaving Rita and all his possessions behind, his mind cleared suddenly, as if he had walled himself off from the worrisome regions of his mind and was free at last to look outward beyond himself. He just needed to get away for a day. No destination, no luggage. Tomorrow he would come home to the woman he loved and try again.

As the bus fled north through the spring afternoon, the sun broke through in the west every few minutes, and it seemed to him that the coach was trying, and failing, to turn east to escape the sun. Ahead, the spring green hills were like broccoli under a nuclear cumulus cloud, marking hell just over the hill, where he imagined infernos of red coals smoldering in deep valleys under a bruised and bloodied sky. At his left and right the hills reminded him of the bellies and pubic mounds of reclining women, and Rita's dark eyes stared into him with resentment as he raised his hand to strike her across the face. And he had done so—because she thought he wouldn't, softening the blow as much as he could; but she hadn't noticed that as she fell back onto the bed and wept into the pillow. There was just no way to convince her that he had been faithful to her. But it wasn't any of that. It was the lack of money, the bad job he had, their inability to plan for anything more than a month ahead. It was the disappointment and pity they saw daily in each other's eyes.

The driver coughed into the microphone and said, "Sir, please keep your boy seated. Standing is not permitted while the bus is in motion." The man, a Hasidic Jew wearing a hat, long bushy beard, and forelocks, motioned for his son to sit down, then glanced with embarrassment at his fellow passengers. In a few moments the boy was up again, and the driver repeated his request, sounding even more irritated, and the father looked even more uncomfortable as he pulled his son back down into the seat. Rick noticed that the driver had resumed his animated conversation with the middle-aged woman in blue jeans sitting just behind him, ignoring the sign above the windshield that prohibited passengers from talking to him while the bus was in motion.

As evening came, the bus seemed to gain speed, as if entering a vast cave, with engines roaring to keep up its courage. It rushed by a small lake, whose waters shook in the twilight like the gelatinous skin of a beast. Near a small town, the bus crept by a well-known mental hospital, where the troubled had responded to the world by withdrawing into madness, while their keepers had adapted by becoming unfeeling and objective, wearing the paper blinders of theory. It seemed saner to him to lose one's mind in the world's circus of unreason than to congeal into a fortress of practicality and convenience. The genuinely insane were often sane among themselves, while displaying all the diagnostic labels to doctors and staff. As refugees from life, they knew amongst themselves who was truly ill—the real monstrosities prowling outside.

At one small town that was scarcely more than a row of old wooden houses separated by a short strip of asphalt roadway, a tired-looking teenage girl, chubby but still vaguely nubile, got on with a sloppily clothed baby and took the empty seats in front of him, putting the child in the one free seat across the aisle. The well-dressed older woman in the window seat looked at the child with disdain through designer glasses, and got up, saying, "I'll go sit up front, and she can have both seats. She seems very tired." The girl did not thank her. After a few moments she crossed the aisle and began changing the little girl's diapers. As the smell escaped, people in the nearby seats began to hold their noses. Finally, the procedure was over, and the girl went back to her seat, avoiding everyone's eyes as she sat down, took out a package of cheese twists from her bag, and began to devour them noisily.

"Mommy," the baby called out, then began to cry. She told it to shut up, and sat back to finish her snack.

When night came, the window at his right became a black mirror, in which his black shape also rode a bus. He leaned back and closed his eyes, dreaming of long-limbed women who smiled at him, and realized that he hadn't thought of Tess in months. "I'll tell my father and he'll make you marry me," she had said happily, slipping on her pink slacks over her long legs. "A dairy farm is not such a bad life." He had been too eager to believe that she was not underage. Maybe next year he wouldn't think of her at all. But as he listened to the teenaged mother crunching her cheese twists in the seat in front of him, he wondered whether Tess had gotten an abortion after he left, or was now a weary, hopeless teen mother like this one. He was lucky that Rita had never found out about Tess. The important fact was that Tess meant nothing to him, and could never have meant anything to him.

He opened his eyes and saw that another bus seemed to be trying to race his own. He peered out through the window, thinking that the drivers must be buddies on the same route. The glass seemed unusually cold against his nose and forehead.

He put up his hands to shut out the light, and across the short distance of no more than five feet he saw a long face with wide set eyes and dark hair peering back at him. He pulled back, startled by the resemblance to himself. The other figure also pulled back in surprise. Rick sat back, afraid that he was losing his mind, then looked again and saw the other figure doing the same.

Several passengers in both buses were now peering out, and he heard people cry out on his side of the aisle. A few figures in the other bus were waving. Both drivers beeped their horns.

"What's going on?" a woman shouted up front. "Someone need help?"

"Stop the bus!" an old man cried in panic.

Both buses began to slow down. Rick saw a rest area coming up—a large asphalt-covered half circle tucked into a wooded area, with a dozen picnic tables on the grass before the trees. There was a break in the trees, but it was too dark now to appreciate the view. A wind waved the branches as if a storm was coming.

The other bus pulled in first. His bus crept in across the gravel and stopped alongside. Rick squinted through the window and saw the other driver come out. His driver also emerged. The two doubles stood gaping at each other, then both men staggered over to a picnic table and sat down, trying to absorb the shock.

As they watched this meeting of the drivers, a cry went up from the people in the seats ahead of him. A few people were getting up and leaving the bus.

"What is this?" a man demanded from his left.

"Can't you see?" the older woman shouted at him, and the man crossed the aisle to look out.

Rick got up from his seat and went past the young mother and her child. Both were sound asleep, oblivious to their surroundings, even though he bumped her with his thigh as he hurried forward.

He came out into the windy spring night and joined the uneasy group that was curious enough to confront the people from the other bus. There was enough light spilling out between the coaches for him to get a good look at his double, who was standing just three feet away, in the same wrinkled tweed jacket and faded blue jeans, with a beaten expression on his face, accepting this strange doubling as if it were a judgment. At his left stood the woman in blue jeans, the Hasidic man, and the well-dressed older woman with designer glasses. Next to her stood two men who looked like plumbers. Rick glanced to his right and saw the same row of people repeated, then noticed that everyone from the other bus except his double was dressed too warmly for spring.

Silently, as their eyes adjusted to the light from the

coaches, the two rows of doubles began to eye each other with curiosity. His own took a step toward him and asked, "Did you do it, too?"

"What?" Rick asked in a whisper.

"You know."

"What?" Rick repeated uneasily, feeling a rush of guilt, as if he were sharing the other's thoughts and feelings. The four plumbers were looking each other up and down. The two old women were staring at each other intently and adjusting their glasses. The Hasidic men seemed to bow to each other, then one spoke in a foreign language. Then they grabbed their hats to keep the wind from taking them.

"Well?" Rick's double asked.

He took a deep, desperate breath suddenly, shook his head in denial, and backed away in fear. The others, on both sides, were also turning away and drifting back toward their buses, dazed, not wanting to know more, he realized, because there was nothing to be gained from talking to their doubles. They were all afraid, knowing that somehow a wall had crumbled, a necessary wall that must never be breached. Rick glanced toward the picnic table where he expected to see the two drivers, but they were both gone. The wind picked up in the trees, and a gust hit him in the face. He turned away.

"Wait," his double said, stepping toward him. "I'm Rick Barrow." The words came out in a strange, distorted roll over the rush of the wind, and Rick was suddenly afraid that it might be dangerous for doubles to touch or even speak to each other. He retreated, mentally struggling to slip behind the wall that should not have come down.

Then, on each side, the passengers turned and got back on the bus. He gave his double a wave; the other did the same, as if in a mirror, and turned away. He looked up and saw the young mother at the window, mouth open as she stared across at her double.

Rick came back to his seat, then decided to move back by two from the mother and her child. He slipped into the window seat and gazed out at the other bus, noticing that even the coach number was the same.

"Where's our driver?" a man shouted up front. "Let's get going!"

Rick looked toward the picnic table where the two men had sat down. There was no sign of them.

"Where are they?" the woman in jeans demanded.

"Can anyone drive a bus?" asked the man across from her.

Rick knew that he could drive the bus, if necessary. Suddenly the driver came back, threw himself into his seat, and closed the door. He gunned the engine and pulled out from the rest area. The other driver did the same.

The buses began to run side by side in the night, each trying to leave the other behind, and failing. Rick wondered what the two drivers had said to each other, then saw that the buses were drifting toward each other, as if trying to merge. Sparks jumped between the coaches, crackling and lighting up the road with flashes of blue electric glare, and he glimpsed himself staring through the other window. People shouted and cursed in panic.

"Get away from it!" a man shouted to the driver.

"Shut up!" he answered. "Something's pulling us together."

Together, Rick thought, wondering if the two buses had been one and the same just recently, and were now struggling to regain that state. He did not feel diminished by half, but would he even remember what had been subtracted?

The buses raced less than a foot apart. He stared at himself across the distance, at the starlit and shadowed face gazing back at him, and realized that there was a whole world behind the man in the other bus, but his movements did not match his own, and were not a mirror image, either, from what he could see. A blue glow came up from the roadway.

Both buses slowed as they neared a causeway that led out across a lake. The other bus pulled ahead suddenly, went through the railing without shattering it, and continued on a phantom road. He realized that there had to be a road across the lake, even if he couldn't see it. The lights of the bus were not reflected in the dark water. The bus receded and disappeared as his own reached the end of the causeway.

The driver pulled up on the shoulder and shut off the engine. After a long silence, someone asked, "Where was it going?"

"Same place we are, I suppose," the driver answered, turning on the engine again and steering the bus back onto the highway. "We're going to be late," he added.

"What are we going to do about this?" the woman behind him asked loudly.

After a moment the driver picked up his mike and said

over the speaker. "Folks, we saw a ghost—I guess. Don't know what else to call it, or who'd be interested in hearing about it. Each of you can do as you wish, but leave me out of it. I've got a wife and two kids to support, and I had to move up here from Texas to get this job when the strike started. I'd forget it if I was you. What good can it do you, or anybody to talk about it? Maybe it was just a delusion of some kind. It'll make you nuts to think about it too much."

No one answered him. Rick could feel the need in the passengers to accept what the driver had said. There were murmurs of agreement, slowly dying away like bad memories into silence.

Listening to the steady rhythm of the engine and the tires bumping across the seams in the concrete highway, Rick sat back and wondered whether he could feel his doubles as they came and went throughout infinity. He had always been more than a little in love with death, or rather with the vision of absolute, sublime peace; but that rest could never be, and had never been, he now realized. *We are forever born and dying in all the infinity of worlds. I am forever,* he told himself, because he was always alive somewhere. They were strangers, all those others. He could not know them any better than he could know himself. He could not choose the thoughts and feelings that came into him like invaders to direct his body. Something that he called himself lived at his center, but it was older and more powerful than the self he knew. That self knew what it wanted to do, and there was no way to resist when it took over. He closed his eyes and felt himself deathless.

In the morning he opened his eyes to fall foliage turning on the hills from green to red, yellow to brown, leaves shrinking and drifting to the forest floor, deathless in their individual deaths, and realized that the spring in which he had begun his bus ride was gone. How could he have been so mistaken about the season? And yet the evidence of his eyes was undeniable. He had dreamed the spring, he told himself as the bus neared the city.

The PA speaker crackled. "Can anyone direct me into the station?" the driver asked. "This is my first time on this route."

Rick got up, went up the aisle and stood behind the driver.

"Take this exit coming up," he said, "then turn left, cross the bridge, turn right, and that will put you into the station."

"Thanks," the driver said.

Rick stood there to make sure there was no confusion, and noticed snowflakes drifting in against the windshield. "That was pretty weird last night," he said.

"What was what?" the driver asked.

"The two buses."

The driver shook his head and smiled at him. "We're the only bus on this route. You okay?"

"What's today?" Rick asked, looking around at a few of the other passengers. They all seemed unconcerned.

"November 21," the driver answered. "What did you think?"

Rick took a deep breath and made his way back to his seat, wondering what had happened to him. No one else seemed to be worrying about the November outside, or what had happened last night.

The young mother was combing her hair and staring at her child, who was still asleep in the seats across the aisle. "That was something last night, wasn't it?" he asked.

She gave him a bored look and said, "I was asleep. We hit something?"

Rick sat down without answering her. Obviously, they had all forgotten. Suddenly he was looking forward to getting on the homeward bus and seeing Rita again, regretting all his violence against her. She was hard to live with, but so was he. She had probably forgiven him by now, and would be waiting for him at the station, as she had done in the past when they had quarreled. He sat back and waited for the bus to pull into the station, anxious to get off and take the return coach home.

As the bus rolled to a stop, he got up, hurried down the aisle, and staggered out into the arms of two uniformed cops.

"Richard Barrow?" the big one asked, grabbing his wrist.

"Yes," he said, as the shorter cop took his other hand.

"You're under arrest for the murder of Rita Malthus," the tall cop said, slipping on the first handcuff.

"What?" he asked, stunned. "But it wasn't me."

"Oh, yeah?" the short cop asked.

"It was . . . the other one," Rick said, remembering the spring outside the windows.

"No kidding?" the tall cop said. "Then you have nothing to worry about."

Rick began to struggle as his hands were brought together and the second cuff snapped shut. "Ask the driver. It wasn't me!" he shouted, choking on the words. "Ask him!"

"Don't worry, buddy," the short cop said, smiling at him. "We'll ask the driver. We'll ask everyone."

"He'll tell you," Rick said, feeling his throat go dry as they began to lead him away. He looked over his shoulder for the driver and saw the Hasidic man and his son staring at him as they stepped off the bus. The young mother, child in arms, was just behind them, chewing gum—

—and he saw Rita's strangled body in his arms, a minute after she had told him about the phone call from a pregnant Tess—

"It was spring earlier today," he tried to say loudly but couldn't. Sweat ran down his back, and he saw his guilty double arriving here, free of his crime, and taking the bus home to an unsuspecting Rita, to kill her again. He was in the station right now somewhere, waiting to board.

"You've got to stop him!" Rick cried, tearing the words out of his throat. They came up like razors. Hot blood burned through his belly and spread into his guts. A fist closed around his heart, and he staggered, but two cops held him up. "You have to stop him," he repeated weakly.

"Don't worry, buddy," the tall cop said coldly. "We've got him."

THE SPIRIT FROM THE NINTH HEAVEN

by William F. Wu

William F. Wu has published more than a dozen novels and numerous short stories, including his classic "Wong's Lost and Found Emporium," which was adapted into an episode of television's 1985 revival of *The Twilight Zone*.

Tom Ong momentarily came awake in his bed, huddled from the cold. In his sleep, he had kicked off the covers. As he reached down and pulled them up, he glanced out the window, through a spot where the curtain always caught on the back of a bookshelf. The outside of the pane was nearly blocked with a drift of fresh white snow. He turned over and snuggled close to the woman next to him. She was a little plump and, he remembered in the darkness, she was blonde. At the moment he didn't remember her name. The electric blanket was warm and he feel asleep again quickly.

Time passed and he dreamed.

As a child, he ran across the uneven asphalt of the playground, then stopped and looked back through the crowd of kids playing kickball and freeze tag. Two older white boys still walked toward him, their faces expressionless. One was tall and bony, the other short with a grape juice mustache. They began to run. He turned and zigzagged through a dodgeball game as he fled again.

In a dream shift, little white girls surrounded him, holding hands in a circle, chanting an admonition from their teachers in their high, singsong voices: *Buy American, buy American, buy American. . . .*

He ran, colliding with two clasped hands, and broke their grip before stumbling away. The two older boys, tall and dark against the sun, blocked his way. He turned and ducked around some kids at a tetherball pole to escape.

The circle of girls enclosed him again, closely this time,

each one of them pulling at the outer corners of their eyes to stretch them in imitation of his own eyes. *Buy American, buy American, buy American. . . .*

"Move! Move! Out of my way!" Muttering, then shouting, Tom jolted to wakefulness, flailing wildly. When he felt a woman's back, he shoved her. At first she barely moved, but when she woke up and tried to roll over toward him, he pushed her onto the floor with a thump.

"What?" Her voice was mild, confused, disoriented.

The room was still dark, except for some indirect streetlight coming in through the window. The red digits of the clock read, "6:03 a.m."

Tom threw back the covers and pushed himself out of bed, stepping over her. He was still groggy even though his heart was pounding. Nude, he walked to the bathroom and used it, shivering in the cold winter morning. Then he looked at himself in the mirror over the sink. His straight black hair was cut stylishly short, though it was tousled now; he was clean-shaven, except for morning stubble.

He went back to the doorway of his bedroom. Carol—that was her name—had moved up to sit on the side of the bed, with her loose, flowing hair nearly covering her face. As she rubbed her eyes with one hand, her pale, pendulous breasts swung slightly.

Suddenly he hated her. "You gotta go," he muttered, embarrassed. "I'm taking my shower." He went back into the bathroom and shut the door.

That evening after work, Tom grinned at his sister, Amy, from inside the glass doors of the local mall as she hurried toward him. The computer store where he worked in the service department was closer to the mall than the car dealer where she sold parts. Beneath the darkening sky, the parking lot had been cleared of snow, which was piled in great heaps around the perimeter.

"Hi, Tommy. Been waiting long?" Her face was flushed from the cold. She unzipped her heavy blue parka, revealing a red turtleneck sweater. "See? Red for Chinese New Years."

"Yeah." He grinned briefly. "No, I haven't been here long. And, look, I'm really not an emotional cripple tonight. Over the phone, you seemed to think I would be."

She tossed shoulder-length black hair from her face and

punched him on the arm. "Of course not. Women dump you so often, I expect you to be used to it."

"I told you, *I* don't want to see her again."

"So *you* say."

He decided to drop the subject rather than tell her what he had done this morning. "You really like the restaurant here?"

"Yes. And obviously someone has to take you around; you're getting to be an old man. You'll hit the quarter-century mark in a few more months." She elbowed him playfully.

"Yeah, yeah. Big talk. Your turn comes next year."

"I'll never be as old as you are, big brother."

"All right, little sister. Anyhow, happy Chinese New Year."

"Same to you."

The mall was crowded, as usual on Friday night. Tom dodged a bunch of giggling teenaged girls, all looking very Anglo-Saxon, and then had to wait for a Hispanic woman pushing a stroller out of a women's clothing store. He hurried to catch up with Amy.

Several doors down, he saw her walk into a novelty shop. Tom stopped outside the entrance, annoyed. His stomach was empty.

"Hey, come on! We'll miss our reservations."

"It'll only take a minute. Come on."

Tom sighed loudly and followed her. "Looks like it's full of junk." As they moved down a crowded aisle against one wall, he saw jigsaw puzzles, humorous greeting cards, and cheap plastic wind-up toys shaped like feet, noses, and hands. On another aisle, something was making a series of fast beeping tones.

"Come on, down here." Amy waved her hand in a quick circular motion, without turning to see if he was paying attention.

When he followed her around the corner, he saw that the back of the store was sectioned off. A stenciled sign over the opening said, "Adults Only." Amy was already walking under it.

Inside the section, Tom first saw shelves with board games that were labeled "adult" and some cocktail glasses with ribald scenes. Amy had gone to a vertical stand of posters on hinged frames. She was turning them in order, pausing to glance at each one.

He found her eyeing a guy in a stylish red swimsuit. The model had pale blond hair, clear blue eyes, and bulging muscles. "You like that look, don't you?"

"Well . . ." She laughed, shrugging, and flipped it.

"Come on. You still seeing the guy who sells cars? He looks like this guy, except he's thinner."

"No, not for a long time." Amy ran past several more posters, all similar. Then she reached a section with female models.

"Whoa." Tom stuck out his hand and caught the frame before she could turn it. "Not bad."

This model was nude, standing at a three-quarter angle with her front leg angled discreetly inward. She was standing on a windy beach with dark blue waves and light blue sky behind her, laughing as honey-streaked hair blew across her face. Droplets of water glistened on her golden tan.

Grinning, Amy yanked the frame away and turned it. The next picture showed a brunette leaning back against a rock. "Must hurt her butt," Amy muttered, turning it.

"Why are you looking at these? All those muscle-bound guys were in the front."

Still flipping frames, she spoke without looking at him. "Why do you always go out with white women?"

"Huh?" He laughed shortly. "I don't know. No reason."

"No, really. I've asked you before. You never answer."

He shrugged. "Don't know, don't care. And what about you? You never go out with Chinese guys—American or otherwise."

"Well . . ." Without realizing it, she used a tone just like his, and even shrugged, too. "They're all too traditional. A bunch of nerdy guys who get shocked too easily." She giggled. "I'm too much for them."

"Yeah?" He grinned. "Me, too?"

"No! You're not like that. You're, you know, more like me."

"Maybe you just know the wrong guys."

She shook her head and flipped a few more posters. "Okay, hotshot, I answered the question. Now it's your turn."

"I told you, no special reason."

"Here it is." She held the next frame. "What do you think?"

This poster was a reproduction of an old pinup-style

painting. The woman was of Chinese descent, also standing at a three-quarter angle, smiling demurely at the viewer and holding a Chinese parasol over one shoulder, with both hands on the handle. Her shiny black hair reminded him of American movie actresses from the 1940s, parted in the middle and swept up on the sides, held in place with tortoise-shell combs. She wore makeup, bright red lipstick, dangling jade earrings, jade bracelets, and an ivory pendant carved into the shape of a Chinese character on a chain around her neck.

"Well?" Amy persisted.

Tom moved his gaze down across her small, round breasts and slender waist. A narrow banner in familiar red, white, and blue stripes rippled modestly across her pelvis. She wore red ankle-strap wedgies and matching red toenail polish.

"I guess you like her, huh?" Amy watched him, amused.

"Funny. All the other posters are, you know, photographs. And it's real long and narrow, like a Chinese scroll. In fact, it's starting to fall out of the holder." He tapped the bottom edge of the poster back up into the plastic frame.

"I thought of you when I saw it yesterday. I'm buying you this, like it or not." She started looking in the shelves under the frames for a rolled, packaged copy of the poster.

"This is pretty racy for an old-time picture. No top. And she's not really wearing that ribbon. It's just floating."

Amy was still sorting through the posters. "So you like her?"

"You'll never look that good." He snickered.

"Hmf. I'll never dress like that, either." She straightened, her hands empty.

"They're sold out? Come on, let's go eat."

"Not yet." Amy reached up and tapped the plastic frame. The poster slipped slightly, dropping one corner out of the crack beneath the frame again. She took it between two fingernails and slowly drew the poster out. Then, grinning at Tom, she briskly rolled it up. "Come on."

Amy bought the poster and shoved it into Tom's hands at the cash register. Then, driven by hunger pangs, he led her impatiently out of the store and down the main corridor of the mall, clutching the rolled poster in one fist. He slipped past an elderly couple with a Mediterranean look and walked briskly past a bunch of young white teenagers, glancing over his shoulder to make sure Amy was behind him. She jogged a few steps to catch up.

An Asian man about Tom's age, an immigrant by his lousy haircut, was coming from the opposite direction. Avoiding his eyes, Tom glanced past him toward the entrance to the restaurant. He hurried inside and got in line.

They did not wait long. At the table, Tom glanced at the menu. "Let's order tonight's Chinese New Year special dinner for two. I don't want to waste time thinking about what to order."

"All right." Amy closed her menu and glanced around. "Oh, look." She pointed across the restaurant. "There's Kathy Lu."

Tom looked. Kathy Lu was having dinner with her older sister. "Must be a night for siblings here, huh?" He grinned.

"Why don't you ask her out? She's nice."

"Hey—did you set me up? Did you know she'd be here?"

"Of course not. It's just Chinese New Year, remember?"

"Yeah. All right."

"Well?"

"What?"

"Why *don't* you ask her out?"

"Aw, hell, I don't know. No reason."

"I should go say hello. I haven't seen them in months."

"No, you don't. Come on, decide what you want so we can get a waiter over here. Then tell me about your day for a change."

"All right, all right."

While Amy frowned at her menu, Tom glanced back at Kathy. His family had known hers since all the kids had been small, but he didn't really know Kathy very well. Kathy was Amy's age, and slender, with prominent cheekbones and fairly short hair simply parted on one side. He looked away, afraid she would notice him.

Kathy and her sister finished and left without seeing Tom and Amy. After dinner, Tom gave his sister a quick hug and drove home, with his poster on the passenger seat. He smiled to himself as he thought of Amy's earnestness. As children, they had quarreled often, being close in age, but he was comfortable with her now. She didn't seem to notice her own hypocrisy, though, in prodding him to ask out other Chinese Americans when she was always dating white guys.

He found his apartment hot and stuffy; he had turned up

the thermostat too high this morning before he had left. Now he turned it down slightly. Then he unrolled his poster in his bedroom and looked around for a place to hang it. As he held it, the bottom edge curled up again from being rolled. He used masking tape to stick the top edge of the poster to the mirrored, sliding door to his closet. After gravity pulled the curl out again, he would decide where to put it permanently.

It was still early. He walked back out to the living room and picked up the remote control. Clicking on the TV, he walked to the kitchen and took a beer out of the refrigerator. Then he collapsed on the couch and started moving through the channels looking for something to watch.

Tom felt guilty about the way he had treated his bedmate this morning. She had already left by the time he had stepped out of the shower. Maybe he would send her a note or something. Then again, he hardly knew her anyway. Hell with it.

Nothing on any of the cable stations really caught his attention. He finished his beer while gazing at the news without interest. Then he dropped the empty can on the kitchen floor, stepped on it, and tossed it into the recycling bag. Living alone brought him a lot of evenings like this.

Not much time had passed, but he was sleepy anyway. After all, he hadn't slept too well last night. He undressed, washed up, and shut off the light. Moonlight glowed softly through the frost at the open spot in the curtains.

He drifted into sleep quickly. His dream began in a black void, from which Cindy Han's seventeen-year-old face emerged from shadows thrown by a streetlight into his father's car. She turned and spoke quietly.

"Well, you must admit, he looks like a movie star."

"Yeah?" With both hands on the steering wheel, Tom looked over at her on the passenger side in near-darkness. Their date was coming to an end. The car sat in her family's driveway.

"He's your classic blue-eyed, blond athlete." Her voice bore an apologetic tone.

He found the apology condescending. Cindy was the first girl of Chinese descent he had ever dated. She didn't look like any blonde bombshell, herself.

"You understand, don't you? He asked me out. I'm going."

"What's his name?"

"What's your name?" A woman's voice spoke close to him, from outside his dream.

Cindy Han faded back into his shadowed memories.

Tom opened his eyes. For a moment, he had been a high school senior again, dreaming of a breakup with his girlfriend. Now the faint light from the open window barely limned the outline of a woman's arm, shoulder, and long, black hair. She was leaning on one arm, her bare legs stretched out on the bed.

"What's your name?" This time she spoke more quietly, gently.

"Tom," he whispered, the dream of the playground and Cub Scouts still swirling in his mind. He gazed up at her, at first feeling that he was just in another dream.

"Why did you look away from that man in the mall?"

Tom suddenly recognized her as the woman in the poster. He looked past her into the shadows, where the closet door was lost in darkness. This didn't seem like a dream.

"Who?" His voice was rough from sleeping. He cleared his throat, feeling more awake now, and started to push himself up. "Hey, who *are* you—"

A cool, slender hand clamped gently over his mouth, shutting him up. She put her other hand on his shoulder and pushed him back down. Then she lay down close, her face next to his.

"The man you looked away from in the mall."

"I don't remember any guy in the mall."

"A man whose ancestry is similar to yours."

"I don't know. I don't remember. Who are you?"

"Who do you think I am?"

"Well, you can't be the woman from the poster. How did you get in here?" He rolled onto one side, starting to get up again.

She laughed softly and pushed his shoulders down again with both hands. Then she swung her body over him, straddling him, leaning on her outstretched arms. She reached back with one hand and pulled loose the combs holding her hair. It fell in long, black shadows around him, tickling his face.

He knew he should be more alarmed, but she didn't really seem dangerous. Instead of throwing her off and getting out of bed, he peered up at her face in the shadows. "Come on. Who are you?"

"If you knew fairy tales, you'd know."

"So you're Cinderella?" He tried to laugh, but it didn't come out right. It sounded more like a nervous cough.

"If you knew Chinese fairy tales, you'd know."

"Yeah, well, why should I?"

"You know European ones."

"Who *are* you?"

She laughed gently and lay down on him, keeping only her head up. "Good night." Her dainty fingertips lightly brushed his eyelids closed and he instantly fell asleep.

The cheerful chatter of the morning news on his clock radio woke him in darkness. He flailed around sleepily and hit the button to shut it off again. Then, inhaling deeply, he remembered the conversation from the night before. He reached out and switched on the lamp.

The poster taped to his mirrored closet door looked the same as before—at first. He felt something was different. Looking it over, he struggled to a sitting position.

The woman's pose had not changed. Her smile was the same and the banner still waved across her pelvis. Only one hand held the parasol now, though. The other one held two tortoiseshell combs.

He looked back up at her face. Now her long black hair tumbled onto her shoulders. When Amy had bought the poster, the woman's hair had been swept up in the back and held with the combs.

Turning away, he climbed out of bed and moved to the bathroom. He wasn't going to think about this now. Maybe he remembered the poster wrong. Anyhow, he had to be at work soon.

When he had showered and dressed, he paused to look at the poster again. The bottom was still slightly curled upward. Now that he was awake, his concern over last night seemed silly. He had been dreaming and had simply woke up remembering the woman's hair wrong. Satisfied, he left for work.

Once he arrived, the familiarity and distractions of the workday took his mind off posters, dreams, and the accuracy of his memory. In the service department of the computer store, he began his day replacing the power supply in a Macintosh and running brief testing programs on two more. Then, just before his mid-morning break, he got a phone call.

"So, have you fallen in love with her yet?" Amy asked.

He was startled, but recognized her voice. "Jeez, you could at least say 'hello' first."

"Well, hello."

"With who?"

"You mean 'whom.' The woman in the painting."

A new idea struck him. "Is this some kind of practical joke? Did you set up somebody to come over last night? You have a key."

"Of course not. What are you talking about?"

"The woman in the painting."

"Look, all I meant was, do you like it?"

"Uh, sure. Yeah."

"Did you put it up?"

"Not permanently. I hung it up to get the curl out of it. Then I'll decide what to do with it. I mean, where to put it."

"If you really like it, you could get it matted. Maybe it would fit a standard-sized frame."

"I'll see." He hesitated, not sure what to say.

"Well, I'll let you go. I just thought I'd say hello." She laughed. "Even if I didn't."

"Yeah, okay. Thanks. Bye."

Tom hung up, the image of the woman in the poster on his mind again. He was sure she had been holding the parasol with both hands the first time he had seen the poster. Annoyed at spending so much time over this question, he went to the coffee machine.

He managed to forget about the poster for the rest of the day, until quitting time. Usually, he was anxious to leave and either go home or swing by his favorite bar. Tonight he knew he had to go back and look at the stupid poster again.

When he got home, his timers had switched on a living room lamp and a bedroom lamp, as usual. The message light was blinking on his answering machine. It sat on an end table next to the living room phone. He pressed the replay button.

"What the hell is wrong with you?" Carol demanded, her voice shouting over the drone of a TV set in the background. "What happened, anyway? I thought you shoved me out of bed because of a bad dream. Then you were rude when you woke up, too. I'd thought you'd call me yesterday!" She yelled something too distorted to understand and then slammed the phone down.

Tom clenched his teeth. He felt guilty. Right now, though, he didn't want to deal with her.

The sudden splash and sizzle of cold food hitting hot oil reached him from the kitchen. A moment later, he heard the fan over the stove come on. Then a spatula pinged against the side of a frying pan or, more likely from the sizzle, his wok. The wok was a present from Amy that he had never used.

"Amy?" He walked to the kitchen, realizing it couldn't be Carol. Even if she had cooled off, she certainly wouldn't cook dinner for him. Besides, he hardly knew her; she didn't have a key. Only Amy did.

"Welcome home." The woman from the painting stood in front of the stove, stirring something in his wok. She still wore only her jewelry, the striped banner now tied around her waist, and her red ankle-strap wedgies. Her shiny black hair was up again, though, held by those tortoiseshell combs.

Tom swallowed, unable to think of anything to say. The pungent aroma of garlic frying in the oil reached him. It reminded him of his mother's cooking.

His rice cooker was steaming away on the counter, causing the lid to rattle. It had been a birthday present from his mother, and he had never taken it out of the cabinet. The button on it clicked.

"The rice is done," she said cheerfully. "The chicken and broccoli need just a couple of minutes. *Furu* and soy sauce are there." She pointed to two cereal bowls on the table.

"Uh—" Tom spun and hurried to the bedroom. The poster was still taped to his mirrored closet door, curling upward at the bottom. It was completely white, though. The woman was gone.

He walked back to the kitchen stiffly, almost in a trance. This time she was more than just a vision in the middle of the night. As he stared at her, she stirred the sizzling dish and then added a little water and cornstarch.

Tom said nothing as she turned off the burner and dished out the chicken and broccoli onto a bowl of rice. Then she moved it from the counter to the table. For the first time, he noticed that her parasol, folded, was leaning against the counter.

She turned and looked at him with dark eyes, still smiling pleasantly. Light caught the carved ivory pendant at her throat. He wondered what the character meant.

She tapped the table next to the bowl, expectantly.

"Uh . . ." He tried to look at her only above the shoulders. "Weren't you afraid of being splattered by hot oil?"

"I was careful." She smiled nicely.

The food smelled very good. He was hungry. Reluctantly, he sat down. She handed him a fork; he didn't own chopsticks.

Unable to think of anything else to say, he looked down at his dinner. She walked away, her steps hard and brisk on the kitchen floor and then silent when she reached the carpeted hallway. He was relieved to let her go.

Carefully, he tasted the chicken. It was very good. He remembered that he had frozen a package of chicken a few weeks ago. He might have had soy sauce left from the last time he had brought Chinese food home from a restaurant. However, he knew that he had not bought any rice or fresh broccoli within recent memory—probably ever. Certainly he had never bought cornstarch or *furu;* the latter, a condiment made from bean curd, was something he had hated since childhood.

He smiled, wondering if she had gone shopping. Dressed like that, no, she would have been arrested. She seemed to be a real person, except for her choice of attire.

Cautiously, he ate a little more. It was all very good, no matter how she had found the ingredients. He relaxed and enjoyed his dinner, trying not to think about the woman who had cooked it. Regardless of where she had come from, he didn't see how an hallucination could cook dinner.

The first bowl only took the edge off his hunger. However, he had become too restless not to get up and look for his strange guest now. Uncertainly, he left the kitchen, peering around each corner to avoid any more surprises.

Tom didn't find her in the living room or the bathroom. That left his bedroom. His heart pounding, he looked there.

The woman was back in the poster again. She had struck the same pose as before, but her hair was up again, as it had been in the kitchen. She held her parasol with one hand and had the other jauntily on one hip. The banner, instead of just floating in front of her pelvis, was still knotted around her.

This was hard to believe and impossible not to believe. He

approached the poster and ran one fingertip across her shapely legs. The surface was smooth and flat against the closet door.

It was just a poster.

With nothing else to do, he went back to the kitchen to see if his dinner was still there. It was, and the second helping was just as good, and just as real, as his first. He finished it all and felt pleasantly stuffed. After another cautious glance into the bedroom, where she was still smiling motionlessly from the poster, he returned to the kitchen to clean up.

When he had completed that chore, he went back to the doorway of his bedroom again. She looked no different from the last time he had checked. For a while, he stood and watched her.

Nothing happened. He wondered if she could see and hear him. Of course, she had never moved in and out of the poster while he was watching.

Suddenly realizing that he was accepting this impossible proposition, he hurried to the living room and turned on the TV.

He ran through various channels, but for the second night in a row, he couldn't concentrate on any show. Every few minutes, he looked toward the bedroom, wondering if he had heard something. He got up twice to look again; the poster remained unchanged. Finally he began to wonder if he really was losing his mind. Maybe he had bought all the groceries and cooked them himself in some sort of memory lapse or trance.

That thought turned him cold inside. It meant he couldn't even be sure that he was sitting in his own living room now watching television. Suddenly he realized that he was soaked in sweat, his face damp and his shirt soggy. Shaking, he considered calling Amy to see if he could make contact with the outside world. He reached for the phone, watching his hand quiver. Then he drew it back. He didn't want to talk to anyone.

Tom pushed himself up out of the couch, walking carefully as though he might faint. He moved with short, stiff steps into the bedroom and looked at the poster one more time. The woman's smile seemed reassuring, though she didn't appear to have moved.

He wasn't sleepy yet, but he was tired after the interrupted sleep—or the fitful dream, whatever it had been—last night.

Since he couldn't get his mind off the poster now anyway, he decided to get ready for bed early. After he had locked up the apartment and washed up, he undressed and turned off the light.

As he lay on the bed, he kept waiting for some sound as the woman left the poster. Then he wondered if she would step out of it silently and just climb onto the bed again and speak to him. Nothing happened. Finally, he fell asleep.

He dreamed of a shy, slender, brunette teenager, the first girl he had kissed. Close to her, he looked into her brown eyes and she lowered her gaze, hiding behind long lashes. The bridge of her nose was high and narrow. Then she looked up again, and became someone else.

Now he stared into the bright blue eyes of a pretty, freckled face framed by frizzy red-orange hair. She smirked at him, on the verge of laughing at something. As he watched, she came even closer, until her blue eyes were all he could see. Just before they kissed, she blinked and turned into someone else.

Black, curly hair surrounded her face and the pupils of her eyes were surrounded by yellow coronas against a dark blue. Their lips brushed. She looked down, ready to kiss.

A gentle arm sliding under his neck woke him. He felt his head turned slightly to his left. Long hair tickled his face. When he opened his eyes, he saw the faint outline of the woman's hair and shoulder as she lay next to him. The pendant in the shape of a Chinese character glistened at her throat in the moonlight.

"You think if you kiss enough of them, they'll make you a white man?" Her voice came in a whisper, warm against his face. "Can you kiss yourself white?"

He just looked at her.

"You like dinner, handsome?"

"Uh, yeah," he whispered sleepily. "But who—or what—are you? Or am I just crazy?"

"Don't I seem real?"

He paused, thinking of how impossible she was. "Yeah," he whispered finally. "But . . . what do you want?"

"Do you think I'm pretty?"

"Yeah." He spoke reluctantly, suspicious of the question.

"You like my body?" Her voice had a hint of laughter.

"Well . . . sure." He realized that Amy was right, though; he had not been interested in a woman of Chinese descent since Cindy Han had broken up with him. Ordinarily, he still might have found this particular woman very attractive; certainly her style of dress was eye-catching. Under circumstances this weird, though, he could hardly enjoy her presence at all.

"No, you don't."

"Huh?"

"You don't like your own either."

"I never said that."

"You've been having bad dreams, handsome."

The room seemed to be floating around him. He felt lost in the darkness. No one else knew about his bad dreams. He had never said a word about them.

"You know what they mean, don't you?"

"I don't know what you're talking about," he muttered. It sounded unconvincing even to him.

"Of course you do."

"Come on." A flash of anger roused him. "I'm sick of this game. Anyhow, who are you?"

"I'm the one you don't dream about." She walked two fingers around on his chest.

"I don't get it. I told you. I don't know what you're talking about." He felt more angry and really came awake.

"No." She snuggled close, angling one smooth, warm, slender leg across his own bare legs.

"No."

"You should apologize to your blonde friend."

"What? What's she got to do with any of this?"

"You wish you were a white man. You're mad at the world, her included. That's why you won't apologize to her."

"What? That doesn't make sense."

"Sure it does. You resent her for being white while you aren't."

"Come on."

"You do."

"You're crazy. What are you talking about?"

"Those guys in the posters. The muscle-bound blond type."

He started to protest, but couldn't think of anything to say. Finally, he muttered, "I'm in okay shape."

"You certainly are, handsome. But you know what I mean."

Tom felt as though he was sinking into the bed. He was

dizzy and sick to his stomach. Right now, he just wished she'd go back into the poster and stay there. He could imagine the long, blank paper, still hanging there on his closet door this very minute.

Suddenly—if she was real and he wasn't insane—he realized her one weakness. He drew in a deep breath, then suddenly sat up and scooted to the foot of the bed. Bounding off it, he felt for the closet door and then snatched the poster off of it.

In the darkness, he couldn't see if it was empty again, but he didn't doubt it. He rolled it up, gambling that she couldn't move back into it that way. Then, holding it tightly in one hand, he reached out with the other and yanked on the curtain pull.

Diffuse, pale light angled into the room through the ice and snow frozen to the outside of the windowpane. The woman still lay on her side on the bed, her body slim and lithe yet ghostly in the winter light. Her black hair once again tumbled down onto her shoulders, but she still wore her shoes and the banner knotted around her waist.

She smirked at him, amused instead of scared, her red lipstick outlining her perfect white teeth.

"I'll burn it," Tom growled, holding up the rolled poster. "I'll find a match and set fire to it."

Her smile vanished.

"Oh, you don't like that, huh? Then answer my question."

She pushed herself up on one elbow, eyeing him carefully. "Don't burn it."

"All right. Who are you?"

She hesitated, studying his face.

"I wouldn't play any more games with me."

"All right." She sighed. "But I'm not allowed to use my human name anymore. I'm just a spirit from the ninth heaven."

"The *what?* What are you talking about?"

"I'm not allowed to explain very much. But because of a sin I committed in my own life, I was required to come into your life to atone for it. We spirits from the ninth heaven must do that. I'm not the only one. If you knew Chinese fairy tales, you would recognize this idea."

"This *is* insane," said Tom. "If I'm not crazy, then you are. This can't be happening."

"I know how it sounds. I'm not some mystic soul from five thousand years ago. I was born in Detroit in 1921."

"1921?" Tom did some quick subtraction. "Then ... I guess you haven't been, uh, dead ... very long."

"I committed suicide in 1946."

"Was that the sin?"

"No."

"What was it?"

"Racial self-hate."

Tom stared at her. She seemed more real, not less, even after telling him that she had once committed suicide and had just come back from some heaven he had never heard of. As he looked at her, she pushed herself up on one arm, and gazed right back at him.

He looked away, feeling that she could see inside him. Folding his arms, he sat down on the corner of the bed, well away from her. "What do you mean?"

"This is the reminder I wear." She fingered the pendant lying against her neck. "It means 'love.' But it's not for someone else. It's for me."

He looked at the pendant, which barely caught the light.

"I wanted my friends to see me as Madeleine Carroll or Betty Grable. I guess I should have aimed for Merle Oberon." She lowered her eyes. "I knew I wasn't Anna May Wong."

For the first time, Tom understood what she meant. All those names were familiar from old movies he had seen on cable while lying awake alone at night. He had watched other movies and imagined himself as Bogart or Redford or Cruise, but never Keye Luke or Bruce Lee. The career of Bruce Lee had been based on virtual cartoon images, no more.

"Some states still had laws against interracial marriage in my time," she said quietly. "Not Michigan. I was going out with an American guy—that's what we called white men then, even if you were born in the Detroit Chinatown like I was. His family had money. I thought I was headed for an engagement ring. Then he told me he was marrying a debutante he'd been seeing at the same time without ever letting on."

"Why didn't you want to go out with ... you know."

She looked up at him again. "You can't even say it, can

you? *Our own men,* is what you mean. Come over here and I'll show you."

Tom dropped the rolled poster on the floor, no longer concerned with it, and crawled over to her on the bed.

She encircled his torso with her arms and drew him close. He felt her breasts flatten softly against his chest. The banner around her waist tickled him. One gentle, slender hand behind his neck pulled him right up nose to nose with her.

The muted, frost-filtered light from the window fell across her dark, slanted eyes and the smooth, nearly flat bridge of her nose. Her black hair framed her face. He felt her warm breath.

"What do you see?" Her lips brushed his as she whispered.

Tom had never seen an Asian woman's face fill his vision as he lay on his bed at night.

"All right, I'll tell you." Her slanted eyes gazed into his. "You see what *you* are. You can't escape it. And neither can I."

"You're very pretty."

"Prove it."

As he kissed her, he brought his arms around her, sliding his palms across her back. For one more moment, he wondered again if she was real; maybe he was merely thrashing about alone in bed, deluded beyond hope. Then she tightened her arms around him and hooked one leg over his hips. He didn't care anymore.

In the darkness, she was lithe and enthusiastic, but totally silent. Her eyes never closed. Instead, she watched his face during every movement, every roll, every shift in the shadows. When it was over, she reached up with a little smile and brushed his eyes closed again with her fingertips, putting him to sleep.

Tom awoke the next morning from a deep sleep, well rested. He had forgotten to set the alarm, but he woke up at the usual time, unsurprised to find himself alone in bed again. The poster, with the woman in it, hung once again on the closet door; he supposed she had put it back before stepping into it again.

He sat up to take a closer look and felt something tickle his throat. When he fingered the slender chain and pendant, he knew what they were. In front of him, the spirit in the poster looked exactly as she had originally, except that her pendant was gone.

A tingling ran up his back. Somehow, he knew that she would not come out of the poster again. He felt a genuine affection for her, though, and was touched that she had left her pendant on him.

Tom moved to the foot of the bed and stood up in front of the poster. Under his fingers, the poster and the image were flat again. The woman remained motionless, of course, but her eyes still gazed at him.

Even now, he still was not sure exactly what had happened to him, but he felt different, more at ease. Whatever he owed the spirit could not be paid back directly, but he knew how to start. If he hurried, he still had time to apologize to Carol before she left for work.

"Morning," he said quietly to the woman in the poster, just in case she could hear him.

Then he remembered something. *We spirits from the ninth heaven,* she had said. *I'm not the only one.*

Tom grinned suddenly. Maybe she had dropped that clue for a reason. Somehow, he was absolutely certain that if he returned to the novelty shop tonight, he could find a poster of a man for Amy.

OLD AS A ROSE IN BLOOM
by Lawrence Schimel

Lawrence Schimel is a poet and short story writer whose work has appeared in over one hundred magazines and anthologies, including *Ancient Enchantresses, Tales from the Great Turtle,* and *Excalibur.*

My fingers trembled as they skimmed across the scroll of roses engraved along the box's sides. I had not touched it in years, and I could barely detect the shadow of my reflection beneath the large curving script on its tarnished silver lid. MFG. Marilyn Francine Gardiner. My mother.

She gave the box to me before she died. Inside, a pair of silver moons slept on a velvet bed beside a matching strand of stars. I had held my breath as I stared at them sparkling under the hospital lights from the box on my lap, like the glitter of sunlight on water.

"My mother gave me these on the day of my prom," she told me, her eyes misty with recollection. "I felt so proud as I wore them, old as a rose in bloom, and as beautiful." She took my hand in hers and made me look into her eyes. "I want you to wear them to your prom. Think of me when you put them on, so I can be with you. In spirit, if not in person." She ran a hand through my hair as if she were combing it for me before the prom, and I nearly spilled the box and its moons and stars to the floor in a flood of silver as I turned to embrace her, crying.

I blinked back my tears again and set the box on the bureau, still not ready to open it.

Downstairs, I could hear Dad and his boyfriend saying good-bye. Ed worked as a drag singer at a bar in town. At work everyone called him Natasha. Dad had been seeing him for four months now, but every night when Ed left for work, they still spent five minutes hugging and whispering as they kissed each other good-bye. Dad was often asleep when Ed got back from work in the middle of the night, since he woke up at six to be at the office on time. But I knew that sometimes he stayed up, worrying, or just waiting for Ed to come home. For a moment I worried what my date would think if he showed up at the door and saw them through the window as he was about to ring the bell. It didn't matter, I realized as I began putting on my makeup. Dad was happy for the first time in years, and I was happy for him. Now, if I could only find the right lipstick to match my dress perhaps I could be happy for myself as well. I was the only freshman girl going to the prom and I wanted to be stunning.

Dad began calling out to me as he climbed the stairs, "Erica, Erica." He knocked hesitantly at my open doorway, suddenly shy or perhaps trying to give me some privacy. Whichever, my chest tightened in response to that tiny gesture and I felt in that moment how much I loved him. He poked his head through the door and in a softer, excited voice declared, "He's here."

I turned to him and smiled, shyly.

"You look stunning," he said, coming toward me. He held me at arms' length for a moment, then kissed my cheek. I felt on the verge of tears, I was so happy. "How long should I keep him busy? Your mother kept me waiting for forty-five minutes. I sat wedged between her father and her older brother the entire time, too afraid to move a muscle, almost too afraid to breathe."

"I shouldn't be much longer," I said. "I just can't find the right lipstick."

"Twenty minutes, then," he said as he walked toward the door. He laughed, and I knew he was just teasing me. "I'll make sure he's occupied. Don't you dare come down sooner than ten, y'hear?"

"Thanks," I whispered as I watched in the mirror as he went back downstairs. I was left staring at myself in the mirror. I really was almost ready, except for the lipstick. I couldn't find the right shade, everything I had was too dark or too light or the wrong color completely. I looked at Mom's box again and realized I couldn't put it off any longer. I held it in my lap for a long moment; the metal felt cool even though my dress. I traced the large, curving letters, remembering her, missing her, let my fingers wander

along the stems of roses around the sides, and finally opened
the box. I'd promised her, and even more, I wanted her to be
a part of this special moment with me.

The jewelry lay on its dark velvet bed, and sparkled as
brightly as that first time I had seen them under the harsh
hospital lights, still untarnished even after all these years. I
lifted the twin moons and held them before me, trying to
imagine Mom as a girl wearing them. I put them on and
stared at myself in the mirror. *I look just like her,* I thought,
as I recalled the picture from her high school yearbook. I
lifted the necklace, the strands of tiny silver stars twisted
gently, almost like a braid, and let the cool metal lie against
my neck. I was amazed as I fastened the clasp how much I
looked like Mom. She was so beautiful then, and now was
again, in me.

I closed the box and placed it on the bureau. Something
nagged me out of the corner of my eye, something I couldn't
quite see. I looked at myself in the mirror again, and realized
that my reflection had not moved at all. My heart began to
pound within my chest. Could it really be her? I wondered.
It was almost too much to hope for. I turned and stared at the
young version of my mother who sat in the chair I had just
vacated. No wonder I looked so much like her when I put
her jewelry on; I had been seeing her!

I was scared, I must admit, even though it was my mother.
And sad, as well. She opened her mouth to say something,
but no sound came forth, and I could not read her lips. What
had been so important to bring her back from the dead? I
was elated to see her again, but felt guilty that I had disturbed her eternal rest, somehow. The ghost stood and
spread her arms to hug me, but passed through me with a
cold chill that froze my tears and made me catch my breath.
Mom did not stop, however, but continued past me, and out
the doorway into the hallway. I hurried after her, unwilling
to lose sight of her when I didn't know if I would ever see
her again. She had walked, or floated I realized later, since
she glided from place to place, to the end of the hall and
waited in front of Dad's bedroom. She was pointing at the
closed door, and when she saw me following her she ghosted
through it.

I hurried down the hall and stood in front of Dad's closed
door. As I put my hand on the knob, I couldn't help thinking
about how he knocked at my open door earlier that evening,

honoring my privacy. But I turned the handle nonetheless, and entered his room. It was dark, but I was afraid to turn on the lights. He was still downstairs, entertaining my boyfriend. What if he came upstairs again to see what was taking me so long and saw the door to his room ajar?

I looked around the room in the light from the hallway, wondering what had disturbed Mom's rest. It looked like there was more of Ed's stuff in there than Dad's. Suddenly it hit me; was Ed the reason Mom had come back from the dead? Was she upset that Dad was sleeping with a man now that she was dead? I looked to Mom for confirmation, and sure enough she was pointing at Ed's stuff on the bed. I felt sorry for Dad; he really liked Ed, and I sort of liked him, too, and most importantly, Dad was happy again. He'd been so lost after Mom had died, and bitter, as if he felt she had abandoned him. But if Mom was so upset by his boyfriend that her ghost came back to tell me so, I guess I couldn't keep thinking things were good. I didn't know what she wanted me to do, however, and I looked at her again for another clue. She was still pointing at the bed.

Suddenly she began to wail in frustration when I didn't understand. It was the first time she had made a sound, and I swear, it was loud enough to wake the dead. But maybe that was what she wanted.

Dad didn't hear a thing, or if he did, he never said anything about it. I moved closer to the bed, to see what she was so upset about. Ed's drag stuff was all over the bed still, wigs and dresses and makeup kits, all the stuff he had been using when he got ready for work a little while ago. Mom kept pointing at one cosmetics bag and, at last, I picked it up and held it out for her, wondering what she wanted me to do with it. She shook her head and kept pointing at it. Finally I realized she wanted me to open it. I felt nervous about going through my dad's boyfriend's stuff. I had no idea what was inside. Drugs? Money? Condoms? At least they used them. Dad had sat down with me and had a long talk about it, since he knew I might be concerned about AIDS and all that. Or did Mom mean them for me? Dad had given me some a year or two ago, but Mom wouldn't have known that. How embarrassing! My mother came back from the dead to explain the birds and the bees to me on my prom night!

I opened the bag. It was full of makeup: rouge, eyeliners,

lipsticks. There was even a shade of lipstick that would match my dress. I didn't think Ed would mind if I borrowed it, so I pulled it out. I looked up at Mom, wondering what it was she wanted to show me in there, but she merely smiled at me and faded away.

I wanted to laugh with relief, or cry. She hadn't been upset with Dad's boyfriend at all! I put Ed's bag back down on the bed, and walked to the mirror. The lipstick was the perfect shade; at last, I was ready. I still looked like Mom, I realized as I looked at myself in the mirror one last time before going downstairs to greet my date. "Old as a rose in bloom, and as beautiful" I whispered, and felt a warm glow of love envelop me.

THE BACHELOR
by Peter Crowther

Peter Crowther has edited such anthologies as *Narrow Houses* and *Heaven Sent,* and has written stories for numerous anthologies, including *Grails: Visitations of the Night* and *Tales of the White Wolf.*

> *"The hurt is not enough:*
> *I long for weight and strength*
> *To feel the earth as rough*
> *To all my length."*
> —Robert Frost

The days flew past faster and faster.

The ground grew harder, the air grew colder, and darkness crept over the world a minute or two earlier every afternoon.

Halloween had disappeared into the fat wedge of Tom's summer memories, along with the flash and bang of Independence Day, the spectacle of Mom trying to get her chuckling, Budweisered husband into bed at the end of Labor Day, the official fluttering-leaf beginning of fall, and, most recently, the delightful formality and bounteous splendor of Thanksgiving.

Food, fireworks, and friends.

Maybe that was what it was all about. Maybe there wasn't anything else. Certainly there was nothing else that Tom could think of. Nor Charles either. Except maybe a new Schwinn or a Daisy handgun—just like Bennie McDonald's—or a complete run of Justice Society of America. *The stuff of future nostalgia* is what Tom's father called it.

"Nostalgia?" Tom had asked, fresh into and still fearful of the pressures of seventh grade. Jack Sinclair had smiled his reply. "Memories," he had said after what seemed like a long time to think of such a simple word. And he had repeated it, with a faraway look in his eyes that made Tom sad and happy at the same time. "Memories."

But not all memories were good ones. Take the usual semester tests. At least they were now out of the way. And the memory of Miss Wilkin and what had happened on a particularly strange almost summery fall day, and the old man with the fairy traps, too. All gone and finished with.

Now, Tom and Charles lazed around in the evenings, reading comic books and reenacting scenes from Riverdale, taking it in turns to be Archie and Reggie ... and Juggie, of course: everyone always wanted to be Jughead. Inventive adventures conjured up by fertile imaginations.

Charles would think along with Tom and then, suddenly, becoming a little too excited by an idea, would suppress his enthusiasm on the grounds that his age (being Tom's senior by a few months) prevented excessive indulgence in childhood fantasies, demanding instead an active participation in world affairs and matters concerning home and family.

On such occasions Tom would laugh, head shaking, full of conviction that life could never be so serious. *Should* never be so serious—at least not to him. Life to Tom Sinclair was one long adventure, a series of breathtaking experiences strung haphazardly together without fashion or purpose.

Every time he drew a breath, Tom learned and drank in the sights and sounds of the world around him. Each sunny day and every single gust of wind was created without design purely for Tom's personal enjoyment and appreciation.

"What will you be like," Charles asked on one particularly cold night in early December, sitting with Tom on the floor in Tom's bedroom, "when you decide to get married?" On his knee lay a tented copy of *Betty and Veronica*.

Tom smiled and placed his own comic book—a copy of *Forbidden Worlds*—beside him on the carpet. "So who says I have to get married?" This was one world that was just *too* forbidden as far as Tom was concerned.

Charles sat up against a chair and removed the comic book from his lap. "Everyone gets married sooner or later," he pointed out impatiently. "Don't you like the idea of your own house and your own things? And your own wife to come home to?" Tom did not miss that this latter element was added purely as an afterthought. And, at least to an extent, he agreed.

There *was* a certain seed of attraction to what Charles outlined. But it was still only a seed, and Tom reckoned if he managed to avoid watering it too much, its roots might just wither and die. He would not be swayed. He knew little about the whole business of marriage, and he cared for it even less. To him it seemed like being caged up instead of being free to roam, to wander at will through rain and sunshine alike. He just wanted to be able to wake up in the morning and decide what he was going to do without reference to anyone else.

"Nope," he answered at last, emphatically.

Charles shook his head in exasperation at his friend's vacant expression. "I'm sure you wouldn't want to wind up like Old Man Milton," he said, frowning for effect.

Tom tilted his head on one side. "How do you mean? What's wrong with Old Man Milton?"

Charles picked up *Betty and Veronica,* satisfied that he was again in command of the discussion, and smiled self-assuredly. "You'll know one day."

And with that the conversation ended.

The following day passed much the same as any other.

School seemed every bit as dreary as usual at this time of year, with everyone simply passing time until the Christmas recess. Tom and Charles sat at their desks and let their minds blow free with the breezes at play in their heads. The only difference being that Charles had perfected a kind of theatrical attention to what the teacher happened to be saying while Tom's face, bathed in far-off wonderment, betrayed his prowling thoughts.

When school let out, the pair walked silently out of the grounds. The winter wind, in full force, played with their hair and blew the tail of Tom's scarf—which he had kept from their meeting with the old man with the traps—out into the void behind him. Occasional scurries of dust bombarded them as they walked against the cold, heads bowed to the ground. Suddenly Tom stopped and looked up. "I've forgotten my math book," he said.

"Your *math* book!" Charles laughed sharply. It was unlike Tom to be thinking of schoolwork when they were not even in school. Come to think of it, it was unlike Tom to think of schoolwork any time at all. "Big deal," he said. "You don't need it."

Tom turned out of the wind and faced his friend. "But I

haven't done that exercise for Mrs. Ross. I promised her I'd hand it in tomorrow."

Charles shrugged and thrust his hands deep inside his jacket pockets. There was nothing he could say, and he knew it.

Tom smiled guiltily and, returning the shrug, started to walk back the way they had come. "Tell my mom I'll be home later," he shouted over his shoulder.

He reached the old house about twenty minutes later. He had not returned to school but then he had not *intended* to return to school, though the story about the uncompleted exercise was true. It would, however, remain uncompleted.

Tom stopped in his tracks and stared into the dark at the house the other kids called Milton's Morgue. The air bit at his face, wafting around him in great sheets of bone-numbing coldness. Inside, he felt a sadness, but the sadness had a warmth—at least, that's the way it seemed, warm and self-satisfying. The house looked bleak and lonely. Weather-beaten walls rose from the earth, stretching into the sky some forty or fifty feet above where he stood, still fifty yards from the front door. Long, rustling, unkempt grass wavered around its base and there were no lights to be seen anywhere.

That did it: nobody home. But Tom knew different.

He scrambled up the slope to the side of Milton's Morgue and, with each step he took nearer, he felt the sadness inside him grow. Here was a man—Old Man Milton, to give him his official schoolyard sobriquet—who had voluntarily cut himself off from the rest of the town and the world; who had avoided marriage, which the rest of the world seemed unable to do. Tom decided he must see him in his natural surroundings so as to compare him and his life to the lives of the other people way back, far behind it suddenly seemed, deep down in the security of the town.

Far above and somewhere over to the right, a crash of thunder echoed and then disappeared into the wintery distance across the fields. Tom turned up his jacket collar and fastened the clasp. With the darkness and increasing cold wind, Tom felt gripped by a feeling of utter dejection and he shuddered involuntarily, shaking his head to throw off the urge to sit down and sob for no reason. He stood and listened. There was no sound save the wind tearing at the trees, and the faint patter of a drizzle which had come in with the thunder to freshen the ground.

He was standing on a small path which led to the door. All was still and dark, although the moon cast a reassuring light when it wasn't obscured by drifting clouds. The walls were dirty gray and stained generously with bird droppings. Around the base, hidden mostly by the long grass, a thick moss had crept, year by year, month by month, inch by inch, up the walls, until it had formed what appeared to be a green, marshmallow cushion upon which the entire house rested.

On the first-floor windows, ivy hung long and spindly from the trelliswork, its unkempt arms scraping the glass with a gentle scratching sound. The roof was flat at the sides, rising farther back, amongst chimneys and an old, bent weather vane, to a pinnacle at the center. The door itself was a majestic oak, hand-carved with tiny figures decorating the surrounds. Tom tried to make out the figures without success.

The rain was falling heavily now and the force of the wind sent violent flurries into Tom's face. He ran along the path to the security of the door and then stopped, shielded by the awning above. After a minute or so he looked around for more adequate shelter, but there didn't seem to be any. He considered going home, suddenly unsure of why he was there in the first place, but it was a long way back down the slope toward town. He would be soaked. There was no alternative. He must sit out the storm. Thunder sounded behind him, rumbling around the back of the house like a prowling animal, and a flare of lightning lit the horizon quickly followed by more thunder. In the glare he saw the rain sweeping across the fields. That was it. He would have to go inside the house.

The door was not locked, opening easily when Tom pushed it, creaking softly. The darkness which greeted him seemed unfriendly but then, he reasoned, darkness was always that way. But he stepped back into the rain until his eyes had adjusted. He stood half in, half out, the sound of the rain in his ears.

Then he moved inside.

After walking a little way straight ahead along the passage, Tom became aware of a light, very faint—just the impression of a light really—over to his left along what seemed to be another short corridor leading to a door. He turned down this new corridor and walked until he reached the door. The light was coming from underneath. Tom stood in the oppressive darkness listening at the door, but he could hear nothing.

Intruder!

The word cut sharply into his head, splitting thoughts like a knife. That was what he was, an intruder, a common thief. The enormity of his crime suddenly hit home with a power that shook him to his shoes and, without another thought, he turned and started to make his way back to the outside. Behind him the door opened and light flooded around him and on down the corridor. "Hello?" said a voice.

Tom turned around and stared into the light. A figure stood framed within the open door, light blazing all around from a room beyond. The face was old but still bore traces of youth, gentle but containing dormant force and strength . . . and wisdom. Above all else, the face looked wise. Wispy gray-white hair combed carefully back over skin sometimes stretching, sometimes sagging, to lay across the ears and curl, lazily, into the nape of the neck. He was wearing a tweed jacket, its side pockets bulging from a lifetime's carrying. And a vest, dark green it looked like, fastened over a white roll-collared shirt at the neck of which grew a large polka-dotted tie, spilling out over collar, vest, and jacket all, like some crazy colorful plant.

Tom's eyes returned to the old man's face—Mr. Milton's face!—and he saw the watery eyes, watery blue eyes, searching Tom's face for some kind of sign, some kind of familiarity, some piece of . . . memory.

"Who're you then, young fella?" the man inquired. "Do I know you?" He hobbled slowly forward toward Tom.

"T–Tom," he said at last. "My name's Tom, sir. Tom Sinclair."

"Mmmm." The man nodded thoughtfully. His head just moved up and down and he muttered to himself under his breath, and then chuckled. "Come on inside and get warm, then," he said and turned around to shuffle back into his room. Tom hesitated and then followed.

The room was small but well lit. In the hearth a log fire sputtered and crackled, giving off a heat which shook off Tom's last half hour in the cold. On the walls hung paintings, some overlapping others, and movie posters and lobby cards. He recognized James Cagney and Laurel and Hardy,

John Wayne and Abbott and Costello, Clark Gable and
Huntz Hall and the Bowery Boys, Bugs Bunny and Tom and
Jerry, Frankenstein's monster carrying an unconscious
woman and King Kong swatting planes while hanging from
the Empire State Building.

And shelves, shelves, shelves.

All containing books and magazines.

On one shelf, in front of a stack of *Argosy* magazines, sat
an almost life-size Jiminy Cricket propped up against a model
of a Chevy van bearing the sign of the Daily Planet newspaper
on the side. And there were other models, too: Mickey Mouse,
Dracula, an old sailing ship, and a Model T Ford here; an Ol-
iver Hardy bust, a huge Tweety Pie, an illuminated Casper The
Friendly Ghost, and a Fisher Price clown-in-a-jalopy. Standing
in the corner, partly draped with a creased sweater, was a tobacco store Indian gazing fixedly toward the far wall—a
framed still of Chilly Willy the penguin, fishing through a hole
in the ice, stared right back. On the shelf beneath Chilly were
several neat piles of baseball cards, a freestanding cardboard
General Mills coffeepot (with a card overlay that said "Spon-
sored by Betty Crocker"), a Vicks inhaler and a signed photograph of Nile Kinnick Jr., the Iowa halfback.

Tom's eyes started to ache. Everywhere was ablaze with
colors and shapes. A Fisher Price schoolhouse clock, a skull
ashtray that had "Smoke gets in my eyes" written across the
forehead, a whole row of packs of cigarettes—all different
brands, a Ventura onyx-base penholder, and all manner of
grocery cartons and packets, from breakfast cereals to cof-
fees, cookie bags to catsup bottles . . . Tom began to feel out
of breath just looking. He turned to face the fire.

On the wall above the fireplace were what seemed like hundreds of photographs, all thumbtacked and overlaid. He recognized the town—the fields out by the sawmill and down
toward the creek; the pond, iced over in some long-ago winter
and covered with skaters, photographically frozen forever,
their scarves flying stiffly behind them; three old men in plaid
shirts sitting out in front of a general store, locked in conversation; a little girl holding the reins of a pony and squinting
into the sun behind the photographer; two boys in impossibly
long short pants putting the finishing touches to a soapbox
flivver; a woman caught in the middle of washing dishes,
laughing in embarrassment; and a boy sitting cross-legged in
the dust of an unswept yard whittling on a piece of wood.

"That one there's me," said Mr. Milton, "mmmm."

Tom spun around as though he had been caught with his hand in the medicine jar "Doc" Grenville kept filled with boiled candies. He started to mutter an apology, but Mr. Milton smiled and nodded and stopped him before he got a word out. "I was eight then, maybe nine. That there piece of cedar turned out to be a genuine—" (he pronounced it "gen-you-wine") "hunting knife like the one made famous by that Bowie fella almost did for Santa Anna."

Tom grunted and nodded enthusiastically.

"An' right next to it's my sister, Kath." He pointed a shaking finger at Tom and then moved it slightly to the left so it picked out the photo of the little girl and the pony. "The horse was called Jessie. She died the next year or the year after, mmmm." Tom decided not to ask whether he meant the girl or the pony.

The old man closed his eyes and smiled, while the fire cast flickering shines and shadows across his face. Tom watched Mr. Milton's eyes moving around in their sockets, skittering first one way and then the other. Then he stepped across a turned-over rug and walked to the shelves at the back of the room.

Books. Books. Books.

Thousands of them, he thought.

And a shelf of phonograph records, old 78 rpms and albums, too. Tom tilted his head to one side and read the spines. There was Sinatra, Rosemary Clooney, The Ink Spots, The Four Freshmen, Stan Kenton. . . .

Tom was suddenly aware that the room seemed crowded. He looked around for the cause of the sensation but could see nothing that he hadn't already noticed. Maybe he had imagined it. But no: there *was* something, nothing he could actually see . . . more a presence. A disturbance. That was the only way he could describe it to himself.

The old man turned first to one side and then to the other, seeming to acknowledge the unseen activity even though his eyes were closed. Then he spoke.

"Hey there, Jack, how's the missus?"

Tom nearly jumped out of his skin. Someone else had come into the room and he had not even noticed. But when he looked around he saw that Mr. Milton was sitting right where he was before, and his eyes were still closed. There was nobody else in the room. But there was *some*thing. . . .

Tom closed his eyes tightly, just the way he used to do

when his father announced present-giving around the tree at Christmas, and then opened them wide.

The room danced before him in the reflected shadows of the fire. But these seemed to be special shadows, forming and dissolving in the room itself and not merely across the walls. Tom blinked again and stared.

There was a mist in the room, a spillover from the fire, perhaps, and the chill, damp air that Tom had brought in with him. As he watched, the mist seemed to roil, slowly gathering itself into some kind of shape—was it a man he could see?—before it lost substance and then wafted away as if disturbed by some invading breeze that had found a doorjamb or a partly-open window.

Tom felt icy fingers touch the skin beneath his shirt. The man-shape—that one-in-a-million coming-together of hot and cold, dry and wet—had registered its presence. For one, single, spine-chilling second, caught in the act of casual but soundless discussion with the old man, it had turned to face him. *Seen* him.

"I wuz goin' ask you, Jack, if'n you could come on over for supper an'—" He stopped and seemed to be listening. "Yup, yup, well, sure enough, I kin see you got all on right now, but—" He listened again. "Yeah, okay. Talk to you again soon, now, mmmm." The old man's left arm flopped off the chair and he lifted it back immediately and laid it across his lap.

Tom tiptoed back into the center of the room and stared at Mr. Milton's face. The old man smiled and started to laugh. Then he coughed and smacked his lips appreciatively. "Nice drop if I do say so myself," he said. "Mmmm." And he shifted in his chair. As he moved, a small white corner exposed itself from the inside pocket of his jacket.

Tom stared at it.

Mr. Milton moved again, more this time, and the corner showed more of itself. It looked like it was going to fall out completely and then it might get lost or maybe fall into the fire when the old man stood up. That wouldn't do at all, nossir. Tom reached out his hand carefully, taking the exposed corner between two fingers, and lifted it clear.

It was a photograph. An old photograph, creased and stained and folded and refolded. A photograph of a woman—*no, a lady,* Tom corrected himself as he stared into the eyes of the sepia image he held in his hand. She wore a

large-checkered dress and was carrying a basket of something—Tom couldn't make that bit out. But the look on her
face . . . well, that said it all. He had seen that look before. It
was the look his mother gave to his father when she thought
nobody was looking, maybe not even his father. He supposed
it was love. And he supposed it was aimed at Mr. Milton, the
picture being in his inside pocket after all. When he looked
again, he saw the picture was signed though the ink had faded
some, but he could just make it out. *To Lawrence,* it said. *All
of my love forever.* And it was signed *Laura.*

Lawrence, Tom thought. *Lawrence Milton.* He looked at the
old man and smiled at his smile. But the smile faded as Tom
watched and Mr. Milton started to shake his head, gently at
first, frowning, and then harder. "No," he said, "nonono-
no . . ." time after time, joining the words up so it was just like
the one word, a long word with only two letters repeated over
and over again. Tom started forward and then stopped. Maybe
he was having a heart attack or something. He looked around
to see if there was a telephone, so he could call for help. And
that's when he saw the woman again. This time she was staring out into the room from a newspaper cutting that had been
framed and hung on a nail by the light switch just inside the
door. That picture would be the first thing you saw when you
switched on the light, and it would be the last thing when you
switched it off. **LOCAL BEAUTY DIES IN FREAK FIRE**
the article was headed. Tom stepped quietly over to the door
and bent down to read the cutting.

"Miss Laura Jane Fenner (22) died last night in a freak fire
which swept through her parents' farm three miles outside
the Forest Plains town limits. Two engines called from the
Delbert County station failed to arrive in time to save the
girl. Fire Chief Dane McClusky told Post representatives
that the inferno probably started through faulty electrical
wiring. Ed Hatton of the Delbert County Sheriff's Office
has called for standards to be agreed on for all electrical
work carried out. Laura Jane's mother was unable to speak
of the tragedy while her father, local farmer F.T. Fenner,
was openly critical of the new facility which claimed his
daughter's life. "I'm going back to simple oil lamps," he
said earlier today. Police have been unable to trace Lawrence Milton of the Delbert branch of Wells Fargo, to
whom Miss Fenner was due to be married next month."

Tom's blood turned ice-cold in his veins. "Is ... is she dead?" a voice asked behind him. "Mmmm," it said. "Mmmm." He looked up and watched Lawrence Milton re-living the moment again, the way he relived so many moments. "Aww, Laura ..." he said softly, and sighed. Then he giggled.

Tom watched.

The mist was re-forming ... but it was not the same one. There was something softer, gentler, about the haze that swirled opaquely in front of the old man.

Tom's heart thundered in his chest like Sandy Nelson's drumbeat as he watched the lady take shape less than two feet away from him. He could make out her dress, the faintest of blues caught in a symmetry of checks. And he caught sight of her profile, leaning down to the old man, a thin, delicate arm outstretched, its hand carrying the faraway, one-time moisture from her own lips to those of Old Man Milton.

Almost as though she had seen Tom watching her, the woman turned slightly, the hand a few inches from its target, and smiled. Such a smile!

She raised her other hand and placed an extended index finger to her lips in the universal gesture of *Shhhh!*

Turning back to the old man, she touched his face with her hand and drifted apart like wood smoke.

Tom watched as the lines of her dress faded into the air, leaving only a lightness in their place. And then that, too, was gone. He looked down at Mr. Milton.

On the old man's face hung the thrills and disappointments of countless years and untold half-forgotten experiences, loves and hates, hopes and fears. He didn't waste time talking: time was too precious for that. Time was for going over and over the old dreams and realities. Time was something in which he must now economize. Right now he was busy somewhere—some*time*—else, years and years ago. Busy doing something, saying something, listening to something, being *with* someone.

Tom stared and watched the expression come and go, the mirth and the sadness. It was a lined face that he watched and this was the reason. Hours and hours spent sitting all alone, in front of the fire, sailing the seas of memory. Alone because he needed no other person to clutter up his thoughts, steal his time and, worst of all, confuse his memories.

That was it, Tom realized: memories.

Memories are what ghosts are made of. Memories with their own existence, their own personalities.

Tom suddenly felt sad. Sad because, one day, there would be no more dreaming for Old Man Milton. No more memories. And on that day, he knew with a conviction that he had never felt before, the old cutting would finally come true: Laura Jane Fenner would finally be laid to rest. It was memories that kept a ghost alive, just as it was flesh and blood which provided living people with their own existence.

He stepped lightly over to where the old man sat and slipped the photograph back into his pocket. He bent down and threw another couple of logs on the fire, then turned and walked toward the door.

Suddenly, behind him, a hollow noise resounded in the room and then blended into the shelves and the photographs and the books and the cards and the cartons and the models, all winking and blinking in the scattered glows and brief darknesses of the regenerated fire. Tom turned to look. Mr. Milton was surrounded by misty shapes, forming, fading and re-forming as Tom watched, and he was laughing, laughing fit to burst, the tears of merriment blossoming from his eyes and sparkling down his cheeks.

Once outside, the cold reality bombarded Tom.

The flickering twilight world of Lawrence Milton was something apart from the wet, dark, windy night of which *he* was a part. He buttoned up his jacket and turned for a last look at the place.

Then, hands firmly encased in the warmth of pockets, he ran, head bowed, back into the wind and the rain.

And as he ran he thought this: *he* could keep the old man alive. Keep him alive by remembering what he had seen and heard and read tonight. And if he could do that, then he could keep Laura Jane Fenner alive, too. The same way.

Halfway down the hill, wet to the bone, he had already started to practice . . . so that he would be ready when the time came.

> "The apparition of these faces in the crowd;
> Petals on a wet, black bough."
> —Ezra Pound

THE NANA'S HOUSE
by Lisa W. Cantrell

Lisa W. Cantrell is the author of the Bram Stoker Award-winning novel, *The Manse,* as well as the novels *The Ridge, Torments,* and *Boneman.* Much of her work is set in or near her home in the foothills of North Carolina's Blue Ridge Mountains.

It was an old house, as houses grow. Old in the way bricks and mortar start to decay with age: cracking, flaking, crumbling. Old in the way wood and plaster begin to dry rot: peeling, splitting, settling. There'd been linoleum once, a gay, checkered pattern of green and white, now stained and dulled beyond recognition. Great chunks of it had come loose, over time been ripped away and discarded, baring the floor to its bones of rough-hewn timber and in places allowing access to the dirt beneath.

Damp, rotting leaves congregated in the corners, blown through gaps where paneless windows provided a lattice-work entry. Some attempt had once been made to cover the holes with plastic; tatters still hung from the skeletal frames, looking like the hair of corpses caught on the rusted nails and splintered fingers of wood.

An old stone fireplace was home only to spiders and cock-roaches now, and the occasional snake or lizard who happened to crawl by. Long-dead ashes of forgotten fires, like forgotten dreams, lay scattered and indistinct, wasted away on the cold, gray hearth, and on the wind.

Rats scurried through the barren rooms, occasionally stopping to gnaw at a rotted wall or floorboard, leaving their droppings to show that they had passed through here, as dogs will mark a territory.

A tangle of naked wires dangled from the center of the kitchen ceiling; long bereft of current, they waved impotently in the sweeping drafts that roamed the empty rooms.

The house had lived and died through countless seasons, moldering away down its dusty, forgotten road like a fastidiously avoided dung heap, enticing only to flies and the odd passing scavenger. Once it had held purpose, and the fruit of that purpose still remained, filling the house with an immensity, a corruption, weighting it down until the very foundation strained with the enormity of it.

For this was a house of sin.

Long ago, people had flocked to the house, bringing their sins to the Nana—the friend, the expiator—who, for a price commensurate with the sin's degree, would accept that sin into her house and send the fortunate soul away, lighter in heart—and pocketbook—untainted, cleansed, and free. Was it the Nana's concern that many of these same, glad souls would soon be back with their coins and cries for absolution?

Time passed, as time will, and the Nana grew old with the house. And the house grew heavy with its burden. Still the people came, and still the sins were taken in until at last the Nana died. It was not a gentle death that visited in the cold black hours of night, but thieves who stole and killed and as a final parting cast their sin into a corner to waste away with the Nana's flesh.

But only the flesh decayed.

Winters passed, and summers, and again winters, and the old house continued to receive the sins—for how could it do otherwise?—growing heavier with each that came its way, unknowingly now, left in passing or by chance:

Once a band of hoboes happened in and made use of the house for a while before moving on, fewer in numbers when they left because Yellow Jake had systematically poisoned off the most threatening of them, leaving himself in sole command.

Another time a small, secret group used the house for unholy rites, communion with the dead, unspeakable acts of debauchery.

Twice, a pair of lovers found refuge beneath the sagging rafters, hiding their sin from all but the house itself, until, in one case, He killed Her in a burst of jealous rage, and in the other a cuckolded husband put a bullet on the mark.

And now the house lay still, unvisited in its shadowed copse—*waiting, waiting*—sated with the sins of the fathers, and of the fathers' sons. . . .

Fast Bobby Lloyd swerved the speeding car in a vicious arc off the highway and onto the rough gravel road, sluicing a wave of rock and dirt in his wake.

"Shut up that gibbering, old man!" He flung a sideways glance at the cowering lump of clothes and bones hovering against the opposite door. "Shut it up, I tell you, or I'll bash your fuckin' mouth in!"

He demonstrated his willingness, even eagerness, to do just this by jerking a hand off the steering wheel and jabbing a fist in the old man's direction. The old man flinched even closer to the door, groping at it desperately; but his gibbering faded to a soft moan.

"Bastards! Goddamn bastards!" Fast Bobby muttered, snapping his attention back to the treacherous road they were traveling at better than seventy miles an hour, and his thoughts to the police cars chasing him. "Think they can pen me up with the old one-two, but I'll show 'em—hah! I'll show 'em."

He leaned toward the open driver's-side window, cocking his head to yell: "Hey you stupid pig bastards! Don'cha know who you're dealin' with here? Don'cha know I useta race the dirt track circuit? Think you can catch me? Hah! That'll be the day."

The snaking road and the pitching car quickly reclaimed his attention, and he slowed barely enough to make an oncoming curve, hanging the left wheels off the edge in a sort of sideways wheelie. The car popped around the curve, the rear end fishtailing for just a second before Bobby brought it back under his control, then stepped on the accelerator pedal again, feeding it more gas.

Sounds of shrieking sirens coasted across the distance between him and his pursuers, filling the air with a keening banshee's wail that set Bobby's teeth on edge. God, how he hated cops. Hated the fuckers! Always ridin' his tail. He wished he could waste them all, always on him, always on him.

He concentrated on his driving, edging the speed up another notch, determined to increase the space between him and the pack of baying dogs yapping at his tail. Like he was on the race course, he would outdistance them, show them who was boss.

"Eat my dirt, cocksuckers!" he yelled into the wind that

went rushing by his window. "You'll never catch me, you stupid pigs, never catch Fast Bobby Lloyd."

The sirens did seem to be fading a bit as they continued to careen down the rough back road.

Bobby smiled, turning the aura of his pleasure on his pathetic passenger, who was holding onto the edge of his seat and the door handle with a grip of arthritic intensity. "What about it, old man—you like the ride?" He laughed, a laugh of pure joy and satisfaction and pride. "Yessirree. Not many's can say they rode to hell with Fast Bobby Lloyd."

The old man's rheumy eyes, glistening with shock, glazed with confusion and fright, tried their best to focus on Bobby's grinning face. Gaunt features strained with the rigor of clenched teeth and tensed muscles. Thin, blue-tinged lips stretched taut and slightly parted, frozen in a rictus broken only by a spasmodic twitch or wince of pain as the bumpy road transmitted each distortion through worn-out shocks.

"Helluva time to be walking past that liquor store, hey Pops?" Bobby laughed again and turned his small rabid eyes back to the tableau rushing toward them.

Trees and scrub brush lay thick on the left-hand side, abandoned cornfields on the right. His glance darted to the rearview mirror.

"Gotta get off this dirt, gotta get off this dirt," he muttered, aware of the snaking dust devil being created behind him and the unwanted attention it could bring. Wasting the owner of that liquor store, plus a couple of bystanders, then making a fireball out of a cop car could only mean an all-out manhunt. But he didn't regret a bit of it. Nosirree! What a blast. What a pure-D blast!

"Hey, bastards," he shouted into the gushing wind. "What about it, huh? You like the ride?"

For a minute he seemed to hear an echo, as if the wind had caught his words and tossed them back at him. Then there was only the wind.

Leaning over the steering wheel, he peered intently at the crisp blue autumn sky, high spirits momentarily evaporating. "Choppers'll be out soon." He spat out the open window. "Sky pigs! Shit. Gotta get off this—

"Whoa . . ."

Braking to a fusillade of gravel, Bobby thrust the bucking automobile into a cavity between a couple of trees and onto an even more abysmal trough.

"Hold on to your dentures, Pops, now we're really sailin'!"

The gibbering had started again, sounded like the old fart was praying, but Fast Bobby was too welded to his wheel to issue threats this time. Let the old fool say his prayers.

"Pig path," he muttered as he twisted and spun the car through thickening foliage, then emitted a high-pitched giggle at this bit of unintended wit. "Just let them pigs in their fancy machines try to find me down this ole wallow—Hah!"

He hit the brakes as he spotted what looked like it might be another, even seedier road branching off of this one. It could lead to nowhere. But it could also be a way out, or at least a place to hide until the search moved elsewhere or night came in to cover his getaway.

It was taking a chance—sure. He wouldn't want to get hemmed in down here. But Fast Bobby Lloyd was one to take chances, always had, always would. You didn't get anywhere in this ole world if you didn't take any chances, nosirree. It was like on the racetrack when you saw a whole bunch of cars do a pileup in front of you, you just pointed your own machine dead center of the pack because when you got there chances were better than good that the fast moving wreck would be gone.

He'd survived more than one wipeout that way.

And he'd survive this, too.

"What th' hell, Pops, let's go for it."

A swerve to the left, and they were plunging through a density of brush and trees, forging their way down a track that seemed more footpath than road. Tree limbs slapped against the windshield and smacked the sides and roof of the car as they plowed deeper and deeper into the forest. Smaller branches got caught in the wipers, scraped along the sheet metal with a screeching noise that sounded like they were in pain. Rocks and potholes and gullies gouged out by the rain lay in wait for them, making the car heave and buck. Bobby had to fight the steering wheel just to hold on.

A series of loud thunks and whacks ricocheted up from the underbelly. A thick, low-lying limb raked stridently across the top. It reminded Bobby of the sound a can opener makes.

He hunched his shoulders over with a reflexive jerk, half expecting the limb to come poking through the metal roof any second and start peeling it back. But it screeched on by without further incident, though he spared a belated wish that he was wearing his crash helmet.

Maybe this hadn't been such a good idea after all.

On the other hand ...

He glanced in the rearview mirror, relieved to see that the branches were closing in behind them, almost as though the road was being swallowed in their wake. It was getting darker, too—Bobby craned his neck—no, he just couldn't see the sky so well through the thick canopy of leaves ...

And then all of a sudden they were popping out of the tangle into a clearing where a dilapidated old house stood rotting away and listing to one side, abandoned and still.

"Hah*hah!*" Fast Bobby crooned to his almost comatose companion, bringing the car to a grinding halt beneath a thick camouflage of branches. 'Here's where we hole up, old man—the holey Hilton, and don't mind the leaks."

Killing the ignition, he thrust open his door and jumped out, quickly circling the car to the passenger side.

"Okay, Pops, outta there."

He swung the door wide, reaching in to heave his terrified hostage from the seat that gnarled hands were holding in some sort of doomsday grip. The old fart seemed bolted down, f'crissake. Bobby had to let go of the door and use both hands, and extra muscle, just to pull him out. On top of that, the old fossil had pissed his pants. Jeez.

Something crunched beneath their scrabbling feet. Bobby looked down and saw the pair of wire-rimmed glasses that had been strung across the old geezer's nose lying cracked and twisted in the dirt. One of the stems had snapped off entirely and lay to one side. A flesh-colored rubber blob hung from the earpiece like a huge, gangly wart—a hearing aid, Bobby realized.

Steadying the old man with one hand, Bobby slammed the car door, then propelled his charge toward the abandoned house, feeling his hand fill with the sharp brittleness of shoulder bone through the meager separation of shirt and skin. It was like grabbing hold of a spike.

"Ya done good, Pops," Bobby said, feeling benevolent now in the wake of his good fortune. He even raised his voice to atone for the lost hearing aid as he thrust the old man through the gaping front doorway, tightening his grip when the old fart nearly fell, then almost stumbling himself as he crossed the threshold and stepped down, not prepared for the unexpected drop in floor level. "Whoa, that'll throw ya."

He stood motionless for a moment, letting his eyes adjust to the gloom, not willing to take the chance that there might be another surprise lying in wait. There were chances, and then there were chances. It wouldn't do to get a broken leg right now.

"Yessirree, Pops, you done all right," he resumed the inane chatter, not particularly liking the thick silence, the heavy sense of oppressiveness that clotted this place, and not sure why. "Kept them pigs from shootin' at us, just like I figgered. Better than a bulletproof vest, that's what you were."

He beamed pleasure at his unresponsive charge and saw that the old man was drooling, spit dribbling unheeded down his chin to form a dollop at the edge and leaving a slimy trail behind, like a slug had crawled out of his mouth. Bobby turned away in disgust.

God, it was gross to be old.

A wave of stale humus had greeted their entry, the dank stench of decomposing vegetation and small animals. There was an almost tangible *presence* to the air. It even looked congested to Bobby, like smog had collected, darker in spots as though long ropy twists of shadows hung from the rafters along with the cobwebs.

No, for some reason Bobby didn't much like this place. But it was all he had at the moment. It would have to do.

"Over there, Pops." He gave the old man a shove toward a back corner of the room, glad to be rid of the cold, bony shoulder that had invaded his hand with the chill of a corpse. "And shut up that goddamn whimpering before I—"

The house shuddered slightly and seemed to dip ever so marginally to the left.

"What th'—?" Bobby jerked a look around him.

Another soft jostle. Had the house sunk into the ground just a bit?

Bobby steadied his balance with a hand to the wall, preparing to duck back outside just in case; but the shaking had stopped now, the house was still.

A gurgling wail erupted from the far corner.

Bobby glanced over and saw that the old man was teetering madly among the dappled sunlight pockmarking the room, hands beating about the air, stirring up sparkling dust motes to join him in his crazy dance.

Old feet struggled to retain balance, making the man appear to be doing some insane version of the Sand Mountain shuffle—a marionette on a palsied wire.

"Shut up, you old fool!" Bobby growled. "This ain't California and that weren't no goddamn earthquake! Friggin' house just settlin', tha's all." He strode toward the still-jerking form. "Probably some groundwater, or somethin', d'ya hear me? Now cut it out, I said!"

He grabbed the old man, meaning only to steady him up a bit, maybe help him over to the wall, give him something solid to hold onto—

The decrepit body erupted in a paroxysm of resistance that Fast Bobby wouldn't have believed possible—and wasn't prepared for.

"Shit!"

Claw-tipped fingers raked down his face, ripping through skin and three-days' stubble to send a searing pain across his jaw. It could have been an eye!

"Goddamn old—"

Bobby made a grab for the swooping claw-hand, warding off another swipe that this time *would* have caught his eye—and a wildly floundering punch connected with his right rib cage.

"Ow!" he yelled, renewing his effort to stem the tide of this unexpected grappling match. "By God, that hurt!"

And then the momentary surprise that had caught him off guard and allowed an old fossil fifty years his senior to score a telling blow transmutated into the viciousness that had always ridden the fast lane with Bobby Lloyd.

Snarling like a wounded animal, he grabbed a flailing arm and jammed it ruthlessly backward from the shoulder, relishing the ease with which he manipulated the papery flesh and fragile bone, savoring the thin scream of pain as he felt it splinter—

A deep rumble cut through the roaring in Bobby's ears, a jolting shudder upset his equilibrium. He let go of the flaccid arm and grabbed the old man's shoulders as another tremor rocked the house.

Earthquake? The neon word lit up Bobby's mind before he erased it with *They don't have fucking earthquakes in Flor-*

ida! But they did have sinkholes. He'd heard not so long ago that one had swallowed up a whole used car lot, f'crissake!

The trembling stopped—but now the old man had begun praying in earnest, a piercing, thready drone that scraped across Fast Bobby's nerve endings like fingernails on slate.

"Shut up *Shut Up!*" he yelled, recognizing the prayer of the confessional. "It's nothin', I tell you!" Hands sprang up from the thin shoulders to close around the scrawny neck.

But the old man was past hearing Fast Bobby Lloyd. Deep within the central chest cavity, a heart already damaged by advanced arteriosclerosis and a massive occlusion began to fibrillate. Eyes, shot through with pain and surprise, glassed over and froze, two gaping, staring pools of sightless ice. The single, undamaged arm made a token gesture toward the chest, hand plucking feebly at the loose cotton shirtfront—or was it the distorted sign of the cross? A gurgling rattle slid between ashen lips—or was it a final prayer for absolution?

"Damn you, old man! Damn your friggin' soul to hell!" Bobby shrieked, squeezing as hard as he could and feeling his fingers dig into the stringy neck, unaware that he was strangling a corpse.

Sudden thunder erupted.

For a moment, Bobby was beyond caring what was happening around him, caught up in the Godlike power flowing through his hands.

And then he realized that something really was going on around him, something seriously weird.

"What th'—"

Flinging the strangely lightened body aside, he whirled toward the gaping doorway, astounded to see that the house had sunk a good two feet below porch level. What's more, it was still settling, slipping downward in little jerks and starts that sent shivers cascading through the structure.

Inch by inch the house descended, until the door was halfway blocked by a wall of dirt. It took a small avalanche tumbling into the room to break Bobby out of the amazed stupor holding him enthralled.

"Hey! Wait a minute. Lemme outta here!"

Fast Bobby made a lunge for the door, feet clambering toward the vanishing daylight like they were plodding through hip-deep water. But it felt like he was attempting to slough his way through an ocean of glue, or maybe quicksand, like the air in here was thickening up even more, and it was sucking at his legs, pulling him down.

Floorboards began to pop loose in his path—warping, twisting, reaching for him as though they were alive. He dodged one, two, tried to dodge a third and fell, the impact shoving air from his lungs and bringing blackness to the edges of his vision.

For a moment he simply lay there, stunned, trying to suck in the gummy, sour air, whimpering himself, now, because at first he thought he couldn't and it was like a barbell was lying across his chest. And then he managed to grab a breath, and another, but still the heaviness pressed down on him, cold and menacing, lying atop him like a thermal blanket that had been dunked in ice water. His limbs felt weak and leaden, movement retarded until even the effort to move became a slow-motion struggle.

His darting gaze found the old man—the old man's eyes were open and staring at him, locked on him with a stabbing, hollow gaze. The bruised mouth had gone slack, jaw drooping against the scrawny neck and creating a dark cavern at the bottom of the face that seemed to echo the throbbing cacophony around them.

It sounded like laughter.

"Shut up, old man. Shut Up!" Fast Bobby screamed, squeezing his eyes closed against the scene being branded into his skull. *What was going on here? This was nuts!*

He had to get out of here.

Making a supreme effort, he scrambled on all fours and began to grope his way over toward a window where a wedge of daylight still stretched like a beacon to a lost ship, shouting curses as once again the house shuddered violently, lurched crazily backward—

And then it was in free fall!

An icepick of pure terror sliced through Bobby's gut as the house dropped out from under him—like a rock in a well, like a jumper off a roof, like an elevator snapped from its cable the house plunged into the ground, taking Fast Bobby Lloyd with it.

"Jezus! Jezus! What's hapnin'? What's goin' on?" Fast Bobby shrieked, clawing at the bucking floorboards to keep from being tossed about like a sack of manure.

How could he know that the tired old house had finally had its fill?

Darkness swooped down, a huge black bird of prey. "My eyes, my eyes, I can't see!" he crooned, then realized it was because he was underground.

He giggled—an insane facsimile of his stringy laugh, drawn to a fine thread and strung like a lifeline to the reality disappearing above him at breakneck speed. Down and down the house plunged, diving through its inky shaft while Fast Bobby Lloyd hung on for dear life, swallowing again and again against the ball of vomit that threatened to spew from him.

Wind whistled past his ears, and he clamped his hands over them as he thought he heard the ghostly, echoing sound of his own voice: *"What about it bastard—like the ride?"*

And then the darkness began to mitigate, becoming a burnished sheen oozing between cracks in the floorboards and seeping in through the door and windows.

As much as Bobby had wished for the darkness to be gone, he now wished it back. It was true that there were things in the darkness that could scare you. But sometimes there were even worse things in the light.

Warmth spread toward Bobby along with the light. An acrid stench invaded his nostrils.

"Where am I? Who's there?" he cried, not wanting to look, but not able to stop himself as the house continued its mad descent into—

"No! No way! This isn't really happnin'! It's a fuckin' *dream!*"

Bobby slung his arms across his face, blocking the insane vision that was rushing toward him, the reality that couldn't be.

The house began to slow.

In the distance, a soft drone had sprung up; a strident, cloying sound like a thousand *thousand* souls in—

"No," Bobby moaned. "No, that can't be true. . . ."

A scrabbling noise came from outside the house. A low, wet slither.

Slowly, he peeled his arms away from his eyes, turning his head toward the window he'd been aiming for.

A little bubble of laughter floated up and out of him. There, beyond the window, grinning with the faces of some drug-ridden nightmare were demons and monsters and squirming, festering worms, all merging toward the house, all reaching through a field of fire with their claws and cankered flesh and swaying tentacles.

Flames rose up to greet the house, and Fast Bobby spun away from the horrors creeping toward him, the nightmare vision that couldn't be—*it couldn't be!*

Scrambling over to the corner where the old man had once sought refuge, he lay panting beside the empty corpse, slinging his head from side to side, trying to force the scalding images from his brain, the maddening sounds.

But it wasn't working, nothing was going away.

Instead, it was coming closer.

He could hear the laughter more clearly, now, and he looked down at the old man, expecting—no, *hoping,* that it came from him. But there was no laughter here, nothing from the slack mouth except what seemed to Bobby to be a lightly mocking sneer.

With a sudden, savage motion, he kicked out at the corpse, scrambling away from it as though this were the old man's fault.

"Goddamn you, old man. Goddamn you!"

The laughter came again.

Bobby frantically searched the room for the source of the hateful sound—and another new grating intrusion, a rhythmic creaking, *back-and-forth, back-and-forth.*

A shadowy form had appeared beside the window. He strained his eyes to see:

It was an old woman. An old woman, sitting in a rocking chair. Moving slowly back and forth.

Had she just appeared? Had she always been there?

She was busily rocking and knitting, rocking and knitting. Paying him no attention at all. Spiders crawled among the strands that tumbled from her needles to her lap.

Bobby flinched away from the form that seemed to shimmer in the light of the dancing flames; there, but not there. He could see through her.

He whimpered.

As though the noise had drawn her attention, she began to turn around and Bobby wanted to scream, *No! Don't turn around. Don't make me look. I don't want to look! No more. No more!* He opened his mouth, but he couldn't scream, couldn't even make a sound.

And now she finished turning to him and smiled, her plump, grandmotherly face surrounding dark sockets where eyes should have been. Flames flickered in their depths. Spiders scampered in her hair.

Bobby felt his sanity floating away on the hot, dry wind.

The old woman laughed again, and the sound ricocheted around and around in his ravaged brain as one by one she dropped her knitting needles, beckoning to him with her soft, pudgy hand.

"Come to Nana, boy," she crooned in her old woman's voice.

"Come to Nana. . . ."

MORE VOICES, MORE ROOMS

by Billie Sue Mosiman

Billie Sue Mosiman is the author of the much acclaimed novel *Widow*, and has been a frequent contributor to numerous anthologies, including *Phobias, More Phobias*, and *The Book of Kings*.

He slipped from that place where he was expected to work and cure his soul of melancholy to find the past where he had been happiest. Only one other soul saw him go and let it be. For brief moments outside of time the dead were allowed to wander. Sometimes the wandering escalated a soul's growth, though more often it crippled it.

Moving back through time, the visitor remembered Monroeville, Alabama, and remembering, appeared in a summer field laced with watermelon vines and dotted with fat green fruit. The six-year-old boy, pale and slight among the black field hands, squinted against the bright glare of noon at an unknown photographer, a ragged chunk of ripe watermelon in his small hands dripping its juice on the earth at his feet.

Cousin Callie called him the sunshine of her home. He might have been, he *tried* to be effervescent and to bring smiles to his elders' lips, but behind his boyish shenanigans lurked an unconquerable well of sadness. The woods were too close by and life too molasses slow. He wanted something he could not have. Family. A real home. And something more, something nameless. If it had not been for his beloved cousin Sook, he might have withered away. A cascade of regret set upon his young heart and it grew, spawning disquieting daydreams as the days passed. He was never truly happy, never the carefree child they thought him.

He turned from the field and soared away, looking for better days. Alabama might have been his first home, but never his last, never his best.

Searching for the beginning of his happiness, he entered a slipstream and found January, 1945. He had rented a room at 711 Royal Street in the heart of the French Quarter. Alone at last! Free to write his novels without a household full of women complaining about how he worked all night and slept all day. Here he had no commitments to anyone.

But not all was idyllic; serpents hid in paradise. Money ran low and his stomach grumbled as he passed the cafés and smelled the rich scents of jambalaya, of shrimp gumbo, and French bread weeping with garlic butter. In order to survive, he tried to paint and sell the canvases to tourists in Jackson Square, but he was not much of an artist and gave it up as a bad job after a little while.

Still, New Orleans provided the first glorious days of his young life. Stories poured from his pen, the first part of his novel came into being. Weren't writers supposed to be poverty-stricken and suffer? He knew it would not be long before the world hailed him as a genius. They would not be able to ignore him. He'd *make* them give him the attention he deserved.

Hovering now near the energetic small youth he had been, he watched him lounging on a park bench, his cherubic face turned up to the starry night sky. It was the night he had decided to leave behind sultry, seductive New Orleans. He had to head for his real home, New York City, where the literary establishment could be made, through whatever machinations he could invent, to give over that glittering jewel of renown he desired.

His youth self came to his feet and entered into the jostling crowds, captivated by the twin excitement of the people around him and the idea of moving to New York. At the edge of Jackson Square, he turned his head slowly east, imagining a glittering, beckoning skyline.

He soared again and in the blink of an eye he was standing beside a lad who waited impatiently before the receptionist at the offices of *Mademoiselle* on East Forty-second Street. "I have a short story I want to submit," he heard himself tell her.

When she asked if he had his name and address on it, he replied serenely that he would wait while it was read.

They didn't take his work that day. They thought he was imitating *New Yorker* fiction, and doing it without any distinction, but he came again, bringing with him a wildly comic tale set in Alabama. He had already sold it. He just wanted to show off and that ploy worked wonders. They bought his next story for the June issue. Suddenly everyone was talking about him, the editor at *Harper's Bazaar* wanted his work; he was *in*.

He saw the day he rushed to a little outdoor restaurant and ordered espresso. While stirring cream and sugar into the aromatic coffee, he idly watched the sidewalks fill with lunchtime workers. He laughed abruptly and people glanced his way. He found it a delicious secret that he would never have to be like them, he was special, chosen, a golden boy. He wanted to grab all of them and shout it out. I am a *writer,* they've published me, I'm on my way to literary greatness. Nothing can stop me now! Aren't you astonished? Don't you know who you have rubbed shoulders with today? I may even win the Nobel. . . .

"You've always been sooo self-satisfied, Truman. Even without the ability to read your thoughts, I know what it is you're thinking."

He turned from the café table where he watched the mirage of his young self scribbling on a pad of paper and stared incredulously at the hunched dark shadow who had crept up behind him. "Tennessee?"

"Do you think I wouldn't appear in your stroll through the past? How were you going to avoid me?"

"But you don't appear in my life for a long time yet. I expected this to go the way it did in life. Along a straight time passage, as it were. Who sent you?"

Tennessee Williams came from the shadows of the café canopy and went to an empty table next to the furiously scribbling Truman Capote. He sat, crossed his legs, smoothed the cloth of his trousers at the knee. He was old and wrinkled and thoroughly sad and misunderstood, as always.

"No one *sent* me. I'm as free to indulge in remembrances as you. It's been years now since we died and not once did you come to find me. You've hurt my feelings before, but this time . . . I thought I'd search you out. And where were you to be found? Gone! Off traipsing like one of those wild spirits who can't rest, revisiting the old life. It's *such* a cliché." Tennessee clicked his tongue, scolding.

"I'd think thirty years on Earth bickering and trading insults would have been enough for you."

The young Truman at the table turned his head to the side as if he were listening to their conversation before he concentrated again on the paper before him, quickly writing down line after line, oblivious to the streets of New York as it rattled and sung and swore, noisy as an old whore hyped up with cheap booze.

"Thirty years was not enough," Tennessee said. "Not nearly long enough. Don't you think God has any sense of humor concerning the two of us? If we'd had fifty years knowing one another, it wouldn't have been enough."

"Why do you call me self-satisfied, as if I were a spoiled rotten child? I had my arrogant tempers, but they were for dramatic purposes, you always understood that, prone to the same fits of pique yourself." He gestured with his hands, sweeping away all criticism, past and present.

"Remember when we met?" Tennessee asked, ignoring the question for the moment in order to approach it in his way, at his leisure.

"I remember everything. Too well."

"I was already one of the country's greatest playwrights. Yet I was *never* satisfied with myself. That's where you made your greatest mistake. Is it what haunts you? Could you have been better if you hadn't thought so highly of yourself?"

"Oh, come on, I don't have to listen to you brag anymore. And I certainly won't be scorched by your tongue now, I had quite enough of that! I didn't come back here to put up with this. I wanted to visit just the best of times. I'd rather be left alone to enjoy it."

Tennessee brought out a silver cigarette case and snapped it open. He took a slim cigarette and lit it, clicked shut the case with a snap, and sat staring at how the light glanced off the gleaming surface.

"Well?" Truman moved closer, his impatience showing in his stance, and the fierce scowl on his face. "Can't you go away and leave me alone in this? Haven't I any privacy, even now?"

"In death more than life, that's what you mean?"

"Please."

Tennessee looked lovingly upon his old friend. "I'm still a fool for your exasperated sighs."

Truman twirled and left the café. In a twinkling the other ghost also disappeared and the young man was left alone, scratching his blond head, struggling for the right adjective to describe his young protagonist in the story evolving on the page before him.

Truman shrugged off the chance meeting and went forward to greet the *enfant terrible,* Gore Vidal. He missed him so much, their rivalry, their heated talks. God surely had humor to have left Gore living and writing while taking the best writers away from their work at the most important times of their careers.

He came through the door just behind his own entrance into Anais Nin's apartment, December 1945. He stood aside, unable to control his smirking, while Gore reached out his hand to shake, that frozen look in his eyes. They both wanted to be immortal, to be the number one American writer. There could not be two of them, they both knew it. One would win, one lose, and the game was deadly serious.

Tennessee materialized at Anais' elbow, smoking his cigarette. "Come to gloat, have you? Why spend time on this business? It's long past and no one cares. If you want to see Gore, go over to Italy, make yourself known, frighten him to death with your presence. I thought ghosts were into revenge."

Truman continued watching the three people seat themselves and banter about the local literary scene. They were so full of light, so vital and bursting with energy. They were cynical, witty, laughing at the expense of their colleagues and their betters.

He remembered Anais giving him an inviting look with those lovely eyes of hers and how he thought what a boy she might have made, with tiny wrists, slim waist, little-boy rounded buttocks that would fit so well and bounce so neatly in a pair of thin silk trousers. . . .

Without glancing at Tennessee, Truman said, "Will you stop following me? I don't *want* to go find Gore and appear to him. He'll join us soon enough for my taste."

Tennessee laughed and coughed on his smoke. "You're a heartless son of a bitch."

"That's what you always said. You never really displayed any originality."

He vanished from the apartment, but speeding forward through the years he heard Tennessee at his back, giggling and saying, "Gore told you all your plots came from Carson

McCullers and Eudora Welty! Remember when we were in my apartment and he said that?"

He remembered that old charge, though he couldn't remember specifically if it was McCullers and Welty. "Tenn, that got published, attributed to you, in the biography of me by that Clarke guy. I'm not sure Gore really said it. I don't recall *everthing* the three of us ever said."

"Oh, you mean Gerald? In CAPOTE: A BIOGRAPHY? But, Truman, I'm sure Gore said it. And then you said . . ."

"I think I told Gore maybe he got his stories from the *Daily News*."

"That's right!" Tennessee whooped in glee.

People wrote down what they said to one another. Sometimes they went to the trouble to make up comments so the feud would deepen and become irreconcilable. People thought they were cruel, but dazzling, and people were right.

He sped faster, hoping to dislodge Tennessee from his coattail. This trip was growing tiresome, it really was. He only wanted to shake free of the past by finding the best of times, but Tennessee was making him remember too much of the pain. He recalled when Glenway Wescott met Gore and commented on how talented, he, Truman, was. Wescott claimed Gore blew up and said, "How can you call anybody talented who's written only one book at twenty-three? I've written three books, and I'm only twenty-two!" The thing was, Truman often said something similarly cutting about Gore Vidal.

Certainly he had not been much kinder, always proclaiming to anyone who would listen that Gore had no talent, none, none, none. If for no other reason he would not now visit the elderly Gore, still alive, still writing. He might bring up the old disputes, which was pointless. The relationship had never been worth so much effort in life, much less after death.

"Petty details, wasn't it? Petty feuds not worthy of great men of letters."

He pulled up short, just before entering a new phase in his life's past, and turned on Tennessee. "Why are you here bothering me this way? It's pure torture to hear you *again* nag at me like you're a fishwife and I'm going off to sea."

"You never went off to sea. You never toiled with your lily-white hands, Truman."

"Oh, hell and damnation! I'd have thought you might have learned something being dead. I know *I* have."

Tennessee drew deeply on his cigarette. As he blew out a cloud of smoke, he said, "You have learned absolutely nothing at all, ask anyone. You're furious you died and Gore didn't. You're furious you were born poor and Southern and had to parade yourself like a circus freak before New Yorkers to gain their attention. You're furious you never finished your last novel. You're furious the world has begun to forget you. You're going purple in the face even as I accuse you because you just won't stop this suffering, Truman. You must like it too much to give it up."

He sank to his knees and leaned back on his heels. He hung his head in the dark blue of nowhere ether, out of time, out of corporeal body, out of synch with the universe. "Who said you know every wise thing there is to know?" He said it quietly, in perfect seriousness. "You were as fucked up as I was and still are. I don't have to listen to you."

Tennessee flicked the butt of his cigarette away and watched the sparks from the embers die out into nothing. "I never said I was all wise and all knowing. I don't pretend to perfection, I never did, did I? But I suggest you listen to me. It could well save you more heartache."

"Did someone send you?" Truman looked up at him like a child in penance.

"I told you before, no one sent me. I saw you leave. I knew where you were going. I loved you enough once to come along to bring you back."

"I shouldn't be here? There's no harm. No one can see me. It's all over and done, I can't change any of it."

"You might. Inadvertently."

"I wouldn't!"

"Wouldn't you?"

Would he? He hadn't tried to rearrange his days as a child in Monroeville, all those lonely, endless days of sun and baked land burning his bare feet. He had let alone the empty evenings that stretched like aeons to sunset, the long bitter nights crying into his pillow, wishing someone could come and carry him in their arms to the rocker to rock him and hold him close and safe.

He hadn't tried to make his starving days in New Orleans any less raw and disturbing. There were nights then when he thought he must be a hundred years old and destined to live in obscurity forever. He looked out over the market square and dreamed he was not so odd, not so driven, that he was like one of the streetcar drivers or a mill worker or a tourist from Birmingham having a wild night on the town. Hadn't he trudged back to his room and sweated and beat those words out right from the bottom of his soul, telling things he might have kept hidden, revealing things that made him vulnerable, things the world might ridicule?

Had he stepped inside the young scared man at Anais Nin's door and made him servile before the new rival, made him grovel for approval, made him less brash and self-destructive?

He had done nothing wrong, coming back. He had no thought whatsoever of interfering, though he had to admit he did not imagine before Tennessee's warning that he had the power to. Not now that he had been a ghost, dead so long.

"Wouldn't you?" Tennessee repeated.

"How do you know about . . . these things?"

Tennessee grew grave and his face folded in upon itself as he prepared his confession. "I tried it. And by so doing added sins untold onto my docket."

"You've done this? You've been back and you . . . what did you do, how could you make any change in what has already been? I didn't know it could be done."

"I can't tell you that. I won't encourage you. I wish now I hadn't mentioned it, though you would have discovered it sooner or later on your own. And that's why I'm here. To dissuade you."

"I'm not going back to that place where we wait until you tell me."

Tennessee vanished and only the scent of his cigarette smoke lingered.

Rising, refreshed and exuberant as he had not been in all the time since his death, Truman smiled, turned, leaped forward to the end time, to those days when he was tormented by writing blocks and his unfinished book, *Answered Prayers,* sat mocking him on his littered desk.

There he was, not drunk anymore, he'd given it all up, but sick at heart and in mind and in spirit, distrustful of love, betrayed, angry at life's turns, failing to meet his own expectations and everyone else's. They were hounding him for the manuscript, for *years* they hounded him, but it was his conscience that was never still and gave him the most grief.

His old self sat in a tired stupor, the New York apartment a Bablyon of empty bottles and dirty glasses (his friends still drank heavily), magazines littering the floor, books opened and dropped where he left them, shoes, clothes, notes and messages to himself on the tables, chair arms, thumbtacked and taped to the walls.

Could he change this human vessel of despair? Could he reach out from the grave and transfer hope, enthusiasm, bright new-penny, creative thoughts? Could he give that broken, sad little man a reason to climb out of his dungeon so he could work again, write again, excel once more?

He might not save him from his death, but it wasn't death so much that mattered, it was the work done while alive, and that had been neglected so badly. Not *willfully,* however, and he thought perhaps he might have a chance to turn it all around.

"You better not."

Truman heard Tennessee at his back, smelled his smoke. "If I can do it, I have to. You know that. It's why I couldn't help coming here."

"It's easily done. Too easily. But it changes your future."

"On Earth?" He must pay particular attention to these hints coming from Tennessee. He didn't want to make a mess of the grandest experiment of his existence. Too much weighed in the balance. His last work. Maybe his last few days alive. His fame! His immortality on the page! Hadn't he died in a dishonorable shambles and left behind a few pitiful bitter pages that were nowhere as important in his literary legacy as what he had done earlier in his career? If he could, he must change all that. Forevertime.

"Your *future,*" Tennessee warned again. "What happens to you *now* will be affected."

"How do you mean? Stop being so cryptic and tell me what I need to know to proceed. Or don't. I don't care. I'm certainly as intelligent as you are. I suppose I can figure it out without your goddamned help. I was never your protegé, Tenn."

Tennessee moved to the dozing man on the sofa. He reached out and ran a finger along the man's bottom lip. "This is how you ended up. Soon you'll fly out to Los Angeles and take shelter with Joanne. You'll talk to her for hours while you are dying, you'll tell her you're tired, to let you go, that you've decided to go to China, where there are no phones and there's no mail delivery. It will be your last, and most dramatic, exit."

Truman sank down beside his sleeping self on the sofa and remembered the words he had said as he lay dying. He thought he saw her, so he called for his mama. The woman who loved him most, his Sook, came drifting into the room and he said, "It's me, it's Buddy." He told Joanne he was cold. Tired. Yes, let him go. . . .

Tennessee continued, "While Joanne watches, you'll go away to this world we look on. To change anything before that event, you change where you stand at this very moment in time."

"I don't care so much about what I endured then. I have to do something about the words. The words, my God, I have to fix them. I have to make something beautiful again before I die. You know what I have to do, Tennessee. Please don't play games with me, help me do it, show me how."

"I'd do that . . ." Tennessee paused and considered his next words carefully. "I'd help you if I could, but right now, you see, I'm being called away myself."

As he watched Tennessee, he saw him fading from reality. "Wait! I have to know where the pitfalls are! Don't go yet."

"That's what I've been trying to tell you, what I hoped to save you from. Where I'm going, I won't be back for a long time, maybe I'll never be back." His voice sounded choked. He had tears in his eyes. "I tried to change my own life, I stepped into my past and took control of it, I manipulated it to my own ends, and this is what happened. I won't be in that place of peace with you any longer. I won't come back here to your past. I'll not be seen by you again, Truman. I go away alone to contemplate my errors—at least that's how I understand it. If you interfere here, in *this* moment of time, if you think your soul is worth the risk, then I pity you as I've never pitied you before."

Tennessee winked out and the room vibrated with his passing as from a stiff breeze. Not even the odor of his cigarette smoke lingered.

Truman's ghost sat beside Truman and knew then what he had left behind of his work was all there would ever be. He couldn't fix it, he couldn't do it over, he couldn't choose another project, write another book, astound the world with another beautiful effort.

He reached out, but just before touching his old sleeping

self, he sighed. He gazed around the room at the tawdry remnants of wasted days and said good-bye to the world for the final time.

"I'm going to China," he said aloud, moving through the walls, through the air, through the ether to the quiet nothingness where his soul knew melancholy and this time let it fill him. "There will be no phones to ring, no mail to check."

He stood there obediently. Waiting. All around him spirits chased through the air or dove past him or hesitated, hoping to ask him how he felt and would he like to join them for a little while.

He ignored the activity and continued his wait time. Loving Tennessee. Wishing him well. Hoping he spoke with another voice, in another room, and that he would be back some day when old dear friends were most in need of his generous company.

LAST MAN IN LINE
by Owl Goingback

Owl Goingback's first novel, *Crota,* was published earlier this year to outstanding reviews. His short fiction has appeared in such anthologies as *Tales from the Great Turtle, The Book of Kings, Grails: Visitations of the Night,* and *Excalibur.* In addition to his writing, he has lectured throughout the country on Native American customs and folklore.

"There it is," Kevin Berry said, pointing through the windshield. Matt Dawsen felt a chill dance down his spine as he spotted the entrance to the park. Memories of fussy black and white photographs flashed through his mind. Photographs of prisoners of war—thousands of them—dressed in the tattered remnants of battlefield uniforms, their bodies ravished with malnutrition and disease. Theirs was a hell that few could imagine, and fewer still could endure. The official name of the prison was Camp Sumpter, but it was best known by the name of the town it was located next to. Andersonville.

Matt lifted his foot off the accelerator. Both he and Kevin were students at the University of Central Florida in Orlando. Matt was a freshman. Kevin a junior. Inspired by a television series about the Civil War on PBS, they had decided to make the five-hour trip to visit the park. The sign at the front gate read Andersonville National Historic Site. The word "prison" had been deliberately left off. Just inside the entrance were the buildings that housed the administration office and visitor center. The rest of the park lay hidden from the road.

"Don't stop. Keep going!" Kevin yelled. Startled, Matt stomped on the gas. The little Nissan shot past the entrance and continued South along Georgia State Highway #49.

"But I thought we were going to the park," Matt said,

somewhat confused. "According to the brochures, it closes in an hour."

"We are going to the park, dummy. We're just going another way." Kevin pulled a piece of typing paper from his back pocket and unfolded it. A map was drawn on the paper in pencil. He studied the map for a moment, then looked out the window. "I got this from a friend of my cousin's, who lives in Macon. Can you imagine living in Macon, Georgia? In the middle of the Bible Belt? God, that must be awful. Anyway, he knows of a back way into the park."

"Why? How much does it cost to get in the front way?" Matt asked.

"I don't know. A couple of bucks maybe. It might even be free. . . . Slow down, we're almost there." Matt slowed down. A plowed field lay off to the left. To the right was pastureland and forest. "There." Kevin pointed.

Matt spotted a narrow dirt road that cut back through the field. He checked for traffic in the rearview mirror, turned his signal on, and pulled off the highway. He had to jerk the steering wheel to the left, and back to the right, to avoid several crater-sized potholes. "Nice road," he grumbled.

"Anyway, as I was saying," Kevin continued. "The place is probably free to get in, but I hear it's pretty boring. Not much to see but a few statues, a couple of old cannons, and about sixteen thousand tombstones. Not really worth driving all the way up here, if you know what I mean. But it makes a perfect place for an initiation."

Matt slammed on the brakes. The car slid to a stop. He turned and looked at Kevin, who was grinning. "What the hell are you talking about?"

"You want to join the fraternity, right? Well the boys at Phi Kappa Alpha have decided that your initiation into the sacred order of fraternal brotherhood is to spend a night alone in Andersonville."

"You're not serious," Matt said.

"Oh, yes, I am."

"And when was this decided?"

"About twenty minutes after I told them that you and I were thinking about coming up here. Imagine, spending the night at Andersonville, where the ghosts of over twelve thousand Union soldiers rise from their graves each night, seeking revenge on the Southerners who imprisoned them."

Kevin grew suddenly serious. "By the way, you don't have any Rebel blood in you. Do you?"

"No, I don't," Matt replied. "But this is a joke. Isn't it? Spend the night? What about food and clothing? What if I get caught?"

"Everything you need is in the trunk. I loaded up last night while you were watching the game. As for getting caught, my cousin's friend says the park is empty at night— except for an old caretaker. And he doesn't get around much. No guards. No dogs. Nothing. After all, what's to guard? It's only a cemetery. Nobody in their right mind would be in there at night."

"Except me," Matt said.

"Except you."

Matt had known Kevin long enough to tell that he wasn't kidding. They had grown up in the same neighborhood, attended the same high school, and now attended the same university. Kevin had recommended Matt to the fraternity president as a possible prospect. An honor not every freshman received. Matt wanted to be a member of Phi Kappa Alpha in the worst way. And if he had to spend the night in a cemetery to become one, then, by God, he'd do it.

Truthfully, the thought of spending the night at Andersonville did have a certain morbid appeal to it. He had always been fascinated by ghost stories, even as a kid, though he considered himself to be somewhat of a skeptic. Andersonville, like many other Civil War sites, was reputed to be haunted. Who knows, maybe he would see the ghost of a Union soldier walking in the moonlight. Too bad he hadn't brought along his camera.

"Okay, you've talked me into it," Matt said. "Besides, spending the night in Andersonville for an initiation beats the hell out of getting spanked with a wooden paddle."

They waited until 7:00 p.m., one hour after the park closed, before putting their plan into operation. Matt took his car keys out of the ignition, hit the trunk release, and pulled a flashlight from beneath the seat. Kevin opened the trunk and removed a gray sweatshirt and a small backpack. He stuffed the sweatshirt and flashlight into the backpack, being careful not to smash the sandwiches he'd already packed, closed the trunk, and handed the backpack to Matt. Kevin's secret "back way" into the park was through a tangled growth of trees. There was no trail. Instead, they had to forge their way through a variety of shrubs, vines, and briers. Luckily, they both wore jeans. The brush would have cut their legs to pieces otherwise. They were muddy, drenched in sweat, and covered with mosquito bites by the time they finally reached their destination.

After reading the history of the prison, Matt had envisioned the park to be as cheerful as a stockyard. But he was wrong. Andersonville was beautiful. Four-hundred-and-seventy-fives acres of gently rolling land stretched before them, dotted with stately oak and magnolia trees, and surrounded by pristine pine forests. Monuments of marble and granite stood like silent sentinels in the fading sunlight, guarding the serenity that enveloped the area.

They entered the park at the southeast corner, near part of the earthworks built to ward off an attack by Sherman's army. To the west, a small brick structure marked the site of Providence Spring. The tiny trickle of water had miraculously appeared in August of 1864 after several days of heavy rain. The prisoners claimed that the spring's sudden appearance was the result of prayer and divine intervention and had named it accordingly.

The actual prison site only covered twenty-six-and-one-half acres. Four cornerstones and a rectangle of white posts denoted where the stockade walls had once stood. Constructed by slave labor, the walls had been built of twenty-foot pine logs sunk five feet into the ground. Sentry boxes had been placed along the outside of the wall every eighty-eight feet. Part of the wall, and a sentry box, had been reconstructed at the southeast corner. The north gate had also been rebuilt. A second rectangle of posts, approximately eighteen feet inside the first, showed where the deadline had run. Nothing more than a simple rail fence, the deadline was designed to keep prisoners from approaching the wall. Anyone who dared to cross it would be shot by the guards.

A paved road circled the prison site and led toward the cemetery. They followed the road and soon found themselves among row after row of tombstones, like ivory dominoes waiting to be toppled. Of the sixteen thousand grave markers, twelve thousand nine hundred and twelve belonged to prisoners who had died at Andersonville. They had been buried side by side in long trenches, shoulders touching, their bodies covered with crude planks of wood. No coffins had been provided for those unfortunates and they were often naked—any useful articles of clothing claimed by the other prisoners.

An additional seven hundred tombstones marked the final resting place for Union soldiers who had died in hospitals, other prisoner of war camps, and on the battlefields. The remaining graves belonged to U.S. veterans of other wars. Matt smiled when he spotted the gravestone of a Robert E. Lee, Jr., a TEC 4 in the U.S. Army during World War II. He wondered if he was any relation to the old general of the South.

Six prisoners had been buried separately from all the others. They were the leaders of the infamous "Andersonville Raiders," organized gangs of criminals who preyed upon other prisoners, robbing and murdering them for the few possessions they had. After a reign of terror that lasted for months, the prisoners rose up against the raiders. The six leaders were given a trial, convicted of their crimes, and hanged. Many of the others were forced to run a gauntlet.

They would have explored the rest of the cemetery, but were afraid of getting too close to the administration office, where the caretaker resided. Trespassing on Federal property was a serious offense. Neither of them wanted to spend the night in a Georgia jail. Instead, they decided to hike back to the prison site.

"Okay, this is where I leave you," Kevin said. "Remember, you can't leave until the sun comes up. After that, you head for the highway. I'll pick you up there."

Kevin wished him luck and shook hands. Matt handed him the car keys and watched as Kevin walked back toward the woods. He smiled. At least he wouldn't have to face the mosquitoes and brier bushes again.

Matt decided to set up camp in the shadow of the cannon. At one time there had been several field artillery pieces in the park, but the carriages had rotted on them, leaving only the barrels. The one remaining cannon rested on a platform of wooden boards, atop the earthworks overlooking the northwest corner of the prison. From where it was located, he would have a clear view of both the prison site and the road to the cemetery. If anyone did come along, he would have plenty of time to hide.

He took a seat with his back against the left wheel of the cannon, and pulled a peanut butter sandwich and a can of

Coke out of his backpack. As he ate, he found himself staring at the prison area, trying to imagine what it was like back then. From his reading, he knew that in its fourteen months of operation—from February 1864 to April 1865—forty thousand Union soldiers had been held prisoner at Andersonville. Of those, nearly thirteen thousand had died.

The prisoners had existed on a tiny amount of cornmeal per day, and an occasional piece of salt pork. Fresh water was also scarce. The tiny creek that ran through the center of the prison was fouled with runoff from the latrines, the bakehouse, and two Confederate camps. Many of the prisoners resorted to digging wells in search of suitable drinking water. All but two of the wells had since been filled in for the safety of park visitors. Raised in a comfortable middle-class family, Matt could not imagine living through such an experience and was certain that he would have been one of those who perished.

He must have dozed off, for he awoke with a start. Matt glanced at his watch. It was nearly four in the morning. Not only had he dozed, he had slept soundly for hours.

Just a couple more hours until sunrise and I'm out of here.

Matt turned his attention to the prison site across the road. Everything appeared normal. The four cornerstones, the monuments, and the section of wall glowed softly in the moonlight. But as his eyes adjusted to the darkness, he noticed a peculiar patch of mist covering the ground like a gray blanket, directly over one of the wells. Matt started to dismiss it as ground fog, when he realized that it occurred nowhere else, especially in any of the low-lying areas where fog is most likely to form.

He rubbed the sleep from his eyes and looked again. The fog was only over the one well. But as he watched, it began to spread, reaching out gray tentacles like a living entity.

The fog rolled quivering across the ground, filling the area between the cornerstones. Statues, trees, and markers disappeared as if swallowed, sucked down into the churning mist. He expected it to drift across the road toward him, but the swirling fog stopped at the boundary posts, remaining inside what was once the prison.

What the hell?

He was dumbstruck. How could fog stop like that if there was nothing to contain it? But stop it did. It had to be a trick. Kevin must have rented a fog machine from someone at Universal Studios and snuck back in while he was asleep.

But if that was true, where would he plug it in? There were no electrical outlets anywhere. And how could he keep the fog in a certain area?

Matt suddenly became aware of how strangely quiet it had become. The crickets and whippoorwills, so voiceful only moments before, had hushed their cries as if someone had lifted the needle from a phonograph. In their place was a soft whistling, a musical sound, like the wind blowing through a hollow reed. But no wind blew.

The skin at Matt's temples pulled tight. He cocked his head and listened. The whistling grew louder, changed its pitch, rose and fell. It sounded like a flute, or some sort of woodwind instrument. The sound came from the direction of the well.

Damn it, that's got to be Kevin.

The whole thing had to be a prank. Kevin, and maybe a few of the guys from the fraternity, were trying to terrify him, hoping to have a good laugh at his expense. He wasn't sure how they were pulling off the effect with the fog, but there had to be a logical explanation for it. Maybe they were using battery powered smoke machines and fans.

"Okay, Kevin, give it up. I'm not scared!" Matt yelled.

There was no response. No peals of laughter. The only sound was the haunting melody of the flute. Angered, Matt grabbed his flashlight and headed toward the well.

Though it still hadn't expanded beyond the perimeter of the old stockade, the fog now reached up into the branches of the trees and smothered the heads of the tallest statues. Determined to call Kevin's bluff, he entered the strange vapor. He'd only gone about twenty feet when he realized he was dealing with something far more sinister than a college prank.

The fog was heavy, oppressive. It blocked out the moonlight and filled him with a feeling of intense dread. There was no wind, but it swirled before him like flowing strands of cotton candy. He felt that it watched him, played with him, enticed him to come deeper within its bosom and dared him to do so. Waves of fear washed over him as slender gray tentacles slipped beneath his clothes to caress his trembling flesh.

Things moved in the fog. Dark shapes. Phantoms. He saw them out of the corners of his eyes, but when he turned toward them, they were gone. Once, he saw a face peering at him from the depths of the mist. No body. Just a face. Pale. Lifeless. A corpse's face. The face disappeared when he turned to look at it.

Matt would have chased after the face, but was terrified of what he might find. All around him he heard whispers. And the odor of something dead filled the air, nearly gagging him.

He followed the sound of the flute to the well. Matt had seen the well earlier in the day. Most of it had caved in long ago, leaving a hole a little over eight feet deep. But now, he wasn't sure how deep the hole was, or what was in it. The fog filled the well, poured out of it, making it look like a cauldron of boiling broth. From the depths of this swirling mist came the ghostly song. He listened carefully, but could not place the tune. Sad. Melancholy. A ballad perhaps.

"Kevin, is that you?" he asked hopefully.

No answer.

"Who's down there?"

Again no answer. The only sound was the haunting notes of the flute. He was afraid to call out again. His voice sounded suddenly too loud, as though he was in danger of attracting unwanted attention.

"Kevin, if that's you, I'm going to kick your ass," Matt whispered, as he climbed over the picket fence that surrounded the well. He was just about to sit down and lower himself in, when something shot out of the well and seized him by the left ankle.

Matt cried out. A hand gripped his ankle. The fingers were long and bony, the flesh a leprous gray. He kicked at the hand, trying to break free, but it held on. He started to grab the fence for leverage, but the ground gave way beneath his feet and he fell headfirst into the well.

He landed on his back at the bottom of the well, dazed, but not seriously hurt. His flashlight dropped somewhere in the fall, he lay in darkness so thick that he could not tell if his eyes were open or closed. And somewhere in the darkness was the person who had grabbed him.

Matt jumped to his feet and stumbled backward. His back

hit the dirt wall. A root scratched his face. He couldn't see. Nor could he hear anything, other than the pounding of the pulse in his head and his own labored breathing. He expected his assailant to rush at him and raised his hands to ward off the attack. A few minutes passed. Nothing happened.

"Kevin?"

Curious, Matt inched forward. He reached the other side of the well. No one was there. He turned to his left and circled the entire hole. Again no one. Whoever grabbed him had left.

Matt found his flashlight, thankful that it still worked. He'd just switched it on, the tiny beam of light barely penetrating the mist, when he again heard the flute. The music came from a spot along the wall, a few feet from where he stood.

Damn it, there's no one there.

Angered, Matt dug his fingers into the dirt, searching for the source of the music. Kevin must have planted a tape recorder in the well. If so, he was determined to uncover the device and smash the thing to pieces.

But it was no tape recorder that his trembling fingers uncovered. It was a tunnel.

"Holy shit!" Matt exclaimed. He'd read about how the prisoners of Andersonville often attempted to escape by tunneling out, though few ever succeeded in getting away. The tunnels were kept hidden from the watchful eyes of the guards by starting them beneath a tent or from a well. Apparently, he had just discovered a bid for freedom that had miraculously survived for over a century.

The tunnel's entrance was about three feet above the bottom of the well and a little over two feet in diameter. Matt pulled a few roots out of the way and stuck his flashlight in the opening. The passageway was narrow and straight, and ran northeast from the well. He couldn't tell how long it was, for the light only revealed the first twenty feet.

Perhaps it would have been best to leave the tunnel alone, but he felt compelled to further explore his find. If he could come up with some type of souvenir—a button off a uniform, a cap pin—something to show for his exploits, he was sure to be accepted into the fraternity.

Matt squeezed into the narrow shaft and crawled forward, using his hands and elbows to pull himself along. In the excitement of his discovery, the strange music and the hand that grabbed him were temporarily forgotten.

He'd only gone about thirty feet when he came to a place where the tunnel roof had long ago collapsed. A pile of dirt, hardened over the years into one solid clump, nearly blocked the shaft solid. There was little space to maneuver, but Matt managed to break the dirt and push it out of the way. On the other side of the cave-in, he found the souvenir he was looking for.

The prisoner had died a horrible death, trapped beneath the ground. Buried alive. His bones were all that remained to tell the sad tale, the rusted remains of a canteen half by his side. Matt shined his flashlight forward and saw a second skeleton . . . and another one in front of that.

All together he counted four skeletons, one in front of the other, but there might have been more. After the cave-in, they had been unable to dig themselves out. Nor had they been able to open the other end of the tunnel. Matt wondered why their friends had not freed them, or told the Confederate guards of their botched escape attempt. Perhaps the prisoners had become so callused by death—with nearly a hundred soldiers dying each day—that they figured one grave was as good as another. Or maybe they hadn't wanted the guards to know about the tunnel, for fear of them looking for others. Matt supposed he'd never know the reason, for the answer lay buried with the dead.

As he studied the skeletons, Matt again heard the strange melody of the flute. The music was much louder than before, and it came from behind him. He pushed himself up on his elbows and looked back over his left shoulder. At first he didn't see anything, but shining his light back down the tunnel, Matt saw something crawl into the entrance.

He watched in horror as a shadowy shape moved down the tunnel toward him. A blackness greater than that which surrounded it, the shape moved like some unknown beast along the passageway, stopping, pausing perhaps to sniff the air, only to move on again. Behind the unnamable shape came the fog. Tendrils of gray slithered like giant anacondas down the tunnel, reaching out to seize him in their crushing grasp.

Trapped with nowhere to run, terrified nearly out of his wits, Matt shut his eyes tight as the blackness reached him. He felt it slowly roll over him, sniff him, caress his body like the tongue of some foul beast. His mouth went dry with fear; his bladder emptied.

Matt pushed his face into the dirt and trembled like a frightened dog. He heard voices. Whispers. Moans of pain. He covered his ears, but still he heard them. The voices spoke to him, called his name. He cried out, begged for them to stop, but they did not heed his pleas.

With the voices came intense feelings of emotion—helplessness, anger, and despair. They slammed into him like physical blows, threatening to tear his soul apart. Tears rolled freely down his face. Sorrow squeezed his heart until he couldn't breathe. He opened his mouth to gasp for air and tasted dirt.

A hand touched his neck, cold and clammy. Another grabbed his leg. Unable to stand it any longer, Matt opened his eyes . . . and screamed.

The tunnel was filled with fog. But it was also filled with men. Ghosts. Gray as the mist itself, they were half naked and skeleton thin, dressed in rags, their bodies racked with disease and malnutrition, They labored one behind the other in the tiny shaft, struggling to gain their freedom. As lice crawled in their shaggy hair and beards, and maggots wiggled about in open wounds, they passed handfuls of dirt back from one to the other. They didn't speak, but worked in silence, their faces grim with determination.

The prisoner in front of Matt, a boy no more than thirteen or fourteen years old, shoved a small pile of dirt back toward him. When Matt didn't take it, he turned his head around and looked at him.

Tremors of fear passed through Matt as the boy fixed his haunted gaze upon him. He wasn't much more than a child, but his face was old and lined, his mouth toothless from scurvy. He stared at Matt for a moment, then pulled something from his pants pocket. A stick, about seven inches long, carefully carved with a pocketknife into a musical instrument. A flute.

My God. He's the one. It's his music I heard. He called me . . . called me to this very tunnel. But why? Why?

He held his flute out and pointed at Matt's flashlight, gesturing that he wanted to trade. The unspoken words came to Matt's mind.

He wants my flashlight. They've been trapped down here

all this time. Their spirits imprisoned. They want to find their way out of the darkness.

The boy reached back and laid a hand, light as a feather, on Matt's wrist. He again gestured at the flashlight for a trade. Matt cried out and jerked his hand back. The boy's face hardened in anger. He placed a finger against his lips and motioned for Matt to be quiet.

Something was wrong. Something was very wrong. Not only could he see, hear and—God forbid—touch the ghosts. They could also do the same with him. Unbelievable as it seemed, he was somehow existing on the same spiritual plane as the ghosts of Andersonville.

When they first appeared, the men in the tunnel were gray as the mist, spectral, almost transparent. But they were rapidly becoming more solid with each passing moment. Matt shuddered to think what would happen when they became real.

I've got to get out of here!

He shoved his flashlight into the boy's waiting hand, grabbed the flute, and pushed backward. He prayed no one was behind him, for then he would surely be trapped, and would probably suffer the same unfortunate fate as the rest of those in the tunnel. Luckily, no one was.

After what seemed like a lifetime of crawling, he reached the end of the tunnel and lowered himself into the well. There was a loud splash as he dropped into water up to his knees.

But this well was empty . . . has been for years.

That might be true, but it now had water in it. And the tree roots that once ran up its side were gone. Also missing was the tree, and the fence that surrounded the well.

Matt tried three times to climb out of the well, and finally made it on the third attempt. He pulled himself up, only to discover that his nightmare was far from over.

"Oh, my God."

What had been twenty-six acres of empty land was now crowded with thousands of makeshift tents. They stretched as far as the eye could see, scattered haphazardly about, with no attempt made to establish any kind of order. The tents faded from view into the fog on the left side, and butted up against the deadline on the right.

Resting in the tents, standing beside them, and walking aimlessly about were thousands of Union prisoners. Like those in the tunnel, the prisoners were as thin as scarecrows and dressed in the ragged remains of uniforms. And like everything else, they were also a transparent gray, as though they were made out of fog.

Matt spun around and was startled to see a wall of squared pine logs towering fifteen feet into the air behind him. He could see the wall, but he could also see through it. Between him and the wall was the wooden fence that marked the deadline, no man's land for the prisoners of Andersonville. At the corner of the stockade wall was a sentry box. The face of a young Confederate soldier peered over the wall from the box.

He stood there for only a moment—witnessing Andersonville in all of its unholy glory—but in that brief period of time everything became a little less transparent, a little more solid. There was no time to lose. He had to get out before it was too late. He dared not think what would happen if the prison became solid—became real—while he was still on the inside.

With a pounding heart, Matt raced toward the stockade wall. He weaved in between the prisoners as he ran, jumping over those lying in his way. The thought of touching another prisoner made him shudder, and he went out of his way to avoid doing so. By the time he reached the west side of the stockade, he knew that the prisoners could see him. Heads turned to watch him as he raced by.

He reached the deadline. The wooden rail felt smooth to the touch, wet from the fog. Matt looked up. The guard in the sentry box watched him. He would have only once chance.

Matt ducked under the rail and started across the deadline. The guard shouted for him to halt, raised his rifle, and took aim. Several of the prisoners shouted encouragements to him, and angry words at the guard.

Dear God. Dear God. Dear God.

A shot rang out. The bullet kicked up dirt by his left heel. From behind him the prisoners cried out in anger.

He reached the stockade wall and pushed against it. The wood wasn't completely solid yet, but it was like rubber and resisted his efforts to pass through it.

It's too late. I can't get out. Dear Jesus, I'm trapped!

Another shot was fired. Matt felt something tug at his sweatshirt and realized the bullet had passed through the fabric, just missing his side. A third bullet whizzed by his head.

Matt spun around. All the prisoners were on their feet, watching him, cheering for him. He looked along the stockade wall. The guards hurried to reload their rifles. If he ran back across the deadline, mingling with the prisoners, he would be safe from the guard's bullets. But Matt knew in his heart that once he stepped back across the deadline he would be trapped in Andersonville forever. He'd rather die first.

He pushed himself away from the stockade wall and ran back to the center of the deadline. The guards raised their rifles and took aim. The sight made his knees go weak.

Damn it, don't look at the guards.

With a scream, he turned back around and charged the stockade wall. Arms outstretched before him, he dove head-first at the log posts. There was a tearing sound as the wall parted and he passed through it. Three shots rang out behind him.

Matt hit the ground in a roll and was up and running. He didn't stop until he was a good hundred yards away. Turning around, he marveled at Andersonville as it had been over one hundred years ago. The stockade. The hospital. The prisoners and the guards. Everything stood out bright in the moonlight. But as he watched, it began to waver and transform back into mist. The mist lasted for a few seconds, and then it, too, was gone. All that remained were the cornerstones, the boundary markers, and a few statues.

The caretaker found him that morning sitting beside the cannon. He probably would have had Matt arrested for trespassing, had not the discovery of the tunnel created an even bigger stir. All told, they unearthed nine skeletons from the tunnel—nine prisoners of war unaccounted for on any of the historic rolls. The park officials also uncovered an item that had them totally baffled. One Everready flashlight, its batteries long corroded, its lens cracked, was found tightly clutched in the right hand of the skeleton closest to the tunnel's entrance.

Matt pulled the flute out of his pocket. For over one hundred and thirty years the bodies had been in the tunnel, waiting for someone to come along and discover them. If Matt hadn't been spending the night, if he hadn't seen the fog or heard the eerie music, they would still be down there. Their spirits trapped in the darkness.

He smiled. For one magic moment, deep in the bowels of the earth, he had transcended time to touch the past. He wondered who the boy was, but doubted if anyone would ever know. A nameless child caught up in the horrors of war.

No, not a child. There were no children at Andersonville, only men beyond their years. To the other prisoners, the boy, whose melody Matt would never forget, had been a comrade, a fellow soldier. And to the men in the tunnel, digging for their freedom, he had simply been the last man in line.

ANCESTRAL CULTURE
by Kimberly Rufer-Bach

Kimberly Rufer-Bach lives in California where she works
as a free-lance editorial consultant.

"Behold! Your shelf," my new housemate said as she bent
bonelessly and put her hands flat on the floor. I instantly felt
like a fat cow. I frowned at the tinfoil bundles and crusty
Chinese takeout containers. "Dee moved out in kind of a
hurry," Sandra explained as she straightened up. She backed
up a couple of paces, put a cross trainer on the ugly gold-
speckled Formica table, and continued her stretches. "She
couldn't sleep, hid in her room, flunked out . . . her parents
cut off her rent. There are all kinds of other goodies in your
room."

"Lovely."

Sandra smiled—she had a great smile—and said, "Hey,
I'll see you later. Gotta get to class."

"I thought classes don't start till next week."

"Yeah, at the university. I am a *dawn*-cer," she said, timed
to a plie, which fluidly led into a leap which took her out the
kitchen door.

Sandra was right; there was almost as much stuff left behind as I'd seen the day I came by investigating the ad for
this pretty-good rental in Berkeley. But this Dee apparently
had good taste, and the room was sunny, the place was near
campus, and I figured the lavender walls would grow on me.
So I laid claim to the dresses and books left behind, rejoiced
over the pine dresser I'd inherited, and headed to the kitchen
to get all that crap out of the fridge before *it* grew on me.

In the back of the fridge, behind some petrified Kentucky
Fried Chicken, I found a beautiful cobalt blue ceramic
crock—the kind with the rubber seal and the metal thing you
flip down to lock it.

When I popped it open (and I mean *popped*), a beery

smell came out. Inside, a thin layer of yellow liquid sloshed over viscous off-white slime. "Jesus."

The other housemate looked over my shoulder and pushed her dark curls out of her eyes. "Dee left the sludge? Amazing. She'll shit kitties when she realizes."

I took it to the sink to pour it out. "What would anyone want it for? What *is* it?"

"No, wait," she said. When she grabbed the crock, maybe two dozen bangles clinked on her wrists. "That's sourdough starter—you use it to make bread. Dee said it was in her family for umpteen generations. I mean, if you want to bake the totally rad bread, Indy, this stuff is it."

I winced. "My name's Denise."

"Oh. What with the fedora and camouflage and work boots . . ." She refrained from mentioning my Raiders of the Lost Ark T-shirt.

"Archaeology major. Egyptology. Denise." I looked right at her for the first time. All that hair, black T-shirt, black spandex miniskirt, torn black fishnets, black combat boots, dangly jewelry, *dog tags* . . . "And do I call you Morticia?"

"Lucy. Psych major."

"Uh-huh." I nodded and looked at the glop again. The smell *was* kind of like sourdough, and I remembered one of the books in the closet was about sourdough baking. "Got any flour in this place?" Anything to put off unpacking, right?

Lucy and I made a hell of a mess. Her self-described "blacks" were now toned down quite a bit, and the counter was covered in flour and bowls and glop. It was my fault for trying to use a bowl that wasn't big enough. And after all this, we were only half done. See, to do this, you add your starter—the stuff in the crock—to flour and water and let it sit around in a warm spot for nine or twelve hours.

We tucked the stuff in Lucy's waterbed with the heater on (the bed was against the rental agreement, but as Lucy pointed out, so was Sandra's cat). Then Lucy said, "Come on, Indy, let's go forth and pound a brewski."

"Huh?"

"You know, drink a beer. Where the hell are you from, anyway?"

Right. A beer. We reeled back after the bars closed. I drunkenly grasped at the Post-it on my door twice before I got it: "Will you please clean up your mess in the kitchen?

Sandra." I giggled at the little circles dotting the i's and went to bed with my clothes on.

I was on the porch of the cabin, in the rocking chair. Virgil sat on the top step, picking out "Sally Goodin" on the banjo . . . my sweet grandbaby with flaxen hair like his daddy's and holes in the knees of his hand-me-down trousers. I looked out across the rolling mountains and my hands knitted almost by themselves, in spite of the arthritis. The chickens clucked in the dooryard and up the hill somewhere it sounded like Daniel was chopping wood. I was thinking maybe I should send Virgil to pump some water, but he was getting along mighty fine with that banjo, considering Daniel had only just made it for his birthday, and maybe the water could wait. And I had best milk the cow, as soon it would be sundown, and time to make supper. The biscuit dough should be almost ready. But maybe I'd just rest here a spell first.

Then there was this strange sound—*unnatural* it was. And I groggily realized it was real, and opened my eyes, and it was morning, and my Mickey Mouse alarm clock was ringing. I slammed the button, knocking over my statue of Anubis, Egyptian god of the dead, and fell back to sleep.

Lucy woke me when she barged into my room. She was dressed in a baggy black T-shirt with a pattern of skeletons having sex in various positions and carried the bowl of bread dough. "You know, when I go out and get wasted, I *never* know what I'm gonna wake up with. Come to my humble pad and bowlify thyself."

I squinted at the bowl. "Huh?"

"Come on, bowlify. Brekky bowl. Wake and bake?"

"You mean the stuff is ready already?"

She shook her head. "Come on."

Turns out, what Lucy was talking about was . . . drumroll please . . . "*Loading* a bowl, *sparking* a bowl, *roasting* a bowl, *smoking* a bowl of the skankiest, most-twisting greenbud of the season. We are gonna get baked like geckos. Come on, let's smoke breakfast." She held out a brass pipe and a Bic.

Well. I looked around Lucy's room with the bright, crazed art all hung at odd angles, and the Christmas lights, and the lava lamp, and all the dried, blackened roses, and thought, "Isn't this part of why you came to Berkeley?" And so I sat down on a pillow on the floor and did it, taking a particular, perverse glee in taking sides in the "War on Drugs." I hardly coughed at all and I felt like a rebel, an outlaw. But I didn't feel *high*.

"That happens to a lot of people their first time," Lucy said. "Don't worry. Later we'll do some more, and you'll look in the mirror and see your eyeballs spinning in opposite directions." She giggled crazily.

We went to the kitchen and had coffee and talked about the classes starting next week. Sandra came in, her Lycra bike shorts and Far Side T-shirt soaked with sweat from her morning run. She pointed theatrically at the dishes and flour on the counter as if she was the Ghost of Christmases Yet to Come.

I started on the dishes while Lucy consulted the cookbook. She dumped some of the batch of sludge back into the crock. "We save this to start the next batch," she said. "Disgusting, isn't it? These little germies have been around forever." Then she made that giggle again.

We added more flour and salt and kneaded the stuff. Lucy pulled on some black jeans and a fringed leather jacket (also black) and went to the store for the cornmeal we needed. I wondered about her driving around in that condition, but I didn't have a car. As she went out the door, she said, "This is your captain speaking. Today we'll be flying at thirty thousand feet. To your left . . ." I wondered what would happen if she got stopped by the police, because I knew we both had to reek of dope.

When she came back, she said, "Flew yet another flawless mission, perfect three-point landing." Then we put the cornmeal on a cookie sheet, formed the loaves and put them on the sheet, and tucked them in the waterbed to rise. I finally went to do my unpacking. I was hanging my pseudo-Egyptian art (painted on real papyrus) when Lucy came in and said it was time.

We put the loaves in the oven with a pan of water—the steam was supposed to make a good crust. It baked, we took it out, and the house was filled with fragrant steam.

Sandra came from her room as we brushed water onto the loaves with paper towels to make the crust shiny. Then we had to pick off bits of paper towel.

Lucy grabbed the only decent-sized knife in the kitchen.

"How 'bout giving the first piece to our long-suffering roomie?" she asked. I nodded as Lucy cut into the loaf.

Sandra asked, "How'd you do the faces? Dee wouldn't ever tell me."

Lucy flipped her hair out of her eyes. "What are you talking about?"

But I saw right away. The bread had risen unevenly on the surface, and the bumps *did* look like faces. "Oh, great, 'Face of Elvis Appears on Bread Loaf,' " I said.

"Hell, say it's Jesus and charge admission," Lucy said as she handed a slice to Sandra.

We watched Sandra bite into the bread. Her eyes rolled. Around the mouthful, she mumbled, "This is really good."

We ate bread for dinner. Then the three of us put up another batch in the waterbed. Sandra said, "Hey, I have *Bladerunner* on video."

"Cool, and I have a six-pack," Lucy said.

So we kicked back in front of the sacred glowing box, drank beer, and Lucy loaded a bowl. And this time, I did get stoned. I closed the curtains first, which Lucy found hysterically funny and paranoid. By the second toke, I was barely able to work the lighter. During the commercials, they'd talk, and I couldn't follow the conversation at all. I'd say something, not remember if I'd said it or only thought it, ask Lucy, and then ask her if I'd asked. She laughed her ass off, and Sandra just shook her head. The room seemed very bright. I would wonder why I couldn't keep my train of thought, remember I'd smoked dope, then think, "Jesus Christ, did I really do that?"

I was pretty upset. Here Henry said we was gonna strike it rich and be farting through silk, and all we was digging up was rocks. Shee-it. I mean, the next claim over they kept pulling great big nuggets out of the stream, and here we were, living on water and bread and not much of that.

I was sick of mud, sick of guarding our "claim," and sick of Nevada City. Lordy, we'd even had to sell the mule for flour—and a trip to that "house" upstairs at the National Hotel.

My, what those ladies'd do for a few silver dollars! Why, that one yeller Chinee—you'd think she had ahold of a stick of horehound candy! She'd—

* * *

And I woke up. The TV was still on, showing a *Three's Company* rerun. I didn't get back to sleep that night.

The loaves we made the next day also had faces. And the day after . . . for days in a row.

I got high with Lucy every day (at least once) and had those *dreams* every night, dreams of being someone else. I dreamed I was the wife of the foreman of a logging operation in the redwood forest near Mendocino, California, chiefly concerned with getting the stains out of a linen tablecloth.

I was a servant in a huge house, looking forward to a tryst with my lover, the head of the house, and he was white and I was *black*.

I was a suburban housewife with three kids and a Chevy and one of the first color televisions in town. And a Valium habit.

I was fourteen, helping Mother in the kitchen, and she was sad, because Daddy was off in Germany in the war, but Bill Greenway had brought me daisies he'd swiped from someone's garden that afternoon. I had already spent half an hour signing "Violet Greenway" and "Mrs. William Greenway" over and over in my diary to see what signature looked best.

" 'Morning, Lucy," I said as I sat down to some of Sandra's usual pot of coffee.

"Bowlify, Indy?"

I shook my head. "No, I think I better cut back. I haven't been sleeping so great, and I think it's the weed."

She nodded sagely and took a long toke. In that grunting stoner voice used when trying not to let the smoke out too fast, she said, "It can happen."

"Thought so. But I had a really vivid dream."

"Me, too." She exhaled as she spoke. Lucy had amazing lung capacity, and her next sentence was also visible in smoke. "Really wild. I was so happy because this dude brought me *daisies*." She giggled. "I mean—"

"Wait. Bill, right? Bill Greenway?"

She put down her pipe without toking. "What, did I talk in my sleep?"

So I related my whole dream to her, and she remembered details I hadn't.

"Lucy, this is too weird. It's gotta be the drugs. The other night, did you dream you just got the first color TV in town?"

"Yeah, and unlimited downers. And before that, I was real worried about this stained tablecloth."

"No, that was a couple of nights ago. Before that, it was working as a servant." I looked at the pipe on the table. "You know, my mom always said something like this would happen if I did drugs. Next I'm gonna be hallucinating, then the cops will get me."

"You're paranoid. It is damned strange, though."

I didn't smoke at all that day, just read a book and baked the daily bread with my housemates. And that night, I dreamed I was baking, getting ready for the big annual family reunion in Cincinnati, and was very happy with my new green dress, which would make my cousin Paula equally green with envy.

In the morning, over coffee, I asked Lucy what she'd dreamed about, and of course it was the same thing. "I suppose this stuff stays in your system for a while," I said.

Lucy shook her head and fiddled with her dog tags. "I don't think it's the weed. I've never heard of this before."

Sandra came in from her run, banged the door shut, and rummaged in the fridge. Then she gulped about half a bottle of Gatorade and gasped a few times.

"Hey, Sandra," Lucy asked, "Did you dream about a family reunion last night?"

"What? How'd you—"

"And before, were you a servant and a housewife and trying to get stains out of a tablecloth?"

"Oh, my God. You guys, what's going on?" She leaned on the table between us.

"We're all having the same dreams," I said.

"This is just too fucking weird," Lucy said. "And Sandra hasn't been smoking, so that theory is out."

My eyes hung up on the perpetual mess of flour and bowls on the counter. "The bread. Making biscuits, living on bread and water, helping Mother bake bread—every night we're dreaming of people baking. Baking sourdough."

"Oh, wow," Sandra said.

We stared at each other and blinked.

Lucy reached for her pipe. "I need another hit."

"Haunted," Sandra said. "The bread is haunted."

I looked at Lucy, who was sucking on the pipe with her

eyes closed. "I bet you're right. Lucy, how long did you say whatshername's family kept this stuff?"

The smoke came out in a skunky rush. "Oh, man. And she had all those problems sleeping. . . ."

"And the faces on the bread?" Sandra asked.

"Come on." I led them to my room, where we went through the pile of books in the corner of the closet. She'd left an album of pictures. And guess what?

There was the fourteen-year-old—Violet—who got the daisies. Also the housewife with the TV.

"Uh, I don't think I want to bake today," Sandra said.

"Right on," Lucy agreed.

So we didn't. We dumped most of the proofed batch, put some in the crock, and shoved it to the back of the fridge. I spent the day getting groceries, notebooks, things I'd need for class, which started the next day.

Kitty was getting worse, and every time the wagon hit a bump she moaned. She kept crying for water, but it came up on her every time. Sam's expression was grim and set as he drove the horses on, hoping we could get to a settlement or at least catch up with the other wagons before our little girl died.

We'd been left behind by the wagon train three days ago when the rear axle broke. It had taken most of the day to fix it. The last cow had died yesterday and the whole plan of going to California was clearly doomed. As I wiped the mucus from under Kitty's nose, I wished to God we'd stayed in St. Louis.

Up in the distance I spied something moving at the top of a little rise. Sam shaded his eyes—he'd seen it, too. I prayed and prayed to myself it was someone who could help.

My blood ran cold at the horrible cry. It was a war whoop, it was Indians. Sam dropped the reins in my lap and reached behind him for the shotgun. By the time he came up with it, the Indians were racing toward us on their spotted horses. By the time he had the rifle up and aimed, there was the crack of the first shot, and Sam fell back into the wagon in a spray of blood.

I heard Kitty cry out, Sam's moans, and I loosed the reins and groped for the gun. The Indians were almost upon us. I leveled the rifle as I heard the crack of their rifles and an arrow shot right through the side of the wagon.

My first shot went wild. The second brought down one of the horses, and the Indian was crushed under it in the dust. I cocked the rifle again, aimed, and then I was slammed back off the bench. It didn't even hurt. I tried to sit up, but couldn't. One of them drew right up beside me on his horse, teeth bared. I realized I'd dropped the rifle. Then the Indian raised his arm, and the sun flashed on the knife in his hand as it came down.

I screamed and bolted upright in bed, covered in sweat. A dream. It was only a dream. My heart raced as I reached over and switched on the light. Three a.m. I got out of bed and went into the kitchen. Sandra was already there, in her Garfield sleepshirt. I put on the light, and Lucy walked in, her hair a tangled mess.

"Indians," Sandra said. I nodded.

Lucy went to the fridge. "I've had about enough of this shit. Let's flush it." She opened the door of the refrigerator. "Oh, shit."

We leaned over her shoulders to look. The glop was all over the place. "Guess we didn't put the lid on tight enough, huh?" I said.

We spent about two hours cleaning it up and then stayed together in the kitchen, drinking coffee.

That night I heard a strange sound, and went to investigate. There was a man in the living room, and he had a gun. He forced me to the bedroom and raped me twice, made me suck him, did it to me the back way . . . and then he put the gun to my head and said, "Say good night, Gracie." Then he shot me.

And I woke up and it was about 2:30 in the morning. We all gathered in the kitchen like the night before. The crock was clean, the stuff was gone, but maybe we hadn't cleaned out the fridge well enough. We threw out everything and cleaned it again.

It didn't help. I died two different ways the next two nights, and so did Sandra and Lucy. The next night, Lucy threw some things in her backpack and went to stay with a friend. I went to Denny's, drank coffee, and tried to study.

Around eight in the morning, I went home. Sandra was pale and shaking and Lucy was offering her coffee, Gatorade, a bowl, anything to try to calm her down.

"What was it this time?" I asked.

In a near-whisper, Sandra said, "Earthquake. I was in a store and the wall fell in and I was smashed under the bricks. I was there for hours. Then there was a fire."

There was nothing I could do, nothing I could say.

"I'm moving out, Indy," Lucy said. "I suggest you both do the same."

Sandra nodded weakly.

"What if we just get rid of the refrigerator?" I asked.

Lucy pushed back her hair. "Fuck it."

"Can't afford it," Sandra added.

So that was what we did. It took me a week to find a new place—a week of trying to stay awake drinking coffee, a week of falling asleep and dying horribly, in terror. Then I moved into a mildewy, cramped studio on the Oakland-Berkeley border (a charming area known as "shooter's row" for all the junkies and dealers). Sandra stayed with me for a few nights, her cat pissing in the closet regularly, then went away to live with her family in Santa Cruz. She said she'd been needing some time off, anyway.

Last week, I went by the old house. There were a couple of guys sitting on the front steps and drinking beer. They seemed pretty chipper.

"Hi," I said. "I used to live here and I think I left a couple of things. Is it okay if I go have a look?"

"Yeah, sure," said this skinny guy with glasses and a book on C programming. He opened the door and watched me as I went to the closet and got out that photo album. Then I searched the cabinets and found the empty crock. "Why'd you move out?" he asked.

"Couldn't sleep."

"Traffic noise, huh?"

I'd never noticed, but I nodded. "Ever have bad dreams?" I asked him.

"No. I never remember my dreams."

I smiled, thanked him, and went to pitch the album and crock into the dumpster behind a 7 Eleven.

Lucy and I still get together now and again to share a bowl or go to Blondie's for pizza. We don't talk about it.

SENT DOWN FROM GOD
by Randy Miller

Randy Miller's first short story appearance was in the much acclaimed *South from Midnight* and his second in the popular *Excalibur*. This is his third short story sale. Dr. Miller lives in Tampa, Florida where he works as a professor of journalism at The University of South Florida.

Vera Truesdale understood that a pastor's wife had few rights in the public presence of her husband. The church's teachings made that clear enough. Women were to be submissive to men in this life.

When she'd attended a seminar on the evils of pornography last month, the leader had shown bondage pictures to the crowd and Vera Truesdale had thought, for an instant, that's just what it's like to be a preacher's wife: silent, bound, and supposedly loving every minute of it. And then she fell into the role of proper spiritual outrage.

In the parsonage, however, Vera ran the show. The two-story house was kept in immaculate condition and was free of religious kitsch. Every time some parishioner gave her husband a carved scripture verse or a sculpted pair of praying hands, Glenn Truesdale either kept it at his office or consigned it to the attic. The reverend was not allowed to snack on the couch and had to watch where he discarded his socks within his own home.

Vera made her stand after the grits and cantaloupe had been finished and the coffee had been replenished. Her husband simply could not believe his wife had doubts about his glorious meeting with Ridley Brown and the others yesterday.

"I still don't understand why you'd want to be vice president of the denomination, Glenn. You've never had the political bug."

"I've always wanted to be whatever God wanted me to be, Vera. Ever since I met you at that pep rally thirty years ago, we've followed His lead."

Vera thought back to those days at the small southern religious college when the shy young coed held hands with the handsome boy she never thought would notice her. True, they'd both had dreams in their eyes then. But, she thought, this didn't sound like the life they'd discussed. She wasn't even sure this sounded like the father of her children, the man who prayed for her after a miscarriage, and the love of her life.

"And now, Vera, He's leading me into an important position within the denomination. Ridley Brown himself confirmed it."

"And all you have to do is stab your friend in the back."

"Tom McKee hasn't been my friend for a great many years, Vera. Maybe once we liked each other back at the seminary. But that was before he lost his way." Glenn Truesdale didn't need to add that his Faith Center church and McKee's Harmony church had been at odds for several years now.

"Liked? We were the Three Musketeers, Glenn. Don't you remember the ski trip to Breckenridge? Don't you remember drinking root beer half the night at the A&W in Trinidad, Colorado when Raton Pass was closed? How about the Friday night cookouts at his house?"

"Yes, I do remember those. But that was long ago when we were young. That was a different Tom McKee. You don't remember the things he's said at conventions? You don't remember that quiet Scottish voice with his loud attacks on our theology?"

"Those weren't meant personally and you know it. You used to get along until his church began growing and he got that television program."

"The better to spread his lies with."

"He was terribly hurt when you didn't visit him after the heart surgery last year."

"And I wasn't hurt when he mocked my preaching in front of the Ministerial Alliance? Remember the line about packing a suitcase for a guilt trip?"

"Is that really what this is all about, Glenn? I thought Clairmont was your dream, Glenn. I thought you were perfectly happy here. We went through four other towns and you told me all the while that this is what God wanted. I wouldn't want you to jeopardize it just because you're jealous of Tom McKee."

The reverend stared blankly, then stood and walked from the breakfast nook. He opened the door to the garage, stepped out of the house, and said, "When you're ready to discuss this rationally, then we'll continue. Many are called, but few are chosen, Vera. Will you pray with me before I go to work?"

Vera Truesdale had noticed for a few months that disagreements were officially closed when he left for church. There, she had to play the good, silent, supportive wife. This prayer was just home delivery of her public role.

"Well, I'll pray for you anyway, Vera, that you'll see God's providence more clearly."

She was afraid that she was seeing things all too clearly already.

Only twenty-four hours ago, in a spacious but impersonal airport hotel suite, in the presence of his denomination's spiritual giants, Glenn Truesdale had believed completely that God would send down his wisdom. The five men were silent, heads bowed in prayer. Truesdale had developed a method in order to maintain his concentration: the more fervently he prayed, the deeper he dug his manicured thumbnails into the ridge between his eyes. "Prayer," he frequently told his congregation, "is worth a little bit of pain and one should always pray with hands held high on the forehead to catch the Holy Ghost."

To his right stood Derrick Reid, Olympic Greco-Roman wrestling champion turned youth evangelist. To his left, Lloyd Langenkamp, the arms millionaire and deacon, and Milton Eams, the firebrand television preacher. And straight ahead was Dr. Ridley Brown, the right-hand man of the Rev. John Jacob Jernigan himself, the man considered the second most powerful non-Catholic preacher in the nation, just behind Billy Graham.

To actually consult with these men, the leaders of the denomination's conservative wing was clearly the highlight of the Reverend Truesdale's thirty-year career in the ministry. He had hoped his suit didn't look too cheap or his shoes too rustic.

Brown had explained why he'd been summoned so secretly: "We have invited you here today, brother, to ask you serve as our nominee as second vice president of the denomination, an appointment which, as you know, will lead to your eventual candidacy for president. We have prayed about it. We have studied your record. The Lord has led us to you. I know you'll want to pray about it, but I'm sure that you'll follow his call."

Truesdale lowered his eyes. "I will take this up in our next prayer meeting back home."

"Let me suggest, Brother Truesdale, that you pray on it rather more quickly than that. We'd like a decision before you leave. And, let me emphasize, the Lord has great need of you for the most important battle in the one hundred sixty-eight years of our blessed church."

Truesdale had expected the discussion to touch on this most important battle—the denomination was gearing up for next year's election at the convention. The liberals, not as so-called moderate as the media would believe, had lost the last three elections. One more victory for the conservatives and the liberals might as well hand over the keys to the seminaries and the denominational offices.

"We know that the liberals are going to have to run one of two candidates," Brown said. "They owe Van Lambert a chance—he's done a lot of organizing for them—but he's too much of a nice guy for his own good. Down deep, he's still hoping for a compromise.

"So I'm afraid they're going to offer it to Tom McKee. And he's trouble for us. He's known and he's popular even with a lot of our own folks."

Truesdale had studied the faces of the committee. Eyes were assessing him, his will, his very commitment to Christ. Brown said: "The Rev. Jernigan and I agreed yesterday to offer you a position within the elite, brother. God wants us to pay the price. These men have paid the price. And your price, brother, is to stop Tom McKee and to do it in any way necessary."

Reid added firmly, "When I wrestled against those commies in the Olympics, I knew I'd have to wrestle on their level."

Eams said, "The man is against us, Glenn. You must stop him."

Truesdale asked if he could pray about it—in his church, the order of services often included six or seven prayer sessions. He adopted his lightning-rod pose again and felt

Reid's massive hand grip his skull and then other hands were laid upon his shoulders. After three minutes, he stood and addressed these men of God.

"Gentlemen, in dealing with Tom McKee, I've found only one biblical passage can apply ... If thine eye offend thee, pluck it out. I hope the only thing he'll be running for is the border."

Truesdale needed a rumor and he had learned in fifteen years at Faith Center exactly which sources were adept in the fine art of gossip. One of the deacons could spread the good word at his barbershop and two of the women were connected with more than half of the social clubs in town. He had private conversations with them as well as with a caterer who handled most of the men's service clubs' banquets.

He also needed an impersonator and he knew he wouldn't find a Tom McKee look-alike in his church. Truesdale decided to check the local comedy clubs first; he'd settle for a university drama major if necessary. He found what he needed at the second comedy club, Laugh Til You Stop: a 5-foot-7 performer named Bert Drummond looking for a gig. They met at the club and Drummond, blond and thin with a remarkably unnoteworthy face, was unsteadily gripping a gin-and-tonic. Glenn Truesdale was wearing a purple baseball cap, an old yellow leisure suit and red sneakers—he'd decided an eyepatch was too obvious.

"Can you imitate this man? You won't be under close scrutiny so no one will be able to see that you're a little tall and not quite the same body type. All you have to do is fool someone at about 10–20 yards."

"I can impersonate anyone for money, pal. I've done Jerry Lewis, Jimmy Cagney, Kirk Douglas. For enough money, I'd try Kareem Abdul-Jabbar. What's the deal?"

"What's your going rate for this kind of performance, Mr. Drummond?"

"Hell, if you're paying and you're not drinking, I figure about $1,500 will cover it." Drummond stared at his well-chewed fingernails and figured the guy would talk him down to $500, which would cover back rent.

The preacher took out a roll of John Jacob Jernigan's money and peeled off two C-notes. "The rest you get after the job." Drummond managed to spill some of the drink on the preacher's sleeve and the preacher recoiled as if it were sulfuric acid.

"Just my luck," Drummond said, rolling his eyes. "You'd have paid $5,000, right?"

"Maybe, maybe not," said the preacher, dabbing at the liquor with a napkin.

"Well, I don't exactly have a lot of options open right now. Maybe if I could get to Orlando. Try to crack the tourist crowd. You know, I got a family routine. No profanity."

Truesdale reached into a bag and pulled out a burnt-orange sweatshirt with the words Texas Football imprinted on it—Tom McKee had preached for several years in Austin and was known for wearing that hideous color. "This is what you'll need to wear. I'd be happy to throw in a bus ticket. Now, this is what you'll do and when you'll do it . . ."

Later, the Rev. Truesdale discarded the disguise in a Goodwill box and stopped at a self-serve Exxon. He made sure to spill some fuel on his wrist. Preachers couldn't afford to smell like a gin mill, and gas fumes could cover a multitude of smells. And he drove home in the muggy darkness with all four windows of the Lincoln rolled down.

The Rev. Tom McKee had long refused speaking engagements and other tasks on Thursday nights in order to spend the evening at home. While he and wife Margaret watched NBC comedies and snacked on pretzels, a group of protesters assembled outside of the town's most notorious gay bar.

The protesters included members of a Faith Center Sunday School class that included three of Truesdale's primary gossip hounds. It had been presented during last week's class as a "unique opportunity to put your faith into action." The Rev. Truesdale, through his Sunday School director, had suggested the proper time and place for such an enterprise. He also made sure that other Clairmont churches were represented in the group. After all, other churches read the Apostle Paul; their members knew the score on gays.

Truesdale was conveniently visiting a new deacon and his wife across town. Despite his praise of his weight room and her decorating, the preacher couldn't help but sneak frequent looks at the couple's Christian clock that spouted a different Bible verse every hour on the hour. Vera would have heaved it into the trash can.

The clock was telling Truesdale that in God's heaven

there were many mansions at the very moment when Bert Drummond, hair dyed gray and false nose in place and wearing the burnt-orange sweatshirt, bolted from his chair where he'd downed three gin-and-tonics, pushed through the door, and dashed for a nearby yellow cab in plain sight of the protesters. Sure enough, voices from the crowd yelled, "Hey, that's Tom McKee!" as the cab raced away.

When Truesdale met Drummond behind the comedy club at 8:30, he handed the poor sot his money and told him, "A word of advice, seek God and be on the next bus out of town. Perhaps He will lead you to greener pastures elsewhere."

Truesdale went home and waited for the storm to envelop Tom McKee.

By Monday, the storm was over. Tom McKee had died of heart failure in his sleep after what must have been the longest weekend of his life. He had fielded phone calls from the press, the Ministerial Alliance, several deacons and finally, a secondhand source said, from the liberal wing itself. He had denied rumors about his sexual preference, but the whispers wouldn't stop. They'd asked him to pray about whether to continue as a candidate. Sunday, he'd had to defend himself from his pulpit.

When the cameras showed up at Faith Center Church that Monday afternoon, the Rev. Truesdale stood in his best gray suit with the faint turquoise line in the weave and the silk tie with the turquoise crosses and proclaimed: "God has sent down his lightning and taken away one of the spiritual leaders of our city. I respected Tom McKee even when I did not agree with him. He's in a better place now, of that I am sure." It was a shame Tom had died, Truesdale thought. Glenn wondered if God would call him home in such a painless manner.

He received proper, respectful calls from Brown and the rest that afternoon. Brown told him: "It was a terrible thing that God had to call Tom McKee away, but the Lord has cleared the path for a convincing victory for us next year. You've been a true blessing, brother."

He'd taken his wife to the church for a Youth Department dinner and returned home to find a message on the phone recorder: "Glenn, this is John Jacob Jernigan calling from Jerusalem where I'm on a Holy Tour. I just heard some news about our brother preacher and I want you to know that I feel for his family. I also wanted you to know that I appreciate your fine work for the Lord. May He bless you in the coming year."

When they buried Tom McKee on Thursday, Truesdale stood well behind the crowd. He knew his rival would get a good sendoff—Van Lambert had flown in from Tennessee to do the honors. As a fellow eulogizer, Glenn Truesdale recognized a good service when he saw one. He owed himself a glance at the casket going into the ground and he'd been willing to put up with a Lambert sermon to get it. This one had a decent mixture of sorrow mixed with hope, he had to admit, but the service was far too much like a wake for his liking. Wakes, he knew, were of the Catholic Church and therefore unsuitable for his denomination. Too much humor in the reminiscing. Not enough sobriety.

There'd been one angry look, though. Margaret McKee had spotted him and given him a vicious stare. The Rev. Truesdale would pray for God to relieve her pain, he decided. Vera, who had actually wept with her, told him later that she was thinking of visiting her sister in Oregon for a month.

When he returned home, the message light on the recorder was flashing. He punched the oblong Play button and suddenly bent over.

"Be in your sanctuary tonight at midnight," the voice said softly with a trace of Glaswegian lilt. "Or prepare to suffer for eternity." And the line went dead.

The fingernails were gouging into the ridge between Truesdale's eyes. He'd been praying, knees bent before the altar in the Faith Center sanctuary, for an hour now, waiting for a ghost.

He tried to concentrate on appropriate Scripture verses, but found himself remembering a foggy morning in Edinburgh thirty years ago. He'd been attending an international missions conference—he and Vera, newly graduated from college, were praying about serving overseas—and had planned to take a night train down to London. With some free time, he'd walked past a castle and old buildings until the fog descended. He'd leaned against a lamppost on an unfamiliar street and heard the sound of bagpipes wafting out of the mist. For a short, blessed time, Truesdale had imagined a regiment of Christian souls marching forth to claim victory over Satan's hordes on an eerie moor. It was invigorating.

When the fog cleared, though, he'd walked into a small park and found an old man rehearsing the pipes from an ancient bandshell. He learned not to believe in ghosts on that foggy afternoon. He didn't think he believed in them tonight either.

Truesdale opened his eyes and glanced at his Seiko. Three minutes after midnight. Glenn Truesdale resumed his prayer stance, and heard footsteps softly scooting down the center aisle.

His last prayer was that the trip wire, carefully looped between pews, would catch this ghost. He did not dare to watch.

He could hear the sudden gasp and crash on the floor followed by a low moan.

And when the Rev. Truesdale unfolded himself and walked cautiously to the body, he found Bert Drummond, makeup in place but wig askew, grimacing with both hands around his left ankle.

"You bloody bastard," the actor hissed. "You bloody bastard."

The reverend stood in genuine surprise. "Brother, why are you doing this to me? Why call me here at midnight?"

"You killed him, you bastard," he said through clenched teeth. The ankle must have been sprained pretty badly. "And you got me to help. I didn't even know what I was doing, but I figured it out quick enough. One of the comedians had a joke in his routine about the guy Friday night and I figured it out. Even went to his church Sunday. Saw the man's eyes and knew I had helped drive him to the edge."

"You don't understand, brother," Truesdale said. "I, or I should say, we had nothing to do with his death. Don't you understand that God called that man home to heaven? Don't you understand that the man apparently had a bad heart? It was his time, plain and simple."

"Well, you damn well pushed him. And you don't have an ounce of sorrow about it, do you?"

"There's not anything to be sorry for. It was God's will . . ."

And his voice stopped. The sweet, discordant sound of bagpipes began to fill the sanctuary and the ghost of Tom

McKee drifted slowly to the two men and said, "And what would you know about God's will, Glenn?"

Truesdale turned and ingloriously stumbled over his own trip wire. From the thick silver carpet, he craned his neck around and the ghost said, "Don't go fainting away on me, Glen. We're going to have a fun time, you and I. I'd better untie this wire before you break your little neck."

The ghost turned to the fallen Drummond. "And you, my friend, need to go to the hospital. Stop worrying about the past. I don't blame you a bit." The actor, face frozen, stood shakily and limped as quickly as he could out of Faith Center church and into the night. In the meantime, Truesdale had twisted onto his back and was crawling on his elbows and feet up the aisle.

The ghost, at once visible yet somehow less than visible, began crawling up the aisle right next to the reverend. "Aren't you going to ask me how I've been, Glenn? Aren't you going to inquire about my health?"

"How you've been, Tom?" Truesdale said uncertainly, getting to his feet.

The ghost snorted and the sanctuary shook. "Never better, Glenn. That's the funniest thing. Your heart goes out on you and suddenly you're never better.

"Of course, you can imagine my surprise when I learned about your little meeting at the airport. I know about your deal with our friend Drummond. You've been very busy, Glenn."

And the ghost smiled. Truesdale feared the smile more than the words. For some reason, the grin was worse than a hurricane.

"Vera's expecting you and I wouldn't want to keep you out late," the ghost said. "When you return here tomorrow morning, we'll talk again. And, Glenn, you'll want to have that political bumper sticker off your fancy car."

When the Lincoln pulled into the Faith Center Church lot, the sticker supporting the mayoral challenger—who had made a generous donation last month—remained squarely on the left back bumper. When the Rev. Truesdale, eyes laced with Visine, walked into his pastoral study, the ghost of Tom McKee was waiting.

"I prayed through the night until dawn," Truesdale said.

"And God told me that you couldn't touch me. That's true, isn't it? You can't lay a hand on me, can you? Can you?"

"I can't."

"So you can't levitate me above the ground or devour me like some beast or anything like that, can you?"

"Have you been reading Stephen King, Glenn?"

"You can't even physically attack me in any way, can you?"

"Well, if you've been talking to God, you would know what I could do, wouldn't you?"

"That means you can't make me do anything. Not anything. I have a pre-wedding counseling session with a young couple in ten minutes. I want you out. In the name of God, I command it."

"You're wrong, Glenn. I intend to make you do a whole lot of things. Just remember one word of warning: I'm no Banquo's ghost."

"What is that supposed to mean?"

"I knew the schools were weak, but I'd have expected you to know Macbeth."

"Shakespeare? No, maybe Romeo and Juliet ... Julius Caesar in high school. Unlike you, I preferred to read more scriptural stuff in my college days, as I'm sure you will remember."

"I can understand that you'd know about Brutus, but you'll wish you'd had a more thorough education by tonight." And the ghost vanished.

Vera Truesdale had taken a group of women to a weekend retreat, so the pastor, faced with a freezer of frozen dinners, met some of his deacons for lunch at Paranelli's where they got together weekly to talk football, politics, and church business, in random order. The reverend had just bitten into his piping hot spaghetti carbonara when he sprayed it out onto the fresh breadsticks. He'd glanced at the TV screen over the bar and the reporter was showing a protest site— some people in wheelchairs down at city hall.

And then it showed Tom McKee shouting into a bullhorn.

His deacons stared at him. "I must've swallowed wrong," Truesdale said, rubbing his eyes. "Just had one of those nights when I couldn't get to sleep."

The phone was ringing when he returned to the office.

Suzanne DeWalt, a Faith Center member connected with the Junior League, was calling.

"This man—I swear it was Tom McKee—brought a group of those homeless people into the Plaza and they absolutely ravaged the buffet. Then he whipped out a wad of money and handed it to the manager and the whole bunch of them walked out singing "New York, New York.""

The reverend reached into his top desk drawer and pulled out four Tylenol and then he went home to try to sleep.

When Truesdale awakened, the bedside alarm clock read 11:39 p.m. He stumbled into the kitchen, put on the coffee, and checked the answering machine.

"You . . . have . . . five . . . messages," the voice intoned.

"Hi, honey, it's Vera. We arrived at the campground safe and sound. Call you in the morning. Love you."

Beep.

"Glenn, Calvin Brooks here. Look, a guy in the barbershop just told me he thought he saw Tom McKee playing basketball down at the Y."

Beep.

"Reverend Truesdale, this is Lynette James at the *Dispatch*. Look, I just talked to a doctor who swears he saw Tom McKee delivering supplies to an AIDS hospice and that McKee referred him to you. Please call me at 555-8901."

Beep.

"Glenn, Deacon Terry here. Some Harmony Church people are saying that they went to the Manhattan Transfer concert down at the arts center and—you won't believe this—saw Tom McKee dancing and high-fiving on stage during the concert. Give me a call, will you?"

Beep.

"Reverend Truesdale, you don't know me, but my name's Stan Carbo and I own The Place, a bar south of town where some bikers hang out. This guy who looks like Tom McKee came in here and began to pal around with them. He said you should be sure to call him here when you wake up. The number's 555-2563."

Beep.

They met one hour later in the Faith Center parking lot. Truesdale arrived in his Lincoln, with a freshly scraped back bumper. McKee's ghost arrived in a convoy of Harleys driven by the most disreputable crew of humans Truesdale had ever seen. The ghost was wearing a black leather jacket and a black T-shirt emblazoned with a neon skull.

The ghost waved to them. The group waved back and revved their engines for the return trip.

"A fine group, Glenn. The leader's name is Diamondback and he's a fine fellow. By the way, I see your car's a little cleaner."

"I looked up MacBeth like you suggested. Apparently, only Macbeth could see Banquo's ghost, but I get the point. Evidently anybody and everybody can see your ghost, if you want."

"Do you understand the lesson for the day, Glenn? I can be anywhere I want whenever I want. So let's forget this commanding in the name of God bit. At any rate, I had a talk with God. She doesn't care at all whether your friends or my friends take control of the denomination."

"I apologize, Tom. For a lot of things, I guess. You know that I didn't intend for this to happen."

"I'm happy to accept an apology. And I should apologize to you as well. By the way, you can expect my friends the Road Dukes for Sunday services as well as my friends from down at the AIDS hospice. You'll need to put in a sturdy ramp for my friends in the wheelchairs, too.

"What? I'm not going to do that."

"Oh, yes, I'm afraid your attendance rolls will decline, but you'll be so much happier in the long run. It's either that, Glenn, or the National Enquirer will send a reporter down to ask if you're going to hire Elvis as your new music director."

"There's no way I'm going to let you take over my church."

"But I'm not taking over. You'll be preaching every Sunday. Do you think your fundamentalist friends are really going to keep you around after today, anyhow? When they see bikers and homosexuals here Sunday, they'll forget they knew you."

The ghost began to describe changes—a food kitchen for the homeless, work with ghetto churches, ordaining women as deacons. "You know, it's about time you let Vera share in your ministry a little bit."

"Why are you doing this to me?" the preacher asked.

"Because, Glenn, God and I think you'll make an excellent presidential candidate for the moderates. You see, I wanted that nomination as much as you wanted to stop me. No offense, but I just never figured that they'd use you.

"The thing is, I'm actually kind of grateful. I really like this disembodied stuff. There were a lot of chains on me and there're just as many on you. Don't you think it's time to loosen some of them? Did you know I'd never ridden a motorcycle before last night? Never played pickup basketball anywhere except a church gym? Never been inside a real bar? I think you're going to like trying new things. I know Vera's ready to stretch her wings, too. We'll be the Three Musketeers again. Be seeing you soon."

Glenn Truesdale crouched by the altar and placed folded hands to his forehead. He wondered just who would be invited to Dr. Brown's next meeting in the impersonal hotel suite. He wondered if it were possible that he could win a presidency with the help of Tom McKee's ghost. And he prayed desperately for God's guidance.

After a long while, he heard the click of the sanctuary door. He straightened slowly and turned to confront the apparition, but saw his wife, wearing her plaid flannel pajamas and a black leather jacket and clutching a motorcycle helmet. He ran up the aisle to embrace her. She seemed to glow with excitement.

"The ghost told me that you needed me and that he'd take me to you. That rascal Tom McKee got me on a Harley in the middle of the night roaring down the interstate picking bugs out of my teeth. . . ."

Vera Truesdale stopped talking, stared at her husband, and rubbed the palm of her hand against his brow. When she removed it, there was a small smear of blood from her husband's forehead.

THE FRUIT OF HER WOMB
by Douglas Clegg

Douglas Clegg's novels and stories often deal with the
psychological, supernatural, and technological aspects
of human potential. His recent works include *The Children's Hour* and his epic, *You Come When I Call You.*

1.

I woke up one morning, after a nightmare, and turned to my
wife. "I feel like there's no hope left in the world," I said. I
felt all my sixty years seeping through in that one sentence.

Her voice was calm, and she held me. "Old man," she
said, her sweet voice mocking, "you need to get your joy
back. That's what you need."

After several such mornings, she and I had to make some
decisions. We had some savings, and the leftovers of my inheritance, and I felt it was time to retire to the country.
When my first pension check came, I told Jackie it was time
for the move while we were still fairly young and able, and
she went along with it because she always adapted herself to
whatever was available. The truth was, I had lost my love
for life, and I needed a plot of earth; I just didn't know
where or when I would need to be buried in it. I wanted a
small town, with woods, with groves, with jays bickering at
the window and the sound of locusts in the summer
evening—and then, when I turned seventy or so, I wanted to
die. These were my projections, and having been an
actuarist, I knew that given my height, weight, and
predeliction for tobacco, that death by stroke might come in
the next decade.

And we found all the birds and gardens and quiet in
Groveton, not two hours out of Los Angeles, and more, we

found a house and I found a reason to wake up in the morning.

The house was beautiful on the outside, a mess within. It had a name: *Tierraroja*, because one of the owners (there had been nine) was named Redlander, and decided to Spanish it up a bit in keeping with the looks of the place. An adobe, built in the '40s, it had been a featured spread in *Sunset, The Magazine of Western Living* in 1947, as "typifying the California blend of Spanish and Midwestern influences." Its rooms were few considering its length: three bedrooms, living room, kitchen, but enormous boxcar corridors connecting each chamber around a courtyard full of bird-of-paradise, trumpet-flower vine, and bougainvillea. Beyond the adobe wall to the north, crisscrossed thatches of blackberry vines, dried and mangled by incompetent gardeners, providing natural nests for foxes and opossums. Beyond this, a vast field, empty except for a few rows of orange trees, the last of its grove—ownership unknown, the field separated the property from a neighbor who lived a good four acres away.

We loved it, and the price was reasonable as we'd just moved out of a house in the city that was smaller and more expensive. Jackie had a carpenter in to redo the kitchen cabinets the same day escrow closed. I asked the realtor about the empty field, and he reassured me that the owner, who was a very private person, had no wish to sell the vacant lot. We would have the kind of house we had dreamed of, where I could relax in my relatively early retirement and where Jackie could put in the art studio she'd dreamed of since she'd been twenty.

It was on the third day of our occupation of the place that we found the urn. It was ugly, misshapen from too much tossing about, a bit of *faux* Victoriana, dull green nymphs against a dark green background. Jackie found it at the back of the linen closet, behind some old Christmas wrapping papers that had been left behind, presumably by a previous resident. The urn was topped with a lid that looked as if it were an ashtray put to a new use, and sealed with wax.

My wife shook it. "Something inside."

"Here," I said, and she passed it to me. I gave it a couple of good shakes. "Rocks," I said. I sniff everything before I let it get too close to me; this is an odd habit at best, annoying at worst, and applies to clothes, my wife, the dog, and

especially socks—a habit acquired in childhood from observing my father doing the same, and feeling a certain pride
in a heightened nasal sense as if it were an inherited trait.
So, I put the urn to my nose. "Stinks. Like cat vomit." I
looked at the pictures. Not just nymphs, but three nymphs
dancing with ribbons between them. On closer inspection, I
saw that the nymphs had rather nasty expressions on their
faces. In one's hand was a spindle of thread, another held the
thread out, and the last held a pair of scissors. "It's the Fates
in some young aspect," I told my wife, remembering from
my sketchy education in the Mediterranean myth-pool, "see,
this one spins the thread of life, this one measures it out,
and this one cuts it. Or something like that."

Jackie didn't bother looking. She smiled, and said sarcastically, "You're such a classicist."

"It's pretty ugly," I said. I was ready to take it out to the
trash barrel, but Jackie signaled for me to pass it to her.

"I want to keep it," she said, "I can use it for holding
paintbrushes or something." Jackie was one of those people
who hated to waste things; she would turn every old coffee
can into something like a pencil holder or a planter, and
once even tried to make broken glasses into some unusual
sculpture.

My wife turned the garage into her studio. The garage
door opened on both sides, so that while she painted, she
could have an open-air environment; the fumes would come
up at me, in the bedroom, where I stayed up nights reading,
waiting for her to come to bed. But she loved her studio,
loved the painting, the fumes, the oils, the ability to look out
into the night and find her inspiration. I played with my
computer some nights, called some buddies now and again
from the old job, and read every book I could on the history
of the small California town to which we had come to enjoy
the good life. I was even going to have a servant, of sorts:
a gardener, name Stu, highly recommended by our realtor, to
tend the courtyard, to keep the blackberry bushes, ever-
encroaching, in check, and to bring in ripe plums in August
from the two small trees in back. I was happy about this ar-
rangement, because I knew nothing about dirt and digging
and weeding, beyond the basics. And I didn't intend to
spend my retirement doing something that I seemed incapable of. Stu and I got on, barely—he was not a man of many

words, and, although only ten years or so younger than me, we seemed to have no common ground to even begin a conversation. He liked his plants and bushes, and I liked my books and solitude.

Within weeks of being settled, I knew I had nothing to do with my time. I found myself going into town on small, useless errands, to get paper clips, or to see if I could find *The New York Times* at some newsstand within a fifteen-mile radius. The town, while not worth describing, was less planned than it was spontaneous: it had been a citrus boom town before the second world war, and after, it was a town for people to find cute places in, but to not do much else. From the freeway, it looked like stucco and smog, but from within, it was pretty, quaint, quiet, and even charming on a cool October afternoon. The library captivated my interests, since I had once been a history teacher, and was an avid reader. It was full of documents about the town and its architecture, fairly unique to southern California, because most of its buildings were a hundred years old rather than twenty.

I found our house, Tierraroja, had at least one story about it. This I learned, briefly, at first, from a local newspaper account from 1952. It seemed the Redlander family had left suddenly, and the house was empty; no one could discover the mystery of their whereabouts. When I went to the librarian, a man named Ed Laughlin, he asked me why I was so interested in the house.

"I live there," I said.

He smiled. "Yeah, right."

"No, really. My wife and I moved in the middle of September."

He chuckled, "Who's your realtor?"

I told him the name.

Again he laughed, "Should've known. She's been trying to unload that place for two years."

"Are there ghosts?" I asked, hoping that there might be, just for something different.

He shook his head. "Nothing that unbelievable. Just that old Joe Redlander chopped up his wife and kids one night. Nobody knew it until about a year after they were gone. The new owners found body parts all over the place, hidden in secret places. They found Joe eventually up in Mojave, but he claimed he didn't do it. He'd found them like that, he said, but the police weren't buying because first off he ran and second off his prints were all over the ax. Heard he blew his brains out up in Atascadero or someplace like it."

2.

I parked in front of my wife's studio; the doors were open, letting in the last of the October sun, almost a light blue sunlight, through her canvases and jars, making her brown-gray hair seem cool and icy. I went up to her, kissed her, and looked at the painting she was doing. It was from memory, of the pond that had been behind her mother's house back in Connecticut. She had just put the light on the water; and it wasn't New England light, but sprays of California light. I waved to Stu, our gardener, who was trimming back what had, in mid-summer, been a blossoming trumpet vine, but which was becoming, as winter approached, a tangle of gray sticks.

"He's so dedicated," Jackie said, "I think I'm going to ask him to sit for a portrait. His face—it has those wonderful crags in it. He's just about our age, but he looks younger, and then, those lines. And the way he holds the flowers, sometimes." She shook her head in subtle awe, and I wondered if my wife was in the throes of a schoolgirl crush on our gardener.

"We had some murders in our house," I told her, figuring it was the best way to make her think of something other than Stu.

She grinned, shaking her head at me as if I'd been a bad boy. "Good God, you'd think you'd have better things to do than make up stories just to frighten me."

"No, really. I was down at the library. The guy who named our house killed his family. You're not afraid, are you?"

She gave me what I had come, through the years, to call her Look Of False Brain Damage. Then, she set the large flat board she used as a palette down on the cement floor, and began dipping her brush in turpentine. "Well, I'm finished for the day," she said. "You making dinner, or me?"

I shrugged, "I guess I can. Spaghetti or chicken?"

"Spaghetti's fine," she said, and then, bending over, picked something up. It was the urn. "I still can't get this lid off. I've been prying and prying. Think my Mister Strong-Man can do it?" She passed it to me.

I tried, but could not get the old ashtray off the urn. "You tried melting the wax?"

She shook her head. "Not yet. You're so smart and strong," mocking me, "I'm sure you can get it open for me."

I gave the urn a good shake, and heard that thing inside it, again. Hard. Like a large rock. "You know," I said, "this guy Redlander chopped his wife and kids up—there were three—and then put their body parts in weird places in the house. Maybe they didn't find all of them. Maybe one of them's in here. Maybe it's the missing hand of little Katy Redlander."

Jackie made a face. "Don't you dare try and scare me."

"Maybe," I said, "it's Mrs. Redlander's left breast, all hardened around the mummified nipple."

I didn't bother trying to open the urn until after dinner. Jackie went into the living room to watch TV, and I stayed in the kitchen. I turned on the gas stove, and put the edge of the urn's top near it. Wax began dripping down into the flame, making blue hisses. When the wax seemed to be loosening enough, I pulled on the ashtray, and it made a sucking sound. Then, I twisted it, and it came off. I wondered if, in fact, little Katy Redlander's missing hand might not be inside the urn. I sniffed at it, and it smelled of tobacco. I held the urn up and tipped it, and out dropped a pipe.

I picked it up off the floor, setting the urn on the edge of the counter. I sniffed the pipe. Smelled like cherry tobacco. A very uninteresting find, although the pipe was quite beautifully carved in rich red wood, a satyr's face. A satyr, I thought, to chase the nymphs of fate on the outside of the urn. Carved clumsily, as if by a child, into the base of the satyr's bearded chin, were the initials, J.R.

Joe Redlander.

"So that's why it's covered with an ashtray," my wife said when I showed her. "Somebody was trying to quit smoking."

"So he seals his pipe up and hides it."

"Or has someone else hide it for him."

"Joe Redlander," I said.

"Who?"

"The guy—you know, the guy I told you about."

"Oh, right. The Lizzie Borden of Groveton, California."

I paced about the room, holding the pipe in one hand, the urn in the other. Jackie kept shooing me around so she could watch TV in peace, but I kept crossing in front of her. "His wife wants him to quit smoking the pipe. But he wants it. So she seals it up, and hides it. He begs her for it. He begs the kids, maybe even bribes them, to show him where Mommy put it. But the kids know better, or else they don't have a clue. And then, when it gets to be too much, he gets the ax he's chopped up all the wood with, that afternoon, and he says, 'Dolores,' "

Jackie interrupted, "Dolores?"

"Whatever," I said. "Joe says, 'Nancy, if you don't tell me where my pipe is, I'm taking you and the kids out.' And she thinks he's joking, so she laughs, and he," and here I mimed whacking my invisible wife with the pipe.

As if she had a moment of supreme victory, Jackie said, "Ah, just like you and your Baskin-Robbins pistachio ice cream?"

"I never chopped you up for that, did I?"

"You would've liked to. You were going to become a blimp the way you ate it, it was a kindness to throw it out. The way you whined for days after that, you'd think I took away your soul."

I made a Three Stooges eye-poking gesture at her and an appropriate noise. "Okay, anyway, so then he goes to the kids, and they're screaming, so he does them, too. And to think, if he'd only looked behind the old wrapping paper . . ."

"The paper was old," Jackie said, "but I don't think it was from the fifties. And that pipe could've belonged to anybody. Jesus, Jim, you need a hobby."

"Look at the initials," I said, to further prove my case, passing the pipe to her.

She looked at the pipe, its carved face, and then squinted at the satyr's beard.

"J.R.," I said, "Joe Redlander. The man who killed his family."

"Your initials, too, Mister Smartypants. Could be James Richter," she reminded me, "maybe the pipe's meant for you."

Later, I put some tobacco in the pipe (for I was an inveterate smoker), and lit it, as if this would give me some inspiration.

3.

I found the old crime, and the pipe and urn, occupying my thoughts after that. The wrapping paper wasn't from the 50s, I discovered, but a kind that was sold by Girl Rangers in the mid-seventies. So, I figured, someone else had found the urn, too, and had hidden it. Maybe someone else knew of its secret. I went to the linen closet, and looked back at the cubbyhole where the urn had been secreted; I reached back to it, and found that, by pushing one of the shelves aside, there was another hiding area. I moved the towels around and brought out the shelf. I leaned forward, reached back into this newfound hole, and only came up with a wadded scrap of notebook paper. It was wrapped in a spiderweb, which I dusted off, and then unfolded the paper. It was yellowed, with large gaps between the thin red lines—the kind of paper elementary-school age children use before they've become adept at rocker curves and the like. In scraggly block letters in ink, it had several figures written across it. It actually looked like a pictographic language, until I realized that it was not some ancient tongue recorded, but the doodlings of perhaps a six-year-old. At the bottom, an initial "K." I folded it neatly and put it in my pocket. I would ignore it; perhaps throw it out. I didn't even tell Jackie about finding it, because I didn't want her to know the extent to which I was fascinated by the story of the Redlander family.

I went back and read the obituaries in the old local newspaper, *The Groveton Daily*. For 1952, March 17, it listed Virginia Redlander, and her children, Eric, 11, May Lynne, 9, and Katherine, 7. So, there was a Katy Redlander, after all, I thought. How clairvoyant of me to have guessed it, considering I couldn't predict weather or my own wife's mood with anything greater than five percent accuracy. So little Katy had written what looked like highly-stylized hieroglyphics and had put it back in her secret place, not far from the urn.

"Or maybe you're just bored to death," Jackie said, when I finally showed her the wrinkled piece of paper that had occupied my mind for three nights in a row.

We were in bed, and she was feeling amorous, while I was being indifferent to sex. "These diagrams," I said, pointing to the one that looked like it had an eye in the middle of it, with some kind of strange animal (a unicorn?) in its iris, "you think a second-grader really did this?"

"My exact question to you," my wife said, turning over, finally. "I think, Jim, maybe you need to go back into teaching at least part time or as a substitute, because you're driving yourself and me crazy with all this weirdness."

I hadn't even noticed how weird I had become in the past few nights. I looked around my side of the king-sized bed, and there were books on Egyptology, and runes, and Greek mythology. I had checked out half the local library's classical section, because those diagrams of Katy's resembled a mix of mythic-images, and I wondered if there were some key to it all.

But I was being weird. So I leaned into my wife, kissing her neck. "I love you," I said.

"I was sure you were enamored of Katy Redlander's ghost."

"I'll throw those things out tomorrow," I whispered, and she turned her face so I could kiss her, and we made love that night, but it was not like it had been when I'd felt more vital. I knew, at my age, I was still fairly young, but I did not believe it, and as my wife and I held each other, afterward, I wondered why it was not as interesting as when I was twenty, or thirty, or even forty, why sex and even food were pleasures that were losing their taste for me; and I wondered why life had to slip like that. Why, I thought, looking out the window at the few deciduous trees in the yard, their leaves having turned the pale yellow of California autumn, why can't we be like leaves, more beautiful when we are closer to the ends of our lives?

I thought I saw something there, as I looked at the trees, something dark against the floodlights, not quite human, trotting away from the window as if it had just watched us.

4.

In the morning, I went to check the window, as if I would see footprints, but there were none. Jackie skipped her painting that day, and was going to drive into Los Angeles to visit with a friend, so I took to wandering. The empty field that bordered us beckoned me with its orange trees, for they held small but juicy yellow-green fruit, and I decided it was high time to pick an orange right from the tree. The grass in the field was just turning green again, because of a recent rain, and I waded through it, mindful of snakes and fire ants. When I approached the fat orange trees, I glanced back at my house: it seemed tiny, like a house on the edge of a toy train track. The trees were powerfully aromatic, for some tiny white blossoms still clung to the branches; most of the oranges were wrinkled and inedible, but there were a few, at the highest branches, which were plump and only just mature. I got a stick and knocked on the uppermost branches until I managed to bat one down. It rolled into the rich earth that was dark and grassless between the several trees, and I went to retrieve it.

There, on the ground, someone had drawn, with a stick, one of the same diagrams I had seen on Katy's paper.

The eye with the unicorn.

I looked around the other trees, and by each of them, another drawing or diagram. A sketch of a dog? Or a pig? And then, several lines with forked endings—snakes?

But something else, too, there, in the dirt, beneath one of the orange trees: an animal, torn up beyond recognition, the size of a small dog.

Dressed as if for a celebration with dozens of tiny orange blossoms stitched with a gay red thread through its mouth and around its eyes, and sutured along its guts.

5.

It was a pig, as best I could determine, because in spite of its mutilations, its corkscrew tail was intact, and rather than stink of slaughter, it smelled fragrant with orange and just the scent of mint and sweet pepper—both of which grew wild in any direction across the field.

Children, I thought, and then: Katy Redlander.

The conflicting thought: but she's dead.

Then, a playmate.

Some friend of hers from 1952, who giggled over arcane rituals they'd found in—a book? *The Golden Bough?* Or Jaspar's *The Birth of Mythology?*

Some friend who grew up—would be, what? Forty-nine or

so now? And still believed in ritual sacrifice in a sacred grove?

I had read reports of Satanic cults in surrounding towns, and of fringe fundamentalist groups which held snakes and drank poison—how far from that, was this?

I left the animal there, and went to spend the rest of the day in the library. I looked up pigs in both the Frazier and Jaspar texts. In Frazier, pigs were associated with the Eleusian Mysteries, the rites of Demeter, and the loss of Persephone for half the year—a resurrection cult. But it was in Jaspar's *Birth of Mythology* that I struck gold. In the fifth chapter, on mystery cults, Jaspar writes:

". . . what 20th century man fails to realize about these so-called 'cults' is that these rites brought the god or goddess closer to man, so that man, in his ignorance, would be inducted into the mystery of creation. The virgin would be buried with the other offerings for a moon, during which time the participants would dance and sing themselves into a frenzy, and fast, and often commit heinous acts as a way of unleashing the chaos of the human and divine soul, intermingled—all in the name of keeping the world spinning the correct way, of keeping it all in balance. Thus, when the virgin was buried alive, it was not an act of cruelty, but of unbound love for the child and for the very breath of life, for the virgin represented the eternal daughter, who died, was buried, and then resurrected into the arms of the Great Mother after a time in Hell. This is not so different from the rites of crucifixion, and burial of Christ, after all. And in this act, the young woman who was sacrificed mated with the God, and returned to impart wisdom to the other participants in the Mysteries . . ."

Beneath this, the diagrams I had found in the wadded paper.

On the following page, a color plate showing the urn, of which mine was an obvious replica, of what I had thought were the three fates, dancing.

The caption beneath it read:

The furies in disguise, dancing to lure youths into their circle, so that they might torment them into eternity.

I remembered a quote from somewhere.

Those whom the gods would punish, they first make mad.
And the story of Orestes, who had brought tragedy and

dishonor down upon his House, tormented by the Furies in their most horrible aspect.

Joe Redlander with an ax in his hand, holding down little Katy's neck while he went chop-chop-chop.

I could picture the house in disarray, the walls splattered with red, the boy trying to crawl away even while his father slammed the ax into his skull; and the mother, dead, cradling her other daughter, as if both were sleeping on the small rug in the hallway.

I closed my eyes, almost weeping; when I opened them, I was still in the armchair of the reference room of the library. Ed Laughlin, the librarian I'd spoken with before, stood near me. He wore a pale suit which hid most of his paunch; his hair was slick and white, drawn back from the bald spot on top of his head. He squinted to read the cover of the book I had in my hands.

"You feeling okay?" he asked, then, before I could answer, he said, "ah, the ancient world. Fascinating. Coincidentally, I hope you noticed who donated most of our reference works on mythology, particularly fertility cults."

He gestured for the book, and I handed it to him. He flipped it closed, and then opened it to the inside cover. He passed it back to me.

I was not surprised.

The bookplate read: From the Library of Joseph and Virginia Redlander.

"He kills his family and then donates books?" I asked.

Ed didn't smile. "Believe it or not, Joe was a smart man, well-read, quiet, but strong. Admired, here in town, too. When a man cracks, you never know where the light's gonna show through. I guess with Joe it just showed through a bit strong."

"Did you know them well?"

He shook his head. "Barely, I was involved in the library here, but also the County museum over in Berdoo. Joe was always nice, and careful with books. That's about how well I knew him. A hello, good-bye, nice weather kind of thing. It bothers you, too, though, huh?"

I assumed he meant living in the house, knowing about the murders. "Not too much. I find it more fascinating than frightening."

"Well, always got to be some mystery in life, anyway,

stirs the blood up a little, but it seems strange to me she never showed."

I asked, "Who?"

"The oldest one. Kim. She was sweet and pretty. Fifteen. Some say she ran about a year before the killings—she may have had a boyfriend here, met on the sly because her folks were real strict about that kind of thing. Maybe she ran off with him. Maybe she did the killings, gossip was. But I don't think so—she was fifteen and sweet and small, like a little bird. Me, I think she got killed, too, only Joe, he did it somewhere else. I hope I'm wrong. I hope that pretty little girl is all grown up and living across the world and putting it all behind her best she can."

6.

My wife was sitting at her canvas, painting, and I arrived swearing, as I went through the area packed with art supplies that surrounded her. "Damn it all," I said, "this is the only garage in creation without garage things."

"Damn right," she responded, "now take your damn language and get the hell out of here." All of this in a calm, carefully modulated voice.

I gave a false laugh, and slapped the inside wall with my hand. "Now, where in hell would a shovel be when I need one?"

Jackie pointed with her paintbrush to the courtyard. "He'd know, Mister Brainiac." She looked more beautiful now, with the late afternoon light on her hair, her face seeming unlined, like she always had, to me, and it amazed me, that moment, how love did that between two people: how it takes you out of time, and makes you virtually untouchable.

I turned in the direction of her pointing—it was to Stu, our gardener, kneeling beside the bird-of-paradise, trimming back the dying stems that thrust from between the enormous, stiff leaves. I went out into the yard. "You have a shovel I can borrow?"

He didn't hear me at first.

He was humming; then, he saw my shadow. He turned.

He was only a few years younger than me, but he actually looked older. Not on the surface of his skin (except in laugh and smile lines) but in something I'd seen mainly in cities:

a hard life. Not difficult, for all lives are difficult to varying degrees, and some people suffer with more relish than others, but hard, as if the lessons learned were not pleasant ones. I had always thought the gardening life would be a fairly serene one: the planting, growing, flowering, seasonal, balanced kind of thing.

"I need a shovel," I repeated.

"No problem," he said, and stood. He led me out to his truck, and reached in the back of it, withdrawing a hoe and a shovel. "I assume," he said, "you're planting."

"Just digging," I said.

He nodded, handed me the shovel, and set the hoe back down.

"You've done a good job around here," I said.

He almost smiled with pride, but another kind of pride seemed to hold him back. "It's my life," he said simply, and then returned to work.

I watched him go, his overalls muddy, the muscles in his back and shoulders so pronounced that he seemed to ripple like something dropped into still water. Then, I turned. I didn't know if I was going to bury a dead animal, or to dig something up, something that had been in the ground for four decades. I used the shovel to press my way through the blackberry bush fence that had become thin with autumn, and headed into the field.

The stink of the dead pig came back to me, along with the scent of its orange blossom garlands. There was a wind from downfield, and it brought with it these, and other smells: of car exhaust, of pies baking, of rotting oranges and other fruit ripening. It almost made bearable the task I was about. When I got to the brief clutch of orange trees, I saw the flies had devoured much of the dead animal, but, oddly, the local coyotes had left it alone.

Behind me, a man's voice, "You planning on burying it?"

I turned; it was Stu, the gardener. He shrugged, "Decided to follow you out here. Figured you could use some help."

He reached up to a branch of one of the trees and plucked off a small blossom. He brought it to his nose, inhaled, and then to his lips. It seemed, to me, that he kissed the blossom before letting it fall.

"Do you know anything about this?" I asked, indicating the pig. "Local kids?"

Stu shook his head. He had kind but weary eyes, like he'd been on the longest journey and had seen much, but now, only wanted sleep. "You won't be burying the pig, will you, Mr. Richter?"

"No," I said.

"What the hell," he said. "I know you know all about it."

"What's that?"

"I hear her, sometimes," he said, "when I touch the leaves."

"Who?"

He looked at me, almost angrily. "I don't have nothing to hide. I didn't put her there." He pointed to the ground beneath the dead pig.

"The dead girl."

He whispered, "Not dead." His eyes seemed to grow smaller, lids pressing down hard, like pressing grapes for wine, tears. "I don't believe it."

"You were her friend," I said.

"I love her. I always will love her." Stu wiped at his eyes. "Look around. This field, used to be nothing. Dirt. Nothing would grow. No orange trees. And your house, dead all around, a desert. But she's done this." He spread his arms out wide, as if measuring the distance of the earth.

"Did you do it?" I asked, even though I didn't want to.

"I killed the pig, if that's what you're asking. It's an offering."

"To whom? To Kim Redlander?" I glanced at the ground, wondering how deep she had been buried; buried alive for a Mystery more ancient than what was written down in a book.

"To the goddess," he said.

We went out into the field, as two farmers might after a long day of work, and spoke of the past.

He said, "I have faith in this. I have faith. It wasn't strong at first. Her dad told me he and her mother went all crazy and it was their festival time or something, and what he did ... to the other kids ... and to Kim ... it was 'cause she didn't come up that spring. He went wild, Joe did. I read all the books, later, and I came to a kind of understanding. I spoke to Joe before he killed himself. He lost his faith, you know? He didn't believe anymore. But I had nothing but faith. I know she's there. Look," he showed me the palm of his dirt-smeared hand. "She's in the earth, I can see her, there."

Joe Redlander and his family buried their daughter alive, I thought.

For the Mother of Creation buried her in the earth, Persephone going to the underworld to be with her sworn consort, and they must have expected her to return in the spring. A family of religious nuts, and one teenaged boy, hopelessly in love with a girl.

In love forever.

"It never happened," Stu said, "that's what her dad told me. They waited in the spring, and she didn't return. But I knew she was still here. I know she'll come back, one fine spring day. Til then, gardening seems to bring me closer to her."

"She's dead, Stu. I know you weren't responsible. But she's dead. It's been over forty years." I was shivering, a little, because I sensed the truth in his story.

He looked across the land, back to the orange trees. "She's in everything here, everything. You may not believe, but I do. I've known things. I've seen things. She's down there, fifteen, beautiful, her hands touching the roots of the trees. She's going to come up, one day. I absolutely know it."

As we both stood there, I knew that I was going to have to fire Stu, because there was something unbalanced in his story, in his fervor. I didn't think I could bear to look out the windows and see him gardening, thinking of love and loss as he tended flowers.

I knew I would lose sleep for many nights to come, looking out at that field, wondering.

7.

Then, one night the following April, someone set fire to the field, and, in spite of the best efforts of the local firemen, my wife and I awoke the next morning and found we were living next door to a blackened wasteland. I got my morning coffee, and went to the edge of the field, near the road. The orange trees were standing, but had been turned to crouching embers. I walked across dirt, stepping around the bits of twig that continued to give off breaths of fugitive smoke.

Where the girl had been buried: a deep gouge in the earth.

I watched the field after that, but saw nothing special. In a month, new grass was growing, and by summer, only through the dark bald patches could anyone tell that there'd been a fire at all.

And today, while my wife painted a picture of the courtyard, I went into the garage and found an old tool, a scythe. I took it up and went out into the field to mow. This action was not taken because of some fear or knowledge, for the Mystery remained—I didn't know if some animal had been digging at the hole where Kim Redlander was offered to the world, or if Stu himself had dug her up days before, moving rotting bones to another resting place. I didn't go to the field with any knowledge. I went singing into the field, cutting the hair of the earth, propelled by an urge that seemed older than any other.

Some have called this instinct the Mystery, but the simpler term is Stu's:

faith.

I swiped the scythe across the fruit of her womb, and gave thanks and praise to the Mother all that day, for I could feel Her now, walking among her children; I spilled my own blood in the moistened dirt for Her.

My wife called to me, waving from the yard, and I turned, holding fast to the bloodied scythe, while I heard a young girl whisper in my ear that faith demands sacrifice.

Life was precious, for that moment, full of meaning and wonder.

I walked wearily but gladly across the field, and when I reached my wife, her face brightened. "You've found it," she said.

"What's that?"

"Your joy," and she seemed truly happy for me.

"I have." I thought of Joe Redlander, and Stu, and Kim, the believers who brought me to this place.

The scythe seemed to shine like a crescent moon in my hand as I brought it across my wife's neck.

GHOST CAPER
by Wendy Hornsby

Wendy Hornsby's writing is more commonly found in mystery anthologies, where she's highly popular and critically acclaimed.

Rollie had to run through three backyards and under a dozen dark windows before he got his hard on. More effort than usual, and that worried him. But now the boner felt good, rubbing against the inside of his sweats with every step he took.

The night was ideal for capering. Rollie imagined how the crime report would read: At 0100 hours, the weather was dry and overcast, the temperature in the low sixties range. The crime scene area was residential with commercial activity along the major cross streets, Sunset Boulevard to the north and Santa Monica Boulevard to the south. A nice, clean report, he hoped. He would put in a request for a copy. The best part of it, he smiled to himself, would be the last line: No suspect description.

Rollie ducked down a short alley off Hampton and cut through the first yard he found that had no yapping dog. The yard was small and well-kept, behind a small, well-kept house. The only light came from a TV in a den at the back. In the flickering blue light he could see two shiny bodies undulating on the couch, layered one on top and one below.

Dense oleander bordered the redwood patio deck. He slipped into the shelter of its clipped branches to watch the lovers. His dark clothes made him feel invisible, powerful like a ghost on the couch between them. He stroked himself in the rhythm they set, breathing hard for them.

The night air was soft, fragrant with jasmine and clipped lawn. So nice, he could have finished himself right there. But he forced himself away, to stay focused, stay on task, because he knew *they* would be in the next block, or the next. Finishing without them would be a big-time disappointment.

He backed away from the cover of the oleander, his black sneakers as quiet as a shadow's steps on the damp grass. He went through a gate at the side of the house and, staying low, crossed the sloping front yard.

When he came out on Genesee, walking, Rollie saw the first unit parked less than a block away, facing north toward Sunset. For a moment he savored the discovery. He had known they would not fail him, but now it was a sure thing. If they looked into their rearview mirror, they would see him, and, if the light hit just right, they would know him. He smiled wide for them as if they had asked him to say "cheese." With a sudden sadness at the transitory nature of this delight, he wished he could have a snapshot, a memento from a memorable evening.

Rollie was sorely tempted to tease at that point, to do something closer to the edge of dangerous, to test them, see how much they had learned from him. Resisting the urge prolonged the pleasure. Already, he felt that if he so much as touched himself he would explode. But it was still too soon.

They never traveled alone. If there was one car out looking for him, he was certain there would be others. They could try to be unobtrusive, but he would easily spot their cars, generic American makes with dark paint jobs, oversized blackwalls, and a little antenna on the trunk. They might as well have sent black and white units after him.

It was mid-week and nothing else was happening in West Hollywood—he had checked the radio calls before setting out. There should have been enough units available to stake out the entire neighborhood, double the normal: West Hollywood straddled the jurisdiction between L.A.P.D. and the county sheriffs. If the call was heavy enough, they would both roll out. Rollie didn't worry about their number, only that they were good at their work.

The target he had picked was two blocks south, on Norton. Walking casually, he stooped at the end of a driveway to scoop up a throwaway advertiser. He slipped off its rubber band, awkward work with masking tape wrapped around his fingertips, and made a show of looking the paper over as he walked easily up the drive toward the lighted house. At the first sculpted shrub, he ducked out of view from the street.

He vaulted a low picket fence that separated this yard from the neighbor's, then skulked through the prickly shrubbery and climbed over another pair of fences, until there was only a vacant house with a room addition in process between him and the target he had scouted on Norton Street. The building debris, bits of two-by-four, bent nails, twists of baling wire, made the going treacherous underfoot. Still, it was a good launching pad. There were no house lights, no inhabitants to rouse if he made a misstep.

The play was on: he spotted a second car. Taking cover behind an untrimmed hedge, and then a pile of new lumber, he made his way to the side of the dark vehicle.

Once again he felt the little electric trill in his groin as he rose to peer into the car window. He had his hand halfway to his waistband before he stopped himself. Instead, he reached into his pocket to finger the card he had tucked there, his ace in the hole, proof of membership in the club if things suddenly went wrong.

The car was empty. So, they were out on foot, hunters looking for him. That was good. He smiled, loving the ultimate challenge to date. They had parked directly across the street from his target.

Using their car as his cover this time, he stopped to listen. He heard the ordinary sounds of night birds, TVs, households after bedtime. No police radio static, no cop talk. Satisfied no one had spotted him, he crossed the street standing up.

He had chosen his target with care, watched it, scoped the neighborhood for a week, explored every possible route between target and home base. A good challenge, plenty of variables.

Other than location, the target was just ordinary, a duplex he figured rented in the fourteen-hundred-a-month range. By the standards of West Hollywood it was modest, but not impoverished, rent well within the grasp of a young executive laboring in the corporate proving ground. No big deal, no hotshot security system.

The front unit of the duplex was heavily landscaped with politically-correct, drought-resistant foliage that would help to conceal his movements. Assholes, he laughed under his breath, as he slipped silently through the shrubbery toward the rear unit. Dues-paying, card-carrying assholes.

He saw no sign of *them*. They could be hiding in any of

the houses in the neighborhood, even behind the dusty junipers lining the driveway he was walking down. But they
weren't. He knew them so well—he was them—he would
have felt them.

Even if he were sure they weren't around, he would have
been as cautious. Heightened awareness was an essential
factor in good capering.

He approached the rear unit and tried the front door. Why
overlook the obvious? The door was locked, as were the
windows on either side. He walked around to the small back
patio and tried the sliding glass door. It was locked, but the
slider was loose in its track, a cheap aluminum frame.
Grasping the top edge of the slider, he slowly, carefully
lifted it. At first, the door resisted, but the latch popped free
of the jamb and the whole side came out of the track without
so much as a squeak. He moved it aside just enough to slip
inside.

The first thing he did was walk through the dark apartment and unlock the front door, in case he had to leave in a
hurry. Then he went back and replaced the slider into its
track and locked it. In the morning, while the investigating
officers and deputies wrote their reports, the tenants would
beat themselves up about forgetting to lock the front door.

Preliminaries taken care of, Rollie was free to roam.

The apartment was smaller than he had expected. Two
bedrooms, living room, dining alcove, kitchen, a single bath.
The furnishings were relatively spare, more taste than cash
evident in their selection. The VCR was new, the TV was at
least six years old. There was a decent CD-tape player combination in an expensive glass-fronted cabinet—the nicest
piece in the room.

He walked down the short carpeted hallway that led to the
bedrooms, being quiet, but not so quiet that he eliminated all
the possibilities.

The first bedroom seemed to function as a study or small
office. Accustomed to the dark, he picked out a PC, a FAX
and a modem hookup on a desk that was no more than a
hollow-core door on two sawhorses. Opposite this desk,
there was a Stairmaster exerciser like the one in his den at
home. Works hard, stays fit, he thought, judging again the
path of escape.

With the apartment's layout committed to memory, Rollie
went back out to the short hall. The bedroom door opposite

was slightly ajar. Taking his time, moving like a ghost, he pushed it open.

In the soft yellow glow of a small night light, he saw two nude figures in the queen-size bed. He looked at them closely. This was West Hollywood; if they were both men, he would leave. But he saw painted toenails sticking out of the tangle of sheets, a spill of long hair across one of the pillows, and, below, a dark triangle with nothing protruding between the legs.

The single blanket had fallen to the floor, atop a pair of slacks. Rollie picked up the slacks and rifled the pockets. The fabric was nice, a step above Penney's, a step above this neighborhood. In the left front pocket he found a money clip with about a hundred dollars. He slipped it into his own pocket with his emergency Pass-Go card.

There was a matching suit coat draped over a bentwood chair, but its pockets held nothing more interesting than a tiny vial of coke and a narrow tie clasp. Nothing that couldn't easily be replaced, so he left it intact.

He picked up the watch on the nightstand, an older model Rolex with a crack in the crystal, changed the time and the date, and put it back. Never take anything with a serial number was rule one. The bedside alarm clock was set for five A.M. He shut it off.

This was a man's bedroom. A single man's, with no women's clothing in the deep closet. He picked up the woman's high-heeled shoes from the floor beside the bed and stuffed them inside his sweatshirt.

The woman stirred in her sleep, tossing off the sheet to expose her firm, surprisingly large, young breasts. He went over to the bed and ran one finger along his erection, the other along her slender calf. She sighed softly and rolled against her bed partner, nestling her face into his hairless chest. Her partner drew her close and sleepily stroked her buttocks. As her lips began to move against his small, dark nipples, the intruder traced the graceful curve of her neck. Just to do it.

As the sounds in the bedroom grew heavier, he slipped into the bathroom. It was a little messy, the counter cluttered with the sort of hair goos and sprays he expected from what he had learned about the occupant. On the glass shelf under the mirror he found an old-fashioned shaving mug and a straight razor, like he'd seen in old movies. He picked up the

razor and opened it, ran his finger lightly along the fine
blade. So sharp it sliced through a layer of the tape on his
fingertip. At least, he thought, here was a yuppie toy that
was worth something. He closed the razor and put it back on
the shelf next to the soap mug.

He left the bathroom and walked through the bedroom and
out into the hall. The couple in the bed had settled back to
sleep. The woman had rolled away from her partner, who
was facing the far wall, snoring lightly.

He gave the house one more going over. In the kitchen, he
found a candle, placed it in a cereal bowl, and lit it. He figured it would take a few hours to burn down. When the occupant and his guest came up for air again, and found they
had overslept, the candle would give them one more thing to
worry about.

His second pass through the small office turned up a nice,
gold overlay pen and pencil set. He could use them for writing burglary reports, so he slid the set into his pocket. There
was nothing else he could think of to do.

He went to the front door, opened it, then paused, looking
toward the street, feeling unusually unfulfilled. No one
was waiting for him. The pressure against the inside of his
sweats had collapsed.

The entire caper had been nothing. He felt disappointed,
depressed. Deprived of his due.

In the very beginning, merely thinking about capering had
done it for him. Now every nocturnal outing demanded more
of him: more danger, more challenges, more close calls.
Push yourself to the limits, he always told them. But for
himself, the limits kept moving away from him, always just
beyond his grasp.

When he turned on his heel and walked back inside,
headed straight for the bathroom, he was fueled with anger.
There were hot tears in his eyes the second time he entered
the bedroom, this time with the folded razor in his left hand.

The woman breathed softly, embracing her pillow. Rollie
leaned over her and kissed her lightly on the ear. Still asleep,
she turned toward him. He put his lips over hers, drew in her
warm, sleepy breath. As her mouth opened to receive him,
he opened the razor and drew the blade across her throat.

He kissed her hard now, pressed her shoulders against the
bed, held her still as she struggled against death. The throes

lasted only seconds, made no more noise than the sighs she had made in her sleep.

When she was gone, Rollie moved his mouth down over her surprisingly erect nipple, tasted the warm, salty blood that flowed from the wound.

The power of what he had done almost overwhelmed him. He felt a surge, like the rush of the sea filling his head, threatening to sweep him over. For support, he backed against the wall and took a deep breath, her scent still on his face, the taste of her on his tongue.

In the dark, the blood streaming from her neck looked like a long, sinewy black ribbon that trailed across her shoulder, coursed down her slender white arm. She was beautiful. He loved her.

With his wrapped fingers, he lifted her arm, placed it gently over the man's back. Desperately, Rollie wished he could be there to watch the man discover that, right there in the bed next to him, his lover had been unfaithful. Unfaithful with a ghost.

For a moment, he felt a pang knowing he, too, had been unfaithful. Of all the transgressions Valerie had accused him of, adultery had never been among them. The secret knowledge of his conquest cleared his head, cheered him.

Planning was the key, and he was way off schedule, had spent far too much time inside. Meticulous even in his hurry, Rollie picked up a dirty white gym sock from the floor beside the bed, pulled it over his hand and carefully, lovingly, wiped the razor clean before he returned it to the bathroom shelf.

The front door was ajar as he had left it. Still with the sock on his hand, he went out, locking the door behind him.

Concealed again by the junipers at the edge of the front yard, he stopped to view the stakeout car across the street, saw that it was still unoccupied.

He knelt down and dug a small hole in the freshly turned garden, then buried the sock and the tapes from his fingers. Sometime in the future someone might find it all, but crusted with dirt, rotted from the sprinkler water, none of it would be of value to the hunters.

Where were the hunters, Rollie wanted to know, feeling distressed that they had fallen down on him after all of his efforts. He knew that when police reached the point in their careers where they were put on plain-wrap stakeout they definitely did not like to be out on foot. They liked to be in their cars, warm and comfy. He knew from his own experience that the cardinal rules for experienced police were never go hungry, never get wet, never get cold, and never breathe hard. That's what they had rookies for. Didn't these guys know that? Hadn't he taught them anything?

He looked down the street both ways, but still saw no sign of anyone. He reached inside his sweatshirt sleeve and pulled out the poster he had lifted from the drugstore down on Beverly, at least, a Xerox he had made in quantity of the original poster. Using the wiper to hold it, he stuck the poster to the windshield right in front of the driver's seat so the driver couldn't miss it: Casper the Friendly Ghost. Then he took the woman's shoes out of his shirt and arranged them carefully on the hood. Shoes of a lover met and lost in the course of an evening; he wanted to keep them.

Once they saw his trademark on the car window, every black and white unit in the area would deploy, not to mention helicopters, and, if they got excited enough, L.A.P.D. units circling the outside perimeter. Looking for the ghost.

Feeling a little better, thinking about the reaction of the stakeout team when they got back into the car, he headed for home. After the first rush, though, thinking didn't do it for him any more. He felt robbed.

"Hey you! Halt."

He spun toward the voice, saw the uniformed figure and the mobile police radio in his hand. He knew he had virtually no time before the deployment began—cops, dogs, and that fucking helicopter. Police cars were certainly rolling in to seal off the area. He knew they expected him to behave like any other burglar. Run, and try to find a place to hide. Then they would bring in the dogs and sniff him out. And, if he were like the others, that would be the end of him.

What made it fun, he grinned, was that he wasn't like the others.

He sprinted between the houses, vaulted the first cinderblock wall in his path, and kept running. He reached Lexington and glanced back toward Genesee, saw the first black and white pull up to the intersection. They had been fast, so maybe they were good, too. With all his heart, he hoped so.

He crossed Lexington in mid-block at a dead run. As he reached the far curb, he heard the car bearing down behind him. He knew he had breached the first line of containment, but the good part was, there was more to come.

The first helicopter came whooping in the sky, maybe thirty-five or forty seconds away from where he was. But in thirty-five or forty seconds, he could be a long way into somewhere else.

In his black shoes, Rollie ran down a driveway, through an open gate and into a back yard that blessedly had no loose dog. Like all yards in the area, it was small and separated from its neighbors by an easily scalable fence. His mind was clear, his movements sure. This chase is what it had all been about. The fresh boner slamming against the inside of his sweats was the proof.

As he hit the grass on the far side of the fence, he disturbed the dreams of a German shepherd sprawled, chained, next to a redwood doghouse. The dog got up and barked at him, but made no attempt to chase him. Rollie slowed to taunt the dog just a little. But the dog saved his energy for old ladies and paperboys.

A wooden gate blocked the driveway. He hardly broke stride as he rolled over it. The gate wasn't latched, so it moved with him. He rode it into the front yard, waved at the shepherd as a farewell, then bounded across Hampton.

He ran full out between houses, expecting the helicopter to pick him out at any moment. He made it to Fountain Avenue, and took a big chance: he ran along the sidewalk, in the open, to Curson. He could hear the helicopter overhead, feel the disturbance in the air, see the trees move, making shadow monsters in the night. But the light hadn't yet found him so he continued to run in darkness.

All around, he heard the approaching cars as the police tried to seal him inside their snare. He had only a little farther to go. The best for last.

When he turned north on Curson, he was sweating, but he wasn't winded. All the training in the hills of Elysian Park above the police academy was paying off. He would have energy to spare when the payoff came.

He heard a car brake close behind him, heard the two sets of footsteps and the shouting. He risked a glance, felt relieved when he saw they were no one he knew. At this point, the card in his pocket had lost its magic to save him, had become instead a ticket to the wrong side of the barbed wire.

Both officers were in full stride behind him, wiry little

guys in good shape. If he had been the pursuer, he would have relied on the car for as long as possible. Maybe, he thought, the officers liked it better this way, the excitement of the chase canceling out the obvious and efficient. He could relate to it, but not condone it.

At Delongpre Avenue, he turned right. He knew he could outrun almost any cop, but he couldn't outrun their radios, or their helicopter. With only a couple of short blocks to go, the chase was more a matter of timing than strategy. He sprinted across Sierra Bonita and found himself in the vortex of approaching red lights. The helicopter spot played all around him, making the shadow monsters dance with him.

The street was a cul-de-sac that dead-ended in front of a library. He knew, because he had done his research, that neighborhood kids had cut shortcut holes through the chain-link fence around the library. He found his hole and was through it without missing a step. Across a slippery wet lawn, another parking lot, then one last fence with the same ease. He came out on Gardner and saw his goal two houses further down the block.

At the moment the helicopter finally passed directly over-head he was sheltered by a huge old pepper tree. His move-ment was lost among the shadows of the wildly blowing branches as the chopper moved on.

An L.A.P.D. cruiser careened off Sunset and roared down Gardner, headed straight at him. He grinned, risking a quick touch to his full-on erection: they were too late.

He rolled under an oleander hedge and emerged in his own sideyard. Without straightening all the way up, he reached the door, turned the knob, and was embraced by the warm after-dinner aroma of his kitchen.

Overhead, he heard the circling helicopter, saw the revolv-ing shadows it cast as it passed over the street. They had come close this time, beautifully close.

The sounds of the search continued outside in the night around his well-kept bungalow as he hurried down the hall, struggling to get out of his shirt, dropping it to the carpet as he ran. He was in pain; the pressure in his testicles was al-most more than he could tolerate.

Valerie was asleep, curled up on her side of the king-size bed. He stumbled out of his sweatpants, spilling from the pocket the stolen money clip, the gold pen and pencil, his own police photo I.D. card.

Before Valerie could waken and protest, he stripped the
covers away from her and rolled her on her back. He knelt
over her, put his mouth over her small silk-covered breast,
groped under the slippery gown fabric to find her warm pu-
bis.

She opened her eyes and pushed her hard little fists
against his chest.

"You've been running again," she said. "You stink. Be a
sport this time and go take a shower first."

"Can't wait," he moaned, spreading her legs apart as he
lowered himself down on her. He thrust himself deep inside
her, ignoring the sharp intake of her breath, her nails digging
into his shoulders. Three long, shuddery strokes, and the caper was over.

Once again, the ghost had won.

TIGER, TIGER, BURNING BRIGHT

by Christopher J. Morgan

Christopher J. Morgan is a recent graduate of the University of California at Riverside where he received a degree in political science. This is his first professional sale.

February 11, 1911
Aboard the steamer, the HAMILTON

It so happened that I was bellying my way through a quag of some officious slime in the middle of a Sumatran mangrove when I first got the telegraph. My best boy, Singh, and I had been slithering through pulpy, dark mulch that smelled vaguely of pig shit for the better part of the morning, trying to capture a live spitting cobra that the London Royal Zoo had commissioned me handsomely to catch. Singh and I had spotted one that would scare the daylights out of the Brit Zoo patrons, thick around as a man's arm and well over six feet of fight, and we were edging through the awful, earthy mess when a coolie came running out of the trees between the snake and ourselves.

"Stop moving!" I fairly shouted.

The coolie smiled, thinking nothing the matter, and told me in broken English that I had just received an urgent message over the telegraph. Singh, not one for delicacies, explained to the young man that he was standing three yards from the deadliest snake in the world and was about to die. The coolie turned and froze. He was greeted by a cobra standing high as his chest, dancing forward with a boxer's lethal measure. When it was a yard from him, it stopped still. The coolie stared at the snake before him, and the glossy black head of jungle death stared back, eyes immobile as two yellow pushpins stuck into the head of a toy. The mangrove, always thick with noise, was suddenly silent. Respect for the eternal standoff. Who would fight and who would run? Who would die? In an instant, the decision was made. The snake turned its head away.

"Cover your eyes!" I yelled.

But it was too late. The cobra swung its head around violently, spitting a shotgun burst of venom at the face of the young servant. He sank to his knees, screaming and clawing at his eyes. The snake glided forward, intent on sinking its fangs into the softer tissues of its crippled prey. Just as the head reared back to strike, I managed to dive and knock the coolie from under the fangs of the cobra. As we lay motionless in the soddy muck, the black demon sidled up to my face, citrine orbs gazing into blue. The cobra yawned its huge eggshell-colored mouth open, filled by two knitting-needle-sized fangs, and reared back, hissing, for the strike.

"Singh!" I cried at the top of my voice.

The head snapped forward with terrible speed, fangs aimed surely at my eyes. Suddenly a bolt of brown lightning struck the sinuous beast from behind, lifting its anguine form off the slurry soil. It was Singh's hand.

"They gonna like this King of all snake in Londonland, eh, Master Finn?"

"Yes, Singh," I said, trapping the coolie's arms behind his back, "they certainly will."

By this time, two other coolies appeared from the trees, having been only a few hundred yards off cutting down some of the mangrove's iron-strong timber when they heard screams.

"Take this man back to camp and tie him to his bedposts. And don't let him so much as touch his eyes. If he breaks the skin, that venom will kill him as surely as a gunshot to the head," said I in Malay.

They nodded and carried him, arms locked akimbo, back through the forest.

"My eyes! They buuurrrrrnnnn!! Help meeeee!! Let me go! They iiitch! They iiiitchhh!!"

"You'll die," I reasoned.

"Let me die!!"

"No," I said flatly. "I've survived this twice. So can you."

"Nooooooo. . . ."

His screams died in volume as he was carried away, but

I was too busy searching for the cable the coolie had brought, now lost because of the tussle. I found it mixed in a ripe pile of detritus, picked it up, and wiped it free of slime. It read:

MR FARROW STOP YOUR PRESENCE NEEDED URGENTLY IN BANGALORE INDIA STOP 5000 U. S. DOLLARS ALREADY TRANSFERRED TO YOUR ACCOUNT VIA BOMBAY GOLD TRUST STOP NO STRINGS STOP PLEASE COME STOP

MAHARAJA NANAK RANJIT BAHADUR OF JAMMU

"What it say, Master Finn?" queried Singh, who was deft enough to thumb a plug of betel nut leaves neatly into his mouth while retaining his hold on the thrashing cobra.

"It says, 'Pack your things, Singh. We're going to India.'"

I boarded the steamer the *Ben Franklin* within an hour of my return to camp. Instructions were given to Han, the pen carpenter, to make transport cages for all the animals to be shipped to several zoos upon my return. The thirty roustabouts I kept in my employ were told to move the animals into Han's crates as soon as they were ready. No easy task that. Trying to budge an angry orangutan is like wrestling with a hairy circus strongman that has a penchant for biting. *Finn Farrow, Inc., Purveyor of Rare Animals,* was in full swing.

Singh was my natural choice to accompany me on the voyage. Although I speak fairly fluent Hindustani, knowledge of one language in a country that harbors over 800 separate languages and dialects can, statistically, be only so helpful. I met Singh about thirty years ago when I was on one of my earliest expeditions. He was a young Hindi boy who belonged to the caste known as the Untouchables. When I first saw him, he was being punished by a teacher for daring to listen outside a schoolroom window, trying to learn. The teacher, bound to the social ties of nonrecognition of Singh's caste, threw his heavy cane at the boy's small back, and Singh had to throw it back so he could be pummeled again. That sight moved me to such anger that I took the boy into my employ then and there, and he has proved a valuable asset ever since. He speaks over fifteen languages and various regional dialects, and has the finest mind for understanding animal behavior I have ever seen.

We sailed north from the port of Djambi, through the Straits of Malacca near Siam. At Victoria Point in the Andaman Sea, we headed due west through the Ten Degree Channel in the Bay of Bengal for over two weeks. Singh, whose geographic perspective was limited to the chew of betel nut leaves, three chews per mile walking, wondered just how far India was from our camp at Djambi.

"I hope you brought *a lot* of betel leaves, Singh," I joked.

Singh, looking sadly down at his last plug of chaw, wasn't amused.

We landed two days later and immediately got into another boat, a shikora, and were paddled by the pole coolies up the Cauvery River. The odor of India was strong in our noses, a sickeningly sweet mixture of mangoes and trash. At first, our noses rebelled against the foul effluvium, but when they realized the smell didn't intend to leave this land *ever,* they chalked it up as inevitable and noticed it no longer.

The following day, we landed in the city of Mysore and hired a team of elephants, from an establishment translated literally as *Abdullah the Unclean,* to walk us the rest of journey. I don't care how romantic it looks riding the back of those behemoths, but let me tell you now, those buggers have sharp spines! After three days of wincing at every lumbering stride, I was greatly gladdened to arrive at the principality of Jammu.

When I descended from my gargantuan mount, I was greeted by the short barrel of a British Martini rifle, thrust quite indelicately in my face.

"Sahib Farrow?" said one of the hirsute and beturbaned Sikh guards.

Figuring it to be in my best interest to avoid startling them with sudden gestures, I nodded slowly. The lethal "o" of the rifle barrel disappeared instantly from my face, and I was escorted into the most beautiful palace I have ever beheld with these aged eyes. It wasn't the kind of estate my hometown of Hollywood makes movies about, all rolled in gold and sprinkled with jewels. Rather, it was an unflattering building that complimented the natural beauty of Mother India surrounding it. No forty Rolls Royces in this garage. A tastefully humble cart drawn by water buffalo stood alone. No gilded trellis; no fountain that gushed fine 1863 French champagne in the courtyard. The gems in this palace were the stunning assortment of brightly colored birds that sang in the eaves and kept the stinging insects away. On the steps of the entryway, a family of king cobras slithered lazily into the doorway. A *bhisti,* or water-carrier, stepped carefully over them, his indifference to their lethal presence a sure sign that a pregnant woman resided within the palace. Cobras, after all, are considered good luck in India.

Singh and I were led into a large dining hall, and seated cross-legged on pillows that felt more like sitting atop wiggly gelatin than the plumes of birds. The low table before us stretched well over thirty feet, and was set for what I assumed to be a feast. Large bowls of *pilao,* a dish of wheat with spiced mutton, curried chicken, and sticky sponge cakes filled with sweet custard were found in plenty. After such a long journey, the decanter filled with *arrack,* an alcoholic spirit distilled from coco sap, was a much welcome sight. Singh almost cried out in joy when he saw the large *hookah* pipe filled to overflowing with the lush leaves of the betel nut tree. It was almost an hour until the Maharaja actually entered the room.

"Presenting His Exhalted Highness, the Maharaja of Jammu."

The Maharaja stepped into the room with twenty of his young, nubile wives following giddily in tow. I elbowed Singh in the side.

"Looks more like 'His Exhausted Highness' to me, eh, Singh?" Singh smiled wide between half-chewed leaves of betel nut.

"Mr. Farrow," said the Raj, "your reputation precedes you."

"I hope it was a polite guest," I joked.

We finished our introductions from across the length of the table, and made small talk over gin slings for the better part of two hours. It was obvious that the fellow wanted to discuss some matter, but was unsure of how to begin. I let him take his time in broaching the subject, filling up the empty space by feeding pats of butter to the Raj's pet cheetah instead. The rough tongue of the cat scoured the pads of my fingers, searching desperately for any trace of the fatty treat.

"I think my Beebee likes you, Mr. Farrow."

As if in answer to the Raj's statement, the cheetah purred loudly and rolled over on its back, pleading in an unladylike fashion to be scratched on her tummy. We all laughed.

"Please, call me Finn."

"All right, Finn, then," said the Raj, "I have been reluctant to bring up the reason for which you were called to my palace, but I feel the time has come. I was afraid that you might not take this journey, thinking me a fool, or being superstitious yourself. The animal I'm asking you to trap, Finn, is indeed to be feared."

"I indulge Your Excellency's warnings, but I have crawled into underground pits chasing after twenty-foot pythons, wrestled poisonous tarantulas bigger than your head from their burrows, and slept not ten feet from a hungry pride of lions in Africa. Now I ask you, what could be more fearsome than that?"

"We need you to catch a demon, Mr. Farrow," the Raj said solemnly.

"Call me Finn, and let's talk."

Over the next few hours, I learned that the Maharaja's lands were presently being besieged by a man-eating tiger that he was convinced was unnatural. I tried to assure him that tigers were exceptionally cunning, and that, as he well knew, were hardly uncommon in his part of India. Apparently, the first victim of this animal was the eldest of the Raj's two sons, Prince Sikkim. The likeness of the ex-future Raj of Jammu peered down nobly from a portrait at the far wall of the dining room. He looked the very picture of a young Indian prince, watching the world detachedly from two piercingly green eyes that were obscured above by a puce-colored turban and below by a thick black beard. His razor-edged *tulwar* distinguished him as an accomplished swordsman.

"My oldest son was the first victim of this beast. His body was found in a tope of pepper trees two months and three days ago by a *chowkidar*, a watchman, employed in my youngest son's entourage." At the mention of his name, Prince Bagh Ali, the Raj's youngest son, stood and spoke.

"I would like to think that my brother's death was without suffering or overmuch pain, but I know this not to be the case. His body had been completely mauled. His skin was shredded, and his insides were pawed through as if the beast were looking for something hidden in his innards. A tooth had popped through his closed left eye, and the tiger's thirsty tongue had sopped up the wet humors like a piece of bread in the yoke of a fried egg. His left hand had only the thumb left, attached by a thread of skin, and there was nothing left between his legs save bloody tatters of flesh. No part of my brother was left unravaged by the filthy *boorao,* even the soft soles of his royal feet had been punctured straight through by the demon's vile claws."

The Raj nodded and motioned his overly descriptive son to sit.

"You will excuse the vivid tongue of Bagh Ali. He is suffering much from the loss of his brother," apologized the Raj.

"I feel his pain as if it were my own," said I, bowing slightly to Bagh Ali. The Maharaja tutted silently, pleased, no doubt, by my deference to his blood.

"But, yes, all this is true. My son died the most terrible death that I can imagine. I was so consumed with anger at this blasphemy that I placed a bounteous price on the head of the man-eater responsible for the pains of Sikkim. Within three days of the announcing of reward money, hunters from around India came to my palace. The first to arrive was the Sultan of Krishnagiri, who practically beat the jungle flat without result. He was followed by the arrivals of the Nizam of Hassan, the Wali of Hyderbad, and the Badshah of Tonk. All of them left well fed, but without tiger or money. We became so desperate that we hired a man who was recommended as the best hunter in the world. . . ."

"Not Pierre LeBeau!" I interrupted.

"You have heard of him, then," said the Raj.

"I ran across him recently in Tanzania. He had just completed a successful capture of a rare black rhinoceros. I counted over twenty-five 30.06 rifle rounds in the poor animal's carcass. I exchanged words. He exchanged bullets."

I pulled open the khaki riding shirt I was wearing to expose the two fist-sized scars that have covered my left shoulder like pink putty ever since my encounter with LeBeau.

"So, he is not a friend of yours?" the Maharaja queried.

"Not since he put two slugs in me and left me for dead, no."

"Good. Then you will be pleased to know that Monsieur LeBeau lost his footing on some slick clay during a monsoon and fell, face first, into one of his own steel-jawed tiger traps. He died most unpleasantly," the Maharaja said, smiling.

"Keep giving me good news like that, and you're going to make me a believer in Karma yet, Raj. Too bad he couldn't have been gored to death by a rhino, though. . . ."

"Yes, it is too bad."

"Father, tell him of the others." The voice was that of Bagh Ali.

"Others?" I asked.

"Quiet, you damned fool!" The Raj was visibly angry.

"But, Father, he must know."

"Must know *what*?!" I fairly yelled.

The Maharaja then flew into a string of obscenities in Urdu so obviously rich in color that I had to blush, though I couldn't make out a word of what was said.

"Singh," I whispered into the young Indian's ear. "What are they saying?"

Singh scrunched his forehead and listened, a sure sign that he was trying to translate vulgar rusticities in the most professional manner possible.

"He say that Bagh Ali gonna scare you away because of the bodies."

"What bodies?" I asked.

The voice of the Raj bellowed its way forcibly into our whispered conversation.

"I should be perfectly honest with you, Mr. Farrow."

"Finn, and if you wish to retain my services, yes, you should."

"Since Sikkim's accident, there have been others."

"How many others?"

"About two every week."

"Good God, that's nearly sixteen men!"

"In truth, Mr. Farrow, the number is seventeen. And I am sure that the same beast is responsible, although none of us have witnessed it. But more unusual than that is that the attacks have no pattern; they occur during the hottest time of the days with equal frequency as they occur during the depths of the night. For the most part, the men have all been well-trained warriors, much like Sikkim. They have all been good men, strong fighters in Bagh Ali's military entourage, but their bodies . . . the bodies are horrible."

Just then a young coolie burst into the room with frantic eyes the size of two polo balls stuck in his head.

"Your Highness, come quick. Another one! Another one!"

We all erupted from the table and flew quick on the heels of the coolie into the courtyard. The body, rather I should say what was left of it, was less than three feet from a bonfire which I assume the victim had going in hopes of warding off predators. The insignia on his rent tunic denoted his position in Bagh Ali's guard. As for the rest of him, the only way to even guess at his identity would be to have a palace role call and see who didn't show up.

"Shiva!" was all that the young coolie could say before turning and vomiting ripely on his own feet.

Something had happened to the body. Before my eyes lay a human mass that had undergone extreme ill treatment. It was no longer shaped in the two-armed, two-legged, one-headed form to which I had become accustomed to viewing dead bodies. It was as if this man had been mashed into raw hamburger. No, much worse. All that was left of this soldier was a lump of red muscle slop, floating slothfully on a thick bog of coagulated blood. The Bot flies, and their ropy maggot larvae, had done their hungry best to reduce the gore to mere bone splinters. Scavenging beetles tenaciously caked themselves to bits of dewy tendon like chitinous brown scabs, opting for their heads to be pulled off, embedded greedily in the meat, rather than be plucked from the delicious mess. And the smell. God, the smell! The fetor of organic decay rose in heady plumes, raising the bile of the faint-hearted along with its ascension. The whole scene was nightmarish.

As the Raj paced nervously about, Singh walked by calmly and knelt over the body with me.

"This is not done by tiger, Master Finn. Look more like scratches from snake fang to me," he said, spitting a black gobbet of betel nut juice into the jellified pool.

"Yes, Singh, but hundreds? One thing's for sure. This is not the work of any tiger I've ever seen."

The Maharaja sat his plump bulk down on the stump of a banana tree.

"I feared this would happen. You will not take this hunt,

and the rest of my royal staff is sure to flee from my lands because they are cursed. I am ruined."

"Now hold on there a minute, old man," I said, patting his shoulder. "You've got a deal. I accept the job."

"But . . . why would you risk your life, so?"

"Because you've piqued my interest."

So, a bargain was struck between the Maharaja and *Finn Farrow, Inc.* in which I was to capture the "tiger" responsible for the mutilations. In return, I was to receive $50,000 in gold certificates from the Bombay Gold Trust, Co. In order to expedite the matter, the Rajah stipulated that for every palace inhabitant killed by the beast whilst I was attempting to trap it, the reward lessened by $5,000. So, since I was officially on the clock after the promissory handshake, and also apt to lose money through some hapless native's death, I immediately commandeered Bagh Ali's guards as roustabouts and heavy laborers to assist me in my plans.

Having surveyed the palace grounds on a snuff-colored gelding earlier that morning, I located the most probable entrance that a jungle animal would take to enter and decided to set my trap there. It was a narrow, eroded opening in the clay security wall around the premises, and was located only meters from where the Prince Sikkim met his violent end. Also, the area was nearly pitch-black every hour of the day, as the sunlight was bedimmed by dense overhangs of pepper tree boughs. All in all, the place seemed a likely trail on which to find a rogue tiger. But I'll tell you, standing alone in that swarthy grove, wondering if gilded lemony eyes were fixed on me from somewhere in the tall grass, I was never more thankful to have my Colt 1911A .45 caliber pistol holstered to my side.

The pit that the eight bruisers and I dug was half finished when a heat-lightning storm hit. Thoroughly flushed and slathered with gamy sweat from shoveling hard earth in 108 degree weather and 100 percent humidity, the hot *simoom* was as unwelcome to the men as a priest would be on their favorite red-light street. Phosphorescent lightning flickered like the quick white tongues of reptiles through the black brain-mass of the cumulus clouds above. Ground strikes charged the air near the excavating men, sending frenzied blasts of hot air in all directions, making the work doubly hard.

When the final pail of dirt was pulled from our hard won chasm, the pit measured fifteen feet deep by twenty feet long. Just enough to keep the springiest of enraged tigers from leaping over the top. Singh, having avoided the chore of digging, covered the mouth of the trench with a canopy of wide-leafed banyan branches. This done, all that was left was to place an irresistible lure on our side of the pit to coerce the cat into a misstep over the trap. For this, I brought along a young lambkin that I took from the Raj's animal pens. I leashed the tender-looking runt to the ground, who bleated weakly and accused me painfully with innocent brown eyes. Dark and light warred in the maelstrom above, bursting in strobes of sudden bright light, only to be countered by volleys of suffocating, still darkness. We ten waited in the grasses, well-armed and weapons in hand. The lamb trembled with fear in the clearing, utterly alone.

Tension among the men grew as time passed. Although none would voice it, we all wondered if the tiger might already be on our side of the palace compound rather than on the other side of the pit. Just as I was giving this notion some serious thought, I saw a brief flash of movement through the crumbled-down section of the old wall. I unfocused my eyes, an old trick I learned over the years to spot motion rather than color and shape. In a business where your life depends each day on seeing that camouflaged Boomslang snake three feet from your face, it's a talent worth cultivation.

"There he is," I whispered to the men, not sure in the slightest if I was correct, but more concerned with allaying their fears.

"Where?"

"All eyes strained into the darkness, but saw nothing. Just then, an animal shriek that sounded like a thousand sharpened fingernails screeching across a giant slate ripped open the night sky. But the animal did not come.

"Why isn't it coming?" asked a fat guard by the name of Churi Chari. Sweat was streaming from his greasy, black mustache in rivulets, unnoticed, into his mouth.

"Because it sees us," I said.

The tiger snarled in the dark, the sound of smooth river stones tumbling together in its throat. The sound of feline laughter.

"COME ON, YOU!" yelled Churi Chari, running into the clearing, unable to take the pressure of waiting any longer.

As he stood there, I saw a great form bolt upright and run toward the pit. But the thing running was no animal. It was as if I were looking at a tiger twice again the size it should have been . . . and it was clear as glass. Clearer, even. I could only make out the barely perceptible tiger form by the way it slightly distorted the things it coursed by. It was like looking at something through water; objects wavered and shimmied like mirages when it ran in front of them. One thing I could tell without having to see the expression on its translucent face, was that it was definitely pissed off.

The image squeezed through the wall and ran full bore at the pit. And not even a leaf bent under its weight as it ran straight across the branches and exploded into Churi Chari. The man's body disintegrated into a spray of what looked like bloody tapioca pudding. I drew my Colt and fired all eight cartridges into the phantom beast with absolutely no result. The thing sprung forward at two other guards that had tried run to Churi Chari's aid. Lightning touched down suddenly near the fray, and the tiger shimmered from head to tail with fuzzy particle brilliance.

One of the men, who I recognized quickly as Bagh Ali's Master-At-Arms, swung his great *tulwar,* hoping to bisect the creature's head. His sword swung through the phantasm, unslowed, and buried itself in the soft abdomen of his compatriot. The tiger snorted and thrust a paw into the warrior's head. His face stretched at impossible angles, as if it were a balloon with a hand pushing out from the inside. The guard's scream sounded like it came from a young girl, and then his head just burst like an overripe melon dropped onto concrete.

Another bolt of lightning struck nearby and I could again see energy snicking up and down the length of the spectral animal. It turned to me. And ran.

So did I, not realizing until I was halfway down that, in my panic, I had fallen into my own trap. I landed hard, winding myself on the soft, cold earth. The tiger roared at me thunderously from the lip of the pit, and then leaped down on the other side. I tried to stand, but found my legs too weak. The beast sauntered slowly toward me. I found my strength and stood defiantly in the giant grave. The tiger bellowed in rage and ran full at me. Ten feet away, it lunged, and its horrible face sped toward mine. It was the face of a man screaming demoniacally, baring his teeth, gnashing with insane fury. When the monster hit, it knocked me to the ground. No explosion of flesh. The animal looked baffled, and savagely opened its jaws and bit down on my face. I could feel slight pressure, but no punctures. No damage. The tiger roared in anger and leaped up the side of the pit, disappearing into the night. The last thing I remembered noticing as it ran off was that it glowed no longer.

"The pit must have bled off whatever strength it had on the surface," I said to no one in particular. And then the fall into the pit asserted itself, and I passed out cold.

There's an old trapper's saying that goes something like, "You can't catch a monkey by throwing a line in the ocean." The events of the night before proved that. In spades. Essentially, I had been trying to trap what I had come to realize was an honest-to-God ghost with laws of gravity that didn't apply. It wasn't a totally useless venture, however. I sat down and started piecing together bits of information, and I figured a lot of things.

Starting with the basics, the phantom tiger was obviously able to inflict great damage to physical bodies. Simple physics tells us that in order to do so, the tiger must have at least a minimal physical structure. Molecular, maybe atomic. Any thoughts that the animal used complex camouflage or was simply invisible were ruled out when the guard's *tulwar* didn't so much as scratch the beast, even though it swung clear through its head. No, scientists have proven that everything we can see, or touch, or taste has a molecular base structure. All things are composed of atoms, so I argued that it was likely that the demon tiger, on some level, was as well.

Further, this accounted for the odd pattern of attack and sudden flashes of energy the spectral beast displayed. Having inquired thoroughly, I found that the victims, strangely all guards in Bagh Ali's brigade with the exception of Prince Sikkim, died either during the heat of the day, by a fire, or during the dry storm last night. This made me wonder, why was the tiger able to virtually liquefy others, and not myself? Surely not by choice. Again, I believe the answer is found in primary physics. When molecules are heated, they move faster, creating energy. During midday, when temperatures are soaring, the molecules of the ghost tiger were frenzied. When it attacked, its molecular particles could collide into the physical structure of, say, a person, and essentially disintegrate their flesh by blowing away the inherently weaker cellular bonds. The fires and heat lightning excited the same result. In the cool dankness of the pit, the tiger's molecules were slowed by the lack of heat energy and, thankfully, I didn't end up a pile of separated cells, rippling wetly on the ground.

There were several other things that bothered me about that night. Foremost in my mind, the Rajah and Bagh Ali both said that Sikkim was found tiger-mauled. His body had been slashed and torn by sharp claws. Every body I had seen since resembled more a soggy heap of human sawdust than a human in repose. They recognized Sikkim's body by face; all other victims had no face. They had no eyes, no legs, no spine. Nothing. Just a fly-feeding mass of human compost. Sikkim, I determined, could not have been a victim of the apparition that attacked us in the pepper grove.

Other thoughts tried to crowd into my mind. I speculated about the fact that the phantom tiger had a human head where that of a Felidae should have been. And why did it look so damnably familiar? I also wondered why all the victims had belonged to Bagh Ali's soldier entourage. Mustn't there be easier prey living in the ramshackle shanties down the trail, or did it really make any difference in the end? More importantly than all this, though, one question remained, bouncing in and out of my thoughts like a rubber ball in my head.

How does one go about catching something that cannot be caught?

After a few foamy draughts of ale, I sat down with a chemistry book and tried to find out.

It was two weeks before I could put my plan into action. In the interim, I had everyone confined to the palace's interior. This seemed to do the trick, because, for the first time in over two months, there was only one death in the period of fourteen days. This was a guard, presumably on his way to spend his service pay on some minxy little nymph down at the local brothel. Like the others, Officer Unao's remains were ladled into a bucket and were ceremoniously immolated.

I had sent a letter by courier to a friend in Trier, Germany, telling him of my unique situation. Although he thought that a fever was having the better of my good sense, H. Kamerlingh Onnes sent me the supplies I requested. The coolies and other native roustabouts helped me to construct the trap I hoped would catch the ghost. It was a simple design, just a long, open-topped metal box that attached to the hole in the wall by the pepper grove. It had a six-foot runway and a metal door at both ends that slid down and sealed into place. To get the phantom tiger to run through the box, we needed a bait. Human bait. Me.

One might be tempted to wonder why I just didn't leave. I certainly wasn't hurting for money, and Singh will vouch that I have no death wish. The answer is that in my business, if you're not the first, you might as well be dead. I was the first to bring a pygmy elephant to the Brooklyn Zoo. And I was the first to finagle permits from the Chinese government to capture a pair of Pandas. And I was the first to bring back a live Nile crocodile to the Royal Canadian Zoo. How many people remember the second or third person to have done that? Zero. No one. I refuse to be that person. I have never been skunked on a capture, and I was not about to let some Pierre LeBeau-type get the better of my reputation. I am Finn Farrow, damn it, and this is my job.

Besides, if another native died, that was more money gone from the pot.

Outside, Singh called.

"Master Finn, we ready."

I took a slug of some strong Indian gin, walked out among the men, and then squeezed myself through the hole into the other side of the wall. The metal clanged jarringly against the hard clay wall as it was slid into place. I looked back through the metal runway, and saw Singh's smiling face, happily chewing more Betel nut.

"We only have one shot at this," I told him for the twentieth time.

"Don't trip," he mused.

I rolled my eyes at his attempt at humor and turned to light the bonfire. The kerosene-soaked timber ignited almost instantly into a raging conflagration. Somewhere not so far off in the jungle, I heard a roar that was not coming from the feasting fire.

"Get ready," I yelled over my shoulder.

I turned back to look off into the far darkness for a sign of the beast, and was shocked to see it rise from the earth thirty feet in front of me. The demon lifted its man-head and blasted me with a cacophony of screams both shrill and deep, and so powerful that I could feel the sound waves reverberating off my skin. Then it smiled.

I spun around so fast that I threw off my equilibrium for a moment, feeling a queasy sickness in my bowels at having almost made Singh's joke a painful irony. I regained my balance and threw myself toward the hole in the wall. When I squeezed through, I caught the image of the beast in a peripheral glance. It was huffing forward like a freight train, all speed and power and screeching insanity.

My heart pounded as loud as my feet hammering on the metal runway.

"Do it now!"

I dropped to my knees and skidded down the length of the chute. I had just about cleared this giant metal coffin when suddenly the endpiece slammed down on my chest, pinning me to the floor. I craned my head back and saw the inverted figure of the spectral tiger running at me at full gait, howling madly at seeing its prey trapped helplessly on the ground.

"Oh, shit!"

I gave it a desperate effort to bench-press the crushing endpiece from my chest, but the mechanism was engaged and refused to budge. With adrenaline coursing through every cell of my body, making me shake like the lambkin I set out for sacrifice, I snatched a glance back at the surging demon. The ghost tiger burst into the bin, laughing and shrieking and lunging with animal bloodlust at my exposed throat.

"Si-i-i-inggghhhh!"

Just as the beast moved to clamp its massive jaws shut on my face, I felt two small hands grab my legs and pull. I will never forget hearing the deafening *clack* of the tiger's teeth snapping shut, empty, inches from my face as Singh pulled me from the metal trap. The noise haunts me still.

The second I was clear, and I suspect it was even a moment before, the ten coolies standing to the side of the trap dumped in huge insulated bowls of steaming liquid. The tiger jolted to a stop when the liquid hit the floor, as if one of its legs had been nailed to the ground. The stuck beast looked up and bellowed furiously at us, time and again, until its howls were cut short by the liquid flowing over its head.

When I peered over into the roiling vat, I looked into the eyes of the creature, a piercing green I had never noticed before. Then I knew.

The Maharaja was talking with Bagh Ali in the dining hall when I wheeled in the tank.

"What is this?" he asked, dumbfounded.

"This," I said, "is what $30,000 in gold certificates would look like if it were a ghost."

"You did it?" the Rajah said. The hope was embarrassingly unguised.

"Yes, Rajah," I answered, putting a hand on his shoulder. "It's over."

The Rajah grinned a gold-capped smile, threw his hands into the air, and moved his fat in a joyous Hindu dance.

"It's moving inside there." This from Bagh Ali, who was peering with horror over the metal rim. The tiger with the man's face contorted infinitesimally in the blue liquid.

"Yes. And it will keep moving. Slowly. Millimeter by millimeter for years until it finally gets out."

The Rajah stopped his merriment and came over to the bin. He reached his hand toward the liquid.

"What kind of stuff is this?"

I grabbed his hand inches short of the ice-blue bath.

"You don't want to touch that. It's liquid helium."

"But how does it . . .?"

"It's physical science," I said flatly. "See, a ghost is a physical manifestation on a molecular level, and I thought if I could stop a molecule, I could essentially stop a ghost. I remembered reading in a scientific journal one night that researchers in Germany discovered that all molecular activity comes to a stop at -273.15 degrees Celsius, or Absolute Zero. So, I used this tidbit of information and created a trap out of it, in which I dumped -268.7 degree Celsius liquid helium on the molecular phantom to slow it down."

The Rajah beamed with pride.

"I knew we chose wisely in hiring you. The reward will be $50,000 in gold certificates, not $30,000. Plus another $50,000 in U.S. currency. You've saved my people, Mr. Farrow."

"That was the good news," I muttered to the Rajah, but squarely matching the wary gaze of Bagh Ali.

"Do you mean to say that there is bad news to follow?" asked the Rajah. "How could any news be bad on such a perfect, perfect day?"

I turned seriously to the Rajah, knowing I was about to enter dangerous grounds.

"Did you ever stop to wonder how improbable it is that your son Sikkim, an armed and battle-wise warrior, was so easily killed by a plain jungle tiger?"

As I suspected, Bagh Ali piped in.

"This is no ordinary tiger, Mr. Farrow."

"Yes, Bagh," I said, "that is true. But this tiger did not kill your brother. His wounds were of another nature."

The Maharaja clearly noticed the growing tension in the room and decided to try to quell it as fast as possible.

"Of course this tiger is responsible for Sikkim's death, just as all the others. Now, we've all had a long day, why don't we just sit and relax. . . ."

"Your Highness, listen to me. I would not say these things if I weren't absolutely convinced that they were true. Isn't it a coincidence that all of the victims of this tiger belong to Bagh Ali's division? You have seen the gore left by this ghost. Your son's wounds were different, made by some sort of blade."

The Maharaja reddened with anger, and Bagh Ali stiffened perceptibly.

"What are you saying?" yelled the Rajah. "I will not listen to this!"

"I'm saying look at the face on that tiger! That is your son's face!"

"Blasphemer!" shouted Bagh Ali.

"Your son, Prince Sikkim, was set up by another. By someone who wanted him dead because he had something to gain."

The Maharaja covered his ears and shook his head. Bagh Ali listened, all glaring attention.

"He was killed by someone who thought he deserved all of your inheritance after your death, rather than allowing it to go only to the firstborn."

I walked straight up to Bagh Ali.

"He was killed by someone who would carry *shokatar*. Someone who carries metal tiger claws."

I patted Bagh Ali's tunic, and a glove with razors attached to the fingers fell to the ground. The Maharaja stopped in shock.

"And that's why Sikkim's ghost has been attacking Bagh Ali's men. He is revenging his own murder!"

"Bhainchute!" yelled Bagh Ali. "Sister Violator!"

"That man in there," I said, pointing to the bin, "is your son. And he was butchered in the pepper grove by Prince Bagh Ali and his men."

Slowly, Bagh Ali reached down and put on the bladed glove.

"We don't want to be doing anything rash here, Bagh." I said, drawing my Colt. In the blink of an eye, Bagh Ali flicked his wrist, and the next thing I knew, my gun was spinning away crazily across the marble floor. Blood spilled freely on the ground from where his *shokatar* opened me up. I tried to cover the series of three parallel gashes running from my second rib down to my hip with my free hand, but found it a lacking suture.

Bagh Ali advanced and sliced straight down, trying to section my face like a hard-boiled egg in a wire cutter. Years of collegiate boxing carried me inside the range of the blades, where I proceeded to clip the young prince on the chin with a series of short right jabs. He flew back, stunned for a moment, and then ran at me again. His lethal hand was cutting through the air like the propeller of an aeroplane. I matched his footsteps, backing up, looking desperately for something to throw.

"Do you want to know how I killed my brother, Farrow! Do you want to see?"

"Bagh!" the Maharaja cried.

I was beginning feel light-headed from all the blood running out of my body. Then my right foot slipped in a slick of my own blood, and I tumbled to the ground. Bagh was on me in an instant, his face as lunatic as the beast's. I was too weak to even fight.

"Let me show you! I started with his eyes. . . ."

Bagh Ali cocked his arm back, readying to thrust the two thin daggers into the soft tissues of my eyes. Something that Bagh had said earlier kept going around in my mind.

A tooth had popped through his closed left eye.

Suddenly an eardrum-tearing crush sounded behind me. I strained my neck around to see that the Rajah had overturned the bin of liquid helium. The phantom tiger, lying in a heap on the steaming floor, rose to stand. I couldn't believe my eyes. The form that stood was that of Prince Sikkim, his image matching the portraiture on the wall exactly. Except for the large *tulwar* he held out menacingly before him. And the green eyes burning with rage.

"No, Brother!" Bagh Ali shouted.

But it was too late. Sikkim ran across the room and buried his sword deep in the guts of Bagh Ali. Nothing happened for a moment, and then black blood began running from the impaled man's mouth. Bagh Ali's whole body started quivering, and then suddenly it collapsed on itself, creating a wet, oatmeal-looking pile on the floor. Sikkim shook still with fury.

"Son."

Sikkim turned to see his father, arms opened, empty. The young prince walked to his father, knelt at his feet, and filled the emptiness, embracing. And for a moment he was flesh.

"I am sorry, Sikkim. I am so sorry." The Rajah cried unrestrained, his tears falling onto the weeping prince. And every tear that ran down the prince's body, erased a trail of his corporeal self. Soon there was nothing left. Sikkim had gone.

The Maharaja looked up.

"Where did he go?"

The Rajah's eyes scanned the room desperately for some sign of his son, but never saw him. I unfocused my eyes and looked into the small puddle of tears on the ground. Very far away in the reflection, almost imperceptible to the human eye, I saw the image of Prince Sikkim walking off into the distance.

PALE GHOST
by *Gerald Hausman*

Gerald Hausman's short fiction has appeared in numerous anthologies, including *Tales From the Great Turtle* and *Wheel of Fortune*.

After burning his suit of clothes, Hansen sat in the shade of an ash tree.

Soon, the ghosts would come. They always did.

The sweat lodge, made of mud and stone, was so hot when he stepped into it, it singed the hairs inside his nose when he tried to breathe. How did the old people do this, he asked himself, the sweat flowing in rivulets down his chest.

City-bred skin.

Soft, city hands.

City, city man.

He tapped the lava rocks with the deer antlers, moving them into place. Then he pulled the old blanket over the doorway. Immediately he was swallowed up in darkness, and the sweat of his steaming body ran into the dirt. Prepare a place for the ghosts, and they will come. . . .

He went outside for the third time and walked into the river, rolling like a dog in the shallows, sending minnows flying in all directions.

One more time.

For the fourth and final time, he pulled the blanket. The daylight was again sealed from him. He was in the womb of time, bathing his skin in the old life, birthing himself in the original wetness of being.

The ghosts, the parts of himself that kept him alive . . .

. . . Not there, but soon . . .

The sweat rolled from his cheeks, collecting in pools around his navel.

For some reason he remembered his grandfather. Maybe it was the antlers. Remembering his grandfather made him remember his grandfather's tractor, the first one ever brought into the canyon.

That was years ago, before he was born.

Brought in on muleback, one piece at a time. They thought, the other elders, that it would ruin the way things were, but it made things better. The peaches could be harvested more easily, the earth furrowed faster. In time, everyone used the tractor.

Hansen had seen it just the other day.

Rusted-out, datura blossoms like moons grew out of the rotten tires. Once, he remembered, when it broke down, his grandfather had put a deer skull into the hub of one of the wheels. When it broke down for the last time, after his grandfather died and he was about to go away to school in Lawrence, Kansas, he and his brother put the deer skull back in the hub. The skull still had the bullet hole that had killed the deer. The boys painted a portrait of Bob Marley on the skull, and the hole where the bullet went through was the singer's open mouth.

Now, nine years later, all of them were in the earth—the deer, the grandfather, the brother, the tractor, the singer.

Soon they would come to soothe him . . .

He sang the old song of thanks then.

Song to the roundness of things, to the beaten bracelet, the sun-shaped basket, the moon-shaped basket, the lodge made of earth, the cedar trunk, the river that wound round the earth, the stars that embraced all of them. He sang the song of first-breath, the song the river makes in the new morning when the sun is first-seen, first-felt.

Then he threw back the blanket . . .

. . . Ghosts . . .

The river cooled his hot skin. He rolled in the shallows for the last time. He came out of the cold into the hour of deception, just before evening, when shadows are being born, the time when warriors strike upon the unwary. The time when the eye is not sharp. The time when things are not separate, the lost time when things are tied together, when one thing becomes another.

He stood there in the crackling starlight and he knew that the cracks were crickets.

Crickets and stars. Stars and crickets.

Cri, cri, cri, Str, str, str.

Cristr, cristr.

Then, listening, he remembered his grandfather's tale of how as a young boy he ran one hundred and fifty miles to see the train pull into the town of Williams. He had not stopped, he had run the whole way.

The language, the old words, came back to him now in clicks and clacks, like the song of the cricket-stars. The language of ghosts. He stood by the river, dry. Hot as an ear of roasted corn, dry and songless, trying to remember more, trying to squeeze the juices of memory.

The words were like flat rocks rubbed together and they were like the rushes of yucca plaited one-over, one-under, until, miracle—there was a basket. Words, he thought, were like this.

Ghosts . . .

At first he thought it was a cloud of pollen on the wind.

Grandfather?

Allen?

Tractor?

Deer?

But the ghost was all of these, a thing of permanent parts, like the tractor itself, brought in, piecemeal on muleback.

Hansen saw, quite distinctly, his grandfather. He was made of the blue pollen that rests on ponds. Out of his body came the tractor, the way it looked when it was new. And sitting on the big metal seat shaped like a leaf was his brother Allen, the way he looked when he was alive, before he took his life, jumping off the cliff. And the deer, bounding like a legend, sprang out of Allen's mouth.

Going down on his knees, Hansen cried.

He cried for the missing parts, for the parts that rust in the sun and rain, for the bones that do not stay, for the people that blow away.

Lastly, he cried for himself.

When he stopped crying, he looked up.

Allen was there, his skin like shining pollen.

"I have loved you like a living brother," he said.

"You are my brother, aren't you?" Hansen asked.

"Yes," Allen said, "I will always be your brother." Then: "You've called on me to tell you something?"

"Yes," Hansen cried, "what shall I do?"

"What shall you do? What you always do. That is what I have been saying all these years."

Hansen still looked uncertain.

Allen laughed gently.

When he stopped laughing, Allen was Allen again. He looked very real to Hansen. Not pollenlike. Real. A man of flesh and bone.

"You—"

"Yes," Allen said. "It is what I have been saying to you all these years."

"—are the one who is alive!"

It was Hansen, then, who dissolved, his face full of surprise.

The meeting done, Allen walked down to the village where his grandfather was waiting up for him.

He was one with his brother for another year.

ISLES

by Pamela Sargent

Pamela Sargent's most recent novel is *Ruler of the Sky,* an ambitious novel about Genghis Khan, told from the points of view of the women in his life. She is the editor of *Women of Wonder, The Classic Years* and *Women of Wonder, The Contemporary Years*. Her many novels include *The Shore of Women, Venus of Dreams,* and *Earthseed*. "Isles" was inspired by her travels in Italy during the autumn of 1993.

Their hotel was near the train station, close enough for Miriam and Alan to walk there. She hefted their carry-on bags while he picked up their two suitcases and followed her down the steps. At the docks along the Grand Canal, people were getting out of a long flat-topped passenger boat as three gondolas glided away across the greenish-blue water. The air smelled of sulfur and salt water and gasoline and faintly of rotting fish.

Alan had a map showing the location of the hotel. Miriam knew that he would not look at it and would only get annoyed if she stopped and rummaged in her bag for her own map. He would never look at a map or ask directions. In Florence, it had taken them forty minutes to get to the Uffizi from the Piazza Santa Croce because Alan knew exactly where the Uffizi was and how to get there and you couldn't miss the place because it was only a five- or ten-minute walk from the Piazza Santa Croce.

He led her away from the Grand Canal to a narrow cobblestoned walkway that ran between a row of buildings and then past kiosks and booths offering postcards, marionettes, newspapers, magazines, cheap jewelry, T-shirts, toy gondolas, and masks. The hotel, a square yellow six-story structure, turned out to be only a five-minute walk from the station. Miriam sat on a sofa in the lobby while Alan checked them in, studying the map she had bought after getting off the train. Her friend Leah had told Miriam that she would need a good map in Venice. Her hands shook as she refolded the map. The strain of trying to be calm during the train trip was catching up with her. If she dwelled too much on the problems awaiting her and Alan when they got home, she would panic and lapse into one of the fits of hysterical weeping that so enraged him.

"It's Room 414." She looked up as Alan handed her a metal key attached to a small plastic cylinder bearing the room number. A porter in a red uniform was with him, carrying the suitcases.

She followed her husband and the porter through the lobby to the elevator. Like the lifts in their hotels in Rome and Florence, the elevator was a closet-sized conveyance barely large enough for the three of them and the luggage. The elevator shook as it stopped at their floor. The hallway to their room had pale walls with gold trim and dark red carpeting. The porter opened the door, then led them inside, setting the bags down near a wooden closet.

"Grazie," Alan murmured. *"Prego,"* the porter replied. Alan handed him a tip; the door closed behind the porter. Another minefield now lay ahead of them, that dangerous stretch of time when they would rest in their hotel room before unpacking, when one or the other of them might say the wrong thing because there was nothing else to distract them from each other. An invisible band tightened around her chest.

"Our gondola ride's at seven," Alan said. Miriam looked at her watch and saw that it was only five. "I checked at the desk. We have to go over to that dock near the train station. It'll cost about 140,000 *lire*."

"Isn't that kind of high? That's something like a hundred dollars, isn't it?" The Italian currency still confused her, even with a pocket calculator, and the unfamiliar bills seemed like toy money.

"More like eighty, but you can't exactly come to Venice without taking a gondola ride."

The small room had two twin beds pushed together and a narrow third bed pushed against the wall. "It's sweltering in here," Miriam said.

"Better open the window, then, because there isn't any

air-conditioning. They told me at the desk. They're doing repairs. Maybe we won't need it. I mean, it is late September."

Miriam pulled back the curtains, then opened the large windows. The room overlooked the watery green span of the Grand Canal, a walkway alongside it, and, just below, an open area dotted with kiosks. Another hotel, painted pink, was across the way, its flower-lined courtyard filled with empty tables covered with pink tablecloths. The miasmic air still smelled of sulfur, salt, and decay.

She said, "It isn't what I expected."

Alan let out a sigh. "Don't start, Miri."

"I didn't mean—" Miriam stopped herself. She had almost risen to the bait. She had meant to say, but in a light, bantering tone, that she didn't expect her first sights in Venice to be a lot of shops and booths selling tacky souvenirs. Alan would have retorted with quiet but bitter words about how he was sorry they couldn't afford some place closer to Saint Mark's Square. She would try to apologize, but by then he would have retreated into one of his silences. He would be thinking that she was after him again because nothing had turned out the way they had hoped, and he knew that she blamed him for a lot of that. She was not blaming him for anything at the moment, but she had done so often enough in the past. She probably deserved to feel guilty now for all the times she had cut away at him. He had picked at her, too, usually when she was at her most vulnerable, as if her unhappiness made her give off pheromones that only made him want to hurt her more.

He had told her six months ago that they should go to Italy, because they had never been and had always wanted to go. "We can't afford it," she had told him. "You're right," he had replied, "we can't. We also won't be able to afford it later, and by then we'll be too old to enjoy the trip. We'll never be able to afford it. So we might as well go now." His mouth had twisted in the expression she thought of as his not-quite-smile, the look he had whenever he was feeling especially bitter.

Miriam turned away from the window and sat down in the room's only chair, next to the small desk. Alan was sitting on one of the beds. He reached into his jacket pocket and took out a pack of cigarettes. Miriam lit one of her own. She did not have to feel guilty about smoking over here, where nonsmoking areas seemed nonexistent. Alan, after quitting for three years, had relapsed last spring, so she did not have to feel guilty about smoking around him either. She no longer had to listen to him harp at her about the dangers of side smoke and how he would not come to visit her in the hospital if she developed lung cancer and that he could barely bring himself to kiss her sometimes. He did not kiss her that much anyway.

"There's actually kind of a nice breeze," Miriam said. "We probably don't need any air-conditioning." She still felt too warm, but did not want to admit that out loud. He would blame her discomfort on menopause and tell her to pester her gynecologist for more goddamned hormones so that she wouldn't be so bitchy and have so many hot flashes. She would have to remind him that larger doses were more dangerous and that the estrogen made her gain weight and that he was already nagging at her to lose a few pounds. They had gone through that particular argument before.

"Want a drink?" Alan asked.

"Sure."

He reached into one of the carry-ons and took out a bottle of Scotch as Miriam went into the bathroom to look for glasses. There was a drain in both the floor and the shower stall, which had no curtain. The stall looked forlorn without a curtain; the curved metal soap holder made her think of a hand held out in supplication. Tears sprang to her eyes; she swallowed hard. Tears came much too easily to her lately. She could not start crying now. Alan would explode if she did. "I'm doing my best, Miri. I'm trying as hard as I can, but I can't control the world. Do you have to cry so much? Do I have to worry about you all the time on top of everything else? Can't you ever be happy?"

Three glasses were near the sink. Miriam brought them out to Alan. He poured a couple of fingers of Scotch for each of them, then began to unpack. She drank while watching him hang up his clothes. She would wait until he was in the shower before she unpacked her own.

"Someday," Vera Massie used to say, "I'm going to move to Venice. I'll live in a *palazzo* and have a gondolier for a lover." Vera had been her best friend in college. Strange that Miriam should think of her now, when she had lost track of Vera long ago. They had said such things back then, believing that at least a few of them might happen. Vera would paint and Miriam would write articles for magazines. They would travel to Venice, Nairobi, Amman, Istanbul, Sydney, Monte Carlo, and Rio de Janeiro, fall in love with guides, adventurers, gamblers, artists, and mysterious men with no visible means of support, and somehow pick up enough at odd jobs between trips to support themselves.

Well, Miriam told herself, at least I made it to Venice, and wondered what Vera would have thought of the circumstances. Her old friend would not have imagined back then that Miriam would travel there only in an effort to shore up a failing marriage and to pretend, for a while, that her troubles were not that serious.

It was probably just as well that she had lost track of Vera, who had possessed an enviable talent for being cheerful and enjoying the moment, whatever problems might lie ahead. Vera would have been disappointed in what Miriam had become.

The sky was grayer, but still light when they met the gondolier by the dock. Alternating between Alan's halting Italian and the gondolier's slightly better English, the two men finally managed to agree that the ride would be an hour long and would cost only 110,000 *lire* and that it would take them along some of the side canals.

The gondolier helped Miriam into the stern of the craft. She sat down as Alan climbed in next to her, followed by the gondolier. The gondola rocked slightly as they drifted away from the dock. Four gondolas carrying small groups of graying and white-haired passengers were gliding toward them; in a fifth gondola, a man standing on the platform next to a gondolier sang as a man in the middle of the gondola played an accordion. The elderly passengers lifted their plastic cups in a toast, saluting Miriam and Alan as they passed.

The gondolier behind them shouted to one of the other gondoliers, who responded with a stream of Italian. "What are they saying?" Miriam asked.

Alan leaned back in his seat and slipped his arm over her shoulders. "Can't tell," he said. "People say that even other Italians don't understand this dialect too well." He smiled. "Bet they cultivate it deliberately. Probably don't want any of the passengers to know what they're saying." He had been listening to language tapes and practicing with a phrase book ever since they had decided to take this trip.

In some sense, Miriam thought, she had married the adventurer she had hoped to fall in love with when younger. Alan was, however, an adventurer who had failed at being truly adventurous. He picked up languages easily—French during a summer abroad in high school, German during his Army days, when he had lucked out and ended up in Europe instead of Vietnam, some Spanish when his business had started hiring more Latino construction workers. His plans for their life had been both straightforward and risky. His business would grow, even if they had to stick their necks out in the beginning. People always needed new houses, and he knew he could not stand working for someone else. When they were bringing in more money, Miriam could quit her job and they would travel, as they had always intended to do. After their children came, the plan had been to wait until they were old enough so that the family could travel together.

They had gotten no farther away than a winter vacation in Cancun and a summer vacation, years later, in the Canadian Rockies, because the business had required more and more of Alan's time. By the time they had been ready to abandon armchair travel for the real thing, Alan was struggling to keep his business afloat, Miriam was hanging on to her job wondering when the insurance company would lay her off, their daughter Joelle had dropped out of her third college in a row to move in with her boyfriend, and Jason had developed his substance abuse problem. Substance abuse, they called it, as if her son's difficulties were somehow metaphysical and might have been solved if he didn't have to live in a material world made of substance that even physicists couldn't understand.

Alan's arm tensed around her. "What's the matter now?" he said, and she heard the tightness in her voice, the sound of exasperation that could quickly turn into anger.

"Nothing," she replied, trying to smile. They were here to have a good time, to live in the present, not to worry about failing businesses, troubled children, and lost dreams.

A motorboat passed them, making the gondola rock a little. Their gondolier was steering into a side canal. The sounds of motors, singing gondoliers, and accordions abruptly ceased.

The sudden silence startled her. This canal was narrow, with stained and peeling pastel walls rising up on either side. A few motorboats were tied up near walkways and stone steps leading to doors. The shutters of several overhead windows had been opened, and clothes hung from ropes stretched between windows, but the buildings seemed empty. Miriam heard no voices and saw no movements inside the windows. The silence was unnerving, as though the crowds of tourists and residents had suddenly abandoned the city. Perhaps all the people were out, riding in gondolas and walking along the narrow streets and meeting friends for dinner.

How fanciful of her to imagine that Venice was populated by people who had nothing better to do than to take an evening stroll or boat ride, sit around drinking wine, make their own contributions to the city's works of art, and admire the decaying beauty of their atmospheric homes. Many of Venice's citizens would still be engaged in the necessary tasks of guiding herds of tourists to various sites, cooking and serving hotel and restaurant dinners, selling souvenirs. Some of them might work in the refineries across the lagoon during the day, coming back only at night. Most of the people in this region apparently lived over there on the mainland, under smoggy gray clouds and amid factories and storage tanks. Many of them might not even get to this graceful city that often.

The gondola was approaching a small arched bridge. A few people stood there, unmoving, gazing down at the canal. How still they were, Miriam thought, almost as if they were made of stone. The air shimmered, making auras glow around the people on the bridge. She touched her head reflexively, afraid a migraine might be coming on. Alan would blame her for ruining her vacation and tell her that she had brought the attack of migraine on herself.

"What's the itinerary for tomorrow?" Alan asked then, his voice sounding strangely hollow.

Miriam pressed her lips together. He could not simply enjoy the gondola ride; he had to keep thinking ahead. They had to make sure that they had plenty of sightseeing planned, so that they could keep up the illusion that they were having a vacation, an escape from which they would return refreshed, that this trip would somehow heal everything that had gone wrong between them. They had to keep busy, or otherwise there might be too much time to think and to brood and to argue.

"There's that place Leah told us about, that showroom

that sells Murano glass," Miriam said at last. "It's near St. Mark's Square, so we can see the church afterward. The tour for English-speaking tourists starts at eleven." If they were lucky, they might meet a congenial couple during the tour of the church, people they could have lunch with so that they wouldn't have to get through lunch by themselves. "Then we can see the Doge's Palace."

"Let's do that by ourselves, okay? I don't want to be following a herd around for that, too."

"Fine," she said. "I'm sure we can buy a guide at the entrance." That might keep them busy until dinner, and Alan had taken the precaution of making reservations for that already.

"Have to remind myself," he said, "to call Bernie after breakfast." Bernie was Alan's attorney. Lately, Alan had not told her much about his ever more frequent meetings with Bernie. Maybe he was thinking of declaring bankruptcy. He would come home one day and tell her that his business had finally gone belly-up. He would say that he had kept it from her because he did not want her fretting over everything and making herself sick, even though she had been worrying about everything and making herself sick all along anyway.

"Is it so important it can't wait?" Miriam asked.

"Yeah, it is," and she knew that he would not tell her what it was.

The gondola glided around a corner into another canal. Miriam was growing used to the odor of decay, and the dark green water was still. For a moment, she was at peace, taking pleasure in the silvery light and the soft sound of water lapping against stones. Had they come here when they were younger, while they were still living together or after they had first been married, by now Alan would be trying to kiss her. She would have protested, wondering what the gondolier might think, and Alan would have assured her that the man had probably steered plenty of lovers deep in the throes of passion along this canal. They would have giggled and cuddled and then gone back to their hotel room to make love before dinner.

She could not imagine that happening now. They should have come to Venice when they were younger, when they would have loved Venice for what it was and not only as an escape. She thought of how Venice was slowly sinking, of the hordes of tourists who came here trying to recapture the sense of beauty, joy, or romance they had lost, whose demands had turned so much of this city into more of a theme park than a place of romance, who roamed over these islands and along the canals in herds. One day, they would all come back to find their beloved city underwater, forever lost to them.

She turned toward Alan, about to speak, then forgot what she was going to say. His brown eyes stared into hers for a moment, then looked away. He had lost some weight recently, and now the tanned and leathery skin of his face sagged more, making him look older.

A longing for what she and Alan had once been to each other overwhelmed her. He had once loved her enough to resent every moment away from her; she had always trusted him to be at her side when she needed him. Now their troubles had poisoned even the wellsprings of love she used to think could never be tainted.

A movement caught her eye; she looked up. A woman was watching from a window up ahead, gazing down at the canal. Somebody was home in one of these houses after all. Miriam caught a glimpse of masses of pale hair, then lifted a hand to wave. The woman moved her hand in an arc, as if wiping an invisible window; the gesture seemed oddly familiar.

I know you, Miriam thought. She blinked, and the woman was gone.

Alan touched her hand. She was suddenly worried about him, afraid that he was keeping too much from her. Tell me what's wrong, she wanted to say. Tell me about all the problems, and we'll work them out together, the way we used to do. It doesn't have to be like this; I can meet you halfway. I won't pick at you, and in return you can listen to me, stop turning away from me, stop looking at me with that not-quite-smile on your face that tells me you're sorry you ever married me. All we have to do is remember how we once felt about each other, and everything else will fall into place.

The sounds of voices suddenly washed over her in a wave, nearly deafening her. The gondola drifted toward another bridge, this one crowded with Asian tourists. Miriam raised a hand tentatively; the people on the bridge grinned and waved and chattered among themselves. The water was slightly choppier, rocking the gondola. Up ahead, beyond the walls on either side of them, she could now see the broad, greenish expanse of the Grand Canal.

They ate breakfast in their hotel, in the indoor dining room next to the outdoor tables where they had eaten last night. Miriam had gotten used to the strong Italian coffee, but still had to put milk in it to make it palatable, something she never did at home. Alan had asked the waiter to bring butter and was putting some on one of his hard rolls. His doctor had warned him about his cholesterol, but the butter would probably do him less harm than his cigarettes.

At the tables on the opposite side of the room, which each bore a marker near the flower centerpiece with the words "American Express," a tour group of older, gray-haired people were eating bowls of cereal. Despite their advanced age, the tourists all looked fit and energetic and blatantly cheerful. Almost all of them were couples. Miriam wondered how they had managed to live for so long and stay married to their spouses without looking as though they had regrets.

Alan finished his coffee. "Maybe you can buy a map of the *vaporetto* routes," he said, "while I go upstairs and make that call to Bernie."

She would not ask him about the call. They had managed a pleasant dinner the night before, largely because a couple in the American Express group, a retired engineer and his wife from Tampa, had struck up a conversation with them from their table. They had not gotten off to a good start that morning. The noise of boat traffic, loud talking, and singing gondoliers outside their open window had kept Alan awake for much of the night. Miriam would not allow herself to ruin breakfast with questions about his business.

"*Vaporetto* routes?" she asked, not sure of what Alan had meant.

"*Vaporetto,*" he said as he crumpled his napkin. "The public boats, the water buses. The plural is *vaporetti.*" He got to his feet. "Go to one of those booths and get a map. Just say, '*Vorrei comprare una carta di vaporetti.*' That ought to do the job. If you want to be polite, throw in a '*per favore*' and say '*grazie*' afterward. Even you ought to be able to manage that."

He turned and walked away. How odd that she could feel hurt by his remark. She should be used to such comments by now.

Miriam stood up and headed toward the lobby. The retired couple from Tampa waved at her as she passed their table. She wondered if she and Alan would ever be able to afford to retire. She thought of what he had said last night, just before they had gone downstairs to have dinner. "You know what would solve our problems? If I dropped dead. Darrell could take over the business and then he could decide who to lay off next year. The insurance would take care of you, and Jason and Joelle would just have to look out for themselves. And I wouldn't have to be bothered any more, which would be one hell of a relief." She had been too shocked to do what she should have done, embrace him and tell him that she could not bear to have him think that way.

She went outside. The narrow street was already crowded with tourists; they seemed to be everywhere. She wandered toward the open area where several vendors had set up their booths and asked in English for a map and schedule of the *vaporetto* routes. The man in the booth handed them to her; so much for Alan's sarcastic language lesson at breakfast.

She walked toward the Grand Canal. In a few minutes, she would go inside and wait in the lobby, trying not to look too impatient when Alan finally met her there.

"Miri," a voice said. "Miriam Feyn."

Miriam looked up. Near the stone steps leading down to the water stood a tall, slender woman in a red T-shirt and baggy jeans. Her unruly long hair was gray, almost white, but she still wore it as she had when younger, in a mass of waves that fell nearly to her waist.

"Vera Massie!" Miriam said, and hurried toward her. "I can't believe it!" They clasped hands and then hugged each other. "We just got here yesterday, on the train from Milan." She stepped back, gripping her old friend by the elbows. "We actually got to Venice at the same time."

"Actually, I've been here for a while," the other woman said.

"You mean you live here?" Miriam asked.

"In a manner of speaking."

Miriam felt a pang of envy. Maybe Vera was leading the kind of life they had once imagined for themselves. The other woman guided Miriam toward the courtyard of the pink hotel across the way; they sat down at one of the tables.

No one else seemed to be sitting here. Miriam looked

around for a waiter, then turned back to Vera. "Vera Massie," she said. "I can't believe it."

"Vera Langella," Vera said. "I thought of hyphenating it, but I never much cared for the name Massie anyway. Frankly, I was glad to have an excuse to ditch my last name when I got married."

"Well, I'm not Miriam Feyn any more either. I tried, but after a while, it was just too much trouble to keep telling people my last name was Feyn and not Loewe. Finally gave up when my daughter started kindergarten. Her teacher kept calling me 'Mrs. Loewe,' and seemed to resent it when I tried to correct her."

Vera smiled. "You have a daughter."

"A son, too." Miriam glanced toward the Canal. The traffic had been heavy only a few moments ago. Now the broad waterway was quieter and even emptier than it had been at dawn, when she had looked out from her window to see shards of golden light dancing on the still green water. "I remember when you used to say you'd live here and have a gondolier as a lover."

"Yeah, and that I was going to live in a *palazzo*. Afraid I didn't manage either the *palazzo* or the gondolier."

Miriam could see her hotel room window from here. She lifted her head, thinking she had seen Alan looking outside. She noticed then that the vendors in the open area did not seem to be doing much business; the knots of tourists buying marionettes, postcards, and maps had disappeared.

"I didn't manage much of anything," Miriam said. "I'm a claims manager for an insurance company, and my husband's a builder and contractor—he owns his own business. He's in our room, calling his lawyer, and he won't tell me what that's about, so it probably means he's doing even worse than I think he is. My daughter dropped out of college to live with a guy named Rich who wears his hair in dreadlocks and works at Burger King while he's waiting for his band to make it. My son's out at Hazelden going through his second thirty-day program for substance problems." She wondered why she had told her old friend all of that. Maybe it was because of all the times Vera had nursed her through her black moods in college, finally convincing her that things weren't as bleak as they seemed.

"What do you think of this guy your daughter's with?" Vera asked.

Miriam thought of Rich's gentle brown eyes. "Oh, in some ways, he's not so bad. He's reasonably mannerly, and he seems to care about Joelle. I just wish he were more ambitious, and those dreadlocks—" She sighed. "God, I sound just like my mother when she met Alan. She used to say he'd be so nice-looking if he just did something about his hair."

"And your daughter? What are her plans?"

"I don't really know. Right now, she's doing some sort of free-lance computer stuff, graphic design and such. I don't really understand it that well, but she gets paid for it, however modestly."

Vera said, "Things could be a lot worse, then."

"I suppose." Miriam leaned back in her seat. "I just hope she doesn't get pregnant. She'd probably go ahead and have the baby, even if Rich bailed out. That does seem to be the style nowadays."

"Maybe he wouldn't bail out," Vera murmured.

Maybe he wouldn't, Miriam thought. She already felt a bit more kindly toward Rich. "Actually, I'm more worried about Jason. He had everything going for him, a fellowship at Stanford and a wonderful fiancée, and he threw it all away. Let me reword that. He snorted and freebased it away. I think he might have died if a friend of his hadn't gotten him into detox."

"What happened then?" Vera asked.

"He came home. Promised he'd stay clean. Alan found him an apartment near us and gave him a part-time job. Within a couple of months, he was out scoring again. I found out after he stole some of our silver to pay for the drugs."

"What did you do?" Vera asked.

"Alan was so pissed off he was ready to call the cops. Before he could, Jason came over, really wrecked, and said he was sorry, that he knew he was out of control, and that he had to go back into treatment."

Vera rested one arm on the table. "Then your son was acknowledging his problem. That's a good sign, isn't it?"

"I suppose so. He flew to Minnesota a week before we left for Italy. Alan refused to cancel our trip. He figured we were better off taking the opportunity to travel while Jason was safely in Hazelden. God knows how we're going to pay for everything when we get home. We'll probably be paying off this trip alone for years, assuming we don't go bankrupt first."

"At least you'll have had it," Vera said.

"Oh, yes." Miriam could not keep the bitterness out of her voice. "We'll remember it every time the Visa bill arrives. And there'll still be a lot of sights we'll miss, because there just isn't the time to see everything."

"You know what I always say?" Vera lifted her arms and pulled her long hair back from her face with both hands, exactly as she used to do in college. "You shouldn't try to see and do everything, no matter how much time you have. You should always leave something for when you come back again."

Miriam's mouth twisted. "What if you know you'll never come back?"

"You shouldn't look at it that way, Miri. It used to help me when I'd tell myself that I'd come back to do something I hadn't done, that I'd left unfinished, even if I knew the chances were against it. What did I have to lose by hoping?"

Miriam shook her head. "That's the worst thing about getting older, losing hope. I used to think it was other things, getting creaky and arthritic and gray and just not having your physical and mental shit together the way you did when you were younger, but it isn't. It's knowing that nothing's ever going to get any better, that you're just going to drag yourself through life until you finally cash in your chips, that all the things you hoped might happen aren't ever going to happen and that your whole life was probably for nothing. Hell, I'm almost fifty years old, and what have I got to show for it? No wonder Jason and Joelle are so confused. Why should they look forward to anything when they see their parents going down the tubes?"

"Are you going down the tubes?" Vera asked.

"Alan won't talk about his business. He used to discuss it all the time with me. All we do now is worry about money and wonder month to month how we're going to get by— we're in so much debt now that everything could cave in on us tomorrow. I keep waiting for him to say he wants a divorce, even though we can't really afford one. We're not good for each other any more. We'd probably both be better off alone."

Vera had opened something inside her. Miriam could not stop talking. She spoke of the constant financial pressures of the business and their children, pressures so overwhelming that she and Alan rarely talked of much else. She spoke of how they tore at each other, of how their friends were starting, very surreptitiously, to avoid seeing them quite as often, of the times she and Alan had gone out and their bitterness had pushed them into angry arguments and public scenes, of how horrified she was at some of the things she said to him even when she could not stop saying them.

"Oh, Miri," Vera said. "Don't you understand? That's why I'm here, to help you."

Miriam swallowed, struggling to control herself. She must have been unloading on her old friend for a good half-hour at least. She peered at her watch; it had been only a little after eight when she left the hotel. Now it was barely eighten. The Grand Canal was still empty of boat traffic, the nearest arched bridge abandoned by the tourist hordes. A gondola was tied up across the way, the gondolier resting against his long pole, so still he did not seem to be breathing. She could almost believe that she and her friend were alone in the sinking city.

Perhaps she was having a nervous breakdown. She had felt on the verge of one for quite a while. She turned toward the booths selling souvenirs, but saw no vendors there. She was imagining it, that everyone in Venice had vanished in the way she wished that her troubles would.

Vera was sitting with her left ankle resting on her right knee, the way she had when they used to sit around in the Student Union. Strange, Miriam thought, that Vera should look so much as she would have expected her to look, older but basically unchanged. Vera would not have cut her hair as Miriam had and colored it to hide the gray, or put on a blazer and a pair of tailored slacks with an elastic waistband because she was too old and carried a few too many pounds to wear jeans.

"Miri," Vera said, "you loved your husband once, didn't you?"

"More than anything. We weren't just lovers, we were pals, best friends. He'd get so annoyed when he had to work late. I'd put the kids to bed and have supper with him, even if it was ten-thirty at night, just so we'd have that time together."

"Miri, he needs you. You need him, too. Don't let a bunch of bullshit get in your way."

"That's exactly the way you used to put it whenever I got depressed." She had been going on and on about herself, never even asking Vera about her life. All she knew was that her old friend had married a man with the last name of Langella. She suddenly remembered the pale-haired woman she had glimpsed the night before, from the gondola.

"That was you," Miriam said, "last night, in one of the houses along that side canal. Everything stopped, and I thought I was going to get a migraine, and then I saw you."

Vera was on her feet. She seemed translucent, as though she were an image about to flicker out. "I have to go."

"I'm imagining you. I really am going crazy." Miriam could see the row of flowers behind Vera through her friend's hazy form. "I dreamed you up, and now you're fading away."

"Go to your husband. I'll see you later, I promise."

Before Miriam could speak, voices around her rose in a roar. Crowds were thronging past the nearby kiosks. Miriam gripped the edge of the table, suddenly disoriented as she looked around her. There was a crowd on the nearest arched bridge, and people were milling around in front of the train station and waiting near the docks for the *vaporetto*. The pathways on either side of the canal had rapidly filled with strollers.

When Miriam turned back, the chair across from her was empty; Vera was gone. She squinted, but could not see Vera's red T-shirt anywhere among the crowds.

Alan said nothing about his call to Bernie as they left the hotel. She could not tell him about Vera, about the long-lost friend who had appeared out of nowhere and disappeared just as mysteriously, who could apparently block out sound and make everyone in Venice disappear from view. He would tell her that she was going nuts and then accuse her of trying to drive him crazy. It was almost a relief to think that she might be cracking up. Having a breakdown might be the only escape from her problems that she could manage.

Miriam studied the map of *vaporetto* routes and discovered that both lines 1 and 2 would take them along the Grand Canal to the docks near Saint Mark's Square. "Line 1 is the local," she explained.

"Let's take it anyway," Alan said. "No need to rush."

They bought their tickets and boarded the passenger boat

at the docks by the train station, managing to slip through the knots of passengers and get seats in the prow. Alan seemed content to enjoy the view as the *vaporetto* made its slow progress along the Canal, crossing from side to side and backing water as it made its stops. By the time they reached the Rialto, Alan was smiling as he watched people bargaining over the prices of flowers, fruits, and fish in the open-air markets near the high arched bridge. Maybe, Miriam thought, Bernie had given him some good news for a change.

He was still smiling as they walked from the landing toward the Piazza San Marco, taking her arm as they entered the huge open square. Mobs of tourists were already swarming through the square as hundreds of pigeons swooped above them; Miriam ducked as one bird barely missed flying into her. Alan consulted his map to get them through the narrow streets and over a small bridge to the glass showroom. She had been prepared to resist the salespeople there, but Alan ended up buying earrings for Joelle, a necklace of glass beads for her, and arranging for the shipment of a ridiculously expensive hand-blown glass sculpture of two long-necked birds that Miriam had admired.

"You certainly turned into a spendthrift," she whispered as they made their way past a group of Japanese tourists just entering the showroom. "Exactly where are we going to put that sculpture anyway?"

"We'll find a spot. Call it an investment. If things get tough, I can probably sell it for more than I paid."

His good mood held throughout the tour inside the Basilica San Marco and during their lunch, which they ate at an outdoor table at an overpriced restaurant in Saint Mark's Square. They exchanged vacuous but pleasant commonplaces about the beauty of the Basilica San Marco and reminisced about all the art they had seen in Florence and the Vatican Museums. Alan lit her cigarette with a flourish after the meal and then lighted one for himself.

He abruptly fell silent, then slumped over the table with a sigh. When he sat up again, his face was sallow under his tan. "Are you all right?" Miriam asked.

"Just some indigestion," he muttered, crushing out his cigarette. "Miri, what would you say if I gave up the business, had Darrell buy me out?"

"What?"

"That's one option. I could subcontract with him, so I wouldn't actually be quitting. He probably couldn't do it, though—he's about as short of money as we are." He pulled his pack of cigarettes from his jacket pocket, then put them back without lighting one. "I could try selling to someone else, but there probably wouldn't be any takers, or else I'd have to take too big a loss. I might be able to get another loan, but a lot of that'd have to go toward what's coming due now. Or there's always Chapter 11. All I know is I can't go on the way I've been going."

He was giving up. That was what he was telling her now. He was saying that he was no longer willing to hang on until times got better because he no longer believed that they would get better. They would be cutting back and living from month to month and trying to fend off disaster until they had nothing left.

He said, "I haven't decided anything yet. We're still discussing the options."

"Why the hell did you buy that glass sculpture, then?" she said before she could stop herself. "Why the hell did you pile up even more debt for this trip?"

"Because, at this point, a few thousand lousy bucks isn't going to put us much deeper into the hole." His expression softened. "It's not just that, Miri. I wanted to give you something now, while I still could." Alan got up slowly. "Finish your coffee. I have to go change some more money."

"Don't change too much money," she said. "You might just be tempted to spend even more if you do."

He walked away. The only reason he had been pleasant up to now was so that he could spring his news on her, his talk about his options, his admission that he had failed. Miriam stirred her coffee, feeling rage and remorse.

From the Bridge of Sighs in the Doge's Palace, Miriam peered through the grille at the harbor. On the isle across that lagoon, she could see a church of red brick and marble, a false promise of sanctuary. The Bridge of Sighs, she had read in her guide, had been named for the prisoners who sighed as they were led across it to the Doge's prisons, knowing that this would be their last glimpse of the lagoon. It would probably be close to her last glimpse of the harbor as well, since they would have only two more days in Venice.

The enclosed bridge led them to a dark and bare stone room. A group of Japanese tourists were there, taking photos of one another. She followed Alan back across the bridge. "What an ostentatious display of wealth," she said as they made their way through an ornate hallway to an exit. "And those paintings! They're gorgeous, but my God. 'Doge So-and-So Worships the Virgin Mary.' 'Doge So-and-So Accepts the Tribute of Venice's Subject Cities.' 'Doge So-and-So and His Son Adoring the Holy Eucharist' and looking mighty damned full of themselves as they do. All they needed was 'Doge So-and-So Kicks Some Serious Butt' and 'Venice Accepts the Tribute of the Universe.' "

Alan usually chuckled at her witticisms, even when they were not particularly funny. As long as they were cracking jokes or making ironic remarks, they would not be fighting. Alan was not smiling; he did not even seem to be listening.

"What time is it?" he asked as they went outside.

Miriam glanced at her watch. "Almost four."

"I'm not feeling too well, Miri. Maybe I'll head back to the hotel."

"Oh." She repressed the comments rising to her lips about how it had been his idea for them to take this trip and now he wasn't even making the most of it and that he could have taken a nap at home for free. "What are your symptoms?"

"I think lunch really disagreed with me." He stepped closer to her. "Isn't anything important. I just need to rest. Wander around some more if you want—you can come back when it's time to get dressed for dinner. Reservation's not until nine." His brown eyes looked watery and bloodshot. His voice sounded as though he was pleading with her.

"Go ahead," she said. "I'll meet you later."

He made his way through the crowds on the walkway, passed a row of gondolas, and moved toward the *vaporetto* dock and ticket booths. Miriam wandered back toward Saint Mark's, wondering what to do now. She could walk along the Grand Canal to the Rialto and do some window-shopping there. She could have ridden as far as the Rialto with Alan, but was afraid they would have been lashing at each other again before they got that far.

"Miri."

Miriam lifted her head. Vera was coming toward her, still in her T-shirt and jeans. "I told you I'd see you again." Vera reached out to take her hands.

"Vera." Miriam clasped her friend's hands tightly. This woman could not be an apparition; she was here, as solid as Miriam herself. "We've been sightseeing." She was determined this time not to let Vera see her distress. "We did Saint Mark's Basilica and the Doge's Palace." She would have to make excuses for her husband's absence. "Alan went back to our room. He had indigestion from lunch. I hope you get to meet him eventually." Her voice had risen slightly.

"Then you have some time," Vera said.

"Oh, I have a lot of time. If Alan isn't feeling well enough to have dinner, I guess I'll have even more time."

Vera slipped her arm through Miriam's. "Why don't you come with me?"

"Come with you where?"

"You'll see."

They walked toward the landing. For a place that had been swarming with people only a few moments ago, the walkway along the harbor was surprisingly empty. Out in the harbor, two large cabin cruisers were embedded in the water, brought to a stop by the waves that had seemingly stiffened around their hulls. It was happening to her again, the disorienting and yet welcome sensation that time had stopped and that she and Vera were somehow apart from the rest of the world.

"What's happening?" Miriam asked.

"You must know. I've come to help you. I'm your friend, Miri, and you need me now." Vera gestured at a shiny black motorboat. "Get in. Thought you might like to see the outlying islands. You can get there on the *vaporetto* lines, but this'll be easier."

Miriam hesitated, then climbed into the boat. Vera got in next to her and sat down in front of the steering wheel. The motor began puttering almost instantly, as if the boat were starting itself.

Vera took them out of the harbor toward a broad canal that ran between islands, slowing down as they reached the open water of the lagoon. The boat slowed still more until it seemed that they were hardly moving at all. Miriam looked back. Venice was a pastel city adrift on a gold-flecked sea.

She could not recall seeing the other woman actually start the boat or put any keys into the ignition, although she noticed that a key was there now. Being in a strange place and seeing someone she had never expected to see here had disoriented her. Maybe Vera's home was on one of the other islands. Perhaps Vera was waiting until they were there, in the place where she lived, before she told Miriam about her life and what had brought her to Venice. Miriam clung to those strands of rational explanation for what was happening to her.

"That's the cemetery," Vera said, waving toward a distant island on which a church stood. "Some famous people are buried there. You can hear the water lapping at the island when you're among the gravestones. Trouble is, if your survivors don't keep up the payments on your gravesite, they dig you up after fifty years and dump you somewhere else. The Venetians always find ways to make more money."

"I wish some of that ability would rub off on me," Miriam said.

"I used to wish the same thing," Vera said. "I had some pretty desperate times after we graduated from college. Then I ended up with a fair amount of money and found out that having it didn't matter as much as I thought it would."

"I've been finding out that not having it matters more than I ever imagined."

Vera had slowed their boat nearly to a crawl, following the darker blue waters of a channel through the green lagoon. In the distance, a fisherman with a net was standing to his knees in water next to his boat.

"Water seems awfully shallow," Miriam said.

"Most of the lagoon's like that. All the boats have to take certain routes to keep from running aground, and they have to go slowly, too. That's partly because the water isn't deep, but it's also to keep from damaging seawalls like that one with a lot of waves from boats going too fast." Vera pointed at a long stone wall bordering the church on another distant island. Miriam wondered why this nautical traffic was nowhere in evidence now. No other boats were on the water except theirs, no cruisers, no *vaporetti*.

"I should have kept up with you, Miri," Vera went on. "I could have at least written to you."

"I sent a wedding invitation to your parents and asked them to forward it to you."

Vera smiled. "They did, and I actually thought of going. But I couldn't afford the plane ticket, and I hadn't seen you for almost three years and—well, I figured a lot had changed."

"You probably couldn't believe I'd gotten so conventional," Miriam said.

"That was part of it, I guess. I was going to write you a letter, but I tore it up halfway through. My life wasn't exactly in order back then. Then I thought, Well, there's plenty of time, I can always get in touch later."

Ahead lay an island of brightly painted houses, long drab buildings that looked like factories, and a precipitously leaning belltower. "I drifted for a while," Vera continued. "I'd get a job and tell myself I'd work on my art in my spare time. Of course I never did. I've been a receptionist, a nursery school teacher, a case worker, a proofreader, and a few other things. I lived with a guy and we broke up, and then I lived with somebody else, and that ended, too. Basically I was just waiting for my real life to begin, or maybe just waiting to grow up."

"Were you unhappy?" Miriam asked.

Vera shook her head. "No, but I was frustrated. The whole excuse for living that way was to get my painting done, and I wasn't doing it. I had to keep pretending I would, because otherwise it was just a wasted life, really."

They had passed the island with the leaning belltower. The light was fading, and Miriam wondered how close they were to their destination.

"Then a lot of things happened." Vera rested one hand across the wheel. "My father died, and I lost my job, the one I had then, and—well, to make a long story short, I started doing free-lance commercial work and using my free time for painting and taking classes. I wasn't exactly a great success, but I was happy. Had my first show in a local bank." She wrinkled her nose. "It was a start. Then I won a prize in a local art show. That's where I met Al, my husband."

"Sounds romantic," Miriam said.

"He'd wandered into the art show by mistake on his way to a Chamber of Commerce thing in the same building." Vera shook back her long gray hair. "We got married almost eight years ago. I've been really happy with him. We tried for kids, but I couldn't have them, and at least we had each other. Never set the art world on fire, but I did a couple of shows in New York galleries and got part-time gigs in the local schools and community college. I got some critical attention. I could always hope—" Her voice trailed off.

Ahead of their boat stretched empty water, still and gray,

and the sun had taken on a strange metallic glow. In the distance, an indistinct dark shape sat on the horizon. Miriam glanced at the other woman apprehensively. It suddenly seemed the height of recklessness to have gotten into this boat with Vera, to have come this far out on the lagoon.

"Al sold his business a few months back," Vera murmured. "Our plan was to go to all the places we always wanted to see and never had, Venice and Paris and Istanbul and so on. The deal was this—we'd stay in one place until we felt like moving on, and then we'd go to the next city. Venice was the first stop."

Miriam said, "So everything worked out."

"You could put it that way." Vera turned toward her and rested one hand on Miriam's arm. "I've had some happiness."

"And how long do you think you'll be here?"

Vera drew away. Miriam saw now that they were approaching an island. A church of russet-colored brick sat just above a low sea wall; beyond the church were clusters of houses painted green and red and purple and yellow. The landing was a long wooden dock, but no boats were tied up there.

"Where are we?" Miriam asked. Vera did not reply. Miriam thought of pulling her guide and maps from her purse to check on the location, then peered at her watch. Four-fifteen, which was impossible; they had left the pier just below Saint Mark's not long past four. Miriam squinted and saw that the hand marking the seconds had stopped.

"Damn this watch," she muttered. "It died on me. Battery must be defective. I just had it replaced before we left home."

Vera said, "I should have written to you. I should have been a better friend than I was. You could have used a really good friend, I think, someone to help you treasure what you have, keep you from tormenting yourself." She steered the boat smoothly through the water to the dock. "Go ahead. I'll tie up the boat and follow you. That path there will take you to the square."

Miriam climbed out of the boat. Darkness had come, even though it could not be that late; the shadows were deep under the broad-limbed trees that stood along the cobblestoned footpath. She followed the path up the gently sloping hill until she glimpsed the empty space of a town square above. She picked up her pace, and the silence seemed to thicken around her.

She entered the square. A church of pale stone stood in one corner; three-story houses with shuttered windows surrounded the square on three sides. A tiered fountain in which no water was running stood in the center of the square near a flagpole without a flag. There were no signs of people, no signs of life.

"Vera," she said, and the air seemed to swallow the word. "Vera!" The emptiness of the place frightened her. "Vera!" She looked around frantically for the other woman. Why had her friend brought her here? She ran toward the church, wondering if she might find people there.

"Miri!" Someone was calling her, someone at a distance. "Miri!" She recognized the voice now.

She hurried toward the voice, out of the square and past a long row of houses. Alan was standing near a narrow canal; he held out his arms as she rushed to him.

"Miri." He pressed her to him; she hugged him tightly, feeling suddenly that she had to cling to him, then looked into his face.

"What are you doing here?" she gasped. "How did you get here?"

He smiled, the way he used to before his not-quite-smile had become a habit. "I'm here now. Can't you just accept that?"

Vera had arranged this. That was the only rational explanation. She and Alan had planned this in secret and he had pretended he wasn't feeling well so that he could get to this island ahead of her. She could not be imagining it; he was here, solid and real. "You should have told me," she said. "You didn't have to—"

He took her arm. They strolled along the canal, past the few gondolas tied up there; she had not known that there were gondolas on these outlying islands. "Vera certainly fooled me," Miriam murmured. "I never would have guessed. How did you plot all this? When you went to change money, I'll bet. Did you know Vera was living in Venice all along?" He said nothing. "You saw her, too. You've met her. She talked you into coming here and surprising me. That means I'm not going crazy after all."

Alan slowed his pace. "I haven't been treating you well lately," he said. "I wanted this trip to be something special for us, sort of a new start. Or, if things don't work out businesswise, something we can remember."

She clutched his arm more tightly. He had on his favorite dark blue cashmere sweater over his shirt. She did not recall seeing him pack the pullover, or the navy blue slacks he was wearing either. They had both decided on his pin-striped suit, his white dinner jacket and black slacks for evening wear, and brown, beige, and tan jackets and pants for the rest of the time. She remembered the details because they had ended up arguing even over the clothes he would take, and he had insisted on throwing in two pairs of jeans at the last minute.

"Footloose and fancy-free," he went on. "That's what I figured on for myself. Never thought I'd seriously consider getting married until I met you, and then I knew I just didn't want to go through the rest of my life without you. Knew that two hours after I met you."

"Two hours?" Miriam smiled. "I thought it took you two days to fall in love with me."

"I told you it took me two days because I didn't want you thinking I was too rash, or rushed into things. That's why I waited a week before proposing, too."

He had waited barely a week. She had insisted on living with him for a while first, to make sure they were truly compatible and things would work out, and it had not even occurred to her that moving in with a man she had known for only a week might be precipitous. They had been married six months later, and she had felt no qualms about that, either, despite her mother's doubts about Alan's new business and her friends at work who felt that marriage was an outmoded institution. They had to be doing the right thing. Otherwise, they would not be feeling so much for each other, would not have made the decision to share their lives so quickly.

Often she had thought of her early self as naive and deluded and too trusting. Now she felt as though she had seen things clearly then, and that her vision had become more clouded and blurred with the years.

"We were happy then," she said. "Even with all the problems—"

"And then the kids came—"

"And then I was so damned exhausted all the time that there wasn't time to think about whether I was happy or not." Joelle had inherited her father's lanky frame and his dark hair, while Jason had Miriam's blue eyes and her father's broad, pleasant face. Everyone had always complimented her on her good-looking children.

"We had some good times," Alan said. "I think I appreciated them more later, when I'd be remembering them, than when they were actually happening."

He led her away from the canal toward a narrow passageway that ran between buildings. The doors were closed, the windows shuttered or their curtains drawn. She wanted to ask Alan how he had gotten here, why no one was on this island, why Vera had gone to all that trouble to get her to this deserted place, and then she gazed into his composed, serene face and forgot her questions.

A door was suddenly flung open. Miriam stepped back, drawing closer to Alan. She gazed into a small sitting room, where a young man sat at a table; the pretty young woman by the door giggled.

"Buona sera," Alan murmured.

"Buona sera," the young woman replied. She was wearing a long red dress and holding a mask in one hand. She lifted the mask to her face and tilted her head.

Miriam could now hear the sound of voices. At the end of the passageway, they came to a broad cobblestoned street and found it filling with people. Couples, a few in masks, strolled arm in arm and stopped to peer into brightly lighted shop windows. The younger women were in colorful long dresses, the older ones in subdued shades of purple and dark blue. Most of the men were in black pants and loose white shirts with full sleeves. They had to be locals; no one was wearing the tourist costume of jeans, T-shirts, and athletic shoes. Perhaps this was some obscure Venetian festival the travel agent and guide books had neglected to mention.

They stopped by one shop window. Behind the panes, two terra cotta marionettes danced. The male marionette took the hand of the female puppet and bowed. A dark-haired young woman was manipulating the strings; she caught Miriam's eye and smiled.

Evening had come. People were sitting at outdoor tables and wandering inside restaurants while others laughingly disappeared into alleys. Alan stopped at a display of lace outside one shop, fingered the delicate work of one shawl, then draped it over Miriam's shoulders.

She shook her head. "It's beautiful, but it'll cost too much."

A slender blonde woman had come out of the shop. *"Quanto?"* Alan asked. She answered him in Italian, he murmured something else, and Miriam saw their hands touch for a moment.

"It's a gift," Alan said as he took Miriam's arm again. Before she could speak, he had led her toward a small table outside one of the restaurants.

The waiter brought them glasses of a sparkling wine, and then a white wine with an unfamiliar label. Miriam let Alan order the food. They nibbled at mushroom tarts, bean soup with pasta, and calamari. The wine was making Miriam light-headed. She laughed as Alan spoke of the early days of their marriage, of the years in their cramped apartment and first house before they had moved into the one he had built for them. Memories were spilling out of her, too—Jason's valedictorian's speech to his high school class, Joelle's home run for the girls' softball team during the state championship game, the morning during their trip to Cancun when they had sent the kids down to the beach, locked the door, and made love until lunchtime.

Their waiter brought them a concoction of chocolate, cream cheese, and cake for dessert. Alan stirred his coffee. "I used to tell you then," he said, "that we'd look back on those years with some fondness, even the rough times."

"Yeah." Miriam leaned toward him. "Funny—I don't even remember how panicky I got when I was trying to get a job and couldn't find one. You remember, after Joelle was in nursery school. Took me three months, and we had to keep holding off the bill collectors, and all I really remember now is how ecstatic I was when Freedom Mutual hired me."

"I kept looking forward," Alan said. "That's what kept me going—that and you. I think I could handle things now if things were right between us. I could face anything then."

Her head was clearing. She suddenly wondered where Vera was. Vera had wanted to leave them alone, to settle things between them, to have a romantic evening on this little island. Why? What did Vera want with them? Why had she gone to all this trouble for a friend she had not seen for years until today?

Alan got up. He was quickly at her side, helping her out of her chair. She did not see if he had left any money for the waiter as he led her along the street. The shops were closing; women were carrying displays of lace, glass, and marionettes inside and locking the doors. The tables outside the restaurants had been abandoned.

Along the canal where Alan had been waiting for her, gondolas were gliding silently toward the open water. Her hand rose to her neck and she realized that she must have left the lace shawl at their table. "We'd better go back. I forgot that beautiful shawl."

"It was a gift, Miri."

"Just because you didn't have to pay for it—"

"You can't take anything away from here. They won't let you."

"Are we going to Vera's house?" Miriam asked. He did not reply. "Does she live here, on this island? How did you get here, anyway?"

"Miri," he whispered, "I need you. Don't leave me," and let go of her arm. She reached for him and clutched air. She spun around; he had disappeared.

"Alan!" she cried out. "Alan!" She hurried along the canal, not seeing him anywhere in the darkness, then ran toward the square. "Alan! Alan!" She kept calling his name until tears filled her eyes.

Lights were going on in the houses around the square. She looked up at the nearest windows and saw people gazing down at her. The square looked smaller, the buildings around it shabbier. The flagpole, painted red, was still there; the fountain had disappeared.

Two men were coming toward her, one in a dark blue uniform, the other in a striped shirt and loose dark pants. *"Signora,"* the man in the striped shirt said.

"Mio sposo," she said frantically. *"Signor Loewe."* She did not know enough Italian to make herself understood. "Help me, please. *Per favore.* My husband—" She paused. "Where am I?"

"You do not know, *Signora*?" the man in uniform said.

Miriam struggled to control herself. "Vera Langella," she said. "She's the woman who brought me here. Where does she live?"

The uniformed man shook his head and thrust out his hands. "I do not know the name."

A joke. It was all a cruel joke. Vera had thought it up and talked Alan into playing along. All the tender words had been only another bitter jest. Maybe these men were in on it, too, and if they weren't, they might assume she was demented if she went on and on about her husband and her friend. She would not go along with this horrible joke any longer.

"How do I get back to Venice?" she asked.

The man in uniform pointed in the direction of the landing. "The *vaporetto*," he replied.

She hurried down the slope. Vera's boat had vanished. Out on the water, she could see the lighted decks of an approaching *vaporetto*.

The boat took her to another island. She looked at her watch, which was running again, telling her that it was only seven o'clock. She consulted her schedule, questioned the people waiting on the landing with her, and found out that she was on the island of Murano and that the number 5 would get her back to Venice itself. That water bus took her to an unfamiliar landing. An older woman who spoke English pointed her in the direction of the Grand Canal.

She walked there and caught a *vaporetto* to the landing near the hotel. The boat traffic was as heavy as it had been during the day, and it seemed that flotillas of gondoliers were ferrying passengers along the Grand Canal. People were still roaming the streets, loading up on souvenirs, or finishing coffee and wine at outside tables.

As she came into the lobby, the desk clerk looked up, and then a man in a dark suit was bearing down on her from the left. "Mrs. Loewe." He bent forward from the waist, then took her hand. "They came for your husband."

Miriam tensed. "Who?"

"They took him, the ambulance. He is in *l'ospedale,* the hospital. He was in the lobby, and then he fell—" Miriam hung on to him tightly. "He came to the desk. I heard him say this word, something like 'Miri,' and then he fell."

The hotel manager walked her down to the docks. A powerboat was there, one much like the boat Vera and she had been in that afternoon. The hospital looked like a Renaissance *palazzo* from the outside. Inside, stretchers were lined against the walls and white-jacketed men, nurses, and nuns moved swiftly through the corridors. As she followed the orderly who had met her at the entrance, Miriam heard the sound of electronic beeps and then a voice over the public address system summoning a physician.

A console beeped next to Alan; an intravenous needle was in his arm and wires ran from his body to the console. A man, apparently asleep, lay on a bed next to Alan's; he was also hooked up to a console. The other two beds were empty; a small marble statue of the Virgin Mary stood at the other end of the room. She lifted a hand to her mouth.

"*Signora* Loewe." A man in a physician's white coat came toward her. "It will be all right." He squinted at her through wire-rimmed glasses; he seemed young, maybe still in his twenties, with light brown hair and a closely trimmed beard. "Your husband was lucky. He was brought here immediately. It is a myocardial—" He paused. "A heart attack, but he will recover."

She leaned over her husband and touched his hand. Alan opened his eyes. "Miri."

"You'll be all right. The doctor just said so."

"Went to the lobby. I don't know why, I was thinking—" His throat moved as he swallowed. "I was thinking about you. Thought of going over to the *vaporetto* landing, to meet you, tell you I was sorry—I was dreaming about you. We were walking around in—I think it was some kind of village. Wanted to stay there, and knew I couldn't. I needed you, I was trying to hang on—"

"It's all right." She moved her hand gently over his. "I can't lose you, Alan. I love you."

His mouth curved up; he was smiling, as he had on the island. "You won't." He closed his eyes.

She found the young doctor out in the hallway. He introduced himself as Dr. Palmieri and led her to an alcove with two chairs, a sofa, and a crucifix hanging on the wall. He explained that her husband could be flown home in a week to ten days, that it could have been worse, that if he had been alone in his room instead of in the hotel lobby among people when he collapsed, where help could quickly be summoned for him, he might not have survived.

"He must see a cardiologist when he is home," Dr. Palmieri said. "It may be he needs more treatment, but I can assure you—"

"Thank you," Miriam murmured. "*Grazie.*"

"I am much relieved myself," the physician said softly.

"Only two weeks ago, I was called to tend to another tourist, an American like yourself. That was not so good an outcome. She had cancer—it had spread to her lymph nodes and internal organs. Her husband said she had been afflicted for almost four years. They were traveling on what he called their farewell tour, because they knew—" He looked away for a moment. "She was a strong woman. She would not admit her illness. She said that I had better put her together because she had not been to see the Peggy Guggenheim collection here yet. She was gone that same day. So I am glad this will not also be the case with your husband, *Signora*."

Miriam bowed her head. "So am I." She would not lose Alan. Nothing else seemed to matter at the moment.

"*Signora* Langella." Miriam realized that she had expected to hear her friend's name. "*Signora* Vera Langella. That was what the American woman was called. She was fighting, but when she was finally gone—" Dr. Palmieri let out his breath. "She seemed at peace."

On the day before they were scheduled to fly home, Miriam took the *vaporetto* to San Michele, the cemetery island she had seen from Vera's boat. Vera had not been buried here; Dr. Palmieri had told her that Vera's husband had taken her body back to the States. But somehow she felt that her friend was here, that she might remain here for a while.

Miriam walked among the tombstones. Other tourists had come, to gather by the graves of Pound and Diaghilev and Stravinsky and the other artists buried here. She stood and listened to the lapping water as she whispered a thank you and a farewell to her friend.

Phantoms of the Night
by Richard Gilliam

Richard Gilliam's stories have appeared in such diverse anthologies as Esther Friesner's tabloid magazine tribute, *Alien Pregnant by Elvis,* and Fred Olen Ray's pulp magazine revival, *Weird Menace.* His nonfiction writing credits include *Sports Illustrated* and *Heavy Metal,* and the motion picture trivia section of the CD-Rom project for cable television's *The Sci-Fi Channel.*

I, Gaius Caesar, write this, though it has been many years since any have known me by that name. My current reputation varies, depending upon whom I am with and where it is I am traveling. In my childhood I was given the name Little Boots, a name which I cherished, though it is a name I seldom smile to hear now that I have reached my elder years. Some know me as Gerald, a merchant trader from great Athens, and sometimes I am Titus of Ausa, though I seldom use the latter name now that the Emperor Vespasian has elevated his slack-headed son Titus to be his co-ruler. My names are like phantoms, figments of persistent thought which I place upon the contemplation of the unwary. It is what we do those of us who live by deception, allowing others to see us as it benefits us most. Long have I lived by controlling the illusions of others, or when illusion failed, by sending the spirit of those in my way deep into that night that is death.

It has been thirty-one years since I have been known by the designation of Emperor, though I am certain many would be surprised now if I were to tell them who I was in that part of my life. There were six who knew, officers of my guard, who warned me of the disloyalty of others, and of the gravity of the plot against my person. It was they who helped me to pretend my assassination and then to escape; first to Aquitania, which was not much to my tastes, and later to other places, and finally here to Mt. Titano. Of my various fugitive residences it is the one closest to that place which I once ruled, and yet within which until now it was the one where I have felt the most secure.

The regrets of a ruler must be few. To allow oneself an emotion when taking a necessary action is a luxury of great price. There are those things which a ruler must do, and by which a ruler must not weaken himself with regret. The doubt of the government is the doubt of the people, and no leader such as I who truly loves his people can allow himself hesitance.

Upon settling near the Liger, I took the guise of a corn factor and pretended to seek new crops to broaden my base of commerce. Adopting the name Marcus Lucius, I purchased at a very inexpensive price the estate of a family recently slaughtered by brigands, and settled in quietness to a life far retired from public service. The six were with me, indeed it was they who had been the brigands who helped me find my bargain. They were my own contact with my former life, and I accepted this risk comfortably until one day in the second year when the youngest of the six asked for permission to visit Rome to see his wife and young child. There was no choice in the matter. I hired local mercenaries and executed the six, giving them the pristine and ethical end which men of their honor deserve. They each accepted my decision, though the youngest cried when he understood what his homesickness had done to the others. One more step made me yet safer. The coins I carried bore my likeness, and without the six, there were none left that I trusted to handle my transactions. I found an artisan skilled in metals and had the lot recast in the image of my uncle who now ruled. The craftsman, to his regret, shorted a tenth part more than the price agreed upon. I would have killed him anyway, for he had curiously studied my face, though his breach of fiduciary ethics cleared me to dispose of him by a more recreational means. He lingered for a month, but died quickly when I tired of his screams and removed his tongue. My ties were thus severed. I was secure.

As my wealth increased and as time passed, I began to travel more, becoming less concerned that any would recognize the Emperor they thought dead. I visited Britannia, and laughed when I saw the temple dedicated to my uncle who had become Claudius, the god. It was he who had talked me out of naming a month in my honor—on the logic that my hubris would be offensive to those same gods which he had now presumed to join. I merely wanted Septemus. Julius had taken Quintilis, which I do not begrudge him, for if any of us deserve a month, it is the divine Julius. Augustus the Pompous, had taken not only Sextilis, but had stolen a day from February, the festival month. Tiberius followed Augustus. No one should ever want to name a month after a loathsome pederast like Tiberius, though I perhaps should not too badly denounce him since he named me his coheir equal with his grandson Gemellus. I shall speak instead of my virtues. The people were fortunate that it was I who followed Tiberius and rid them of Gemellus, and who restored dignity to the office of Emperor. I never tortued, nor physically used anyone without just cause, and never, in the entirety of my life, abused a child nor had any child killed in any manner that was not quick and painless.

Alas, virtue so often goes unrewarded. I became neither a god nor a month. I deserve to be better remembered. The plotting of my uncle now became all too clear—he had my throne, my godhead, and most probably would someday take my month. O, the scheming that men of ill will do to those of us who serve the public.

Fortunately, my uncle had received his deserts, poisoned by his fourth wife, my sister and thus his cousin, so that Lucius Domitius, her son whom my uncle had stupidly adopted, could ascend to his title. And as so often occurs, the son—who you may know as Nero, his adopted name— poisoned his co-conspirator after her presence became inconvenient. A sister of mine should have known better than to have opposed her son's mistress, the comforts of younger flesh often overcoming the ties of blood, and all the more foolish given that Poppaea Sabina was Rome's preeminent foul-tempered whore.

I did not travel to Rome myself, of course, but heard these stories from passing merchants, or from my agents, whom I rewarded generously for such information. Never did I return to Rome, never until earlier this year, when faintly I heard the voices for the first time.

"Little Boots," they called, gently and with a warmth that reminded me of childhood summers, so lovingly spent along the Rhine with my father and his troops. "Little Boots, it has been much too long. Why do you not honor us?" They called again, over and over, till I was visited by a sadness that I knew could only be satisfied with a journey to Rome and to the personal temple of my family. So I traveled, taking the little trafficked roads where those of us of secret ways often move faster and more safely, unimpeded by the intrusiveness of modern life.

My mother, the Lady Agrippina, was the epitome of Roman virtue, though somewhat more sentimental than practical when coarser action was required. She died at the orders of Tiberius, banished to the island Pandateria, where to the embarrassment of Tiberius she starved herself to death. I have long suspected the complicity of Tiberius in the death of my father, the noble Germanicus Caesar. Tiberius was an envious tyrant, and in the third year of his reign he recalled my father to Rome, soon after the time when my father had won great military victories at which Tiberius had failed. The triumph shamed the Emperor, so much more did the people love my father.

Tiberius had him poisoned. Twenty years later my revenge was to be Tiberius' heir.

I think he chose me heir in part because he knew Rome needed my skills, and in part because I had refused to join his bed. Gemellus had no such reservations, and at my earliest opportunity I had no reservations at all about putting Gemellus to death in a very unpleasant manner. A state can only have one master, and I had been selected by the Senate and by the people. Gemellus cursed me before he died, and for that insult I granted him three days of additional life, each of them excruciatingly worse than the day that had preceded it.

During my reign I lavished great expense on the upkeep of my family temple. It rested on a hill near the center of the city, visible to those who passed in the distance. I was dismayed when I saw it in ill repair, and even more shocked as I drew closer. Too firmly had the hated Nero been associated with my family. Seven years earlier tales had reached me of the fire that had destroyed two-thirds of Rome. The evidence of the charred temple proved their truth. My hopes that my family shrine had been spared ceased to exist.

Slowly I approached. Outside the entrance stood a penitent, his clothes ragged and his alms bowl held near his chest. A smile came to my face. There were those left who remembered. I took a spot behind a collapsed pillar, near a pool of water from which I could drink, and paused to watch.

Not many visited this area—indeed, the broken buildings had been growing more distressed for some distance now. The remorseful beggar seemed to pray silently, though his head remained unbowed, watching for those who might draw near. Much of the day passed and yet no person neared the temple. Finally, as the sun lowered, two men approached the beggar, who eyed them cautiously.

"Travelers, a warning," spoke the mendicant. "You are not of this city."

"No, Antium," said the taller of the two. "Just trying to find our way back to the main roadway."

"It lies south," said the beggar, a look of concern on his face.

"What is wrong?" spoke the traveler again.

"Antium. It is the place of his birth."

"Nero? Yes. Nero is four years dead now and Vespasian rules in his place. All of Antium is not so bad as Nero."

"No, not Nero," said the beggar. "I speak of Little Boots."

"Caligula?" laughed the smaller traveler. "The Emperor Caligula has been dead for thirty-one years, killed by his own guard. You would have been but a child when Caligula died. Why worry about one gone for so long?"

"Little Boots is not dead," said the beggar. "My father helped him escape, and for that he had my father killed."

"Your father?" asked the first traveler.

"One of his guards. Killed when I was six. My mother died the following year and I have lived at this temple ever since."

"But why?"

"I wait to greet Little Boots," said the beggar. "I wait here till his return and warn others of the evil that is this place. They're all here, you know, his whole mad family. All here. Only one mad Claudian not among them."

A bolt of pain shot through me, and involuntarily I turned my sight from the beggar, only to find myself staring into the pool near my feet. I looked at my reflection, maybe for the first time in years. I was advanced in age, sixty by true count, and I knew that what I saw was myself from younger days. The first images were pleasant, with my father Germanicus, the day I bruised my toes and was given manly shoes much too large for my feet. I saw the soldier who first called me "Little Boots," and remembered how I liked the name. I saw my mother, the soft and gentle Agrippina, as she hugged me and told me stories of Rome long past. And then the later images. The debauchery of Tiberius, the last cries of Gemellus, the staging of my death and the execution of the six who helped me flee.

I saw then a young boy, sleeping at the temple, first clandestinely, and later with the blessing of the priests who he helped with their chores. I saw the temple darken on the day of the death of my uncle Claudius, and then darken again on the day when Lucius Domitius put my sister to death. Through this all I watched the beggar, as he grew into manhood, and as he waited in vain.

The scenes from seven years ago were a surprise. I saw the beggar spread the oils and start the fire. Destroy the temple where he lived, and yet afterward remain. Destroy most of the town as well, though I think this was not his purpose. I saw Lucius Domitius kick his mistress to death and marry another. Then I saw him fall on his sword outside of Rome. A loss to the arts, indeed. This image was the last.

How much time had passed while I watched I cannot say. The sky was dark and the moon was down. That it was the middle of the night was a reasonable presumption.

My carelessness of thirty years earlier was quickly corrected. As the reflection had shown me was his custom, the beggar slept behind the ruined altar at the center of the temple. In deference to the service of his father I slit his throat without disturbing his rest. Let this be a lesson harshly learned. Do not kill a man lest you kill his sons also. A thing is not complete till there are no progeny left to bring vengeance. It is a lesson I should have learned long, long ago, and one which I had often so foolishly ignored while laughing at the failure of others.

O, that I had not entered the temple that night.

"Little Boots," came the wail, almost as soon as my knife had creased the beggar's throat. "Little Boots, please join us."

"We are yours, Little Boots," came a snickering voice, which I recognized as that of Gemellus. "We have waited for you to return."

My father spoke next. "We bribed the wind, my son, after so many years of not knowing where you were. We thought you dead and your spirit lost. What a great rascal you are!

Only the wind could reach your ears upon so high a mountain. Come, Little Boots, we want you here. The last Claudian should not be away from his kind."

I ran. And how I ran, not recalling leaving the temple or the city, or climbing through the nearer Apennines on the way to Mt. Titano, my feet and boots well bloodied as I found my house on the eastern slope of the third peak.

They were waiting when I arrived. I should have known. I had not the power to outrun their spirits.

"You have a nice home, Little Boots," said my mother. "I am pleased. The temple was never the same after the fire, and this is a much more pleasant place to wait with you till you join us."

"Hee, hee, hee, hee, hee," cackled Gemellus. "Till he joins us."

"You'll join us soon, won't you, son?" said my father. "Join us under your name, not one of those disguises you used to hide from us for so long."

"Soon," said my mother, her voice ever so soft. "He will join us soon."

All I have tried has failed. I have tried donation, sacrifice, penitence, and exorcism. None have freed me from my burden. I am mastered by my past. The voices remain. The blood on this parchment is from my ears where I have pierced my drums in vain. I no longer know the real from the unreal, or whether I am already among them. They toy with my hope, granting me sweet brief moments of peace. Like phantoms of the night, they ceaselessly return. My choices are few. Perhaps my pain will be less if I join them. I shall take a honeycake with me to pacify Cerberus. By whatever name I undertake this journey, I shall be found. May the gods accept me, their Little Boots.

Welcome to DAW's Gallery of Ghoulish Delights!

☐ **DRACULA: PRINCE OF DARKNESS**
   Martin H. Greenberg, editor
A blood-draining collection of all-original Dracula stories. From Dracula's traditional stalking grounds to the heart of modern-day cities, the Prince of Darkness casts his spell over his prey in a private blood drive from which there is no escape! UE2531—$4.99

☐ **FRANKENSTEIN: THE MONSTER WAKES**
   Martin H. Greenberg, editor
Powerful visions of a man and monster cursed by destiny to be eternally at odds. Here are all-original stories by such well-known writers as: Rex Miller, Max Allan Collins, Brian Hodge, Rick Hautala, and Daniel Ransom. UE2584—$4.99

☐ **THE TIME OF THE VAMPIRES** May 1996
   P.N. Elrod & Martin H. Greenberg, editors
From a vampire blessed by Christ to the truth about the notorious Oscar Wilde to a tale of vampirism and the Bow Street Runners, here are 18 original tales of vampires from Tanya Huff, P.N. Elrod, Lois Tilton, and others.
UE2693—$5.50

☐ **WEREWOLVES**
   Martin H. Greenberg, editor
Here is a brand-new anthology of original stories about the third member of the classic horror cinema triumvirate—the werewolf, a shapeshifter who prowls the darkness, the beast within humankind unleashed to prey upon its own.
UE2654—$5.50

☐ **THE YEAR'S BEST HORROR STORIES: XXI**
   Karl Edward Wagner, editor
A "bad girl" is taught a lesson no one else in her life will ever forget . . . a sketch artist takes from his model more than just her likeness . . . a Vietnam vet survives only to return to a hell worse than any he has ever known. Karl Edward Wagner once more leads readers into the heart of the horrific! UE2572—$5.50

Buy them at your local bookstore or use this convenient coupon for ordering.

PENGUIN USA   P.O. Box 999—Dep. #17109, Bergenfield, New Jersey 07621

Please send me the DAW BOOKS I have checked above, for which I am enclosing $_____ (please add $2.00 to cover postage and handling). Send check or money order (no cash or C.O.D.'s) or charge by Mastercard or VISA (with a $15.00 minimum). Prices and numbers are subject to change without notice.

Card #_____ Exp. Date _____
Signature_____
Name_____
Address_____
City _____ State _____ Zip Code _____

For faster service when ordering by credit card call **1-800-253-6476**

Allow a minimum of 4-6 weeks for delivery. This offer is subject to change without notice.